Fa

The Story of ...

Book II of the Plantagenet Embers Trilogy

Other books by Samantha Wilcoxson

The Plantagenet Embers Trilogy

Plantagenet Princess, Tudor Queen: The Story of Elizabeth of York
Queen of Martyrs: The Story of Mary I

Middle Grade Historical Fiction

Over the Deep: A Titanic Adventure

Middle Grade Inspirational Fiction

No Such Thing as Perfect

Faithful Traitor

The Story of Margaret Pole

Samantha Wilcoxson

Faithful Traitor

The Story of Margaret Pole

Samantha Wilcoxson

ISBN10: 153017404X
ISBN13: 978-1530174041
Printed in the United States of America

For my husband, who believed in me long before I did.

Family Tree of Margaret Pole
and the York Remnant

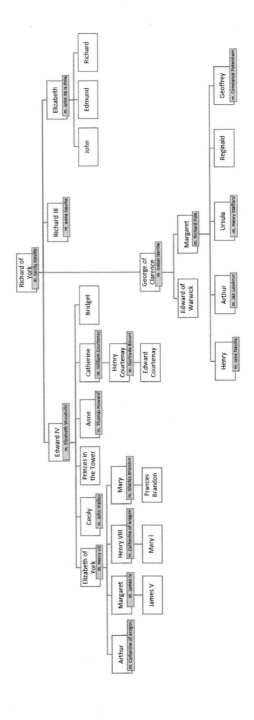

February 11, 1503

The Queen of England was dead.

The parchment bearing the news fell to the floor as Margaret grasped for the closest chair and collapsed into it. She forced herself to swallow the lump in her throat and closed her eyes in an effort to form a prayer.

Margaret fought the conflicting feelings churning within her upon hearing about the death of her cousin, Elizabeth of York. Elizabeth had done what she thought was right when she married the last hope of the Lancastrians, Henry Tudor, but Margaret would always hate the man for sending her brother to his death.

Edward had been innocent, of that much Margaret was certain. What she still wondered was how much Elizabeth had truly done to help him as his youth wasted away while he was imprisoned in the Tower. Elizabeth had loved him once, Margaret knew, but she had also allowed him to be executed on the Tower Green.

Grief threatened to rise in Margaret's chest as she remembered Edward and Elizabeth running through the moor at Sherriff Hutton, laughing and being chased by the puppy that Edward had adopted upon arrival. They had both boasted the bold red-gold Plantagenet hair that glimmered brightly in the sunlight. It was difficult for Margaret to convince herself that they were both gone now, and she would not see either of them again until they greeted her in heaven.

She remembered that Edward had a sprinkling of freckles across his sun-kissed cheeks, while Elizabeth's skin had been smooth and pale like Margaret's own. Elizabeth's relationship with Edward had begun, in part Margaret was sure, to fill the gap left by the disappearance of her own brothers when their uncle Richard had taken the throne in 1483. It seemed so long ago now.

Margaret sighed and opened her eyes, memories had come

more easily than prayers. She leaned to retrieve the unpleasant missive and wondered if she should have been there with Elizabeth in her last moments. Allowing herself to become lost in reminiscences again, she reflected upon the times that she had attended her cousin during the birth of other children. The one that had taken Elizabeth's life, baby Katherine, had quickly given up its own as well.

"Oh, Bess," Margaret sighed and briefly wondered if the gentle spirit of the first Tudor queen could hear her.

Though Margaret had loved her golden cousin with an adoration akin to worship, that devotion had wavered when young Edward of Warwick was led to the scaffold. With Elizabeth gone, there would be nobody to soften the rule of Henry VII, England's unexpected Tudor king. Margaret was thankful that she had her husband to lean on through turbulent times.

She rose from her seat to go to him now. Richard would know how to comfort her, even as she had no idea how to cope with the feelings raging inside of her. He had been with her through most of the young Tudor dynasty, and she thanked God daily for him. Henry had given Margaret, a prize of high value because of her royal blood, to his devoted follower, Richard Pole, but she had surprised herself by falling in love with him.

Margaret strode from her chamber in search of her husband, taking in her surroundings with the renewed appreciation of someone who has been reminded that they are enjoying a day that a loved one has missed. The estate at Bockmer was a relatively simple one for the niece of two kings and cousin to the latest queen, but it was the place that gave Margaret the greatest happiness.

As she moved through the corridors, remembering special moments and dreaming of more to come, she was struck strongly by the memory of her sainted family members of whom there were so many. Shaking her head, she vowed to focus on the present. Thinking of all who had gone before her through her thirty years of life would only drag her into a dark pit of depression. She must find Richard.

He would be catching up on his personal business, a task that he had more time for since the death of Prince Arthur. Richard had been the steward of Henry and Elizabeth's firstborn son until his passing ten months earlier. The time since they had returned to their own estates from the prince's at Ludlow had been used to bring the Pole family holdings into order.

Margaret reached the heavy wooden door of Richard's study, but paused before entering. Would Elizabeth have risked another pregnancy at age thirty-six if Arthur had lived? Her eyes searched for patterns in the floor rushes as her mind sought answers that it never could obtain. Prince Henry was now the heir to the crown and the only surviving royal prince, since Elizabeth's final effort at childbearing had not been fruitful.

Shaking herself from her reverie, Margaret lifted her head and knocked upon Richard's study door. Not waiting for him to call out, she pushed the door on its creaking hinges and entered the sunny room. While some men preferred dark, cave-like studies for carrying out their business, Richard preferred his well lit by the glazed glass windows and an abundance of candles. It was one of his few indulgences to keep the room bright, saying that it improved his disposition.

He rose from behind his desk and neat piles of documents as she entered, swiftly reaching her side and taking her hands. His were smooth except for the calluses caused by wielding his sword in the service of Henry Tudor.

"What is wrong, my Meg?" he asked her, his dark eyes searching her brighter sea green ones.

She lowered her face from his analysis, wondering how he could read her so easily. "It is Bess," she whispered.

"Queen Elizabeth?" he asked, not as comfortable with family nicknames for his sovereign as his wife was.

Margaret nodded and shifted slightly toward him. He took her in his arms, sensing her need. "The baby?"

All had been concerned for the beloved but aging queen. Though her mother, Edward IV's queen Elizabeth Woodville, had birthed many children for well into her forties, childbirth remained a risky but vital business of queens.

Margaret simply nodded, finding herself unable to speak. She buried her face in Richard's doublet, losing herself in his strong, supportive embrace. She could not place enough blame at Elizabeth's feet to not mourn for her. "I have just had a letter from my cousin, Cecily," she began before the lump in her throat made speech impossible.

"Dear Meg," Richard said, holding her tighter. "Tell me."

She forced herself to look up into his eyes though hers were shining with unshed tears. Only seconds passed, but it was long enough for her to drink in his features and discern where their children had inherited small elements of their appearance from him.

Henry, their eldest, whom Richard had insisted be named after his king and benefactor, had received Richard's serious yet caring nature. His forehead creased in concern just the way Richard's was now. Arthur had the same thick, dark hair that was the envy of many young ladies. Sweet Ursula was the image of her mother except for her quick smile that was all Richard. Finally, little Reginald showed all signs of becoming Richard's physical reflection with no sign of Plantagenet features visible thus far.

"Meg," Richard whispered, pulling her from her wandering

thoughts.

Taking a deep breath, Margaret forced herself to say, "She has died, Richard. And the baby, too."

The tears that had been threatening to fall now streamed unashamedly down Margaret's face, and Richard directed her toward a bench and pulled her down beside him. He gently stroked her thick auburn hair and whispered comforting platitudes as she sobbed.

"She died on her thirty-seventh birthday," Margaret whispered when her breath came more regularly. "She always did sicken when with child. She should not have risked another."

"She only wished to perform her duty to her king and her God. She was a devoted queen."

They were quiet as each mentally reviewed images of the copper-haired Plantagenet princess who had become Henry's wife. After a few moments, Margaret raised her head and gave Richard a weak smile. "You have held me through so many tears, my love. I do not know what I would do without you."

"Or I without you, sweet Meg," he said softly, giving her shoulders a squeeze. "You have endured much, and I only hope that our family has been some small comfort to you in these last fifteen years."

Margaret pulled away to meet his eye, "I would not have survived had we not been married, Richard. Henry may have believed that he chose you for me, but it is God who knew that I needed you. As a lost and confused fifteen-year-old girl, you were my safe place. You still are."

She rested her head on his shoulder, feeling exhausted by her emotional display.

"Henry has lost his wife and child then?"

Margaret nodded, feeling the rough fabric of his doublet

against her cheek. "The baby was a girl. She was named Katherine and died shortly before Bess."

"It will be a burden for Henry. He believed that their relationship was healing."

"It should not take the death of a child to mend a marriage," Margaret snapped with more venom than she intended. Her emotions were too raw for self-control.

"It should not," Richard quietly agreed. He would say no more. Now was not the time, and they had argued about Queen Elizabeth's right to blame Henry for the death of their children of illness or Edward of Warwick by execution far too many times already.

"I suppose we should tell the children," Margaret sighed.

"You retire to your rooms. I will send Molly to attend to you, and I will speak with the children."

Margaret did feel overcome with weariness despite the early hour. "I believe some warmed wine and a few minutes to rest would do me wonders," she admitted.

Richard kissed her forehead after walking her to her rooms. Margaret extinguished the candles and pulled the curtains around her bed so that it was as dark as night. As she lay her head down, she could not escape the ghosts from taking over her mind, bringing her to tears once again over losses that still felt fresh after several years.

Her last thought before passing into heavy, dreamless sleep was that maybe Elizabeth was the lucky one, for there were more of their shared family members in heaven than on Earth.

February 1503

Richard and Margaret traveled to London where Elizabeth's body lay in state for a fortnight. As Margaret entered the chapel of St. Peter ad Vincula, leaning heavily on Richard's arm, she fought against the spirits of others she had prayed for as their souls sought heaven.

Elizabeth's coffin was surrounded by hundreds of candles, but the light was quickly absorbed by the black fabric hung generously over every surface of the room. Catherine, the queen's sister, led the other ladies in their constant vigil around the body.

"Cat," Margaret whispered as the cousins embraced each other. The fierceness of Cat's grip did not surprise Margaret. She was a young woman who did everything with passion. She had recently lost her young son during Elizabeth's final progress, and her husband, William Courtenay, was currently being held at the king's pleasure within the Tower.

"Meg, it would mean much to Bess to know that you are here."

"Of course, I am," Margaret protested with a blush. She did not like inferences to any possible family issues outside of private conversation with Richard. "Bess was my beloved cousin," she added, and found that she meant it.

"And she loved you," Cat agreed, turning and leading Margaret to pray, kneeling before Elizabeth's casket. Cat took people at their word and had a liberal attitude toward treasonous thoughts. She would not blame Margaret for anger regarding her brother's death any more then she blamed William for his treasonous words about Henry Tudor. Emotions could not be ruled by law, she felt.

Once they had prayed, Cat and Margaret rose, crossed themselves, and retired to a quiet corner of the dim chapel.

"You were with her in the end, Cat. Was she . . ." Margaret paused, searching for the right word, "satisfied?"

"I believe she was," Cat confirmed with her lips pressed together and her brow furrowed. "There were events that she found difficult to forgive Henry for, but I do believe she loved him and was willing to give her life in order to bring him another child."

"If only that child had lived."

"Bess would say that God in his wisdom has planned this course."

Margaret raised an eyebrow at her cousin. Cat made it easy to say things that shouldn't be said. "But you do not believe so?"

Cat shrugged irreverently, "I do not claim to understand what God has had in mind since my father died."

Margaret nodded, thinking that the chaos went back further in her own life to the execution of her own father, Cat's uncle, in 1478. Would things have gone differently had another brother survived to assist Richard of Gloucester when Edward IV died or would the infighting only have been taken up again much sooner?

The women sat in companionable silence that seemed misplaced in the dreary place of mourning. Both had experienced too much death in their lives to feel uncomfortable with it. "How are your little ones?" Margaret asked, wishing to think about the future rather than the past.

Cat's face visibly brightened. "Dear Henry is beginning his studies, and shows great promise. He is as smart and outspoken as his father."

Margaret smiled, not pointing out that William would likely be at Cat's side rather than residing within the king's fortress were he slightly more tactful.

"Little Margaret, who I like to think of as your namesake rather than the king's mother's," Cat said with a wink, "is lovely and obedient, much more than I ever was."

Now Margaret's smile was sincere as images of her own daughter, Ursula, flowed through her mind. She was only a year older than Cat's daughter, and the two seemed to be of a similar mold.

At that moment, the women were reminded of their purpose for being in this place as King Henry VII entered the chapel. He looked less majestic than ever, his shoulders stooped and hair hanging drably about his face. Margaret and Cat rose from their seat only to lower into expert curtseys before the widower king.

Henry's eyes were red-rimmed and darkly shadowed, as if rest had been elusive since the loss of his queen. With some shame at the satisfaction this gave her, Margaret took in his wasted appearance. Did he feel guilt that Elizabeth had died attempting to grant him a son to be his spare in case young Harry followed his brothers Arthur and Edmund to an early grave?

Margaret felt the sudden desire to have Richard at her side. She felt that Henry never looked upon her graciously unless Richard were present. She need not have worried. Henry had eyes only for the empty shell that contained what remained of his beautiful Plantagenet bride, the woman who had helped him unify England after decades of familial infighting.

There were many details of this reign for Margaret to take issue with, the greatest being the execution of her innocent brother four years earlier. Henry had predated his reign to the day before he defeated her uncle Richard at Bosworth, forcing all who had fought for their anointed king to beg him for mercy and forgiveness. He had put off his marriage to Elizabeth and then her coronation to ensure that all understood that he claimed his crown through his own conquest rather than her royal blood.

However, as she looked at him today, bowed low before his

wife's lifeless form, she could feel only pity for a man who had lost someone dear to him. The fact that he appeared so lacking in stateliness only made him more worthy of sympathy in her eyes.

He had not taken note of the women's obeisance, so they rose and waited for Henry to finish his prayers for the souls of his wife and tiny daughter. When he finally stood and crossed himself, he opened his eyes and appeared surprised to realize that others were in the room. Margaret could not bring herself to go to him, but watched as Cat did.

"Your grace," she said with a shallow curtsey. "I have prayed without ceasing for my sister and for you."

"I thank you," Henry said distractedly, as if he knew not who was speaking. Then his eyes found Margaret.

"Lady Pole," he said, then paused, seeming unsure about his reasons for addressing her. His gaze wandered about the chapel, taking in the crying women and flickering candles. Once his focus again fell to Margaret, he continued. "My dear Bess held you in the greatest esteem, and spoke highly of her time with you and your brother."

"Thank you, your grace," Margaret said as she curtseyed low to hide her face. Her pity for him did not extend far enough to speak of her brother as if Henry were not the one who had framed him for a crime he did not commit and then executed him for it.

If Henry noticed her discomfort, he made no sign of it. He was lost in his own grief and did not appear in good health. His face was flushed with heat though he pulled his cloak tightly around him to ward off chills. A frequent cough racked his body with pain.

"You should be resting," Margaret said as she stood to her full height.

Henry was staring again at Elizabeth's body, as though he hoped there had been some mistake and she might suddenly open her eyes. "What? Oh, yes. The strain of . . ." He held his arms out to indicate his surroundings, and Margaret wondered if he meant Elizabeth's death or the challenge that had been his reign. "I will be retiring to Richmond with my lady mother to restore my health and spend time in prayer."

"Yes, your grace."

Margaret curtseyed again. She did not know what to say or if the king desired her to say anything, so she silently watched him lightly run his fingers along the coffin. He hesitated as they reached the edge, before striding quickly from the room without addressing anyone else who promptly knelt before him as he passed.

~ ~ ~ ~

Nobody would believe the rumors of Henry VII's penny-pinching ways if the funeral of his widely mourned queen was their only evidence. Right of conquest or not, Elizabeth had been the reason that many consented to Henry's rule, and the people grieved for her and their own future.

A carriage swathed in black velvet carried the queen's remains from the chapel to Westminster Abbey, where Elizabeth would spend her eternal rest. The procession following the beloved queen stretched as far as Margaret could see from her place next to Richard. They were largely unnoticed amid the other esteemed families who shared a blood relationship with Elizabeth of York. She tried to ignore the crowd surrounding her by bringing up lines of verse that she had read earlier. Many poems of lamentation had been written since the Queen's death, but this one, by a lawyer named Thomas More, had captivated her with its eloquence.

Riches, honor, wealth, and ancestry
Hath me forsaken, and lo, now here I lie.

11

It could be the motto of the Plantagenet dynasty, Margaret thought woefully. So few of us are left.

The effigy of her cousin had disturbed her, though she was accustomed to the sight from so many other noble funerals. The artistically rendered form of Elizabeth captured her wide-eyed beauty and small, prim mouth, but the face was so cold and void of soul that it gave Margaret shivers to look upon it. Henry had spared no expense on the craftsman, who had found copper hair of just the right color and carved the wood until it was almost Elizabeth's mirror reflection, but it held no more vibrancy than the queen's cold body.

The chilly starkness of the February day suited Margaret's mood and the state of her heart. It felt fitting to be suffering, as if it made mourning more effective. God would look down and realize the pain he had caused in taking this particular woman from Earth too soon.

The procession made its slow way toward Westminster and Margaret almost stumbled as she remembered the last time she had followed this route. Richard kept a strong hold of her arm and leaned to her ear.

"Are you alright, my love?"

"It was her coronation," Margaret said barely loud enough for him to hear with his ear turned toward her. He shifted to search her eyes.

"Elizabeth's?"

Margaret realized that she was making no sense. "The last time I walked this course, it was in the procession for her coronation."

Richard said nothing but held her more firmly, his lips pressed together in frustration. How he wished that he could take some of Margaret's pain into himself and spare her. They made their way as Londoners solemnly watched the procession through tears, unguarded fear for the future etched into many faces.

April 1503

By spring, Margaret was settled at Stourton Castle with the children while Richard attended duties in Wales. It was his service in the wild lands in the west that had earned him the undying gratitude of the Tudor king, and had won him the hand of a noblewoman many would have considered too far above him.

Margaret did not mind if others saw her marriage that way, for she had found peace with Richard in the midst of the tumultuous times that she had lived through. She would have loved him had he been a stable boy.

Warmth and new life was in the air as she led the children into the gardens to enjoy some exercise and the fresh scents of spring. With her little ones surrounding her, it was easier to push aside the thoughts of the loved ones who would not be experiencing this change of seasons with her.

Henry dashed away though, proving that he was too old for the immature play that his younger siblings were capable of. Margaret's smile that had come with the flood of warm sunshine faded as she watched her firstborn son sprint across the lawn. He should be at court, as was his blood right. He may be a young boy, but he was right in one thing. He was too old for the company of his mother and young siblings.

Margaret mentally chided herself for finding things to worry about. She made a note to speak to Richard about the boy's education and placement in a suitable home while taking a deep breath of fragrant air to center herself.

Arthur was not far behind Henry in needing his future considered. At eight years old, he too could be placed in the household of one prepared to teach him the skills of a gentleman. He giggled with his sister as unruly dark locks of hair fell across his forehead, and Margaret smiled. She would hold him a while longer.

No need to rush things.

Ursula's auburn tresses flew in a tangled mess, causing Margaret to call her over to her side. The young girl skipped joyfully to her mother and sang a quiet tune as Margaret pulled grass from her hair and tamed it into a simple braid.

"There you are, you imp," Margaret said, giving her a playful push toward the waiting Arthur. The two were as inseparable as a brother and sister could be expected to be. Just like Edward and I, Margaret thought with a sharp pain stabbing at her heart.

"Thank you, mama!" Ursula shouted in an unladylike fashion while running to take her place in some secret game.

Reginald's nurse sat with him beneath an apple tree that was budding and showing promise of a bountiful harvest come the autumn. Having just turned three, he was anxious to leave her and join his older siblings as they tumbled and laughed.

"Oh, set him free for a bit," Margaret said to the nurse's relief. "I do not believe he can outrun us yet."

"Many thanks, my lady," the shy nurse mumbled with her eyes downcast. She was outgoing with the children but clearly intimidated by their mother. Margaret was unsure what she had done to make this so and made every effort to be kind to the tender hearted young woman.

"Visitors!" Henry shouted from his vantage point halfway up an ancient oak tree. He scampered down before Margaret could shout a warning to take caution. He seemed to hit the ground running toward the courtyard gate.

By the time Margaret caught up with the younger children in tow, Henry had already tossed himself into the waiting arms of his father.

"Richard! I was not expecting you for days," Margaret exclaimed, rushing toward him with unbridled enthusiasm.

"Papa!" shouted Ursula and Arthur in unison.

"Such a greeting!" Richard laughed, hugging them each in turn. "One would think that I had been gone a year rather than a fortnight."

"A single night is too long sometimes," Margaret said low enough for only his ears to catch.

He was surprised but pleased by her uncharacteristic display of public affection. "You need not worry," he whispered in her ear with his beard scratching at her neck. "You will have no way to be rid of me this night."

Margaret pulled away with a blush racing across her cheeks, and the children quickly took her place in Richard's arms. They squealed as he lifted them into the air, and he favored his wife with a quick wink before giving them his full attention.

~ ~ ~ ~

Later that night, long after the children were tucked into their own little beds, Richard and Margaret lay together with the bed's curtains pulled tightly closed. Margaret basked in the sensations coursing through her, knowing that Richard would soon have to leave her again on the king's business. She felt his muscles, firm from hours of riding and sword drills. The scent of him was musky with slight traces of horses and wine. Resting her hand lightly upon his chest, she closed her eyes and counted his heartbeats, not wanting to consider that they may be finite in their number.

"I hate to leave you again, my love," he said as though reading her thoughts. "His grace has need of those he can trust during this difficult time."

"Henry will always have need of you. There will always be difficulties."

"Do not begrudge him," Richard said, pulling her firmly to his side. "It was he who gave you to me, after all. Who else would have treated a poor knight with a Plantagenet princess?" He playfully pinched at her side when said it, holding her tight so that she could not wiggle from his grasp.

She shrieked and slapped at his chest to no avail. "I will have to speak to the king about assigning high born ladies to such curs!" she gasped through her struggles.

Richard claimed her mouth with his own to stop her protests, and his hands became gentle yet needy rather than playful. Margaret happily submitted to his caresses.

Within too few days, she was forced to watch him and his men as they rode from the courtyard to attend to the king's business.

September 1504

It seemed that he was always leaving. As the autumn leaves gilded their green with rich golds, Margaret was once again asking, "Richard, must you leave again so soon?"

"You know that I have no choice, my sweet Meg. I would do nothing but spend my days in bed with you if it were up to me."

Margaret swatted at Richard's chest, but his reflexes were quick and he grabbed her wrist and pulled her to him.

"You are scandalous, my lord," she protested with a giggle. "You know that it is impermissible for us to indulge in my condition."

He released her to place his hands on her rounded stomach. Though they had four surviving children, Richard appeared to be in awe of the changes that her body was going through as if it were the first time. Margaret knew that many other wives did not appear without clothing in front of their husbands during this time, but she adored watching him and feeling his hands upon the little life within her womb.

"There's my boy!" he said as his touches were rewarded with a firm kick.

The adoration on his face brought a smile to Margaret's.

"What makes you so sure that it is a boy? Ursula is counting on a playmate, which she feels she deserves after enduring three brothers already."

Richard chuckled without removing his eyes from the rolling motion of Margaret's womb. "Surely, our Ursula is correct, and may our Lord reward her with a golden haired sister."

They each chose not to make mention of the tiny sister that had been born, taking only a few breaths before joining Margaret's great extended family in the heavenly realm. This was too happy of a time for bringing up heartache. Margaret was too filled with thankfulness for her husband and their healthy surviving children to dwell upon the loss.

~ ~ ~ ~

Too soon, Richard was in the saddle preparing to ride out with his men once again. The horses snorted and pawed the ground, the only ones eager to be on their way. The crisp autumn air was perfect for traveling, and Margaret thanked God for that. She hated it when Richard was gone during inclement weather and she had no way of knowing if he had caught a chill.

She struggled to keep her emotions at bay, but her natural aversion to him leaving combined with the moodiness of her heavy pregnancy was causing tears to shine in her eyes. Blinking quickly, she ignored the urge to wipe her hands across her eyes. Richard's last view of her would be a happy one to help him endure their separation over the next several weeks. Her lashes feeling heavy with moisture, she gazed at him with a gleaming smile.

"Woman, you are no better liar than you are a cook."

"Richard!" His comment was successful in bringing a sincere upturn to one corner of her mouth. "It is a good thing that we have Nan then."

"Otherwise we would all starve," he agreed with an exaggerated sigh.

"Richard Pole! You would disrespect your wife in front of your men?"

"Would you like me to share with them some of the tasks you are particularly good at?"

His wink was quick but she did not miss it. Nor did he miss the blush that it brought to her face. He leaned down from his perch upon his favorite horse, bringing his face as close to hers as possible.

"Fifteen years and our sixth babe, I suspect they already know."

"You are a cur," she whispered as she stood on tiptoe in order to give him a lingering kiss.

They separated reluctantly, and Richard turned his horse, leading the small party away from the manor and the woman that he loved.

"God go with you," Margaret said, though she knew that he would not hear her over the thunder of hooves and laughter of men. To the rest of them, this was a welcome adventure away from the boring monotony of country life. Did Richard secretly feel that way as well?

At that moment, he paused and turned his horse just enough to lock eyes with her. The longing she saw there reassured her that he most certainly did not want to go but would do so because it was his king's bidding. She held up her hand in silent farewell. He nodded and turned away one final time.

October 1504

"Push, my lady!"

Margaret screamed in pain and with the effort of giving life to her sixth child. Visions of her last child, small and blue, kept flitting around the edges of her mind with the threat that the same thing could happen this time

"No."

"Yes, my lady. You must," the confused midwife insisted.

Margaret fixed her eyes upon a knothole in the wall across the room. Ignoring all but that imperfection in the wood, she pushed with all of her might until she felt the burden of the child leave her body. Her ears waited anxiously for the sound of the babe's first cry. Only once she heard it, could she relax and know that she had been successful.

"God be blessed," she whispered as she closed her eyes in exhaustion.

"A robust little boy!" announced the midwife as the baby's wails increased in volume.

A weary smile crossed Margaret's face, but it was interrupted by the sound of commotion on the other side of her door. The door was swung open, and Richard's squire entered, suddenly looking as shocked as the women at his actions.

"You will remove yourself from this room!" the midwife ordered with authority of her many years of experience.

"But . . . I" he seemed unsure of what to do now that he had forced his way in. He glanced at Margaret and a blush raced up his neck to cover his face.

Margaret's midwife looked as though she were preparing to physically remove him as the baby screamed its displeasure in the arms of one of Margaret's women.

"This is not an appropriate time for whatever message you

are bringing," she said, giving the boy a rough shove toward the door.

"It is Sir Richard," he stuttered uncertainly. Maybe the midwife was right. He had ridden all night to arrive as soon as possible, but now it seemed that his news could have easily been postponed by a great deal.

Margaret's eyes flashed open at her husband's name. "Wait!" she called just as the midwife prepared to shut the door in his face.

"My lady, it is most improper," she mumbled, but acquiesced.

"I am sorry, my lady," Richard's page said, his eyes downcast and his hands crumpling his cap. "I can wait in the hall until . . ."

"Nonsense," Margaret insisted. "What about Richard?"

"He" the squire looked toward the midwife for support, but he searched an unsympathetic countenance. "I wish our Lord had not left this news to me to bring."

Margaret's insides clenched with a kind of pain completely different than that which had recently brought her child into the world. "Where is he?"

"I believe at the abbey at Chester, but, my lady I do not think you understand," his nervous worrying of his cap had left it nearly unrecognizable, but Margaret was out of patience. She had just given birth and had no energy remaining for tongue-tied squires.

"You're right, I do not. That is because you have not told me." She tried to calculate how soon she could convince her women to allow her to go to Richard. She should stay in her rooms until her churching, but she would not stay abed if Richard had need of her.

"I'm sorry, my lady." Tears filled his eyes, reminding the women in the room just how young he was, and the pain in Margaret's gut reached into her chest. "He was ill, Lady Pole." He fell to his knees, as if to beg her forgiveness. "It was so quick, my lady."

"No," Margaret whispered. She wished she had allowed the midwife to send him away.

Sensing that Margaret could take no more, the midwife moved once more to shove him through the door.

"Is he?" Margaret could say no more as she felt her world crumble and she wished to be swallowed up into the depths of the earth.

"I beg your forgiveness, my lady. He was taken up by our Lord two days hence."

With that, the midwife did shut the door in his face before she rushed to Margaret, who was already sobbing uncontrollably.

"Not my Richard," she moaned, punching at the bedding with knuckles that were still swollen from pregnancy.

"Wine," Margaret's midwife said to the closest lady, who stood, like the others in astonished stillness.

"Of course," she said, and rushed from the room glad to have a task to attend to.

"Please, stay away," Margaret said, holding up a hand to ward off anyone who would go to her side.

The baby's wails became demanding, and the midwife ordered the wet nurse to take him from the room.

"No!" Margaret forced her voice to steady. "Give him to me."

The woman looked between her lady and the midwife, uncertain which she should obey.

"He is my child, and you will give him to me," Margaret insisted.

"Yes, my lady." The young woman rushed forward and placed the red faced infant in Margaret's waiting arms.

Tears continued to stream down Margaret's face, though she

no longer shook with emotion. "I will nurse him myself."

"What? My lady, your wet nurse is waiting to take the baby for you," the midwife needlessly pointed to the curvy young woman.

"No. He is mine," Margaret said, her voice thick and strained, "and he is the last bit of Richard that I will ever have. Our baby will be fed by his mother."

The midwife shrugged, and turned back to her own business. She had not become successful at her trade by arguing with noble ladies.

Margaret gazed at the tiny boy, now suckling contentedly at her breast, but could see only Richard's face. Maybe there had been a mistake. He could not truly be gone. Would her Heavenly Father do this to her? After her parents and brother, surely her husband would not be taken from her as well.

The women carried on their work around her, and it was almost as if the devastating announcement had not been made. If it were not for the fact that the infant fed at her own breast rather than that of the wet nurse, she could convince herself that she had imagined it.

But she had not. Richard, the man she had grown to love though under different circumstances she would not have even known him, was gone.

She watched their baby fall into peaceful sleep through the tears that she felt would never cease.

December 1504

"Is this young Geoffrey? Isn't he the spirit and image of his father?"

The jovial duke of Somerset lifted the infant's chin with a stubby finger for a moment to express interest that he knew would please Margaret. She was well aware that he saw no resemblance to her late husband and would be hoping that she would send the baby away with his nurse as soon as possible. He was a kind man, but still a man with no room in his schedule for young children. With that in mind, Margaret beckoned to Molly and sent her off to the nursery with her precious bundle.

"Did Richard have our accounts in good order, Henry?"

"Of course, of course," he said as he fumbled with papers in one hand while balancing a quickly acquired wine goblet in the other. "I am happy to cover the costs of Richard's funeral arrangements. He was such a dear friend."

Henry did not look at Margaret as he said this, and she wondered if he hid tears or did not want to see her shame in the admission that she had not the funds to cover the cost of her husband's funeral. While she wanted to argue and decline his generous offer, she had to think of her children's future rather than her own pride.

"Thank you, Henry. When I am in a position to return your kindness, you can rest assured that I shall."

The duke continued to shuffle papers with no obvious objective other than keeping his hands busy. "You will remain here with the children?" he asked, gazing around at the large estate clearly wondering how she would keep it up.

"I think not," she said and continued before he could object. "I will spend some time at Syon Abbey while I am in mourning. The peace and prayer will restore my state of mind, and the children can begin their lessons."

"A wise plan, dear Margaret." He took a slow sip from his wine while studying her over the rim. "And then?"

She sighed. She was not in the mood to plan further than the next day, but her circumstances did not allow her the luxury of procrastination. "I will likely spend some time with Catherine. We shall see."

Margaret and Princess Catherine had become quick friends during the latter's brief marriage to Margaret's cousin, Prince Arthur. Had he not died, Catherine would be a happy bride and mother, and Elizabeth might still be alive. Margaret shook her head to clear it. What might have been didn't matter and only served to distract her from important decisions. "Yes, I will spend some time with Catherine," she said more confidently.

April 1509

"Long live the king! Long live King Henry!"

Margaret wasn't sure how to feel about the death of Henry Tudor, who had committed the legalized murder of her brother and defeated her uncle in battle. She certainly wouldn't be shedding any tears for the man who had turned her future upside-down when he walked away from Bosworth as the victor. She had tried to find the good in him for Elizabeth's sake, but now they were both gone. Their son Henry, who looked so much like his grandfather, King Edward, stood in his father's place.

Henry was tall, handsome, and charismatic - everything that his father had failed to be. He made people laugh, and they felt special to be spoken to by the king himself. His red-gold hair gleamed in the sun like a Plantagenet crown. But he was not truly a Plantagenet, Margaret reminded herself. Whatever resemblance he had in appearance and personality with Elizabeth's father, Henry was a Tudor.

As he made his way toward Margaret, she forced herself to think about Richard. He was the one gift that the late king had given her that she could be thankful for. She still missed him and caught glimpses of him in the way Geoffrey laughed and the curl of Reginald's hair. Before her thoughts ran away with her, she dropped into a deep curtsey.

"Cousin!" Henry boomed. "Rise, dear Margaret and give me a kiss!"

Margaret smiled in spite of herself and grazed her lips against young Henry's cheek. "You look very well, your grace."

He did. All of the women of marrying age in the vicinity looked jealously at Margaret for gaining his attention. The fact that she was his close relation and twice his age made little difference.

"I pray that your reign will be long and prosperous," she

added, curtseying again to indicate that he was free to leave her for more interesting members of his audience.

"Thank you, Lady Pole. You can be sure that I will be sharing my bounty with you and your family."

Margaret opened her mouth to inquire his meaning, but he had already moved on, closely followed by a herd of sycophants hoping to profitably attach themselves to him.

It was true that she had struggled in the years since Richard's death, though she had refused to marry again in order to ease the burden on herself. Her reluctance had only partially been due to loyalty to the one she had loved. She had also been hesitant to inquire who Henry Tudor would choose to pair her with a second time. It was safer to be alone and focus on her children. Would this Henry choose to raise her up to a status more suitable to her ancestry?

Her answer came within weeks. Margaret was asked to come to court and wait upon her closest friend, Princess Catherine, who was soon to become Henry's queen.

May 1509

"Margaret! You will not believe the good news!"

Margaret rushed to Catherine's side, overflowing with thankfulness to see her friend so full of joy after years of uncertainty and doubt.

"What is it?" she asked, taking Catherine's hands into her own. The younger woman's eyes were shining with happiness that had been adding beauty to her countenance since the new King Henry had announced that he would finally marry her.

"He is releasing William Courtenay from the Tower!"

Margaret was touched that this news brought Catherine such delight. William's wife, Margaret's cousin Cat, would undoubtedly be thrilled to have her husband back after years of imprisonment under Henry VII. It was evidence of Catherine's deep love and compassion for others that she had taken up the Courtenay cause as her own.

"That is wonderful indeed," Margaret agreed. She allowed her mind to create a vision of the bold Cat welcoming her husband back into his home. Cat was not one to hide her feelings behind decorum and would greet him with passion. Margaret had to shake herself back into the present before letting the vision take her too far into the Courtenays' private moments. She could see that Catherine was watching her, waiting for confirmation that she had used her power over the king effectively.

"Cat will be stunned and overjoyed," Margaret assured her. "You have made a friend and gained a supporter for life."

"The praise should go to God and our gracious King Henry, who has made their reunion possible," Catherine demurred.

"Yes. Thank God for King Henry," Margaret agreed, her years of training enabling her to keep the surprise from her face that these words had ever been formed by her. Maybe this King

Henry would be one that she could indeed thank God for.

"We truly should," insisted Catherine. "Look at how he has lifted up the both of us from our poverty and unhappiness." She made sweeping motions with her arms as she said this, as though to emphasize the bounty gifted to them by their new king. "Cat will have her William returned to her, and all will be pardoned."

"All except the de la Pole brothers," Margaret couldn't stop herself from saying.

Catherine blushed only for a moment. She had lost the innocence that had caused her face to flame at the slightest provocation that had embarrassed her when she first became Arthur's young bride.

"The de la Pole brothers are in open rebellion and should not expect pardon." Catherine proved eager to demonstrate that she would be her husband's most staunch supporter. "He has also had those vile ministers Dudley and Empson executed for their lawless acts," she added in the hopes of encouraging Margaret to look upon her betrothed more favorably.

"That is true," Margaret agreed without emotion. While she liked the henchmen of Henry VII no more than anyone else, she could not rejoice at the tyrannical act that whispered of executions under the former king that had been little more than legalized murder. Margaret was keeping quietly to herself until the son proved a better man than the father, even if he was favoring her and Catherine to a much greater extent.

June 1509

Catherine looked angelic as a natural flush rose to her cheeks and excitement lit her eyes, rendering cosmetics entirely unnecessary for enhancing her beauty. Margaret watched as women bustled about to prepare the princess for her wedding day. If the people expected a second exquisite St. Paul's ceremony, they would be disappointed. Catherine showed every sign that she would be submissive to her husband in all things, but in this she had insisted that her wedding day to Henry would not be filled with mirror images of her marriage to his brother on that autumn day almost a decade earlier.

Though their vows would be exchanged within the palace at Greenwich with only the necessary witnesses in attendance, Catherine was adamant that she look her best for her young groom. When asked if she was concerned that she was five years older than the virile, young king, Catherine simply laughed the idea aside. She had waited a quarter of her life to marry Henry, and nothing would make her think twice now.

Margaret prayed that Catherine's second marriage would be much happier than her first, and much longer. The years that had stretched between these days had been filled with doubt and conditions that most princesses never had to learn to live with. Catherine had been resolute and was now receiving her reward. As Margaret prepared to return to her children at Bockmer, she prayed that Catherine's joy would be complete and that she would soon bear a child.

Seeing Catherine eager for her wedding day had not given Margaret the pangs of jealousy that she had half expected. She still missed Richard, but that emptiness had not given her the urge to find a second husband. For this one thing, she did have reason to be thankful to Henry. He had shown no signs that he planned on asking her to marry any of his followers. As a relatively poor remnant of a bygone dynasty, maybe she was no longer the favorable catch that she assumed herself to be.

Before the evening fell, Catherine was enraptured with wedded bliss. A more intimate party of women prepared her for the night with Henry, and Margaret used this time to say goodbye as well.

"You have your husband to see to your needs, and I must attend to my children," Margaret said firmly when Catherine begged her to stay at court. Catherine was a dear friend, but Margaret had learned through hard experience to give up nothing for the pleasure of kings and queens.

"Just for a short time," Catherine pleaded. "You have been by my side through so much," she added, allowing her open countenance to finish the work.

"Very well," Margaret acquiesced. "I shall stay for a fortnight to ensure that you are well ensconced in wedded bliss before I return to Bockmer." She brushed through Catherine's gleaming coppery hair and changed the subject. "Is there anything else you need from me before I leave you to the attention of your bridegroom?"

To Margaret's surprise, the quick reddening of Catherine's younger years warmed her cheeks. She pulled Margaret close to avoid eager ears. "Is there anything . . . well, anything that I should know?" she asked in a barely audible whisper.

"But, Catherine, surely . . ." she stopped herself before saying more. Remembering the days with Catherine and Arthur at Ludlow, Margaret suddenly understood. "You truly are untouched. Arthur never . . ."

"He was not healthy enough during our short time together. I, of course, did not pressure him, thinking that we had long years ahead of us." The flush had faded from Catherine's cheeks, but she looked down to avoid Margaret's eyes.

"Do not worry," Margaret said, embracing the shockingly naïve little queen. "You will know by nature what to do."

She could hardly add that Henry certainly had the experience to guide her. It was one of those things that was understood but not spoken of. Margaret kissed Catherine on the forehead as if she were her daughter, gave her a silent blessing and the sign of the cross upon her brow, and quietly left the room. Though it had not been her intention, she found herself kneeling in the chapel before returning to her own rooms. Please Lord, she begged, let this marriage be blessed and watch over your devoted daughter, Catherine.

~ ~ ~ ~

Catherine would be queen, and it seems one Tudor prince would do as well as the other. Margaret was astonished at first to hear that young Henry intended to make his brother's wife his own. But upon second thought, it made a sort of sense. Henry would be replacing his brother in every sense of the word, as if poor Arthur had never existed at all.

"Margaret, it is such a comfort to have you here with me." They sat working at their embroidery projects, Catherine in a dress more beautiful and elaborate than anything she had worn since Arthur died.

"There is nowhere else I would rather be," Margaret said though images of her children briefly flashed through her mind. "You and I are kindred spirits, are we not?" she added with a smile.

"Ah, but if I were you, I would rather be with my children," Catherine said knowingly. "It makes me appreciate your presence all the more. You alone shared my time with Arthur, before we were

35

both left alone in this world." She worked her embroidery with a small forced smile on her face.

Margaret was impressed by her friend's strength, but she did not want to be reminded of their dead husbands today, nor of the time that they had spent together after Richard's death. Two young widows praying for the king to see their needs but not marry them off to men not of their choosing - it was not a memory that Margaret often visited. Better to live in the present.

"The boys are busy with their tutors, and Ursula may yet join me here. We will get you settled as a happily married woman first." Margaret shared a secret smile with Catherine, shoving aside questions about the age difference between the royal couple and whether or not God blesses those who marry their brothers' wives.

Catherine had been through too much since arriving in England to great rejoicing eight years earlier, Margaret thought. Both women had been raised from the relative poverty and obscurity that Henry VII was comfortable leaving them in. The son had proven more generous.

"Will you marry again, Margaret?"

Catherine may have been a shy and quiet girl when she first arrived to be Arthur's bride with few words of English under her control, but she had gained confidence through her trials.

"That will be up to the king." Margaret evaded any discussion of remarrying and was no longer of an age or level of wealth that would bring suitors. "I am content with my children."

"I could speak for you," Catherine began, eyeing Margaret discreetly. "If there is someone you prefer."

Margaret answered with laughter causing her words to quake. "Do not waste the favors earned in Henry's bed upon me." She was purposely bold to encourage Catherine to drop the subject.

It worked. Catherine focused her eyes on her work as her

characteristic blush darkened her Spanish skin.

"Maybe there is one thing that I would ask," Margaret thought aloud, making Catherine's head bob up in surprise. "When the time is right," Margaret added.

"Anything, Margaret," Catherine gushed. She cast her work aside to take up the older woman's hands. "You were with me through the darkest part of my life. Watching Arthur..." She faltered. Though they were married just a few months, Catherine was still brought to tears by the thought of her young husband's suffering and death. "What can I do for you, once I am crowned queen?"

"It is Cat's William. He remains in the Tower for his impetuous talk. I know that Henry said he would be released, but can you ensure that it does not slip his mind?"

Catherine drew back slightly. She had not expected to speak to her husband about treason quite yet. Margaret held her hands firmly, injecting her with confidence as she continued. "Courtenay is no threat to Henry, even less so than he was to his father. He will be content to raise his children and love his wife. Give them their pride in their Plantagenet blood while Henry has the crown."

Catherine did not immediately speak. She examined Margaret's face as though she would look for hidden motives there. The Tudors feared Plantagenet blood, knowing that they have so little of it. However, this Henry has much more than his father did, thanks to his beloved mother. Surely, he would be less afraid of rival claimants.

"Of course, I will." Catherine suddenly decided. "When the time is right."

~ ~ ~ ~

Additional coaxing from Catherine was more effective than

years of efforts by others, and William Courtenay was released within the fortnight. In fact, he was further honored with the task of carrying Henry's sword at his coronation.

Margaret hoped that Cat's husband accepted the unspoken message that he was welcome to serve the king as long as he remembered his place. Cat watched William with evident pride, her own head held high in a sophisticated posture that comes naturally only to a princess, which of course she was. Margaret had observed them both and prayed that they could focus on their household and rein in their proud tongues.

Shifting her focus to the royal couple, Margaret's smile came easily. Their marriage may have been a private affair, but not so with their joint coronation. Henry was insistent that he had his opportunity to show off his lovely bride, and he had chosen his moment well.

The streets had been transformed by tapestries and rich cloth draped along the path of the coronation procession. In ermine trimmed scarlet and cloth of gold, Henry was magnificent. His bearing was dignified yet approachable and must have come naturally to him as it had his grandfather, for he certainly had not learned it from his father. He was young and golden, and the people shoved and craned their necks for a glimpse of him.

Not far behind her husband in the procession, Catherine was carried in an elaborately decorated litter. Her rich auburn hair, only slightly darker in hue than Henry's, was loose and glorious. Margaret thought that Catherine's hair was her most beautiful accessory, despite the intricacy of the jewels, embroidery, and fabrics that surrounded her. The Englishmen who had cheered Catherine as she became the bride of the first Tudor prince welcomed her all the more now as she finally took her place as queen. Their excitement was palpable as they quickly tore away at the cloth of gold fabric that lined the street to Westminster. It had guarded the procession from dust and worse but now became souvenirs.

Henry was happy to let them have their mementos. He cheerily laughed and waved as the crowd pressed in and collapsed on themselves as soon as the last prancing horse passed. When the Archbishop of Canterbury hailed, "Vivat, vivat rex!" they returned the cry four times. "Long live the king!" Henry and Catherine proclaimed their vows to serve England with dignity before leaving the abbey for several days of jousting, celebrations, and dining.

Margaret took this opportunity to quietly slip away to Bockmer.

July 1509

Back upon her own estate, Margaret felt tension leave her back and shoulders that she had not even realized was there. She loved Catherine and had been happy to serve her in many roles over the years, but she could not live at court. It was more than being away from her children. She simply could not feel as though she belonged there.

Margaret had been forced to reduce her household to the bare minimum following Richard's death and, at times, was only able to maintain that through the generosity and advisement of friends like Henry of Somerset. He visited and reviewed her records as often as he was able, often praising Margaret for her good management.

"You've made remarkable work of it for a woman," he exclaimed, believing this to be a high compliment indeed, and Margaret had taken it for the kind encouragement it was meant to be.

Margaret's attention was shifted by the appearance of her son, Henry. Recently turned seventeen and a heartbreaking image of his father, he had reached the point where he required useful work to put his hands to in order to avoid the evils of idleness. For this reason and because Margaret felt it was more his place than hers, Henry had been given an increasing amount of responsibilities over what remained of the Pole estates. She was happy to see him now for she had greater plans in mind for him.

"Come and sit with me, Henry," she said, patting the seat next to her. She had been gazing out the window of Richard's study, where she spent much more time since his death than she ever had while he was alive. It made her feel closer to him, touching the papers and furniture that had been his.

She had brought in chairs that she placed in front of the

large windows, so that she could comfortably pass the time in the room when not working at the desk. Henry joined her, dropping himself into the opposite chair with the easy grace of youth.

"Are you well, mother?" he asked, making her smile at his politeness while bittersweet feelings made her miss him calling her mama.

"I am, thanks be to God," she responded as she reached out to pat his hand. It was no longer the hand of a little boy, but now carried scars and callouses from training and hard work. "I would like to speak to you on an important matter."

He did not seem surprised and simply waited for her to carry on, his honey brown eyes more serious than his father's had ever been.

Knowing that he appreciated frankness, Margaret did not wait to broach her topic. "I have a marriage in mind for you, Henry. One that I think you will be happy with and will enable you to come into resources that I have not the power to give you."

She had thought that, at this point, her son would have something to say, but he continued to gaze at her with a controlled look on his face that gave away nothing. How had he learned to arrange his face that way, she wondered. It was a skill that she had often wished she had mastered to a greater degree. His stillness made her want to fidget, but she would not be intimidated by her own child. She forced herself to picture his baby face as she stared into the eyes of this man fully grown.

"It is Jane Neville that I speak of, and there are a variety of reasons why I feel she is a good match. Do you remember her?"

"Baron Bergavenny's daughter, of course," Henry admitted that he was acquainted with the girl in question and nothing more.

Margaret sat up straighter in her chair in order to be on eye level with her son. "Indeed," she said. "Jane's father has no sons.

Therefore, Jane is expected to split his estate with her sister - eventually, of course. Bergavenny is in good health, but his wife died last year."

Henry rubbed his chin and furrowed his brow in a thoughtful posture that made him look years older than his true age. Margaret waited for his judgement on the matter while holding her hands still in her lap. After a few moments, a hint of a smile crossed Henry's face.

"Yes, I believe you are right, mother. A match with the Nevilles is a respectable and appropriate one. If King Henry elevates us, as he has led us to expect, Jane and I could enjoy a comfortable future together."

Wondering how a child of hers and Richard's could be so devoid of passion, Margaret nodded and waited for him to continue.

"Have you spoken to Lord Bergavenny?" he asked.

"We have had preliminary discussions," Margaret said with a nod indicating that she had been pleased with the result. "He understands that I have less than I would like to leave to my children while he does not have sons to inherit his estate. You and Jane are of an age and similar temperament. I do not advise you to count on favor from the king, but it shall be a blessing if that were to come to you as well."

Finally, an authentic smile lit Henry's face, and Margaret couldn't help but return it.

"I trust your judgement in all matters, mother, and confess that your plan pleases me as well. When do you see the betrothal being carried out?" he asked. He was attempting to keep his voice formal and his attitude disinterested, but Margaret noticed that a hint of a smile could not be kept from his lips. Maybe there was more than met the eye in her oldest son. Jane would have her work cut out for her.

Margaret assured him that she would see to finalizing the arrangements that would carry her first child far from her. She tried not to think of it that way, but as she watched Henry stroll from the room with a new lift in his step she couldn't help but think of Richard.

He had been gone for almost five years and would not recognize his own children were he to see them today. Henry was ready for the responsibilities that came with marriage, but Margaret almost wished that he were not so she could hold him close and not have to let go.

She walked slowly to the window of the room that would always be Richard's study in her mind, whoever made use of it. She examined the landscape for other changes that had taken place since that day when her greatest joy was mingled with her harshest loss.

Geoffrey galloped across the grounds like a frisky colt, and a lump rose in Margaret's throat as she remembered, not for the first time, that Richard had never held this youngest son. Geoffrey had the red-gold hair that Plantagenets were famous for, and Margaret was thankful that he was not another painful reminder of Richard the way Henry was with his dark ringlets inherited from his father. She turned away from the window with the fleeting thought that even the trees were taller than Richard would remember them. It was necessary for her to change the path of her thoughts before they led her to the pit it was difficult to pull herself up from. She no longer had Richard to lend her a hand upward.

She remembered the example of her cousin Elizabeth as she held to her faith through the many losses and challenges of her life. The same God that had seen Elizabeth through the destruction of her family and the founding of a new one would serve Margaret as well. Leaving the study, Margaret strode with purpose for her private chapel. The time on her knees would encourage her and help her feel linked to all those she missed so sorely.

December 1509

With Henry's future secured to that of Jane Neville's, Margaret had felt she should return to court. She enjoyed Catherine's company and appreciated the king's kindness to her family, but few would understand her preference for her small estate at Bockmer. The Christmas festivities and Catherine's pregnancy would make the time more enjoyable. A smile softened Margaret's countenance as she envisioned herself holding the next heir to England's crown in a few short months. Catherine radiated joy as she happily assured anyone who would listen that she was certain to be bearing a prince.

Margaret prepared to enter Catherine's room now and was overflowing with gladness. The optimistic queen was good company for her, countering her own less cheerful moods with natural happiness. Pausing only a moment at the door to compose herself for the chaos that was likely to be found within Catherine's busy rooms, Margaret entered but did not take more than a single step inside the room, frozen as she was in shock.

Catherine was sitting in the center of her luxurious bed, tears streaming down her face. Her solicitous ladies patted her and offered whispered words of comfort to little avail. Margaret's mind worked furiously for what could have upset Catherine to this extent. No news that she could recall should have been more than a minor disappointment, and who would dare share anything worse with the queen in her condition?

Jolting herself into action, Margaret rushed forward and shoved the more junior members of Catherine's household aside. Placing herself before Catherine, she knelt upon the soft coverlet and put her hands on either side of Catherine's warm, tear-streaked face. She firmly but gently forced Catherine to face her. Raw pain seemed to emanate from the eyes that met Margaret's.

The baby! That was the only reason Margaret could conceive for the anguish in Catherine's eyes, but she did not want to look down and break eye contact. Instead, she added her own shushing and empty words to those of the other women as she softly stroked Catherine's hair away from her face. Finally, something that Margaret whispered captured the queen's attention.

"No, that is not it," Catherine insisted, though her breath caught in her throat as sobs made speech difficult.

Margaret wrinkled her brow. Not the baby? Then what? Finally, she allowed herself to look about the room, taking in details she had looked past earlier. The other women looked guilty but not remorseful. They did not appear to believe that the heir had been lost.

"You may all leave. I will attend the queen," Margaret said as she stood next to the bed, her disdainful glare dared any of them to countermand her.

None did, and the room was soon cleared. Without a crowd gathered about her, Catherine seemed capable of controlling her emotions. The shaking sobs slowed to quivering hiccoughs, and Margaret waited patiently, stroking the girl's slim shoulders and calming her own breathing. Once Catherine seemed recovered enough for speech, Margaret moved to sit before her once again.

"What is it, my friend?" she asked, taking up Catherine's small hands. Her fingers stroked Catherine's, and she couldn't help but admire the lovely rings that Henry had placed there as evidence of the great love he had for his queen.

"Henry has taken a mistress," Catherine said so quietly that Margaret was sure she must have misheard, though she couldn't ask for this to be repeated.

"Surely not," she began, but Catherine interrupted her.

"It is certain," Catherine insisted, with a deep breath

shuddering out of her small frame. "He has taken up with Bess Fitzwalter, and I seem to be the last to know. Well, other than you." A half-hearted smile flitted across her face as she raised her bloodshot eyes to Margaret's. "I suppose I was a fool to think he would not stray while kept from my bed by the babe."

Margaret enveloped Catherine in a firm embrace. "You are not a fool, but Henry is a young man who has suddenly had the entire kingdom placed at his feet. He gives not enough thought to the idea that there are some gifts offered that he should not accept."

As she held Catherine and let the last sniffles leave her, Margaret resolved to speak to her own boys about the treatment of their wives through childbearing. She could not reprimand the king, but she could save her daughters-in-law some heartache, she hoped. Bringing herself back to the present situation, she held the queen and rocked her as she would her own child, for there was nothing to be done but to bear the knowledge that her husband had not taken long to prove that he would put his own satisfaction above her happiness.

Within a few days, Catherine demonstrated her royal upbringing by appearing at supper at Henry's side. The looks of admiration that she gave him were sincere and as enthusiastic as they had been prior to his straying. Like many queens before her, Catherine had chosen to be content that she would be the mother to princes and princesses, if not the only woman in her husband's bed. Margaret was astounded by Catherine's strength but grateful once again for the husband God had joined her to, for he had never caused her that kind of pain.

Sitting near enough to hear the conversation between king and queen, Margaret followed Catherine's example. She laughed at Henry's jokes and showed proper appreciation for his stories as though there were not already secrets building up between the young royal couple.

Exhausted from the façade, Margaret found a quiet spot to sit when the entertainment began. Leaving Catherine's side, she escaped to an alcove that afforded some slight privacy. She wished that she could leave the hall altogether, and felt a desire for her own home and family swelling in her breast. The Christmas revelries would keep her from Bockmer for several more weeks, but maybe she could leave for some time then before Catherine's lying in.

Her soul required time away from the gaudy, gilded beauty of court that attempted to hide heartache, manipulation, and ambition. Circumstances would keep her there as Catherine's needs proved greater than those of Margaret's children.

January 1510

Catherine frantically tore at her bed hangings and grasped at her ladies' hands. Nothing she could do would tighten her womb to hold the baby inside. Margaret winced as her friend murmured, "No, no, no" until her tears made her incapable of speech. In an attempt to calm her, Margaret took Catherine in her arms much as she would have one of her children with a gentle swaying motion that could not ease the pain but demonstrated her love and sympathy.

After a moment, Catherine responded to Margaret's mothering, and a calm peace began to come over her. She laid back on the bed and a tiny child slipped from her womb with little of the anticipated pain and pushing. Leaving her mother before either were ready, the little princess never took a breath of chilled English air.

Catherine's face was vacant, a painful contrast to the joy that had been evident since she discovered she was with child. She had allowed herself only the one breakdown over Henry's infidelity, and Margaret admired her dignity without mentioning the topic again. Remembering her own babes gone to God too soon, Margaret knew that there was little she could do to comfort the young woman in this situation either. Instead, she quietly cleared the room of anyone else and pulled a seat near the bed which looked far too large for the woman cocooned there.

Taking up needlework, Margaret was simply present. She covertly monitored Catherine and waited to respond should she wish to speak.

Enough time passed in silence that Margaret began to wonder if she should try another approach, when Catherine suddenly spoke in little more than a whisper, her voice sounding hoarse with emotion. "What will Henry think?"

Pressing her lips together and slowly filling her lungs with the smoky air emitted from the fire, Margaret did not rush to answer. Henry had proven himself self-assured and remarkably capable in the months since he became king. Would his confidence be shaken by this loss? Some would call it a judgement from God upon the young king's reign, but that only mattered if Henry believed it. Margaret remembered how Richard had mourned as fervently as she had when they lost their little ones. She also knew that Henry's father had not shown anger toward Elizabeth when their royal children had not been protected from illness by their status.

"He will be concerned for you, above all things," Margaret decided. "God will send you more children, but Henry has only one queen. You need not worry that he will blame you for things that only God can control." Setting down the needlework and shifting herself to sit on the edge of the bed, Margaret took Catherine's small, pale hand. "Henry has waited many years to marry you, and even a king expects some hardships in life. He will stand by you and love you as he always has."

Catherine turned her head toward the older woman and seemed to examine her. "Do you truly think so?" Her eyes were swimming with tears, this time for her disappointed husband rather than her dead daughter.

Margaret wished that she could take some of Catherine's pain onto herself, but she could only reassure her, "He loves you more than anything in this world."

She held Catherine until she fell into a deep, exhausted sleep. Turning to take one last look before leaving the room, Margaret was struck by how young and innocent Catherine appeared with her cares removed by dreams. A few reddish blond locks trailed across her forehead and down her cheek, her soft breathing disturbing a few strands. Margaret took a deep breath and pulled at the heavy door, praying that she was right about Henry.

~ ~ ~ ~

Margaret was not present during the private moments shared between Henry and Catherine after a carefully chosen lady had been sent to him with the news of his daughter's death. She was fidgeting outside the door to Catherine's chamber when Henry strode out with his chest thrust forward in confidence though no smile lit his face.

"Please see to my dear wife, cousin," He requested as he lifted Margaret from her expertly performed curtsey. "I know that she still grieves, but I wish for her to be healthy enough for God to bless us with another child. I have no doubt that your attendance will help her."

He was already carrying on his way when Margaret managed to weakly respond. "I will do my best, your grace."

Waiting for Henry to be out of sight in case he should decide to call her back, Margaret tapped her foot until she could spin around and enter Catherine's room. She released the breath that she had been holding when she saw a look of contentment, if not happiness, on Catherine's face. Forcing herself to a more casual pace, Margaret went to the edge of Catherine's bed and waited for her to speak.

"You were right. He is not angry and only wishes to have me back in his bed." The rosy glow of her cheeks gave deeper meaning to the slight lift of the corners of Catherine's lips. "Maybe I will be able to do better than that."

Margaret's brow furrowed, but before she could pose a question Catherine continued. "I do believe that I may have been carrying twins." Catherine's smile broadened, but Margaret was reluctant to encourage false hope.

"What causes you to believe that?" she asked softly as she stroked the young queen's hand.

Catherine peered around the room before answering, though both knew they were alone. "Look, and see if you do not agree."

The bed coverings were swept away, and Catherine framed her small hands around her still bulging belly. "Another child remains in my womb, Margaret. I am almost certain of it."

Catherine nodded to encourage Margaret's touch, and so she did. "I should caution you that many women experience a swollen womb for many days beyond childbearing," Margaret said as her fingers gently prodded and searched for evidence that life thrived underneath. "I will call for a physician to evaluate your condition, but you should remain in bed in either case. You must recover, especially if a child continues to grow within your womb. Did you mention this to Henry?"

Catherine's lashes concealed her eyes as she slowly shook her head. "Not yet," she admitted. "I did not want to be the bearer of false hope."

Margaret tried to stifle her sigh of relief and hide it behind a smile. "That was wise. Let's see what the learned physician thinks before we inform the king."

Busying herself with unnecessary tidying of the room, Margaret awaited the physician's arrival. She had once again sent Catherine's other ladies and servants from the room. Whether Catherine was right or wrong, this needed to be a private moment. After adjusting the fall of a tapestry across the window for the fifth time, Margaret forced her hands to be still. She closed her eyes for a moment of silent prayer before fetching a dish of sweetmeats from a small table. Offering one to Catherine, she said, "You must build your strength."

"Ah, you do know my weaknesses," Catherine said as she eagerly swiped several of the sugary tidbits from the plate.

The sweetness seemed to melt across Margaret's tongue, and she savored this simple pleasure before the disappointment that she was sure was about to come. Soon, a man was bustling into the room surrounded by an air of self-importance. Margaret tried to keep the smirk from her face that this man would demonstrate such confidence in the company of the queen as she licked the last of the sweetmeat from her lips and brushed her fingers on her skirt. She needn't have concerned herself, because the arrogant man did not even glance her way.

"Your grace," he said dismissively, placing his instruments upon a table that had been moved to the bedside for his use. "I have been called to examine you once again."

Margaret bristled at his tone that inferred his opinion of this feminine silliness, and she moved forward to defend Catherine, almost forgetting that she did not believe her either. "Sir, I remind you that you address the queen," she said as she placed herself at the opposite side of the bed and took Catherine's hand.

The physician simply raised a bushy eyebrow at her and murmured, "Indeed."

Margaret contented herself with silent support of her friend as the humiliating examination took place. How she wished that Catherine's suffering would have worthwhile results. Could she trust this haughty physician to break the news with compassion?

With quick, precise movements, he took measurements and evaluated Catherine's bloated womb. A few questions were asked in a clipped tone, the answers recognized by a single nod. Before she knew it, he was closing his case and offering Catherine a shallow bow. "It appears that you are correct, your grace. I believe a living child remains in your womb, and you can expect to deliver it this spring with proper rest and God's blessings, of course."

Words of comfort were already forming on Margaret's lips when she realized what he had said. She looked to him with widened eyes, a silent question within them. He gave her one of his curt nods in response and strode from the room without another word. Margaret realized she was still staring at the door where he had disappeared with her mouth fallen slightly agape when the pressure of Catherine's hand dragged her from her shock.

"You see, Margaret! God is with us, and he protects my remaining child."

Catherine's beauty shone once again in her joy, but Margaret could only manage a forced smile before she excused herself to visit the chapel. She would praise God for his mercy and beg his protection over the child that she was still not quite convinced existed.

As the days passed and Catherine's body continued to show the symptoms of pregnancy, Margaret began to believe that she could have been wrong. Why was she so cynical regarding the physician's diagnosis? Surely, he would receive no reward for false promises that demonstrated a lack of skill. She allowed herself to be caught up in Catherine's joy. Despite the fact that they looked forward to weeks in the confinement quarters, both women looked at Catherine's bulging stomach and saw a miracle.

March 1510

"I think we should have the king's physician return."

Catherine words were barely louder than a whisper, and Margaret had been expecting to hear them for days. Throughout the month of February, they had been filled with excitement for the coming child. In their cozy rooms, Margaret stitched tiny clothes while Catherine worked on new shirts for Henry. They had shared secret smiles and calm contentedness while they patiently waited for the babe to grow strong. However, as more time passed and Catherine's womb started to shrink rather than grow, Margaret's doubts returned.

"Have you felt the babe's movements?" Margaret asked, remembering her own children making their presence well known at this stage.

"I'm not sure," Catherine admitted, her voice even lower than before.

Margaret clamped her lips together as she turned away to put away her sewing before addressing the queen's concerns. "I will see that he attends you as soon as one of Henry's men can have him here." Not feeling prepared to offer continued false hope, she quietly left the room without saying more.

When he arrived, his posture was slightly stooped and the lines seemed to be more deeply engraved on his face. He did not address the queen with any more respect than in his first visit, but exasperation replaced the confidence he had exuded. After a brief examination and a few questions that he appeared to not need the answers to, he stood to his full height and arranged himself into a confident stance.

"My apologies for being the bearer of unfortunate news," he began, and tears were already streaking down Catherine's face. "I believe that your grace has lost the second child as well, or there is a possibility that it never existed."

As sobs shook Catherine's shoulders, Margaret was rooted to her seat. She couldn't take her eyes off this man who refused to take responsibility for his part in her grief. She knew there was no point in asking him why he had given the favorable news in the first place. He would find a way to blame it on Catherine. He did not glance at either woman again as he packed up the tools of his trade and left the room. His job was done, and the aftermath was not his problem.

"Margaret, I don't understand! Wouldn't I know if I had lost another child?"

Watching tears roll down Catherine's blotchy skin and hearing her innocent inquiry, Margaret's heart softened. The doctor no longer mattered. Her task was to comfort this woman who was both her friend and her queen.

~ ~ ~ ~

Henry accepted the news with only a hint of frustration. Whether he was upset over the time lost as Catherine laid in pointless confinement or the failure of the physician serving him to provide him with what he wanted, Margaret was not certain. Catherine was hurriedly churched so that she could return to his bed, and the child, or children, were not mentioned in Margaret's presence again.

After the ebb and flow of the past months' emotions, Margaret was relieved to obtain leave to see to her own estates and her children. She left feeling confident that Catherine's healing would continue in Henry's capable hands.

May 1510

Not only was Margaret thankful to be away from court for a time, but she had the added joy of preparing for her son's wedding and the accompanying celebrations. Negotiations with the Nevilles had gone as expected, with the match between Henry and Jane pleasing all parties involved. After her own traumatic childhood, Margaret was determined to provide well for her own children. She had little to leave them, but her Plantagenet blood still made her children an attractive possibility to those with family details other than money to worry about.

It also pleased her that the young couple appeared to enjoy each other's company. While it was not a requirement for the marriage to be successful, Margaret did hope that her children would also have the opportunity to enjoy the kind of love that she had shared with Richard.

Henry would be well placed within the king's circle, or so she hoped. Surely, the distrust and fighting for position that had been part of his father's reign had no place in the court of Henry VIII. He was quite secure upon the throne, and, though Margaret wanted great things for her children, the crown was not one of her objectives. She had seen what that ambition had done to her father and what the threat of it had done to her brother. No, her family's noble blood would be respected but never suspect. She could count on her close relationship with Catherine to ensure that Henry never doubted her loyalty.

Preparations for the upcoming nuptials were organized and carried out with precision by Margaret alone since Jane's mother had recently died. This arrangement suited Margaret just fine, since Lord Bergavenny would still be paying for half of the cost of the celebrations. The guests were chosen with care, and the event would embrace simple elegance rather than gaudy opulence. This fit both Margaret's taste and her household budget.

Bergavenny had offered a generous jointure to seal the union, which would increase if his daughter gave birth to a son and he continued to have none of his own. Margaret was confident that Henry would eventually inherit half of the Bergavenny estates through his wife, since the almost fifty-year-old nobleman was now without a wife and in possession only of two daughters. She felt she had provided quite well for her oldest son, and was already making plans for the others in the back of her mind.

She was not anxious to see her children married off, but she knew it was the way of the world and would rather see things done on her own terms. None of her children would be married to a relative stranger at the innocent age of fourteen, as she had been, but she also would not wait until the best opportunities had passed them by. Henry's proposed match appeared to be all she could have hoped for him.

As she considered the vast swirling mists of the future, Margaret thought of Reginald. Of all her children, he had somehow found favor with Henry Tudor. She had no marriage plans to make for him because he was firmly entrenched in the scholarly life at Sheen's Carthusian Monastery. Whether the current king's father had made the appointment out of obligation to Richard Pole, guilt toward Margaret, or love for Reginald, Margaret would never know. What she did know was that Reginald thrived in the austere environment and had a great love of learning. Not many young boys would appreciate the setting of seriousness and devotion, but she had seen for herself that Reginald adored living there.

The new King Henry had confirmed his father's commitment to supporting Reginald's education, so Margaret knew that he would have a bright future without an heiress for a wife.

Margaret was hesitant to place her hopes on England's new king, but Henry had provided evidence of his intent to raise the Pole family from the impoverished obscurity that his father had left them in, much as he had lifted Catherine from widow and displaced princess to queen. Margaret's oldest son had a place in the king's household, and, she hoped, he would soon also be given a title. She felt that it was only natural for the king to impart one of her family's titles upon Henry, even if his father had never been more than a knight.

Leaning back in the chair that used to be Richard's, Margaret stretched and looked toward the study's large windows. Instead of bright sunlight streaming in, the purple of night gazed blankly back at her. She blinked as she realized how cold and dark the room had become. Still, she rose with a smile, well pleased with her day's work and planning. When she reached the door, she paused, remembering all the times she had entered the room to see Richard. She hadn't believed that she could survive without him. Her fingers lightly touched the worn wood as though some essence of the man who had made the imprints upon it was still present, but the smile did not leave her face. She could look back with happiness at what she had with her husband, but she was also proud of herself. She was head of the Pole family now, and she would serve with a fervency that would make Richard proud of her.

Returning to the study the next day, Margaret had mixed feelings about a message that had been delivered. The seal, ribbons, and quality of parchment told her who the sender was without reading a word. After breaking the seal, her stomach began to churn uncomfortably. She was summoned back to court to wait upon the queen as soon as Henry and Jane were reasonably settled.

Her peace within the refuge of Bockmer would soon be at its end.

January 1511

Margaret had monitored Catherine with more care than she would deem appropriate for a small child through the months since her return to London. If it were at all within her power, this child would be healthy and robust. She spent her days tempting Catherine with sweet, exotic oranges and wine spiced with ginger, as well as praying for the safe delivery of England's next prince. Catherine's other ladies were strictly ordered to keep to themselves any rumors about where Henry was finding his satisfaction while his wife was unavailable to him.

"You will not upset the queen, or I will see that you are sent home to your families in disgrace," she had informed them. Each of the younger ladies quickly demurred to this cousin of the king, while those who were older smiled as they saw a little of the Plantagenet fire in Margaret that she rarely demonstrated.

By the time January arrived, Margaret felt that her efforts had been worthwhile. Catherine was in full bloom and had encountered no problems. Both women thanked God daily for her good health, and Henry showed no signs that he was concerned about the risk of a second tragedy. Everything went according to Henry's plans, why should the birth of his son be any different?

Thankful to be in confinement rooms warmed by the rosy glow of a roaring fire instead of part of the New Year festivities, Margaret relaxed her watch. Catherine could safely deliver any time now, and Margaret felt tension leave her shoulders that had been building there throughout the previous months. She had to laugh to herself, thinking that she was likely more nervous than the child's father.

The women who had been carefully selected to attend the queen at this time were relaxing in the cozy room. Catherine was working, as she often seemed to be, on a new shirt for her husband.

Although he could easily have them made anywhere, it was a task that she felt strongly should be put to her own wifely hands. Margaret was moved by the idea that only fabric that had gone through Catherine's hands would touch her husband's chest, even if her hands were not the only ones to caress his skin.

There had been no discussion of Henry's wandering eye, and Margaret felt she had scored a minor victory. She had no doubt that Henry had found a buxom companion to keep him warm and that Catherine would have guessed as much, but keeping names and details from her had helped ease the queen's suffering. Little enough was within Margaret's control, so she accepted her success where she could.

"Are you feeling alright?"

Margaret had noticed Catherine's hands falter at their work and the color drain slightly from her face. Immediately going to her side, Margaret wondered if the moment had arrived.

"I'm not sure," Catherine said in a quavering voice. Her eyes searched Margaret's for support, and the older woman was reminded of the first time she delivered a child.

"Let us get you into a comfortable position on the bed and see how you feel." She kept her voice even and calmly helped Catherine put away her sewing before guiding her to the large four poster bed that had been provided for her lying in. Her heart was racing in her chest, but she would not allow Catherine to see any indication of worry or nervousness. She adjusted pillows and wrapped Catherine in blankets until she seemed content. "Do you still feel pain?"

Catherine shook her head with the quick movements of a scared child. "Not now. No. Maybe it was nothing." Margaret smiled at the hopeful sound in Catherine's voice.

"Now," she said, patting her hand, "You do want the babe

to be born, and I will be at your side every moment."

Catherine closed her eyes, her lips forming the words of a silent prayer.

"My friend," Margaret continued when Catherine looked up at her again, "I will ask God's blessings upon your son and send for the midwife to put your mind at ease."

A small alter had been erected within the confinement rooms to serve the women who waited upon the queen. Margaret knelt there now, the coolness of the stone floor contrasting with the warmth of the air in the queen's chamber. She made a note to have the fire's intensity reduced before focusing her mind on her request. She would not want God to punish Catherine for her own distracted prayers. The king must have a robust child this time. Surely, God would agree.

The creaking in her joints and tiredness that overcame her as she rose dismayed Margaret. If Catherine's labor was beginning in earnest, it would be a long night. She took a deep breath and strode back into the connecting room with determined steps. Before too long, she would be present as the next king of England entered the world.

The following hours passed in a whirlwind of activity, but Margaret's exhaustion was forgotten when the midwife proudly held up a squalling baby boy. The room was filled with joy that made all else irrelevant. The fragrance of herbs that had been rubbed into Catherine's skin to ease her trial was rich in the air, covering the less desirable scents that were a natural part of childbirth. Dawn seemed to fill the room with fresh light just as the Tudor prince was presented to his mother. Sunlight glowed through the tapestries that had been hung over the windows to keep the winter chill from the room, insisting on being a witness to the important event.

Margaret had stayed firmly at Catherine's side, as she had said she would. Catherine had been disappointed too many times in her short life for Margaret to ever willingly cause her one moment of pain. The pleasure on the young woman's face as she gazed upon the miracle of life that she had born was the only reward that Margaret needed to make any service she had rendered wholly worthwhile.

Before she knew it, the room had been cleared of all evidence of the women's battle fought there, all except for the babe himself, who suckled contentedly at the breast of a wet nurse. Margaret dozed in her chair, still not ready to leave Catherine's side. The peace that overcame her was soon disturbed by the proud father barging into the tranquil room.

"Catherine, my beloved!"

Margaret winced at the booming voice, but Catherine smiled radiantly, so happy was she to present the king with his first born son. Choosing to leave the two of them to a moment of privacy, Margaret moved to slip quietly from the room.

"Cousin! I am glad that you are here for this," Henry's voice stopped her in her tracks. She turned and curtseyed, keeping her eyes on the rushes. "Stand, stand. There is no reason for that," he continued. "You are cousin to the king and should act like it." A sudden thought seemed to strike him. "In fact, you should also be awarded more appropriately for your station. I will demonstrate to all that I welcome my extended family in a way that my father found difficult to bear."

Henry's chest visibly filled with pride as he envisioned reactions to his generosity. He may have been young, but he had heard the whispers when Margaret's brother, Edward of Warwick, was put to death. Raising Margaret up would establish that he was a better man than his father. It would let everyone know that infighting was over and all members of the royal family were to be welcomed at court with open arms. Looking at the perfect features of his tiny son, he saw no reason why he could not afford to welcome Margaret's brood to higher glory.

Margaret stood slowly and waited for Henry to clarify what he meant by his promising statement. She had hoped to reclaim one of her family's ancient titles, the earldom of Salisbury or Warwick. Her father's title of duke of Clarence was beyond what she hoped to reach for, but desire to see her sons' positions improved motivated her to present a request for something. First, she awaited Henry's move.

"Your grace?"

Still enraptured by his small son, Henry only glimpsed at her, as if he had already forgotten the promise he had begun to make. Reluctantly placing the babe in his mother's arms, Henry took long, quick strides to Margaret and grasped her arms in a viselike grip.

"We shall see your family restored. Your sons shall serve mine, and England will see the branches of our family tree firmly united."

Again, he looked to his son with the rapture of one in the presence of the Christ child himself and then back to Margaret, clearly waiting for her display of gratitude.

"Your grace," she stammered. "I am at a loss. What can I say to properly thank you for thinking of my sons when the joy of yours is still fresh?"

Henry laughed, pleased with himself and his effect upon the older woman. He loosened his grip on one arm to gesture toward his small family, including them in the moment. Catherine gave him an encouraging smile in support of his intentions toward the Pole family.

"File a petition to receive your family title of countess of

Salisbury. I will approve it without delay."

With that, he returned to his wife's side, not waiting for further thanks from Margaret. She stood frozen in disbelief. Had she heard correctly? Should she express her thankfulness? Henry was leaning in intimately toward his wife, his mind already moved beyond Margaret's concerns. She decided to render her praise within the chapel rather than to her direct benefactor and silently left the room.

February 1511

Henry's revelation had given Margaret newfound pride that she did not remember feeling before. The last time her family had been at the wheel of fortune's height, her father was alive and the heir to his brother's throne. That was long before anyone considered the possibility of a Tudor king. Now, after serving her cousin, Elizabeth, and the children she had with Henry VII, Margaret would have a noble position of her own. Let the memory of her brother retain the title of Warwick. She would be countess of Salisbury as her ancestresses had been.

These thoughts buoyed her through her daily tasks. Not that serving Catherine was a chore. The two shared a close friendship that made spending time together a pleasure. Margaret only missed spending time with her own children. With the young prince settled with his nurses and Catherine churched, Margaret could prepare to leave for Bockmer soon. She paused at a window to imagine the countryside surrounding her own estate as it came to life with the new season. With God's help, she would be there in time to witness the greening and blooming.

Sounds of shuffling feet and worried voices reached into Margaret's daydream and sent her feet hurrying to Catherine's room. A weight began to form in her stomach as the words became distinct and weak crying could be heard. She straightened her back and entered, ready to take control of whatever situation presented itself.

She would have given anything to save Catherine from whatever might ever again send her weeping. Had the young woman not been through enough? Margaret's heart ached as one glance at the scene informed her that she would not be able to take charge. All was in God's hands.

"Margaret!" The pain in Catherine's voice caused Margaret

to cringe, but she swiftly moved to her side.

"What has happened?"

She only half listened to Catherine's sorrowful reply as she observed for herself the tragedy that had suddenly enveloped the room. One of Henry's personal physicians examined the small prince who had been baptized only weeks earlier. Margaret had been so proud to be godmother to the robust, copper haired boy. Illness so shockingly attacks the young, irretrievably sapping them of vigor. The babe did not move, only whimpered, as the doctor prodded and manipulated the tiny limbs. Margaret closed her eyes. There was no need to see more.

"We shall trust in God and his great love for each of his children," she whispered to Catherine, hoping she sounded more convincing than she felt. "It is he more than any doctor who can bring healing to your son. Let us pray for him."

Catherine nodded with tears leaving wet trails down her cheeks. Together they moved to the altar that remained in the next room. Although Catherine could leave her rooms now, the evidence of her recent confinement remained unchanged. Would young Henry ever move to his carefully prepared nursery?

If the strength of her own will could save the child, he would have enjoyed immediate healing, for Margaret prayed more fervently than any time in her life. She had been through much and begged God for many things, but this was for her friend, a woman who deserved better from the God of all creation.

God undoubtedly heard the women's prayers, but his plan for the tapestry of their lives was known only to him. The brief life of Prince Henry was but a stitch of color with a more noticeable knot. The morning he died, Catherine sent her attendants away, and Margaret returned to Bockmer in somber acceptance that she was not needed by anyone.

Catherine's dismissal stung, though Margaret was never unhappy to return to her beloved home. It reinforced her belief that she could count upon herself alone for her future, for certainly the king would reject her petition for the carldom of Salisbury in the face of his personal tragedy. Margaret would do her best to ensure that she did not rely upon the whims of kings and queens for the future of her children.

June 1511

Despite the somber chain of events that had sent her home, Margaret felt rejuvenated after spending the season of new life with her own family in her comfortable, if modest, household. She had even enjoyed a lengthy visit from her son, Henry, and his wife, who seemed to revel in the excitement of their new life together. Whether their joy would last was anyone's guess, and Margaret was determined to simply appreciate the gift of the present.

Her call to return to court was expected and not entirely unwelcomed. The bitterness she had felt when Catherine sent her away had dissipated when she reconsidered all that her friend had been through. Margaret held the summons between her fingers as she examined the desktop that had been marred by her husband's work and habits. Her grief at his loss was no longer a burning pain, but she did long for his advice and easy conversation. What would he think of the match she had made for their oldest son or the royal couple's struggle to bear a child?

Reginald had been sent to Magdalen College for continued schooling, a path only made possible through the support of the king. It was one area where Henry was of one mind with his father. Although suspicious of Margaret, Henry VII had discerned an unusual capacity for learning in young Reginald that his son continued to make provision for. Margaret was content that two sons were set upon satisfying paths and looked next to her son, Arthur.

Named for the prince that she had cared for when his hopes were golden, Margaret's Arthur did not yet demonstrate the strength of character of his older brother. She would admit it to no one, but Margaret saw much of her father's charm in Arthur. It was a charisma that was shallow and, at times, manipulative. Knowing how a similarly weak character had led to her father's demise,

Margaret prayed that Arthur would mature and become a better version of his princely grandfather, George of Clarence. The correct wife could make all the difference.

The parchment began to slip from Margaret's fingers and she grasped at it, returning to its words. Catherine's words were kind, and Margaret read an apology between the lines of text. Forgiveness could be freely given to a woman who had been harsh while in mourning for her second child buried in two years of marriage. Margaret began to place things in order for her absence and called her steward in order to provide him with her instructions.

~ ~ ~ ~

"Your presence is a balm to me, Margaret."

The scent of rosewater filled Margaret's senses as Catherine embraced her. She looked healthy enough, even if she would never again be as slender and graceful as she had been when she arrived in England to marry her first Tudor prince.

"My friend," Margaret said, holding Catherine at arm's length and considering her more carefully. "I am privileged to serve you and pray that God sends you blessings."

"He does," Catherine said with a smile that appeared sincere. "He has given me a loving husband and understanding friends to bear with me."

Margaret nodded once, and their conversation was able to fall into the comfortable rhythm of small talk and innocent gossip. By the time they were enjoying a private meal of manchet bread, sharp cheese, and sweet wine, Margaret felt generous enough in spirit to offer her thanks for Reginald's provision.

"Henry is happy to sponsor him," Catherine said, waving away Margaret's thanks. "He enjoys the company of learned men and strives to emulate them."

She sounded proud, like a mother enumerating the many talents of her child.

"From the time he was young, his mother ensured that he had the most sought after tutors and was exposed to modern philosophies. He never tires of discussing ideas and debating with those whom most would never question."

Margaret indulged a grin. "He is the king. He may challenge who he likes."

Laughing, Catherine conceded the point. "I'm sure he looks forward to the day when Reginald reaches an age to face him in healthy debate."

The women sipped their wine as each sent their imaginations into the future to observe the lively discussions that would take place between the king and his favorite young cousin.

"He means to have Courtenay fully restored," Catherine said in an off-hand manner that did not match the information.

Margaret's hand halted halfway between the table and her open mouth. William Courtenay had been released from the Tower, just as Henry had promised. He had even carried the sword at Henry's coronation, demonstrating their new friendship. That Henry continued to favor him, even after the death of the prince, was surely a positive sign of Henry's intentions toward his mother's family.

"Henry is generous indeed," Margaret managed to say. She stuffed her mouth with the bread in her hand to forestall the need to say more.

Catherine nodded slowly, almost reverently, as she considered the actions of her husband. "He is a fair and wise ruler, and he does not forget those who serve him. Courtenay is once again earl of Devon and his son marquess of Exeter. Nor has the king set aside his promise to you, Margaret."

Her heart beating roughly in her chest, Margaret swallowed uncomfortably before responding. Still she was not sure what to say. "Promise?"

"False ignorance does not suit you," Catherine said with a smirk. "You submitted your official request for restoration to the earldom of Salisbury?"

Margaret could only nod. How could she speak when she had completed the application while home at Bockmer. She had been looking to her own advantage while Catherine had mourned her son. Catherine did not indicate that she was offended. In fact, her face brightened.

"Good! I had hoped that you would. Henry will approve it as he said. It is no more than you deserve."

She patted Margaret's hand in an odd reversal of roles that placed Catherine in the comforting position.

Finally, Margaret managed to speak. "I am grateful beyond words. It will mean much to my children as they reach marriageable age to have a portion to offer."

She was surprised that Henry continued to recognize and raise up male relatives while he himself had no heir. It was certainly not the path his father would have taken. As if reading her mind, Catherine carried on.

"Henry will never admit as much, but he is heavily burdened by the execution of your brother. As am I." The brief confidence that had filled Catherine faded, and she withdrew her hand and bowed her head.

"You? What have you to be sorrowful for?" Margaret asked, taking her turn to reach for Catherine.

"It is entirely my fault," she whispered. "I have not spoken of it before, for it will not change the past. You should know, however, that I have never forgiven my parents for insisting upon the execution of your brother."

Margaret tried to interrupt and assure the queen that she had no part in the decision, but Catherine stopped her with a look of determination.

"You are only partly correct," she insisted. "I knew of the terms, and they seemed to make sense from my distant perspective. It was only upon getting to know you and your Richard that I began to question what had been demanded. Queen Elizabeth never purposely revealed her anger to me, but I could see a change in her countenance when Edward's name was mentioned. I began to see the human cost of what had been, to me, only the terms of a negotiation between kingdoms."

Tears filled Margaret's eyes as visions of Edward overwhelmed her. He should be a man with a family by now, the patriarch of the York remnant. Instead, his mind had wasted away in captivity before his head had been struck from his body for a trumped up crime. Margaret could not respond, despite the years that had passed since Edward's execution.

"Henry was too young at the time to fully understand the events that were taking place, but he assures me that his father expressed sorrow regarding Warwick before he died."

The mention of Henry VII stiffened Margaret's resolve. He had made little effort to save the young man he saw as a threat to his position despite his complete power over him.

"I will not speak of the king's father, for he is gone to God's judgement which is always just." She gasped for breath, emotion tightening her chest. "I am, however, thankful that the king strives to compensate for wrongs of the past. William Courtenay may yet enjoy freedom and a position in Henry's court, as he should. I will wait to learn what the king has in store for my own family."

Catherine's lips were pressed tightly together. She had clearly expected more exuberant gratitude that would absolve her of the guilt her part in Margaret's pain caused her. Disappointed, her determination increased to prove to Margaret that blows of the past would not be repeated. She would see that Henry was a different man than his father.

A somewhat uncomfortable silence had settled upon the women, both struggling with the past and with varied visions of the future. They were somewhat relieved by the entrance of a messenger. His presence enabled Margaret to take a deep calming breath, until she lifted her eyes to his face. It seemed that messengers used the arrangement of their face to prepare their audience for the news that they were there to impart. Margaret could see that she must prepare for bad news, and she prayed that it was not regarding one of her children then felt guilty for thinking it. Who would she wish the unfavorable tidings upon?

"Your grace," the young man said as he swept into a low bow at Catherine's feet. They could see only the back of his head, covered with wavy brown hair, left greasy where his cap matted it. Margaret briefly wondered what it would look like freshly washed with lemon water, soft with bright highlights in the curls. Catherine bid him rise and Margaret shook her head into focus.

The man only glimpsed at Margaret, recognizing her with a curt nod. "I pray your forgiveness, your grace, as I bring unwelcomed news."

The fact that he did not even seem to know who Margaret was reassured her, and she was drawn to his honey brown eyes that reminded her of Richard. He would be forever young in her mind as she continued to grow old. Though he had been forty-five when he died and she was yet only thirty-eight, she suddenly felt ancient.

The messenger continued at Catherine's signal. "It falls upon me to inform you of the death of the earl of Devon. A sudden sickness visited him, but his family remains well."

It took a moment for Margaret to connect the title with the man that she had only just learned had reacquired it. William Courtenay, finally released and restored, was dead. Poor Cat. Although she bore hardships well, this blow would crush her. She had stood firmly by her husband's side, even when Henry VII threatened him with charges of treason. His loss would be more devastating than anything else she had endured.

Guilt made Margaret's face burn with embarrassment. She had prayed for her family to be spared, not thinking of who else might deserve a reprieve. Catherine, who did not know Cat well and William not at all, thanked the messenger and sent him to receive food and drink as was expected for his service.

With another glance and brief nod to Margaret, he left the room, and Catherine turned to Margaret. Before she had a chance to speak, Margaret stood and asked to be excused. This was not the most severe blow that she had ever been dealt, but it was one that she wished to consider in private before grieving publicly.

February 1512

Margaret was returning to Bockmer only briefly, not because she was called to return to Catherine's service but because she had other estates to attend to. After difficult years and the reduction of her family's status, she had finally been restored to a place proper for the daughter of a Plantagenet prince.

"Countess of Salisbury," she let her own title roll off her tongue quietly enough that no one was near enough to overhear her. It was impossible to keep her face from breaking into a satisfied grin, and she hoped that her mother, were she able to see her now, was proud of what she had achieved.

Images of her oldest son were tucked away in her memories, precious treasures that she would never forget. He had been the image of his father as he stood before King Henry, dignified and unintimidated by his cousin's magnificence. Margaret's Henry was imbued with a quieter character, and he would serve the boisterous king well. From now on, he would be Lord Montague, rather than simply Henry Pole. That they both held titles that could be traced back through Margaret's Neville ancestors filled her with a sense of family ghosts pressing in upon her, but she welcomed their presence as she wished to demonstrate to the world that not every Plantagenet had been crushed beneath Tudor rule.

With a place in the king's household, Henry would be away from Jane and his estates more than desired, but the rewards would be great. Margaret's income from the lands now granted to her would allow her to keep her household in a state she had not enjoyed since before her father had died. She would not hesitate to make her status known. After visiting Bockmer long enough to gather some belongings and give instructions to the steward, she was immediately undertaking improvements at Bisham, where she intended to live.

Jane would be comfortable in the well known surroundings at Bockmer, the familiarity taking some of the sting from Henry's absence.

"You are to ensure that my son is referred to as Lord Montague by each person within the household," was among one of Margaret's first orders to her steward. The only elevation more important than her own was her son's. "Any decorating or improvements that Jane wishes to undertake have my full approval." Margaret paused before adding, "Except to the study. That room alone shall remain my own and untouched. Lord Montague may utilize another space for his office." This one bit of the past she was not ready to release. She didn't know if she would ever be. The study was the only place on Earth where she still felt Richard's presence.

Turning to her daughter-in-law, Margaret continued, "All is trusted to you, my dear. I know that you have a frugal and sharp mind and, therefore, am completely confident turning this beloved place over to your care."

The corner of Jane's mouth upturned slightly at Margaret's easy transition to grander behavior and speech than the girl had grown used to, but she maintained her own dignity and simply said, "Yes, mother," with her head respectfully bowed.

Margaret could see that Jane was amused and uncertain regarding their new circumstances, but Margaret was dedicated to guiding her family into the upper echelon of nobility, where they were meant to be. Raised as part of the royal family, even after her father's death, Margaret knew how to play her part and would teach her children as well. She had no concerns for Henry and Jane, for they were serious by nature and would take to their new roles quite naturally. Once she was settled at Bisham, she would turn her focus to the younger children.

June 1512

Ancient stone towers soared above the vast monastery grounds at Bisham. Margaret's new residence shared one of the wide Bisham Abbey walls, adding a stunning grandeur to the home. Timbers of unbelievable size propped up the ceiling over the great chamber, an enormous space more than suitable for the Countess of Salisbury to receive supplicants and guests. The adjoining rooms were no less grand, though it all needed some repair and scrubbing. Margaret was anxious for work to begin.

Choosing the rooms with the least maintenance needed, she issued orders for unpacking to begin even as she began dictating the restoration work that was to be done. Tapestries, glazed windows, and fine furniture were all to be ordered without delay. Large additions would allow elaborate parties to be hosted by the generous noblewoman.

As Margaret watched every member of her household scurry to do her will, she noticed that each worked with eagerness. They were as energized by this new adventure as their mistress was. Her advantage was certain to bring benefits to them as well.

She could not rest for a moment. Once her trunks were unpacked, she sat down to write a message to her cousin, the duke of Buckingham. They had marriage plans to discuss.

September 1512

Edward Stafford was not one to leave his estates any more than he had to. Since growing up under the oppressive hand of Henry VII, Stafford had learned to enjoy his riches away from Tudors who watched him with a suspicious eye on his royal bloodline.

The duke of Buckingham's father had been executed by Richard III after leading a rebellion against him. Only five years old at the time, Edward had been forced to live in hiding until the rise of Henry Tudor. The death of the first Tudor king left Edward with a feeling of freedom, and his relationship with his son was, so far, without strain. Edward had carried his cousin's crown at his coronation, hoping to demonstrate to anyone who mattered that the Stafford family was happy to serve under the new dynasty.

Both Tudor kings had been hesitant to give the direct descendant of Edward III too much power, so Edward had sufficient time on his hands to enjoy his estates and father illegitimate children.

Margaret remembered Edward as a kindred spirit growing up at the Tudor court. Although Edward was not an orphan, he had been taken from his mother, Katherine Woodville the dowager queen's sister, and placed within the royal household as a ward of the king. Margaret had also been placed first in the households of Edward IV and Richard III and then in that of Henry VII, who married her cousin, Elizabeth. Margaret could see from an early age that she and Edward shared the sense of being important by blood but a presence that those in power wished they did not have to deal with. Although they had not been close due to the five years in age that separated them, Margaret felt a bond with the duke that she hoped would lead to satisfying negotiations.

Because of Edward's desire to remain at his own estates,

Margaret was traveling to visit him. The autumn was mild and she was happy to escape the dust and chaos of construction at Bisham to enjoy Buckingham's historic family home, Stafford Castle. The motte and bailey structure dated back to the time of the Conqueror, and Margaret could almost envision the Normans slowly creating it with strong timbers, as her caravan approached the sprawling estate. Most of the original timber was gone or hidden beneath the impressive stone towers and walls. Margaret could not help but wonder if the residence's status as an unapproachable fortress was one of the reasons Edward enjoyed living there. It was difficult to recover from the execution of a father for treason, as Margaret well knew, and this castle would make him feel safe.

Edward had clearly set a watch for them because the way was cleared for the party to enter the courtyard without pausing to wait. Margaret was relieved. Although she had enjoyed the trip, taking in the vivacious colors of the season along the way, she was road weary and looked forward to a fire and a flagon of fine wine. She had no doubt that Buckingham would be serving the best in the hope of impressing upon the newly raised countess his own almost royal status. She did not mind and would happily benefit from the duke's insecurities.

Gratefully, she left the horses and luggage to others and allowed herself to be swept away by Edward Stafford. He was a magnificent presence to be in. Five years younger than Margaret and renowned for his handsome features and elaborately tailored clothes, Edward had a clear resemblance to his cousin the king. Tall and broad with auburn hair that gleamed in the fading sunlight, he had no trouble turning the heads of many more women than he had a right to. It was probably best, Margaret thought, that he did remain reclusive. She could see that rivalry would be inevitable if the two men were too much in each other's company. Better to leave more reserved men, like her son Henry, to see to the king's everyday demands.

"Countess, I am honored to welcome you and am eager to discuss our common interests," he said with a grin that Margaret was certain made many a young maid's heart beat a little bit faster. Though she had known him since they were children and considered him far too young for her, Margaret was not completely immune and found herself admiring the way his hair fell endearingly across his forehead.

"Thank you, but I hope we are too intimate for titles, cousin. It is as family rather than peer that I reach out to you now."

He had quickly led her into a lavish hall that was quite literally fit for a king. Henry may not entrust many responsibilities to Edward, but he did endow him with rich lands that were managed with care. Soon, Margaret had acquired her sought after position in a comfortable chair before a roaring fire. She sighed with contentment as she settled into it.

"How are your sons?" Edward asked before concealing his own face behind his glass.

Margaret examined her own wine glass as she considered her response. It was a fine piece of craftsmanship, undoubtedly imported at great cost from Italy. She mentally noted to order a set of her own for use only with the most noble of guests. The impression they made upon visitors was well worth the cost, which she could now afford.

"Henry is doing exceptionally well in the king's service," she began, setting the glass aside. "He and Jane are well settled at Bockmer while I oversee the work at Bisham. I would welcome you to an extended visit once it is in order. Reginald has entered Magdalen Collage with his grace as his sponsor. The boy is well suited for learning and is expected to excel among the Oxford scholars."

"And Arthur," Edward prodded when Margaret paused to consider what was best said about her second son, who was on the cusp of manhood.

She retrieved her glass and sipped slowly to give herself more time. She was less certain about Arthur's future than his younger brother's, but that was of no consequence since she was here to discuss her daughter.

"Arthur dotes upon his dear sister while he awaits orders from the king. I expect he, too, will soon have a position at court to attend to. Ursula assists me in the management of my estates and has become a capable young woman."

Edward raised a single eyebrow at Margaret's turn in the conversation, but his eyes were lit with amusement. "Your daughter is a beauty as well, which is no surprise considering her mother."

Margaret dropped her eyes to her hands which began to fidget in her lap as she cursed herself for blushing. "You flatter me, cousin," she said without looking at him.

"Ah, don't be silly," Edward boomed as he rose to his feet. His natural energy had been confined for too long and he began to pace before the fire. "You know as well as anyone that you have your fair share of Plantagenet beauty. Had you only been free when I came of age."

Margaret's blush deepened and she hoped that it could be blamed on the heat of the fire even as she attempted to shake herself free of his charm. She finally forced herself to raise her eyes to him and saw that he was grinning broadly in clear enjoyment of the effect he knew he had on her.

"That's enough, you devil," she scolded him, though she could not stop herself from smiling in return. "How many women are you able to keep from ever stating their request because you have turned them into shy girls?"

"I cannot help myself, my dear, but I do apologize," he said with a perfect bow that still somehow held the air of mockery. "I also do not mean to keep you from your desired objective. My Harry will be an ideal match for your Ursula as soon as he has been deemed responsible enough to care for a noble and beautiful wife."

Margaret realized that her jaw had dropped, and she quickly clamped her lips together. Oh, it was good indeed that this one was not at court. "How did you..."

She did not get a chance to finish. Edward waved her silent as he retook his seat.

"I have no spies. It simply made sense. I do have greater intelligence and skill in many areas than our cousin the king gives me proper credit for."

"That, I can see, is true," Margaret said, allowing herself to relax into the softness of the cushions with the wine warming her from the inside and the firelight dancing across the scene. "You also favor their marriage then?"

Edward confirmed his assent with a firm nod. "I can think of no better union than that between your noble line and my own. Their children will have twice the royal blood than he who currently sits upon the throne of England."

Margaret sat up and quickly scanned the hall. Even in his own home, Edward should never say such a thing, true as it may be. Edward observed her actions without reacting with more than a smirk.

"Surely, you have considered this and count it as a reason for approaching me," he said as he poured more wine into her only half empty glass.

"Well, yes. However..."

Again he cut her off. "You do not wish me to speak aloud

what we and everyone else already knows."

She sighed. He knew very well that he was making light of treasonous words.

"Before we consider the discussion closed," he said, leaning close and lowering his voice. "You should know of a prophecy that may ease your mind."

His face was closer to hers than anyone other than her children dared to approach. She could see wine glistening on his lips and the specks of emerald in his sapphire eyes that blended to create the hue of a raging ocean. Was it the heretical reference to a prophecy or his proximity that left her speechless?

"It is dependable, Margaret," he clutched her hand, and she wished to look again to ensure that they were alone, but she could not avert her gaze from his. "This prophecy was given to me by a reputable monk. Nicholas Hopkins is his name." He carried on when she demonstrated no reaction to the name. "Our children will take their proper place as God wills it," his voice had lowered to a whisper filled with fervency. "This second Henry Tudor will have no sons. I have been assured. When he dies..."

It was Margaret's turn to stop him. "No! Edward, you must not even whisper of the death of the king. It is treason!" She placed her hand that was not grasped by him on his arm. To anyone secretly observing them, they appeared to be lovers, but Margaret's heart was filled only with fear. "Our fathers have already taught us this lesson. It would be best to remember them and avoid their fate."

He only leaned closer. "I am certain and do not fear, as you should not. Henry will leave no heir, and it will be I who is the next king of England."

Margaret's eyes widened in horror, and she leaned away, attempting to put space between them. Edward seemed surprised by her reaction.

"Do you not see? Your daughter will be queen. You should rejoice at her good fortune and the correction of past wrongs."

She stared at him, seeing that he was entirely sincere. "Maybe you are right, but we can never speak of it again. We must be content with bringing together our families and trust anything else to the Lord."

He pursed his lips, still not satisfied. He squeezed her hand once more before releasing it and leaning back into his own seat. "I will respect your wishes, but you will see. I promise that you will see all that I have said come to pass."

Edward immediately transitioned to more innocent threads of conversation, leaving Margaret wondering if his talk of prophecy had all been in her imagination. Yet, as she lay in bed that night, his stormy sea eyes still vivid in her mind, she knew that she had not dreamt it. She could not deny the knot of excitement in the pit of her stomach. Though she had admonished him for his loose speech, the future he painted thrilled her more than she would admit aloud. Would Edward be the next king and pass on his crown to his son and Margaret's daughter? The idea exhilarated her. The Tudor king may have executed her brother, but he had not counted on the Plantagenet women to be the ones who rose from the ashes of their dynasty.

Her dreams were pleasant that night.

The next day, Edward showed no sign that he had been speaking treason the evening before. He gave Margaret a meandering tour of the castle as they discussed terms that would unite their families. Margaret was forced to confess that the fee she was obligated to pay for the title she now enjoyed left her currently unable to present him with much. As much as the Stafford name, she strove to connect Ursula to the Buckingham riches. She would never be forced to struggle as Margaret had. The estates Henry had provided her with changed her status dramatically, but she would never forget having to borrow the money to bury her husband.

Edward was generous in the negotiations. Whether it was because he truly believed that royal riches were in his future or he felt a fond kinship for Margaret she did not know and would not ask. They agreed that the children would wait a few more years for the ceremony sealing their union. Ursula, at fourteen, was the age that Margaret had been upon her own wedding night, but Ursula had nothing to run from and could afford to wait while she learned valuable lessons at her mother's side. Besides, Henry Stafford was two years his betrothed's junior. While women were occasionally married off at age eleven or twelve, men were not. Margaret was well satisfied with the arrangements and the time that she had secured for herself with her daughter.

Edward had moved on to the topic of his building project at Thornbury. "I have had the former manor house demolished and will build a more fitting home for my family there."

Margaret could not hide her surprise. "You would leave Stafford Castle? You seem to adore it." She made a sweeping gesture with her arm indicating the esteemed surroundings.

"I do," Edward nodded in agreement as he continued strolling the manicured grounds. "Eleanor longs for more modern and manageable accommodations."

He needed say nothing more. Edward's wife was one of the few women who would have taken issue with the fine, aged estate. It was not Margaret's place to comment upon this, and so she did not. Instead, they carried on in companionable silence as autumn leaves swirled around them. Appreciating their glorious bursts of color, Margaret wondered if there was any other example of such beauty in death.

October 1512

Following her visit with Buckingham, Margaret returned to Bockmer, where she intended to enjoy time with Henry and Jane until after the Christmas festivities. The work continued at Bisham, and she was confident that construction would make greater strides if the workmen did not have to tiptoe around her. She looked forward to seeing the results when she arrived in January.

"Have you ordered new windows, mother?" Henry asked.

"I have," Margaret said, her eyes lighting with excitement. "The craftsman you recommended assures me that he is more than capable of etching the arms of my family and your father's into the glass. The clarity and durability of the glass are modern marvels."

Montague smiled in satisfaction that he had been able to serve his mother in a higher capacity than as her child. He wanted her to look to him as the head of the family, and he devoted much energy to making himself worthy in her eyes. "I am pleased that he is equal to your desires," he said, glancing at Jane to see that she too wore a satisfied grin.

"Have you news from court? When does the king expect you to return?" Margaret asked.

"You could come to court yourself, mother, and would then be aware of every whispered rumor," Montague teased.

Margaret waved a hand and shook her head. "I have no desire to be at the center of politics, but would know how my dear Catherine fares."

"The queen is well, so far as I am aware. Were she not, I am certain she would summon you to care for her."

"And the king?"

"He looks to France for several reasons. Richard de la Pole continues to evade his efforts to apprehend him. Henry is not a man to take disappointment lightly, and he sees de la Pole's success as mockery of his rule. He will be sending more than secret assassins in the coming year. For now, he will have Charles Brandon made duke of Suffolk in order to discredit the de la Pole claim and keep Buckingham from feelings of superiority."

"Brandon made duke. Quite a rise," Margaret said evenly, keeping emotion from her features. Brandon's father had been killed defending Henry Tudor at Bosworth, and the son had been shown remarkable favor ever since.

Montague shrugged. "It was bound to happen. He already has greater power over the king than any other person, including the queen." He lightly shrugged again when he saw his mother's raised eyebrows. "It is true. The two have grown up together, and there is no one the king admires or respects more." A glance at Jane kept him from adding anything about Brandon's female conquests that he shared with his monarch as often as he was willing.

"What of Richard?" Margaret asked, changing the subject to one she found more significant. Were it not for her loyalty to Catherine and desire for peace, the cause of the de la Pole brothers would be Margaret's own. With John's death and Edmund's imprisonment, Richard was the last York challenging the Tudor king.

"He is believed to be in France, though, as I have said, the king's spies and assassins are having trouble pinning him down. Henry cannot funnel too many resources into his capture with problems brewing to the north and the south."

"He will take on both Scotland and France? What of his sister?"

"She has failed to give James an heir," Montague trailed off, not sure what to say that could not also be said to criminalize England's queen. "The king will insist upon his rights as overlord of Scotland."

Margaret did not immediately respond. She wondered how Henry would proceed with animosity on two fronts. Who would he send to fight for him? Might he be killed in battle and Buckingham truly left his heir? Would Richard de la Pole press his own claim, leaving them sliding into the depths of civil war again?

"Will he win?" she asked her son.

Montague appeared taken aback. "Against Scotland? Assuredly. I am not yet certain what strategies he will put into place with James or Louis, but there is none like our King Henry against any enemy."

Margaret was thinking of war, not tournaments, but her son could still be correct. They could not count on Tudor's early demise. She must continue to plot a course for her family that assumed his success. Henry had given her much to consider, so she turned her questions to Jane and diverted the conversation to more mundane topics of household and crops.

Alone in her room after the full day, Margaret felt the loneliness that creeps into those who have no spouse to warm them through the winter. Since she was growing too old to bear children, she was not often considered by men who needed a wife to replace one who had been lost to illness or childbed. Usually, she was content with this. However, on nights like this one, she gazed into the dark night glittering with thousands of points of light and wondered what it would be like to have strong arms wrapped around her.

March 1513

Little time had been spent admiring the improvements at Bisham and providing instructions for ongoing work before Margaret was summoned to court once again. Catherine's missive had been brief but cheerful, and Margaret was looking forward to catching up with one of her oldest friends. Barely unpacked from her stay at Bockmer, she had reopened the trunks to prepare for London.

The cold seemed to seep into her bones more than it ever had in the past. Margaret pulled her cloak more tightly around herself as a woolen barricade against the blustery wind. She remembered Richard leading his men away in all extremes of weather. Always worried that a sword would take him from her, it had been seasonal illness that was her true enemy. The Lord could take her as well if it were his will. She was content with her position and what she had achieved for her children. So many of her family members had died young that she felt almost decrepit at forty.

When the conglomeration of tightly packed buildings came into view, Margaret accepted that God indeed had other plans for her. With mixed feelings, she prepared herself mentally for presentation to the queen. Catherine could be greeted with joy and informality, but she must also be equipped for the possibility that Henry would be at her friend's side. The king would choose whether he wished to greet her as a cousin on this occasion or expect her to demurely enter his presence.

The king was with his wife, but Margaret was shown, once again, that she had worried over nothing.

"Our dear cousin," he gushed as he, far from expecting her obeisance, rose to greet her with an overwhelming embrace. His height placed Margaret's frozen cheeks against his broad chest briefly before he held her away at arm's length. She felt like a doll being manipulated by a child but could only smile up at the young man who greatly resembled her uncle, King Edward IV.

"It has been too long since you have been here with us," he said in response to her mumbled greeting, a wide grin on his still boyish face.

"Your grace, I believe the countess would appreciate a seat near the fire and some sweet wine," Catherine suggested even as she kept her head slightly bowed in reverence to him.

"Of course, you are right, my beloved," he said with no less enthusiasm. He even proceeded to pour the wine himself into a pleasantly warm silver goblet.

Margaret thought of Buckingham's fine glasses and smiled that the king did not see the extravagance as necessary to impress her. She held the goblet with both hands, taking in as much of the warmth and sweet fragrance as possible. The scent told her that it was one of her favorites before she took the first sip. That would be Catherine's touch. Henry, as kind as he could be, was frequently too focused on his own objectives and desires to take note of the preferences of others.

As Margaret relaxed and soaked up the heat of the cheerful fire, Catherine and Henry spoke in low voices. She was content to let them carry on without her for a moment and closed her eyes to enjoy the heat seeping into her extremities and the comfortable feeling that was washing over her. Before long, she sensed Catherine at her side and opened her eyes just in time to see Henry stride from the room.

"Does he have to hurry off?" Now that she knew Henry was in a jovial mood, she was sad to see him go.

Catherine gave her a knowing smile. "Henry is always hurrying and can hardly stand to be still, but in this case, he is honoring my wish to have some time alone with you." She had settled herself comfortably near and waved off her ladies to far corners of the room. "He was right. It has been too long. I've missed you Margaret. You have become one of my dearest friends."

"We have shared much," Margaret agreed. "Endured pain and celebrated joy."

Catherine simply nodded as they both considered the deep past that she had so concisely described. Since Catherine's arrival in England more than a decade earlier, the two women had leaned on each other as fortune's wheel turned.

"I hope that you will stay at court and be by my side once again as I await God's richest blessing," Catherine said in a quiet voice that could not quite hide her excitement.

Margaret was instantly more alert, the sleepiness caused by the wine and cozy warmth leaving her in a moment. She turned to examine Catherine's rosy complexion more carefully and forced herself to smile. "You are with child." She hoped she had infused her tone with an appropriate level of enthusiasm. Margaret did wish for a child for Catherine but was not sure if she could watch her continue to go through pregnancies that ended with tragedy.

Catherine seemed unfettered by such concerns, and her face lit up now that her news was revealed. "I believe we can expect our prince in the autumn." Her hand subconsciously had fallen to rest upon her thick layers of skirts, and she demonstrated no sign that she expected this child to befall the fate that had taken her previous babes.

Forcing herself to leave her seat and appear joyous, Margaret knelt before Catherine and took her hands in her own, rubbing them as if they were cold. "Thank the Lord for his many blessings! Of course, I will be here with you. I would not trust your care to another soul in this world."

"Thank you, Margaret," Catherine whispered as she pulled

her into an embrace that revealed the worry she had been so successfully hiding. "God has sent me a great gift in you."

May 1513

Catherine bloomed along with the Tudor roses that spring, and Margaret was pleased to see that she seemed in good health. Watching over her like a mother, Margaret ensured that the queen got proper rest and foods that were known to strengthen children in the womb.

Henry was only slightly less vigilant. He had refused his wife's requests to ride out with him and insisted that she also give up dancing and any other activity that may exert too much energy or jostle the child. Of course, this meant that he was also absent from her bed, though Margaret was unsure who Catherine's proxy was. Maybe he would honor his queen and avoid dalliance this time in the hope of earning God's favor for the precious babe. There were few things that Henry coveted more than a son of his own.

Margaret did not want her charge to become too slothful under Henry's instructions. She understood better than he the energy that Catherine would require when her time can, so the women shared garden walks each day and watched the greenery come to life. New discoveries were made each day as the women noted shoots popping from the dirt, buds exploding into bloom, and leaves creating veils around private alcoves.

During one of these early morning excursions, Catherine voiced her fears for the first time as birds sang a joyful tune and the sun shone with promised warmth.

"What if this babe, too, dies?"

Avoiding her friend's gaze, Margaret took a moment to respond. "We cannot know God's will," she said, but saw that this was not what Catherine needed to hear at present. "Your child will not die," she stated firmly. "You have the best care and a doting husband who just happens to be king. God hears your sincere prayers and is sure to bless you and the country with a prince to be his father's image and heir."

The queen inhaled deeply of the fresh air and squeezed her eyes shut for a moment. "Thank you. I do not only need you as a helpmate and guide, but your faith boosts my own when the devil attempts to get a foothold."

"Oh Catherine," Margaret said, turning and gripping the younger woman by her shoulders. "I cannot know our future any more than you, but I also cannot believe that God has brought us both to this place only to see us brought low again." She held her close for a moment before continuing, "You will give birth to a thriving child if it is within the poor powers that our Lord has given me to ensure that you do."

The moment was broken by the sounds of chaos from across the courtyard that could only indicate the approach of the King. Henry was a boisterous presence at all times, but an edge of anger could be heard as he demanded to know the location of his queen.

The women hurried toward the sounds, wondering what could have upset him. He had been jovial since Margaret's return to court. Whether it was because he was young or because he was king, he did not seem to doubt that his wife would present him with a healthy son this time. Margaret had begun to forget to be distressed by his presence.

As they approached him, Margaret was alarmed to see his gaze fall upon her rather than his wife. His face was held firm in angry lines, and he sent away those he had just called to him in order to help locate the women. Without meaning to, Margaret hung her head and looked at the ground in an effort to turn his attention away.

"Dear husband, what is it that troubles you?" Catherine asked as she raised her hands in an attempt to touch his face and smooth his hair.

He shook himself out of her grasp and took a step toward his cousin. "Lady Salisbury, you will tell me what you know of your traitorous cousin's location and actions."

Her head whipped up for her eyes to questioningly search his. "Your grace, I'm not sure . . ."

"You know exactly what I mean," he bellowed. "Or maybe so many decades of treason does, in fact, leave you uncertain in a family like yours."

Margaret swallowed the lump in her throat. So, her family was no longer his, then? "Please, your grace."

"Richard de la Pole," he said without listening to her entreaty. "He has evaded me and now gives his loyalty to that French viper, Louis. Have you communicated with him?"

"Your grace, I have not," Margaret stated as confidently as she was able. As relieved as she was to be able to honestly deny Henry's accusations, she could not be at ease until she was certain he believed her. "Richard de la Pole left England while my husband was still alive. My concern has been only for him and then his children for many years." She bowed her head enough to be respectful while keeping it high enough to demonstrate that she did not hide anything from her king.

With a furrowed brow, Henry contemplated her words and considered their truth. "And Edmund?" he asked.

Margaret could not stop herself from a quick, sidelong glance at Catherine, who simply shrugged. She raised her eyes again. "Surely, your grace, he is still held in the Tower at your pleasure."

Edmund de la Pole had been imprisoned since he was turned over to the previous King Henry by Philip of Castile several years earlier. Margaret had never known him well and had not visited him in the interest of protecting her own children. She assumed he was there still.

Henry's face now was smug in an ugly fashion that reminded Margaret of bullies who target smaller children at play. A curl of fear began to twist itself deep in the center of her being. Had she tempted fate with discussing her great position just moments ago?

"He was," Henry gloated as he flexed his chest and stood tall to emphasize how high he towered above her. "His family's treason has resulted in his execution." Leaning in toward her ominously, he added, "Be sure I am the first to hear of it if you are contacted by Richard de la Pole or have any news of him whatsoever."

Margaret could only whisper, "Yes, your grace."

She lowered her head once again and did not move or speak until she heard his heavy footsteps completely fade away. She clamped her eyes shut as she waited, willing tears away as she prayed that God not revisit these feuds upon her family. Not again. Had they not endured enough? But Henry would not remember that. He had not even been born when John, the first de la Pole brother to rebel against Tudor rule, gave up his life at Stoke Field.

Feeling Catherine's small hand upon her back, Margaret allowed the vision of the tranquil garden to once again fill her eyes. The beauty of the day remained, and she could almost convince herself that the interlude with Henry had only been a horrid nightmare. Except that one look at Catherine's face told Margaret that her friend was as terrified by the transformation in the king as she was.

Catherine quickly arranged her face to appear as if nothing untoward had occurred. She slipped an arm around Margaret's waist and informed her ladies that they were going to retire to her rooms for a while. "My dear Margaret does not feel well," she said, though all had heard Henry's attack. "Please give us some privacy until I call for you."

Most of the women mumbled their assent or said nothing. Each had to determine what to say and how to act going forward with the knowledge that the countess of Salisbury was no longer held in high regard by the King. Would he bring her down further or was this simply an explosion of temper aimed at her because Richard de la Pole was beyond his reach? Loyalties must not be too loudly proclaimed just yet.

The door was quietly closed once Catherine had obtained food and wine to bolster them. Sitting together like this with the rest of the world shut out, Margaret could fantasize that they were simply two Englishwomen, not pawns at the whim of a Tudor king. An involuntary shudder drew Catherine's eyes to her.

"It is not you that he holds responsible," she attempted to reassure her. "Richard and Edmund have demonstrated their lack of loyalty since before Henry was crowned."

Margaret pressed her lips together and nodded slowly. Catherine was right about the de la Poles, but why would Henry take it out on her? She was no closer relation to them than he was. She hated feeling like a scapegoat.

"He will soon be distracted from his anger by the preparations to leave for France, in any case," Catherine continued as if she were talking about nothing more serious than the behavior of a naughty child. "You have heard that he sends the earl of Surrey north while he will personally lead his army across the channel?"

His sins forgotten, Catherine glowed with pride as she discussed her husband's plan to fight a war on two fronts with the Scots to the north and the French to the south. Margaret was not sure what to say about the ease with which Catherine brushed aside his cruelty or his questionable battle strategy. She chose to say nothing and sipped her wine instead. For the first time since she had accepted Catherine's call, she wished she could return to her own estates and be with her children instead of participating in the unpredictable game that was the royal court.

She was not surprised or offended that Catherine's first loyalty would be to her husband and king. That was as it should be. She only wished that the babe's birth was closer at hand so that she could look forward to being gone from this place where one's destiny could suddenly reverse at any moment.

Catherine munched on bread and cheese. Her waist thickened quickly and not solely from the growth of her child. Silence, she seemed to have decided, was the best way to cope with this problem. Margaret could not disagree. After all, Edmund was already dead, and Richard was in the service of the French king. She could only pray that her name would not become intertwined with theirs again.

Releasing a deep breath, Margaret finally turned to Catherine, who raised her brows questioningly as she sipped wine to follow most of the food that had been on the serving plate.

"I did know that the king was planning a French campaign. Montague has been included in the ranks of those who will be joining him." Margaret could not decide if she was proud or terrified that her oldest son would be part of Henry's forces in France. It had to be better than being sent into the rugged north.

"Lord Montague will undoubtedly earn his knighthood conquering England's ancient territory," Catherine said a little too brightly, clearly hoping to grasp on to something that would cheer her friend.

"I have every faith in my son," Margaret conceded. "Buckingham goes as well, and he will be the guide to him that his father cannot be."

She was not sure why she had brought up Richard. Gone for almost ten years, he had left Margaret with a wound that she occasionally reopened to ensure that it still pained her.

"Oh, Margaret, my friend," Catherine crooned, holding a tray invitingly in front of Margaret's face. "Try the sweetmeats. They could cheer one in the deepest, darkest pits."

Margaret could not help but laugh as she resigned to accepting a few of the delicacies. "Breeding women always believe that food solves every problem," she said wryly, giving Catherine a gentle nudge.

"Well, surely they are correct then," Catherine assured her with her nose in the air and eyebrows arched.

Their comfortable companionship regained, discussion of Henry's plans was left for another time. Margaret chided herself for allowing the episode to upset her. It was up to her to maintain the calmness and good health surrounding the queen. The prince was her first and only priority until she was free to leave this place.

June 1513

In the weeks since the king's outburst, Margaret had carefully avoided him as much as she could without making it clear she was doing so. During meals, they were often in company, and she put supreme effort into exuding the demeanor of one who is both innocent and demure.

For his part, Henry had neither apologized nor repeated the accusations he had threatened her with. He was also not difficult to avoid as he was consumed by his plans to invade France while the earl of Surrey took charge of English troops in the north against King James of Scotland. When he was in Margaret's company, his mood was polite if not as familiar as he had previously been.

This was fine with Margaret as long as her son would be in good standing with the king while they were across the channel. Concern for her son led her to approach the king during one of the last opportunities she would have before many of the men would leave England never to return.

"Your grace," she said to him with a deep curtsey. "My son is proud beyond measure to serve his king in France, all the more so because you are our beloved cousin."

She breathed a sigh of relief as Henry smiled in what appeared to be genuine bonhomie.

"Montague will be an ideal companion," Henry said in a friendly tone, as if he and Margaret's son were planning nothing more serious than a day of hunting. "He has the intellect to assess the situation between us and our enemy and his training in arms is almost second to none." He said this last with a playful flexing of his own muscles in case there was any question who Montague was second to. "It will be a comfort to have a faithful cousin at my side."

Margaret's smile was sincere as she continued, "I thank you for choosing to take Arthur as well. I pray that he learns much by observing at your side and that of his brother."

In truth Margaret's guts twisted at the thought of her second son enthusiastically tramping off to war, but she could make no excuse to keep him safely home at the age of eighteen. Since he must go, she would choose pride over worry.

Henry threw his shoulders back, making his broad chest seem even more so. "Young Arthur will do well to be a part of the campaign. You can rest assured that I will see to his safety and training."

It took some fortitude to keep her smile from appearing amused at Henry's condescending tone. She was happy that Arthur was not present to hear the king speak of him as if he were an infant.

"You have put this poor mother's heart at ease then, your grace," she said bowing her head low and hiding her face behind the display of humility.

"When we return victorious," Henry continued as if she had not spoken, "you will see that your sons are formed into men. Possibly fortune will shine on them and one will even return with his knighthood."

"I hope and pray only for their safety and that they serve their king well," Margaret said, lowering her face again to keep him from noticing her dismay at the changes she perceived in him. How he had changed since happily greeting her as family at his coronation. She felt like a supplicant and wondered how her sons would manage their interactions with him. Of Montague, she had no concerns, but Arthur too often depended upon his charm to get away with what other men could not. Yes, she would be praying indeed.

She realized that while she had stood there lost in her own thoughts, her head bowed before the king, he had moved on to the next person who he felt certain should be honored by his attention. Margaret took a deep breath, somewhat bolstered by the fact that the conversation had gone about as well as she could have hoped for, and looked for Catherine.

It was easy to spot the queen despite her small stature. She positively glowed with joy and good health. Margaret was certain that the women's prayers would be answered by the safe delivery of a healthy prince in the autumn.

"Margaret, I do believe that it is time that I should rest," Catherine said slightly too loudly as Margaret approached.

Keeping her face neutral, Margaret observed that the newly named Lord Lisle had claimed Catherine's attention. Charles Brandon may have been the king's oldest and closest friend, but the queen quickly grew weary of his coarseness. Margaret lowered her head slightly to the large, overbearing man before turning to her queen.

"Your grace, let me escort you to your rooms and fetch a cool compress for your head."

Margaret moved to take Catherine's arm then turned slightly toward Brandon. He scratched at his bushy beard, and Margaret could not help but wonder what his young ward by whom he took his title thought about being betrothed to him. Poor Elizabeth Grey was only eight years old, but maybe that was a mercy. Even Brandon could not suggest that they marry just yet. Besides, her title was just a small stepping stone on his way to the promised dukedom.

"Excuse me for interrupting, Lord Lisle," she said, knowing that use of his new title would keep him from taking offense at the queen's leaving. "I must ensure that the queen takes every precaution, regardless of how much she enjoys her present company."

She heard Catherine make a low scoffing sound and resolved

not to glance in her direction, hoping that Brandon had not noticed. Her worry was entirely unfounded, as his attention was already captured by one of the younger of Catherine's ladies. Margaret was thankful for his distraction while making a mental note to instruct the girl on handling men like Brandon.

As they turned away, Margaret gave her friend a sidelong glance and could hold back her grin no longer. Only steps away, she whispered, "Your grace, I can only escort you from undesirable situations if you are able to maintain your composure at my lies."

Catherine did not hold back her laughter, and Margaret hoped that they were far enough from Brandon that he would not connect it to himself. She was afraid that Brandon had more power over the king than Catherine gave him credit for. Maybe it was her upbringing, but Margaret saw potential for rivalry everywhere.

Soon they were settling in Catherine's rooms with a window open to allow a sweet summer breeze to refresh them. Margaret solicitously placed a small stool under Catherine's feet and cooled a cloth in rosewater before placing it upon her brow.

"You are too good to me," Catherine sighed wearily. Tiredness seemed to overtake her once the excitement of the crowd no longer enlivened her.

"I am precisely as good as you deserve, your grace."

Margaret was pleased to see a content smile form on Catherine's lips as she seemed already to be dozing in the cushioned chair.

~ ~ ~ ~

Before she knew it, before she was ready, it was time for Margaret to send her two oldest sons off to France to serve their king. She vowed not to spend their last moments together repeating advice and instructions that she had already given them until they rolled their eyes at her and assured her that they were no longer children and did not need to be treated as such.

She stood proudly before them. Though her head was held high and her back straight, both of her sons towered over her. Just as their father had. She quickly dismissed the thought. This moment did not belong to her husband's ghost, although he would have been thrilled to see his sons in the king's service.

Montague knelt before her with Arthur quickly mirroring his movements. "Your blessing, mother?" he requested in a resonating tone that enabled Montague to be a man that others listened to despite his youth.

"Of course, my son," Margaret could manage only to whisper as her throat seemed to swell. As she lightly made the sign of the cross upon his features, she prayed, "May the Lord bless your eyes with discernment and your mouth with wise words. May he give you courage and victory."

Montague arose as Margaret repeated the words to her younger son. The blessing ended with her voice refusing to obey her. The way Arthur's hair carelessly fell across his forehead reminded her of her brother, though Edward's had been Plantagenet red and her son's was dark as a raven. Looking into his eyes as he rose, she wondered why she had never noticed the similarities in them before. Her brother would never have the opportunity to serve his king, but her sons would make up for that loss.

She blinked, realizing that Montague was speaking words of comfort and assurance to her that meant nothing and ensured nothing but were kindly intended. Margaret knew that few men headed into battle believing that they would be the ones to fall. She would not embrace them again. That had been done in private. Now was the time to send them off as men. Each of them raised her hand to their lips and were carried off by the bustling swarm of humanity that looked to make their fortune in France.

Moving to Catherine's side, she was pleased to see the strength demonstrated in the queen's dignified appearance. Margaret had not given voice to the fact that she disagreed with the king's decision to make Catherine regent in his absence. Her ability Margaret did not doubt, but she wondered if it was wise to put the stress of ruling upon the queen while she was with child. Catherine's expression left no doubt that she was certain of her own fitness for the task at hand. Margaret could only pray that God would see the child brought safely forth and England's enemies vanquished.

September 1513

Margaret kept her back straight and stiff as she knelt before the altar that was set up in her room for private worship. Months at court left her buzzing with anxiety and unable to let down her guard even long enough for prayer. The ease that she should have felt with Henry's leaving was replaced by concern for her sons and other people she cherished who had gone to war. She fervently prayed for each of them by name, and was disturbed by the ache in her knees when she finally rose.

As a girl, she had been able to leap from the altar unaffected by the cold stones that left her elders rising more slowly. With chagrin she realized that her younger self would put her in that category of elders with her grown children marrying and following their king to glory in France.

"I suppose I am old," she whispered to the sculpted Jesus who had already listened to her silent prayers. The statue had been a gift from her cousin Elizabeth upon Margaret's marriage. Many times had her eyes taken in the fine details of craftsmanship that made her savior seem so lifelike that at times she expected him to give vocal response to her heavenly requests. His sky colored eyes gazed solemnly into hers but revealed nothing of his divine wisdom.

Returning to the demands of her day, Margaret turned from the unchanging stare with a swish of skirts and strode toward Catherine's rooms. She had not far to go and was thankful, for the narrow corridor was much cooler than her private room with its cheerful fire chasing away the autumn chill that invaded through each crevice of the palace. She pulled her mantle closed to trap the cozy warmth of her rooms close to her body, not releasing her grasp until she had gained entry to Catherine's comfortable quarters.

The queen did not have her fire roaring as Margaret had. Younger and burdened by the weight of her coming child,

Catherine did not feel the cold as her friend did. In fact, she had discarded her mantle and was wearing a dress more suited to summer while her ladies took places closer to the small fire. Her face lit up when she noticed Margaret's arrival.

"I have wonderful news," Catherine said in a low voice meant only for Margaret. "Henry will be pleased with tidings from Scotland as our Lord Howard of Surrey is leading his troops toward an encampment near Flodden Edge. The Scots believe that we cannot bring the battle to them with our troops in France, but they are confidently marching toward their own defeat."

Margaret did her best to appear impressed by the news that Thomas Howard felt himself ready for battle. Well advanced in age, Surrey looked to recapture a bit of his family's former glory, but Margaret was sure the Scots had good reason for their optimism.

Catherine did not notice Margaret's doubt and continued, "He is hopeful that King James himself will be there."

"Will that not inspire his troops to fight that much more fervently?" Margaret asked and then winced that she had allowed the question to escape.

Catherine, however, merely shrugged. "It will not matter. James is ineffective and will fail."

"Henry's faith in you was well placed, your grace. I would not have foreseen your aptitude for war."

With a confident smile that made Margaret wonder where the queen's shy blushes had gone, Catherine stated, "Henry will have every reason to be pleased with me upon his return."

Margaret nodded. A prince in the cradle and the Scots put back in their place. This would please the king a great deal if events went according to his queen's plan. Margaret prayed that they would. Surely, God would bless Catherine this time.

As if her thoughts had prompted the action, Margaret

watched Catherine's eyes widen in fear and her hand reach under the bulge of her belly. Without giving her a chance to speak, Margaret ordered the most senior of Catherine's ladies to clear the room and send for the midwife.

~ ~ ~ ~

The hours of agony had once again paid Catherine poor reward. The child, who was born an almost cruelly perfect baby boy, had struggled to take breath only briefly. One could almost convince themselves that he was sleeping, so finely formed were his outward features that his death was a mystery.

Rather than collapsing into tears, Catherine's face appeared to be carved from stone when she was given the news that strident efforts had not saved her son's life. She was no longer a girl and had grown used to pain and disappointment, but she was also now the regent ruler of England and would not show weakness, regardless of how fractured her soul felt.

After a brief rest taken as women silently tidied the rooms that should have been filled with a newborn's cries and happy celebrating, Catherine requested writing tools to inform Henry of the birth and death of his son.

Catherine was still abed several days later when a messenger wearing the evidence of long travel arrived and requested an audience with the queen. He was ushered into Margaret's presence instead with Bishop John Fisher, Catherine's most trusted advisor, at her side.

"Your grace," the young man said hesitantly, as if uncertain who he addressed or how to properly address her. "I've come with a message for the queen."

"You will have heard then that she has recently born a child and cannot receive visitors at this time." Margaret knew that she sounded harsh but also knew that a woman must in order to obtain authority and respect from men. "Queen Catherine sends me as her proxy, and anything you have to say to her you may tell me."

With a glance at Fisher, the man assented. "I bear her majesty victorious news from Northumberland, my lady. Surrey has taken the day and the King of Scotland lies dead upon the field near Flodden."

Margaret controlled her features to hide her emotions upon hearing that James IV, the husband of Margaret Tudor, was dead. His son, now James V, had not yet reached two years of age. What would Henry think of the ascendancy of his nephew?

The messenger was continuing with details of the battle, men captured, and others lost, while Margaret considered what this battle would mean to her family and the game of royal dynasties with Henry's sister in control of the infant King of Scots. Excusing herself as soon as she was able, Margaret rushed to share the news with Catherine.

An unpleasant smile formed on Catherine's face as Margaret relayed the news. "I will have the head of the Scots' king as a gift for my husband to uplift him as he also prepares for battle."

Margaret was caught with her mouth agape. Of all the things she had thought her friend might say, this was an order she had not anticipated. "Catherine?"

A cruel gleam that Margaret had seen in others but never in Catherine lit the younger woman's eyes. "See it done, Lady Salisbury. The king will be pleased to have the head of that arrogant Scot presented to him before he destroys the French."

Seeing other faces in the chamber no less shocked than her own, Margaret mumbled assent and bowed from the room.

She was thankful when Fisher pointed out the logistic difficulties of transporting King James' head to Henry in a desirable condition and suggested a gift of his bloody doublet in its stead. As gruesome as the business was, Margaret thanked God that Catherine did not have to report a double failure to her mercurial husband.

"Do you believe that Henry will order his sister to return to London?" Margaret asked Catherine as they shared a simple meal in Catherine's rooms a few days later.

"It is the course that I plan to recommend to him," Catherine said as she shoved a healthy portion of fluffy white bread into her mouth. Margaret was saddened that a thicker waistline was all Catherine had to show for her many pregnancies. "He will wish to groom her son for kingship, I have no doubt."

"It will serve him well to have an ally in Scotland, rather than a rival," Margaret agreed. Best to befriend the boy while he was young and develop a sustainable relationship with the Scots.

"Of course, he will be more than an ally, since he will also be Henry's heir."

Catherine seemed to be frequently taking Margaret by surprise. She considered those who Henry might name as his heir besides the young King of Scots. There was Edward Stafford, but of course he would prefer a son of his own sister. "Only until he has a son of his own," she said as her mind flitted through the Tudor family tree for acceptable substitutes.

"That is in God's hands," Catherine stated harshly, closing the subject of her own childbearing.

"As are we all," Margaret agreed, submissively bowing her head before this hardened version of her faithful friend.

June 1514

With Catherine recovered physically, if permanently altered emotionally, and Henry returned from France, Margaret had gladly taken her leave from court to tend to her personal estates. She felt herself slowly relax the farther she removed herself from London, and was pleased to see the progress made at Bisham.

The news that Montague had been knighted in France was received with pleasure second by far to that pertaining to Henry and Arthur's safe return. Henry had made his way to Bockmer and Jane, while Arthur had remained at court to ply his charm upon the king and the fair ladies of England. How he reminded Margaret of her father. She thought this with a smile that disappeared as she prayed that God would grant her son a more prudent mind than George of Clarence had been blessed with.

Margaret had invited the duke of Buckingham to visit Bisham. She told herself that she had done so to hear of her sons' exploits in France and to have his opinion of the ongoing construction project, but the tightness she felt deep within her when she thought of him exposed her private lie. As long as it was only herself that it was ever revealed to, she thought.

Ursula was at Margaret's side to receive Buckingham and his entourage. The carefree smile upon her daughter's face reassured Margaret that she knew nothing of the marriage plans that she and Edward would also negotiate and finalize during this trip. Ursula would not be dismayed by the match, but surely she would be nervous if she were aware that she would soon be greeting the boy that would become her husband.

At sixteen, Ursula was more beautiful than Margaret had ever been. She thought this with pride and not an iota of jealousy. Having grown up surrounded by cousins who were stunning in looks but not always blessed with happiness, Margaret had long understood that there were more important elements of life than youthful beauty. Many of these vital components were also embodied in her daughter. Ursula skillfully managed the household while Margaret was at court and demonstrated none of the infamous Plantagenet temper.

A warm breeze stirred the few loose wisps of Ursula's auburn hair that had escaped their pins, and Margaret's heart ached with love for this girl whom she would soon be sending away to begin her own household. She was not foolish enough to wonder why it had to be that way but did wonder what life might be like if she and Ursula could simply stay together at Bisham, never visiting the Tudor court again. At least with Stafford she would be safe.

The caravan edging closer to the waiting women had the appearance of a royal procession. Buckingham displayed evidence of his royal blood in the finery that clothed his men and horses, the Buckingham coat of arms daring anyone to challenge his superiority. The Stafford chevron was boldly quartered with England's rampant lions and France's fleur-de-lis to remind everyone of whom Edward's ancestors were. Fear tugged at Margaret's heart. Must he be so antagonistic? It was time to accept that the Plantagenet dynasty was over.

A brilliant smile covered the emotions that were at war within her. The sight of Edward genuinely boosted her spirits, and she would have nagging doubts about any family that she was entrusting her daughter's care to. She took a deep breath. She was doing the right thing.

The russet haired boy riding next to Edward had to be his son, Harry. Margaret released the breath she had been subconsciously holding, thankful that the almost fourteen-year-old appeared tall and well-built. Ursula would have balked at being betrothed to one who seemed to be a little boy, and Margaret could not blame her. Before he dismounted, Margaret could see that Harry would tower over her daughter despite being two years younger.

If their looks marked them as family, only a few words spoken established that Harry was a very different man than his father. Leaping from his horse with the ease of youth, Harry did not give the impression that his actions were for show. He had the look of one who takes in much more than they reveal. As his father loudly greeted the ladies and barked orders at servants, Harry quietly and respectfully waited to be presented.

Margaret dared not glance at Ursula enough to give anything away, but she saw enough to perceive a slight flush that rose to her daughter's cheeks. Good. That was a promising beginning.

When the party turned to move indoors, Edward consumed Margaret's attention. When he took her hand and placed it on his arm, she kept her face turned away to avoid revealing her own blush. The anger she felt with herself for feeling this way only exacerbated the problem, and she felt her face flush with heat.

"Margaret, you must serve us some of that wonderful red wine that you have brought in from Spain. The heat of the sun seems to be getting to you."

She dared not look up into his face to see the smug grin that she was sure resided there.

"I will," she responded with enthusiasm, refusing to rise to his bait. "In fact, I have a new one that I know you will enjoy."

He carried on with the descriptions of wines that he had sampled since their last meeting, while Margaret attempted to focus her ears on the conversation between Ursula and Harry. She did not manage to hear them but could see that Harry had either been tutored to treat Ursula with special care or he was an uncommonly refined gentleman for his age. Either was fine with Margaret as long as he pleased her daughter. The sparkle in Ursula's eye when she tilted her head back to smile up at him proclaimed that she was pleased indeed.

The household quickly settled and many retired early after a gluttonous meal that Margaret knew would please the duke. He had been in his element, entertaining all present with his stories of France. Even Margaret enjoyed the meal more than she normally would have since Edward's escapades included her sons. She beamed when Henry's or Arthur's name was mentioned.

"The wine you requested," Margaret said, gesturing to a small table set before the fire in her private sitting room.

Edward smiled sincerely this time as he took up a goblet and relaxed into one of the chairs set between the fireplace and the open window. During the summer, Margaret enjoyed blending the cool evening air with all its seasonal scents with the warmth of a small, cheerful fire.

Taking up a glass herself, Margaret sat next to him. "The children got on well," she observed. "Had Harry been prepared?"

Buckingham laughed. "No, I dared not speak as I know that my own tongue has a habit of running wild once it is set free." After a moment of internal reflection, he added, "He is simply a better man than I am."

"Self-doubt? I never thought I'd see it in you," Margaret teased, placing a hand lightly upon his arm. "But I am happy that they seem well suited to one another."

He examined her hand as if considering his next move, so she pulled it back. "The boy deserves a fine marriage. If he can be happy as well, then he will be richer than his father."

Guilt washed over Margaret. Eleanor and Edward were seen so rarely together that she had a habit of forgetting that the other woman existed. While she would never consider anything inappropriate with Buckingham for her own reasons, honoring his wife should have been one of them.

"You are content that we move forward with plans for them?" Edward interrupted her thoughts.

She nodded with exaggerated motion as if it would clear her head of all else. "I am. Our families are ideally matched. They will be the most notable couple in the kingdom." Glancing at her cousin, she added, "Besides the king and queen, of course."

"Of course," he agreed, though he could not contain himself from saying more. He leaned in close to her in the way that always made it difficult for her to focus on what he was saying. "Maybe they will be the king and queen," he whispered.

Those words. The wine on his breath. The quivering in her stomach at his closeness. She thought she would be sick.

"No, Edward." She forced more strength into her voice. "Do not say anything like that again." Her anger building, she stood and looked down on him. "My father was executed for words such as those. My brother because the king thought he might someday say them. Do not ever utter them in reference to my daughter."

Her hands were on her hips and the fire glowed behind her, making her appear to be a demonic vision. At least to anyone besides Edward Stafford. He laughed.

Margaret wavered in her conviction and her arms fell limp to her sides. She felt foolish and turned to pour more wine in order to give herself a moment free of his mocking face.

"Margaret."

How had she not heard him rise and move behind her? He was too close, with his hands on her arms, almost embracing her as no man, save Richard, had ever done. Her limbs were frozen and her words caught in her throat.

"You misunderstand me," he said in a voice so low and deep

she swore she could feel it vibrating inside her. "I know they will rule."

She swallowed.

"You know what the monks have told me." His breath warmed her neck and excitement pulsed through her. "It will be you and I, Margaret, and our children will follow us."

Margaret closed her eyes. She would not be swept up in this. She was not her father. She pulled herself from his grip and turned to face him.

"And where will your wife be while we rule England? Where will Henry Tudor be? Do you think he is simply going to hand you his crown?" She allowed the mockery that Edward usually utilized to saturate her own questions, but he only smiled knowingly.

He stepped toward her again, keeping his voice seductively low. "Henry will die with no heir. Surely you see that?" He stopped short of touching her. "Who is higher in the kingdom than you and I?"

"I..." Margaret faltered. She didn't know what would happen if Catherine failed to birth a son. She hadn't allowed herself to consider it. "Henry has sisters. Surely they..." were not men, like Edward was. She did not finish.

"You understand now," he said, wrapping his arms around her. "It is our royal blood that is strong. The weakness of the Tudor blood is showing and it will fail." His face was inches from hers, and she forced herself not to prepare for his kiss. She would not close her eyes, would not part her lips.

"I will give you time," he said, releasing her. Edward was gone from the room before she could catch her breath.

February 1516

Almost two years later, Edward's words flashed through Margaret's mind as she heard the first cry of Catherine's baby.

After that night, they had both pretended that the treasonous, intimate conversation had not taken place. They had discussed construction, betrothals, and her sons' action in France. However, she had never been able to forget his certainty or the way he had made her want it to be true as well.

"Lady Salisbury, please attend her grace."

The midwife had addressed her with more briskness than should be acceptable, but Margaret was thankful to be shaken from her memories. The baby's wailing continued. It sounded strong and healthy, and Catherine looked radiant.

"He is robust! Do you hear him?"

"Yes, my friend," Margaret said, smiling. "I wager that all of his future kingdom can hear him."

The sex of the child had not been announced, but Margaret would not be the one to crush Catherine's dreams. That was often enough accomplished by nature.

"You have a beautiful baby girl," the midwife stated with false enthusiasm.

And there it was.

"The king will be so pleased!" Margaret gushed before anyone could express sympathy. "This long awaited and blessed child will warm his heart on this cold winter day."

She may not have a courtier's skill at arranging her face, but this she said as if it were written in scripture. Catherine's happiness meant more than truth right now.

Catherine's face had fallen slightly at the midwife's words, but brightened at Margaret's. "Yes! A princess for England. Someday, she will be a queen."

Nod. Smile. Margaret went through the motions as her mind went off on its own track again. Would Henry be content with a girl as an heir? It seemed natural to Catherine because of her own mother, ruling Castile in her own right, but that was not the way things were done in England. Henry's father had carefully established that he took the throne by conquest, not his wife's royal blood.

Thankfully, others had taken up encouraging and congratulating the queen on the birth of the baby girl named Mary.

October 1518

As Ursula was joined with Harry Stafford, Margaret remembered that day they met four years earlier. Love beamed between them, and Margaret rejoiced that they would enjoy this elusive element of noble marriages. The groom's parents certainly did not, and Margaret had too briefly. She closed her eyes to the rainbow of autumn foliage and prayed that their children would be blessed with the longevity of the Stafford marriage and the affection of the Poles.

Since Ursula could look forward to someday becoming the duchess of Buckingham, she would outrank her mother as peeress. This did not bother Margaret. She had spent too much time with princesses and queens to assume that rank was the equivalent of happiness.

"They look well," Buckingham said as he sidled up to her. His expression indicated that he meant much more than his words revealed.

Margaret surveyed their surroundings before keying her voice for his ears only. "Better than if you had selected a princess bride?"

For once, Buckingham appeared to be genuinely shocked. "I would never marry my son to a Tudor."

Margaret was not sure if she should feel honored that her family was considered higher stock than the king or terrified that Edward still thought that would someday mean something.

"I hear that Reginald has been named the dean of Wimborne," he stated loudly enough for those nearby to hear that they spoke of innocuous topics.

"Yes, the king has been most gracious in his education and placement. Reginald intends to take orders and continue to serve his grace to the best of his abilities." This was all true if unnecessary to express so vocally. Margaret was afraid that the wedding guests could smell the treason simmering between her and her cousin.

Edward's smirk told her that he sensed her discomfort and reveled in it. "Our king has taken me to task for the lawlessness in the Marches. I offered to try any strategy he recommended to convince Welshmen to act with honor."

Margaret paled and almost reached out for support. She envisioned Henry's face when Buckingham aimed this insult at his father, who King Richard had called a Welsh milksop.

Buckingham took her arm and steered her away a few steps. "Margaret, do you think me so foolish? Ah, clearly you do." He shook his head at her naivety. "I believed that I could speak my mind with you. I know that I cannot with Tudor. Have a little more faith in me, my dear."

Maybe it was the way the sunlight gleamed in his hair, perfectly coordinating it with the golden red leaves. She could blame his voice made purposely soft and seductive when nobody had tried to seduce her in years. Possibly, she just wanted to believe the best of him for the sake of her daughter's future. Whatever the reasons, she took him at his word.

"I apologize, Edward. It's just that . . ."

"I know. Your father. Your brother. It is wrong of me to tease you on such a sensitive topic."

She gave him a weak grin as somewhere in the back of her mind she wondered if anyone noticed them so closely conversing.

"In all seriousness," he continued as if nothing untoward had passed between them. "Henry will likely be killed in France. He wants to prove he is the next Henry V, but we know he's not got it in him."

"Please."

"Alright, my little countess. Nothing more regarding our

illustrious cousin."

He grinned again before leaving her alone. By the time Margaret felt composed enough to rejoin the wedding party, Edward was standing tamely at his wife's side.

"Mother, are you quite alright?"

Montague held his arm out to her, but his eyes were on Buckingham.

"Oh, yes. Thank you. Where is Jane?" she asked, taking the proffered arm.

"She is surrounded by other young women and would rather I found alternative entertainment," he said, sounding so much like her Richard that tears sprung into her eyes. Instead of crying, she laughed.

"You are a sensitive husband."

"Sensitive and observant," he replied.

His eyebrow was raised in unasked question. Margaret knew that they had been too obvious. "You know how Edward can be," she said with a nervous laugh. Plucking at invisible debris on her skirts did not make her appear less guilty.

"I do. Better than you know." He turned to face her, and she was suddenly surprised by how far up she was forced to look. Margaret remembered that Henry had spent time with Buckingham in France.

"What has he said to you?" she asked fearfully.

Henry examined his mother for a moment as he considered his answer. "Unlike our cousin, I am prudent enough to not repeat most of what he says. In this case, I am simply ensuring that my dear mother is not his next conquest."

"Henry!" she exclaimed much louder than intended, and heat rushed to her face.

Montague calmly secured a goblet of wine and steered her

clear of crowds. "You must know his reputation," he continued in the same steady voice after she had taken a sip.

"Of course," Margaret snapped. She did not enjoy feeling like the immature one next to her own child.

"I only felt that it was my duty," he began, but she did not let him finish.

"I can assure you that I am more than capable of managing myself."

That eyebrow was raised again. She wondered if Jane found it endearing or maddening. Her anger relented.

"You are right. In part," she quickly added. "He speaks too freely and has a way of..."

It was his turn to cut her short. "I'm aware of the duke's way with women."

Hearing this from her son, knowing that he had watched Buckingham seduce barmaids with the same technique he had observed being attempted on his mother, Margaret hardened her resolve against Edward Stafford.

"You need not worry about me. Thank you for your concern, my dear son, but I am in control of my own destiny."

July 1519

It had been ages since Margaret had seen such a display of wealth. Buckingham must have spent more on preparing for this visit than the king had on his campaign to France. Penshurst was a buzzing hive of activity with servants bustling about to ensure that everything was perfect for the arrival of the royal court. How Edward had convinced the king that he should spend a portion of his summer progress at the duke's estate was beyond her for it was no secret that the two men disliked and distrusted each other. Maybe that would all change now and Buckingham would be content with his rather blessed position in life.

The king and queen would be arriving within days, so every surface had been polished until it glistened in the warm sunshine. Exotic foods and wines imported from places Margaret had never heard of were waiting to grace tables for a few moments before they would be tossed aside because there was too much for people to actually consume. Women would wear fine gowns that cost more than most people earned in their lives, and men would secretly negotiate in corners. It was just the sort of occasion that Margaret despised.

She was here to see her daughter. Since her recent marriage to Harry Stafford, Ursula had been taken from Margaret's arms and deposited onto Buckingham's estates, now part of his family rather than hers. Her shoulders tensed and lips pressed together as she dwelled on the feeling of abandonment that she could only blame on herself. After all, she was the one who had arranged the illustrious marriage. Why could it not be possible to secure your children's future while also keeping them under your wing?

A sigh escaped her as she forced herself to relax, earning a bemused look from the maid who was scurrying past. Margaret hardly noticed. She would not have called herself arrogant, but she had long been trained to think of household staff as something akin to furniture. Except that they had ears. You could never forget that they heard every whispered word and stolen moment.

Her mind was a dreary place today.

The sun shone brightly and she forced herself to squint at it until a yellow and pink glow filled her vision even when her eyes were closed. Could she will the light to give her a sunnier disposition? God help me, she prayed, not quite sure what she hoped to receive from him.

"Mother!"

Bright colors danced across Margaret's eyes and she could just make out the outline of Ursula sprinting toward her as she had not done since she was a little girl. Her voice was filled with joy, so Margaret was satisfied that her daughter was thrilled to see her but not disappointed in her new life.

Ursula almost swept her mother off her feet with her embrace. "I never realized how I would miss you," she whispered into Margaret's hair. Was she taller? Margaret realized that her children had all outgrown her.

"Let me look at you, my love," Margaret said, not wanting to give her mind time to run away with sadness. She held Ursula away from her and admired her healthy glow and smile lit by contentedness that could not be pretended. "Good," Margaret said nodding. "I prayed that Harry would be good for you."

"Yes, mama," Ursula agreed, suddenly remembering herself and kneeling for a blessing. The girlish exuberance was replaced with the respectfulness of a child grown.

Tracing the sign of the cross gently upon Ursula's forehead, Margaret pushed back memories of performing the act since the girl was a newborn infant. "God's abundant blessings upon you, my dearest daughter."

"I am your only daughter," Ursula joked, rising with a playful grin upon her face.

Margaret smiled in return at the familiar retort. "It only makes me treasure you all the more."

Ursula nodded at the expected response that warmed her heart no less because of its repetition. As if they sensed his approach, the women turned as one to greet Harry Stafford. He knelt before his mother-in-law, though he need not have, and Margaret gladly gave him her blessing as well. Harry rose and respectfully tilted his head toward Margaret before holding his hand out to his wife. Her face when she looked at him left little doubt that Margaret and Edward had at least done something right in their lives.

"My father wishes for me to escort the two most beautiful women in England to the hall for the undoubtedly magnificent meal that he has planned."

"And who might they be?" Ursula playfully inquired as she took his arm and pressed herself close to him. Margaret attempted to hide her amusement, taking Harry's other arm more loosely.

"The finest foods should be saved for after the king's arrival," Margaret stated, unafraid as few others were to criticize the duke of Buckingham to his own son and within his own walls.

Harry simply laughed. "You do not know my father as well as I believed if you do not know that he has more than enough gourmet delicacies to entice us all for far longer than the king's planned visit."

Ursula giggled as though Harry was the most hilarious person she had ever encountered, but Margaret only grunted. It was just what she would expect of Edward. How had his son turned out so differently? She supposed that it only mattered that he had.

"How is Arthur occupying his time?" Harry asked, and

Margaret could feel him jostled by Ursula's elbow. Not a single other person had dared to mention her son whom the king had expelled from court in a fit of anger.

"I am putting him to work at tasks more valuable than privy duty," she replied and was rewarded with Harry's laughter and Ursula's gasp of shock. "He has been with me at Bisham since leaving London, but I will soon send him on to Warblington to oversee work there."

"Interesting and useful work indeed," Harry observed mildly. "I enjoyed seeing him joust the last time I was at court. He is the epitome of princely bearing and charm. I am sure that you are proud, of him and all your sons."

Knowing that he meant to be highly complimentary, Margaret only nodded, but her pessimistic mind whispered that people said Arthur was a vision of his grandfather. All charm and no substance. Some months of hard work would increase his skills and build integrity, she hoped.

They entered the hall which was warmed by too many bodies and trays of heated food. The air did not stir, leaving too many cloying scents competing for dominance and turning Margaret's stomach. Outdoor trestles would have been better on such a day, but no one would tell Buckingham that.

"Cousin!"

Margaret heard the greeting from behind her and wondered how the king could have arrived without them knowing it. Then she turned to see Edward Stafford approaching her with open arms. Her body stiffened, causing Harry to glance at her with a question in his chestnut colored eyes.

"Our children were kind enough to escort me in," Margaret said, recovering her etiquette training. "Everything looks lovely," she said, gesturing to the room with both hands. "Stunning," she corrected when his face told her that lovely was not good enough. The right corner of his lips turned upward in appreciation.

"Sit, and tell me how old Bergavenny outsmarted you," he said jovially as he directed her to the seat next to his own.

"I would not say that he has," Margaret snapped. "You should be ashamed to bring it up."

"Oh, come now, Meg," Buckingham said as he relaxed into his seat. "Your Henry will have his own titles and living. My Mary was in need of a good husband."

The topic aggravated her far more than Arthur's supposed scandal. That Edward had married his daughter to her son's father-in-law was a strong antidote to any affection she had thought she had for him. She took a long drink of wine, peering at him over the gold rim before speaking. When he had the grace to look uncomfortable, she slowly lowered it.

"You know better than most that I arranged that marriage with Jane's inheritance in mind for them, but you are also correct. Henry is proving himself quite nicely and will receive his own rewards in addition to the Montague lands from our gracious king."

As soon as she had said it, she wished that she had not. Edward would say something that he should not. That nobody should.

But he did not.

"How long until Ursula is making us grandparents?" he asked, as if they were an old married couple snuggled together before their fire.

The transition caught her off guard, though she was glad that he had not taken the opportunity to insist that their shared progeny would wear the crown. Instead, he sent her mind swirling into thoughts of her child bearing a child of her own. The thought thrilled and terrified her, as it must Ursula.

"These things happen in God's time."

"Of course they do," Buckingham agreed before settling in to his heaped up meal. He had given up attempting to draw Margaret out and wrap her around his finger as he had in the past. She seemed unaffected by his charms. He wondered if he was getting old.

Margaret hid a blossoming smirk with the glittering gold cup and took a sip of wine.

~ ~ ~ ~

The next day's activities centered upon the arrival of King Henry and Queen Catherine. Margaret would have gladly sacrificed her visit with Catherine if it meant that she would not have the anxiety of Henry and Edward together. Someone was certain to say the wrong thing. While excitement flurried around her, she fought nausea when she considered what Henry might hear from the mouth of her cousin, her daughter's father-in-law. Let him be prudent, she prayed.

Margaret had been content to remain at the rear of those who shoved for position to greet their monarch. How could so few people understand that attention from the king was a double edged sword, just as likely to cause their downfall as their rise? She was content with her current position and would rather not be noticed. However, she also could not let the king think that she was avoiding him. She sighed. Thankfully, Catherine was always there to smooth away the wrinkles.

In between those who were eager to present themselves and those who would not dare supersede the countess, Margaret demurely presented herself with a low curtsey and the appropriate praise. Her chin almost rested upon her chest, and Henry had difficulty seeing more than her lashes when he struggled to gauge her ambitions in her eyes. You could always tell by their eyes.

"Lady Salisbury, I am so grateful to have you in attendance. Please join me in my rooms later."

Margaret raised her head to assure Catherine that she was eager to do so. It only took a glance for Margaret to see that Catherine understood and for thanks to be communicated.

"My wife would like to discuss a proposition for you, cousin," Henry spoke for the first time, and Margaret could not have been more surprised by his words. He seemed pleased that her eyebrows came together and her mouth puckered in uncertainty. Good. Ambition scares her, he thought.

"Of course, your grace," she said, curtseying low before him again to complete her servile presentation and hide her confusion. "I am yours to command."

"Oh, I know that," Henry said in a low voice. He was leaning over to draw her upward, and he grinned as she stood before him, small and pale. She could not see any of his father or mother in his face at that moment. The gleam in his eye and movement toward her that was just a little too close reminded her of Edward. She dared not move her gaze from him to see if anyone else noticed.

Thankfully, his attention was quickly drawn away by the next poor soul to kneel before him. He never glanced at her again, and she felt like a dead mouse that a cat had grown bored of.

Once in Catherine's rooms, she knew that she could relax for the first time since arriving at Penshurst. The idea made her laugh to herself. The presence of the queen was not where most people would say one could be themselves, but that was what it meant for Margaret.

"My dear friend, how have you been?" Catherine asked, sighing as she lowered herself to a cushioned chair.

"All is well. Ursula is married and happy. Henry and Jane

have two little girls now." She closed her eyes and breathed deeply, the familiar scent of Catherine's rosewater and fresh summer air washing away her tension. Catherine would not badger her about Arthur or tease her about Jane's potentially lost inheritance. "And our Princess Mary?"

Catherine had arrived looking tired and worn, the years separating her from her husband more evident than they had ever been before. At the mention of her daughter, the fine lines and shadow seemed to disappear to reveal the still young woman underneath. In her passion, she reached out and gripped Margaret's arm. "She thrives and is beautiful. You were right about everything. God rewarded my perseverance and gave me the child I had prayed so fervently for. Henry will name her as his heir."

Margaret was too relaxed to control her reaction and saw the dismay on Catherine's face. "My apologies," she stuttered. "I had not expected this news, but am happy that the king sees his daughter as a fitting queen." Catherine looked only partially mollified, so she added, "As he should."

"Yes, he should," Catherine said, her face hardening into aged lines again. "And he will despite his efforts to get a son through any method required." Seeing Margaret's confusion, she continued. "Elizabeth Blount will soon give birth to a child that Henry has already confessed is his." With a sigh, Catherine settled back into her chair, excitement gone.

"I'm so sorry," Margaret said. It was her turn to reach out as she remembered consoling her friend the first time she had realized that Henry would not be a faithful husband. She could not fathom what else she should say. Many men had bastards, but that was no consolation when you were picturing your own husband ravishing another woman or watching her hold a baby that he seemed to conceive with ease in another womb. Queen or not, that was a wound that never healed completely.

The women sat in silence, each lost in their private thoughts about the hands that God had dealt them. Suddenly, Catherine brightened.

"Speaking of my Mary, I have a request for you."

"Anything," Margaret said without hesitation. "I would fulfill any request for you or my goddaughter."

"I pray that it is a commitment that you will find a joy nonetheless," Catherine gushed, and Margaret watched the years miraculously fall away from her face once again. She wondered if she should inform her friend of the beautiful effect that happiness had on her features.

"No doubt, I will," she said. "As soon as you tell me what it is you require."

"Of course," Catherine laughed, shaking her head. "I am getting ahead of myself." She moved closer and grasped Margaret's hands. "I would like you to serve as Mary's governess. There is nobody else that I would trust with the most precious gift that our Lord has given to me. Please, say yes."

Margaret was speechless. The long awaited princess, the heir of England would be entrusted to her care, just as Prince Arthur once had been. Gazing deeply into Catherine's eyes, Margaret understood that this was why she had been chosen. With her from the beginning as they both fought for Arthur's life, Catherine understood that Margaret's family were neither traitors nor schemers. Margaret would trade her own life for that of her charge if that was what was deemed necessary.

"I am humbled and honored, your grace," Margaret whispered. "And I accept, though I have a feeling that your husband may have instructed you to phrase it as an order."

The serious moment broken, both women laughed and

embraced one another.

May 1520

Fortune's wheel had done Margaret Pole quite a few good turns in recent years. Having undergone extensive rebuilding and improvements under both Tudor kings, Greenwich was breathtaking. Margaret could not ask for a more suitable and enjoyable appointment than to be the governess of the four-year-old Princess Mary within such a beautiful setting. It was a position that placed her high above most others while, at the same time, keeping her from the dramatics of court life.

With Margaret's forty-seventh birthday close on the horizon, this assignment gave her life renewed purpose. Her own children were established on their own, with the exception of Geoffrey, who at sixteen was happy to be out from under his mother's thumb as well. Ursula was carrying her first child. That somehow made her even more Harry's and less Margaret's, but she supposed that was as it should be. Not having grown up with a mother, she was constantly faced with confusing and conflicting emotions when it came to her relationship with her daughter.

Arthur had been invited to return to court, just as she had suspected he would be once the king's anger had the opportunity to cool and he realized how much he missed the younger man's charm and company. Arthur was thankful for the opportunity, the environment appealing much more to him than it ever had either of his parents. As Margaret took up her duties as caretaker of England's next queen, Arthur accompanied the king once more to France, where an unprecedented meeting was to take place between the rival kings.

The Palace of Greenwich was a sprawling, yet somehow still comfortable, estate. Spring gardens that would be perfect for taking the young princess for walks beckoned to Margaret with their fresh scents and peeking buds. She had already toured the rooms that would be utilized for tutoring Mary on the skills most necessary for her education. She would be given a broader range of coursework than many girls because she would not only need to be a wife, she would be a queen. Embroidery and music would still be a part of her lesson plan, but so would be writing, philosophy, and diplomacy, as her age and maturity allowed.

Margaret felt recharged by the challenge and the faith that her friend was placing in her to put England's next monarch under her care. She knew that Catherine, and to an even greater extent Henry, continued to hope for the birth of a son. While Margaret would not naysay them, she knew that Mary stood a very good chance of being their only child. Margaret would raise her to rule.

The courtyard where she stood was only a backdrop as her mind was wrapped up in visions of the future plans and occasions that included her and the child together.

"Lady Salisbury, do the accommodations suit your purposes?"

Catherine had approached unseen and addressed Margaret formally as an example to the Greenwich staff. Margaret was in charge. That must be clearly established.

"Perfectly, your grace," Margaret agreed, greeting the queen with a casual curtsey.

"Princess Mary is eager to see you," Catherine continued as the two women walked a bit beyond those who had accompanied them.

"She must not be aware of the strict schedule I am preparing for her."

They laughed together before Catherine became more serious. "I am glad. I know that you will be firm yet loving with her and ensure that she is prepared for what is to come."

Margaret gave her friend a quizzical glance at her choice of words.

"Blount has given birth to a son, as I am sure you've heard." The words were out of Catherine in a rush and she did not wait for Margaret to respond. "Apparently, the boy is thriving." She could not keep the bitterness from her voice. None of her sons had thrived. "He will someday challenge Mary, and she must be ready."

The idea that she must prepare a four-year-old for battle with an infant made Margaret's stomach turn and her mind drag out memories of deadly family feuds, but she only nodded in agreement. "You need not worry, my dear friend. Mary will be as intelligent as she is beautiful, with an unshakable faith that includes the knowledge of what God has created her to do."

Catherine pressed her lips together and nodded once. Margaret had a feeling that she knew what men felt like as they prepared for battle.

They strolled back to their waiting ladies to see that an addition had arrived. Lovely little Mary was presented to her new governess dressed in an elaborate gown that must have weighed almost as much as she did, but she curtseyed expertly in it without losing her balance. Her light auburn hair gleamed in the sun, reflecting shades of gold and bronze that combined her parents' coloring.

"I am pleased to welcome you, Princess Mary," Margaret greeted her in a firm yet friendly voice. "Our time together will be well spent and you will make your mother proud," she added with a glance at the queen.

"And my father!" Mary exclaimed, suddenly appearing much more like a typical four-year-old.

Margaret smiled and leaned down to place her hand gently under the child's chin. "And your father," she agreed.

November 1520

"I am so happy that you are here with me, mother," Ursula attempted to speak lightly, but Margaret could detect the fear behind her words. I'm so glad you will be with me in case I die, was what she was really thinking.

"All of God's angels and all the devil's demons could not keep me from your side," Margaret said with her voice infused with love. She had grown better than her daughter at keeping fear from her voice, but she, too, was terrified. She had lost so many people she loved. If God took Ursula . . .

No, he couldn't.

"Harry must be setting the whole household on edge," Ursula attempted to joke.

It was true. Harry Stafford was polite, kind, and everything a mother could hope for in her daughter's husband, but he was nervous and demanding right now. He was not accustomed to major events that were beyond his control.

Margaret gave Ursula an unconcerned smile. "Harry is telling anyone who will listen that his son is to be born within the week. He is as proud as a rooster."

This succeeded in earning a bit of laughter from Ursula as she tried to picture her husband regaling the staff with stories of his unborn child's pursuits. Her rounded stomach bounced as though her child were laughing at his father as well. The young woman placed her fine, white hands upon her voluminous skirts, eager to hold the hidden child but scared of the process that must bring it about.

"Thank you for choosing him for me, mother." Her eyes had a faraway look as she focused on secret moments with Harry. "So many daughters are not as fortunate in their parents' choice of husband for them."

"That is because they are counting on fathers to choose," Margaret snapped. She had seen too many men make matches for their children with nothing besides riches in mind. Buckingham's match with his daughter Mary to lord Bergavenny came to mind. "Do not misunderstand," she continued. "I have worked to ensure a future and position for each of my children, but not at the expense of happiness, or at least contentedness," she added, thinking of Arthur and the bride he would soon acquire.

"You are a most loving and considerate mama," Ursula said dreamily, making Margaret snap to attention. She peered at her daughter's face, but Ursula merely seemed sleepy and content.

"We should get you to bed so that you may rest more comfortably."

Margaret directed her daughter to the ridiculously grand bed that Harry had furnished her lying in rooms with. Ursula and all her attendants could likely sleep in it together, Margaret had joked when she first saw it. Taking the mockery in stride, Ursula had simply said that it was her husband's way of demonstrating his love for her and making her think of him when he could not be there.

Now, Ursula melted into the thick covers and was asleep before her mother could even finish the thought that she seemed too young for what she was about to go through.

Harry turned out to be correct. Ursula's labor started without mercy less than twenty-four hours later. Margaret's skill in remaining calm in a storm were harshly tested. No confinement prepared you for watching your daughter go through more pain than she believed was possible. Every time Ursula screamed or moaned, Margaret's insides twisted and she vowed to God that she would never forgive him if her daughter did not survive.

Even the cry of Ursula's newborn son could not distract her from her anxiety. She finally understood how Richard had felt each time she had given him a child. The baby was a blessing, certainly, but it was the mother he could not live without. For the first time she wondered if it was cruel that men were kept from their wives as they brought new life into the world, possibly at the cost of their own.

That made her think of Harry. Dear Harry would have heard his wife's cries, for Margaret knew he could not be persuaded to go far from Ursula's chamber. She must go to him soon.

"Ursula, dearheart, how do you fare?" she asked, gently pushing loose hairs from her daughter's face.

"The baby, I must see him," Ursula said without concern for herself.

Margaret satisfied herself that Ursula's color looked healthy, and she was exhausted but not delirious or ill. The baby was brought to her.

"He is a strong son, milady," the midwife announced as she presented the bundle to his mother.

Tears of joy streamed down Ursula's face, freeing the tears in Margaret's eyes as well. Thank God, she thought. Thank God. She felt that he would forgive her for threatening him. After all, he knew a mother's love.

"Is he not the most beautiful baby you have ever seen?" Ursula asked, her face full of pride and her pain forgotten.

"Second only to his mother," Margaret said in a quiet voice that was almost drowned out by the praise of the surrounding ladies, but she could tell that Ursula had heard. "I will bring the news to your long suffering husband."

"He is long suffering? Men do not know the meaning of suffering!"

The ladies laughed obediently at Ursula's words, while Margaret wondered just how true they were. She did not have to go far to find Harry. He was more disheveled than she had ever seen him, and her heart ached with love for this man who so clearly adored her daughter. When he saw Margaret, he cringed as if he was sure that she brought bad news, but he stood firm as he ran nervous fingers through his hair and down his wrinkled clothing.

"She is well," Margaret soothed, taking one of his fidgeting hands between hers. "Ursula has endured God's work for her and given you a wonderful son."

Harry's eyes widened as if he had forgotten that he would have a baby when all was said and done. "A son?"

Before she could stop herself, Margaret had taken him in her arms. He looked so young and lost. "A perfect son," she assured him when she released him a moment later.

He giggled like a schoolboy and ran his hands through his already thoroughly tussled hair again. "A son! I have a son!"

"Yes, I know," Margaret said, laughing with him.

His feet moved as if he would break out in dance, but instead he grabbed Margaret and kissed her cheek. "Thank you, mother! It is a boy!" he shouted to nobody in particular. He took a few steps to go share his news but turned back looking serious. "And Ursula," he said in a low voice. "You are certain that she is alright."

No, she could not be certain. "Absolutely," she said before watching him practically skip away to tell the household of the birth of his firstborn son.

~ ~ ~ ~

A few days later, Margaret wondered if she would ever see that raw joy on Harry's face again. The baby, who had seemed so perfect from his dusting of copper hair to his tiny, pudgy toes, had died in his mother's arms. As is often the case in such matters, nobody could offer an explanation to the grieving woman who had given so much to bring the small life into the world. It simply was not God's will.

Margaret loved her God, but she hated those words. She had heard them too many times, and would have given anything in her power to save Ursula from having to hear them. But nothing she could do would achieve that desire. The baby, who the proud parents had named Henry after his father, had gone on before them into heaven. Knowing they would see him again offered poor comfort to those who wanted him in their arms now.

Ursula had cried in her mother's arms in the moments before Harry was informed. A piercing ache filled Margaret's chest, she so wished that she could take away this hurt the way she had once mended Ursula's dolls or kissed a scrape. Margaret knew from experience that there was nothing she could do or say, and so she said nothing but offered her companionship and understanding.

When Harry arrived to take Margaret's place, she was both touched and slightly jealous. It was only right that he should do so, but she wanted to hold her daughter in her arms forever. She made herself useful by sorting household issues that neither had thought to attend to. How many mothers in the course of time had offered their love through useful deeds that nobody noticed were accomplished?

Before long, Margaret knew that she must return to Princess Mary. Ursula continued to grieve and would for years to come, but Harry would share that pain with her. It was Margaret's role to give a mother's love and discipline to the heir of England instead.

"Thank you," Ursula said when Margaret's trunks were packed and her caravan was prepared to return to Greenwich. It may have seemed an odd thing for the mother of a dead baby to say, but Margaret understood. She could only bring herself to leave because she knew that Harry would understand Ursula's deepest feelings as well as she could.

She embraced her daughter fervently, not loosening her hold until Ursula did. "Send for me if ever you need me, and I will steal the king's fastest courser."

Ursula normally would have laughed. On this day, the picture of her almost fifty-year-old mother racing across the countryside on King Henry's horse only brought a fleeting smile. "I know you would, mama," she said. She had resorted to her childhood reference for her mother ever since baby Henry's death.

Margaret blinked away tears. Her heart broke for Ursula, and she could never speak aloud that she was thankful that at least it had been the baby and not her that had died.

"I will keep you and Harry in my prayers."

She knew that others would assure Ursula that another child would be conceived soon. God's will would be done. She also knew that was not what Ursula wanted to hear. She did not like people assuming that they knew God's will or that the happenstance of this earth necessarily fit into it. Her God was usually kinder than that.

The hint of a smile. "I know you will do that too, mama."

"God bless you, my dearest heart."

Margaret embraced her again, then strode quickly away. She did not want Ursula to see her tears and certainly could not stand to see hers.

February 1521

"My first joust! I cannot wait to see the knights and their destriers!"

Princess Mary danced around Margaret's skirts, her exuberance releasing pins from the carefully crafted hair style that her ladies had spent almost an hour creating.

"Your grace, you must compose yourself and behave with dignity as those knights expect from their future queen."

Margaret never referred to the princess by anything less than your grace or princess and allowed no lapse in respect in any member of the household. She was quick to remind them that one day this child would be their queen and she should be treated as such. She was just as quick to discipline the young lady for she knew it was better to receive strict treatment now than to make public mistakes later.

"Yes, Lady Salisbury," Mary said, instantly transitioning from energetic five-year-old to demure young lady with her head bowed and hands held loosely in front of her stomacher.

Margaret could not maintain the frowning face of a strict disciplinarian with the lovely auburn haired child so submissive before her. She smiled as she leaned down to the girl's level. She could feel the cold emanating from the hard ground as she did so.

"It will be a fantastic spectacle, and you will even get to see my two oldest sons compete in the joust." Margaret's grin widened at the thought of her handsome sons proudly representing their king.

"I look forward to watching Sir Arthur and Lord Montague as part of the revelries," Mary responded properly and without enthusiasm, making Margaret laugh.

"You will also see your mother, who I know cannot wait to hear about your progress in your studies."

"And my father!" Mary exclaimed, brightening once again.

"Yes," Margaret agreed as she replaced the loose pins in Mary's hair. "Your father will be anxious to receive you as well."

She could say nothing else, though she wondered. Henry sometimes behaved as though he loved his daughter beyond measure and was happy to name her his heir. Other times, he showered such favor upon Henry FitzRoy, as Elizabeth Blount's son was known. Margaret could not imagine how this made Catherine feel because her own feelings were fierce with love and protectiveness for the sweet princess.

The grounds of York Place were as manicured as they could be with the hard frost still upon them and a vast field had been prepared for the competition. It was bustling with men and horses.

Margaret instructed Mary's nurses that they were to keep their eyes on their precious charge rather than the handsome knights. Mary was an obedient girl but had never experienced anything quite like this. Accidents too easily happened when children inadvertently wandered off. Margaret herself would be at the girl's side as much as possible, but she also would be expected to greet certain peers and was eager to see her children.

Princess Mary's eyes were bright with excitement and constantly moving in an effort to take in every detail. However, she made no effort to move from her attendants' sides. Margaret nodded with approval at no one in particular.

Her thoughts were shifted from her royal charge in an instant as Montague approached. For a moment, she had caught her breath, he looked so like his father had at his age. Margaret had to remind herself that this could not be Richard. Had he lived, he would be approaching his comfortable old age, but she would not allow herself to question God about why he had not allowed that just now.

Montague was the perfect nobleman. Handsome but not arrogant, intelligent yet willing to hear the opinions of others. He displayed effortless horsemanship as he easily reined in the giant horse before his mother.

Mary squealed with delight at the dark brown animal whose coat shone in the sun. Montague leapt from its back and knelt before her, even before greeting his mother.

"Your grace, it is more than I deserve to have your blessing before my match."

Mary suppressed the giggle that rose to her throat and attempted to match his serious tone. "Fight well, Lord Montague, with my blessing and God's," she said in a clear, high pitched voice.

Henry rose, bowed before her, and approached his mother. Bowing low again, he said, "And your blessing as well, mother?"

"Of course," Margaret could only whisper as emotion closed her throat. "May God watch over you, keep you safe, and give you victory," she said in a weak voice, crossing his forehead and resisting the urge to embrace him tightly.

He gave her a grin as he rose that brightened the already sun-filled day. Margaret nodded to the other women to carry on with the princess and allow the little girl to see the sights as she enjoyed a visit with her eldest son.

"You could not have made a better impression on your future queen," Margaret admitted as Henry instructed a page to see to his horse. The grin he returned assured her that had been exactly his ambition. "She will never forget the noble Lord Montague." She said it in a light tone but nodded her approval. Royal favor could be elusive, but that earned early would color each thought of him from that point on.

"Arthur has arrived as well," Henry added in a neutral tone.

"It will be wonderful to see all of my children," Margaret

said, hugging herself at the joy of it and feeling like a young mother again.

"He is well, of course."

She heard the inference. Arthur always made sure that he was well, though he would not know the status of others. Again, that fear that he was too much like his grandsire crept into the far reaches of Margaret's thoughts.

"And Geoffrey?" she asked.

Henry paused and squinted as though it made him see his thoughts more clearly. "I've not seen him. Will he arrive with Buckingham?"

Despite her feelings for, or rather against, Edward Stafford, she knew of few better equipped to instruct her youngest son in manly arts and had sent him to Thornbury.

"Yes, and his entourage will likely be impossible to miss."

They exchanged knowing glances, and Henry inquired regarding his sister.

"Ursula travels with them as well. She fares well," she answered the unvoiced question in his eyes.

"Good." As the firstborn, Henry felt protective of his siblings, especially his only sister. "And there they are, I believe," he said, looking toward a long caravan of horses and wagons making camp in a favorable location near the jousting field.

Margaret peered in the direction her son indicated but could discern nothing more than fuzzy activity some distance off. Her eyes were no younger than the rest of her, alas.

"You go to greet them," she encouraged him, patting his arm to urge him on. "I must find the Princess Mary, and you should not be held up by an old woman."

"I would never think of you as old," Henry argued, though his happiness at being released was clear. "I will bring you back news of my brother and sister once I locate them."

"Please do," she said, but he was already gone, his strong back receding through the crowd that surrounded her.

As if sensing her need for company, Mary was almost immediately at her side, filling the air with bubbling conversation about the horses and armor she had seen in her short tour of the jousting grounds. Her enthusiasm was just what Margaret needed to lift her spirits while she waited for her children to find her.

"When will my mother and father arrive?" Mary asked after she had described each scene she had taken in during the short time away from her governess' side.

"Within the next day, to be sure. Now let's take a seat under the canopy and rest."

"But I do not need to rest," Mary started to protest before her tutoring took over and she realized that her governess likely did need to sit. "Yes, Lady Salisbury," she corrected herself with a low curtsey.

Margaret raised her up with a pat on the head, and they settled themselves in a spot with an enviable view of the grounds and those camped around it as preparations for the joust went on around them.

A basket was produced, and the ladies were refreshed with bread, cheese, and watered wine. Margaret was thinking what a charmed life it was when she heard a familiar voice booming voice ranting about the escapades of Richard de la Pole on the continent. She knew only one person who would speak anywhere other than in dark corners of the man so hated by the king that he was the known target of hired assassins. Edward Stafford.

Anger much deeper than any lust she had ever felt for the man threatened to spill over into her countenance. This man currently counted two of her children as members of his household.

Could he not consider the safety and security of those who relied upon him?

"They are lauding him as Richard IV," Buckingham said jovially as though telling a great joke, seeming not to notice that those around him laughed half-heartedly and anxiously scanned their surroundings.

"But we do not here," Margaret stated firmly. She had reached him quickly, not because she desired his company but because few would stand up to him and put an end to his careless talk. It needed to be done, and she was not afraid. Not of him.

A few hangers on took the opportunity to melt away from the circle that the king's spies would inform him were listening to the duke's treasonous talk. They hoped that their presence had gone unnoted. Others clung on, more desperate for the favor of Buckingham than afraid of the king's wrath. Only Margaret stood confident, in every way Buckingham's equal.

Edward only laughed. "Well, that goes without saying, doesn't it?" He placed her hand on his arm and chose to ignore how unwillingly she acquiesced. "We both know that it will not be Richard de la Pole to replace good King Harry."

Margaret swiftly pulled her hand from his grasp and only just kept herself from smacking his mocking face. Her voice was an angry growl. "If you must cause your own destruction, please do so away from my presence and that of my children. Do you not understand the great risk you take just to take verbal jabs at our king? What could you possibly hope to gain?"

"Oh, Meg," he sighed. "You are too uptight."

"You lack common prudence," she countered, letting her fury fuel her words with him for the first time. "Your father died with no opportunity to explain himself to the king or beg for mercy. Do you expect to earn greater reward from a Tudor?"

For once, Edward fell silent and some color seemed to fade from his rosy cheeks. She waited for him to follow his thoughts where they would lead and watched his eyes seem to take inventory of those who remained close by.

"You do not think..." he started in a voice tinged with fear, but it soon disappeared. "It is not as though I have raised troops against dear Henry," he protested, his light tone back in place.

"Do you think he will wait for you to do that?" Margaret asked in astonishment. "He knows the riches and men you could call up and will not wait for you to do so. He is a king, not a merchant hoping to collect your account. My father was killed on the orders of his own brother. You are counting too much on the kind understanding of an arrogant and mean tempered man."

Buckingham looked as though he would argue more, his mouth opening and then closing again like a fish seeking water. Finally, he just smirked and tipped his cap to her. "Good day, Lady Salisbury. Thank you for your kind advice."

Margaret watched him walk jauntily away and wondered if she had chosen a poor ally.

As she returned to her own party, Margaret resolved to enjoy the rest of the day, taking pleasure in Princess Mary's excitement and the company of her children. She would solve nothing by worrying about Buckingham and his lack of self-control.

When time for the joust arrived, she forced all concerns regarding Edward Stafford from her mind. She joined Mary in cheering on her sons. Henry, who was normally reserved and older than many of the jousters, performed remarkably well and even appeared to enjoy himself. Arthur was truly in his element, flashing his irresistible grin at the young ladies and effortlessly defeating his opponents. They were so dissimilar yet still recognizable as brothers when they congratulated each other on their victories. The sight of them warmed Margaret's heart and brought memories of them as little boys together to the forefront of her mind.

Henry had apparently heard whispers of Buckingham's ravings, and asked what his mother was going to do to protect their family.

"I'm not sure what you would have me do, Henry. He is all bark and no bite. All I can do is pray that the king recognizes that."

"Forgive me, mother, but I think it is more serious than that."

Henry's eyes, brown like his father's, bore into her own. She could see that he was serious and he was not known for making emotional decisions. But what could she do?

He seemed to sense her reluctance. "Remove Geoffrey from his care," he insisted, laying a hand on hers in silent pleading. "He can join my household for now. You can tell Buckingham that I have an arrogant older brother complex and believe I have superior knowledge to endow. Say what you must, but ensure that Geoffrey's name is not connected with his."

Margaret felt the blood drain from her face. She had underestimated the situation, assuming that Buckingham said more in front of her than others just to torture her. His reputation had grown and there was not a doubt that the king would have heard of his ramblings.

"I will," she said, lifting her chin to demonstrate she was ready for any challenge where her children were concerned. "And Ursula?"

Henry relaxed and waved a hand at the thought of his sister. "She is safe. As a woman and the wife of Buckingham's son, who all know to be a very different man than his father, the king will not bother to glance in her direction."

Margaret pursed her lips. Was he correct, or was his status as the man of the family clouding his vision? On the other hand, what could she realistically do about Ursula's situation? She was a married woman, Harry Stafford's wife before she was Margaret Pole's daughter. "Very well," Margaret sighed. "Anything else?"

Henry stood, grateful that his task was complete and successful. He did not realize the effect of his parting words. "Be sure that the queen is ready to beg mercy on our family's behalf, should it become necessary."

April 1521

Princess Mary held the hand of her governess in a firm grip as she intensely stared at the creature blocking their way on the garden path. She stood perfectly still in order to avoid attracting the attention of its beady eyes. She had gasped in fear when she saw it and wished they had not set out on this early morning trek.

"Is it a wolf?" she whispered. She had heard terrible stories of grey furred wolves, stealing livestock and even small children. Could that small animal possibly drag her away? She edged closer to the comforting presence of Lady Salisbury.

Margaret held back her laugh, not because she was afraid but because she did not wish to scare away the fuzzy visitor that was sniffing the air, sensing their presence but unable to focus its poor eyesight on them. She slowly leaned down and whispered in Mary's ear. "It is a badger, your grace. He will not harm you and is probably making his way to his bed, for badgers sleep during the day and care for their families at night."

A hesitant smile worked at the edges of Mary's mouth. "Are you sure it is not a wolf?"

"Quite."

They watched the badger sniff and squint for a few moments before he waddled along on his way, telling himself that nothing had been there after all. Once he was out of sight, Mary began to giggle.

"Did you see his stubby, little legs?"

Her joy was infectious, and Margaret laughed in return. "He did not know what to make of us, giants in his garden."

"We must take early walks more often, so that we can see him again," Mary insisted, using the voice that Margaret heard her employ with increasing frequency. It was a tone that informed the world that this was their next queen and they should take note of her desires.

"I think that is a wonderful idea," Margaret agreed. She did not see Mary's order as impertinence, but as the budding confidence of a monarch. A frown formed as she saw one of Mary's ladies hurrying down the path toward them.

"Lady Salisbury," she said in a breathless voice that indicated that she did not usually hurry from place to place.

"What is it?" Margaret asked in a regal tone that never left any doubt of who was in charge at Greenwich.

"A messenger." The young woman's battle to catch her breath would not allow her to say more.

"At this hour?" Margaret said mostly to herself. She was already stepping around the girl and pulling Mary behind her to return to the hall and discover what news would cause a messenger to ride through the night to reach them.

The young man's livery was that of her oldest son and fear gripped her heart. Had there been an accident? Jane was due to have another child, and Margaret prayed for her safe delivery knowing that if the messenger was here her prayers were too late.

"Deliver your message before you take your comfort in the hall," Margaret ordered him more sternly than she aught.

"I apologize for the early hour," he said as he cowered in her presence. "Lord Montague wished for you to receive the news without delay."

"Then do not delay it."

"It is the duke of Buckingham, your grace," he paused until he glanced up and was pushed forward by the impatience in her stare. "The king has asked him to meet him here, at Greenwich."

Margaret's face could have been carved from stone but her emotions reeled within her. It was the moment that her son had warned her about. She willed steel into her spine but could not find her voice. A stern nod released the messenger, and she sat for a full hour contemplating her next move.

~ ~ ~ ~

The days that followed this announcement were filled with dread and indecision for Margaret. She left Mary more in the care of her instructors and ladies while she gathered her thoughts and questions.

Why had the king determined to meet Buckingham at Greenwich? Was he sending her some sort of message? Did he hope to speak with them, and accuse them, together?

She contemplated sending a note to Catherine but was hesitant to put any questions she had to parchment. It was impossible to know if Catherine would have any knowledge of her husband's plans, but he would certainly be privy to her communications.

If the moment came, should she disavow Buckingham or provide for him a character witness. Would exposing his guilt serve her family worse than taking the chance that they would be included in it? In the end, she knew the only one with any knowledge of the future heard her prayers as she frequented the chapel for daily services and meditation. God, however, seemed hesitant to share his answers with her.

Knees aching from so much time on the cold stone floor and mind weary from sleepless nights, she ordered the household to prepare for a visit from the king. Assuming this was a routine visit to monitor his daughter's progress, the staff bustled into activity but not concern. Only Margaret harbored fear regarding the visit's true meaning.

After a night of sleep that was so deep it could only be brought on by complete exhaustion, Margaret received another messenger from her oldest son. This time, she received him in her own rooms after dismissing her attendants.

"What news does Lord Montague send?" she plied him with the question as the door closed behind the last lady to leave. The messenger bowed low and respectfully, but she was annoyed with the delay. "Your message," she ordered.

"My Lord Montague wishes to inform you that the king has changed his plans and will not be traveling to Greenwich. He has intercepted the duke of Buckingham and had him lodged within the Tower of London."

He heard Margaret's quick intake of breath, but her face was arranged by the time he looked up.

"Thank you," she said regally. "You serve my son well. Please see to your refreshment in the hall."

He bowed again. "I appreciate the offer but am to return with all haste. Do you have a return message for Lord Montague?"

Margaret considered what motherly advice she should send forth with the man before realizing that it was Henry who was expertly following events and protecting them all. "Tell him that I pray for God's blessings upon him."

Another shallow bow and her son's man was gone.

May 1521

If Margaret had been anxious before, she was terrified now that Buckingham was under arrest. It was difficult to concentrate upon Princess Mary's tutoring and activities when she was plagued by worries of what it would mean for her family.

Thankfully, she had taken Henry's advice and sent Geoffrey to him. That left only Ursula with close connections, but her husband was not often thought of in conjunction with his father. She thanked God for that.

Margaret was perched upon a window seat in her rooms, facing outward but not seeing any of the spring beauty outside, when movement caught her attention. A rider was approaching, and as the distance was reduced to within range of her vision she recognized him as the man her son had last sent with news of Buckingham's arrest.

She sent her ladies each on errands, one with the task to have the man sent directly to her. If he was shocked by the disarray of her hair and wardrobe when he arrived, he did not show it. He had much more important concerns.

"What message does Henry send?" She asked before the messenger could kneel before her. Failing to refer to her son by his title in the presence of a servant evinced her fretfulness.

"He did not." Seeing the confusion on her face, he continued. "I have come of my own accord because I believe it is what my lord would have had me do."

"Oh, God, no," Margaret whispered.

"You misunderstand me, your grace," he quickly interrupted. "Lord Montague is of good health."

She closed her eyes and took a deep breath in gratitude, but only for a moment. Her eyes flashed toward him. "Yet there is a problem. A serious one."

"I am deeply sorry, but yes. Montague and Bergavenny have joined the duke of Buckingham. In the Tower."

Margaret thought she now knew what it felt like to die.

Memories of Henry flooded her mind from the time he was born and Richard was still healthy and strong at her side to the last time she had seen him, looking much as his father had looked before he rode away for the last time.

"No," she whispered to the empty room.

The years since Richard's death had not dealt her that type of pain again, as if God knew that she had already endured a lifetime's worth of sorrow, but now Henry was in the Tower. Did the king know that Buckingham was certain that his son and Ursula would someday reign? If so, her daughter was not safe either. Margaret had allowed the idyllic days to make her incautious. She had dropped her guard and now her children were in danger.

"No," she said again, but what could she do?

Henry was perceptive. With Edward as good as lost, he would give the testimony that the king wanted to ensure his own safety. Wouldn't he?

"Dear God," she said, falling to her knees in the middle of her room. "Please protect him, for you are the only one who can."

With her skirts pooled around her and her knees angrily protesting that they were too old to be pressed against the unforgiving stone floor, Margaret wept as she had not since the death of her husband over fifteen years earlier.

Realizing that his presence had been forgotten and his task complete, Henry's man crept silently from the room and away from the shocking presence of the weeping countess.

~ ~ ~ ~

Margaret was standing within the courtyard of the Tower of

London, surrounded by people she knew from the best families in the kingdom. The spectacle about to take place was one that no one seemed eager to witness, but they had all been called there just the same. What would occur here was to be an example to them all. Do not cross King Henry VIII.

Margaret took little comfort in the fact that Ursula, Arthur, and Geoffrey were standing near. She wished that they were not here and did not have to see the horrible play of power that was being put into motion. Thankfully, Reginald was preparing to attend the university at Padua. The king still valued this Plantagenet son and was sending him to further his education across the channel. Reginald had a way of remaining sheltered from the low points of life that the rest of them were forced to experience. Maybe his siblings were jealous of that fact, but his mother was grateful.

Let him never return to England again if that is what it takes for him to be safe and happy, she thought as she reached for Ursula's hand. Just as her fingers were almost within reach, Ursula shifted her body away from her mother, and Margaret stood surrounded yet alone as her firstborn son was marched out onto the fresh spring grass.

Henry stood proud, as she knew he would. Nothing in his countenance gave away his fear, his regret that he would not see another summer sun or lift his children into his arms. He knew that his final actions and words would be long remembered and would not spend them groveling. Only Margaret noticed his extended gaze into the sky that was filled with longing. For heaven or another day on Earth?

The scaffold had been prepared, and Henry strode toward it with no urging from those guarding him. He would meet his fate with courage.

Margaret's knees turned to jelly and her stomach threatened

to empty its contents here in front of this noble gathering. How could she watch her son die? She thought of the Virgin Mary, sitting at the foot of the cross as her son was tortured and executed. "Pray, give me your strength," she whispered, though none around her seemed to hear. Everyone's eyes were fixated on Montague, who appeared to be a man but Margaret knew to be her little boy.

He had climbed onto the scaffolding, and Margaret wondered that he did not speak. This was happening too quickly! What about his final words and prayer, the opportunity for the king to send relief at the last moment? They must give him time.

But they did not. Henry's neck was exposed on the block, and the axe was raised.

"No!" Margaret screamed, or she tried to. The word would not come, and the people around her seemed frozen in place. "No!" she tried again, only a guttural moan escaping her.

Ursula finally turned as if just now noticing her mother. She grabbed her by the shoulders and shook her firmly.

"Stop! We must save Henry!" Margaret cried. Ursula's face remained neutral as she continued to jostle Margaret without mercy.

"Margaret!"

It was not Ursula's voice, and she had not been addressed as mother. In confusion and grief, Margaret let the tears fall.

"Margaret, you must wake," the disembodied voice ordered.

Ursula, the crowd, and Tower Green disappeared. Margaret gasped to find herself in bed, her ladies surrounding her with fear plastered upon their faces.

"It was only a dream....a nightmare," one of them dared to explain.

Heat rushed to Margaret's face as embarrassment replaced her fear and sadness. She must have called out in her sleep, but what had she said? Could they discern the content of her dream? She sat up in bed, smoothing the covers and her hair, fidgeting because she did not know what to say.

"Thank you," she managed to mumble.

Her attendants, seeing her discomfort, tipped their heads to her and began to move away. Just as Margaret was catching her breath and the flush was fading from her cheeks, an unexpected knock came at her door. Whispering between the girl who had rushed to it and the mysterious person on the other side of the door ensued for just a moment.

The young woman closed the door and leaned against it for support. She suddenly realized that all eyes in the room were upon her, and she looked to Margaret with an apologetic look on her face.

"It was a messenger, your grace." She paused, looking around the room and seeing that everyone waited impatiently for her news. "The duke of Buckingham has been executed for treason."

Everyone seemed to freeze just as they had in her dream, and Margaret prayed that she would be shaken awake once again to discover that this was not reality either. When her closest attendant laid her hand upon her shoulder in condolence, she knew that this was, in fact, real life. Edward Stafford was dead.

Feelings of guilt washed over her as she realized that her first emotion had been thankfulness that it had not been Henry.

June 1521

"I knew that you would be desperate for news, and I am always eager to visit my princess."

Catherine squeezed Mary so tightly that Margaret expected the girl to squeal, but she endured and even seemed to enjoy the rare demonstration of affection. Margaret was touched by Catherine's visit and bit the inside of her cheek to stopper her words until Princess Mary and her nurses had been dismissed.

Sensing her friend's impatience, the queen gave her daughter a final pat and dismissed her entourage with the wave of a hand.

"You should know that he died well, with none of the foolish talk that took him to that place upon his lips."

Margaret considered this. She had wondered if Buckingham had gone down blustering and debating or proud and courageous. Now she had her answer.

"He denied being a traitor, of course, but also praised Henry for being a 'gracious prince' before his jury." Catherine waited to see if Margaret would ask about the execution, about the three strokes that it had taken to sever the duke's head from his body, but she did not.

"Do you know the king's plans for my son?"

Catherine sighed. "I am no longer Henry's chosen confidant, and certainly not when it is the son of my closest friend that he wishes to discuss."

Margaret visibly deflated, so Catherine offered what she could.

"There were tears in the crowd as Buckingham was led to death. I do not believe that Henry will repeat this act based upon the imprudent words of a dead man."

Slowly nodding at the sense of this, Margaret began to feel

the first easing of concern regarding Henry.

"The king's attention has been diverted to France once again, where he continues his quest for Richard de la Pole."

Margaret furrowed her brow. "He is concerned that he is a threat? We are well into the Tudor dynasty and most have come to fully accept it. Richard de la Pole has few people on English soil who remember him, let alone would support him should it come to an invasion."

"Yet, that is just what Henry fears," Catherine admitted, rubbing a hand across her weary eyes. The years had not been kind to the queen. Years of uncertainty, dead babies, and easing the fury of a temperamental husband had taken their toll in the fine lines, shadowed eyes, and downturned lips. Margaret had not seen Henry in some time but wondered at how the difference in their ages must be evident now as it was not when they married.

"Do you think there is any basis for this fear?" she asked, bringing herself back to the topic at hand.

Catherine shook her head but her face was uncertain. "I do not think so. Richard has made a name for himself on the continent, but would he risk what he has for an invasion that would be likely to fail?"

"Henry Tudor did," Margaret said without thinking, and Catherine tilted her head as if considering the comparison.

"He had nothing to lose. Richard, by all accounts, does. He is in high standing with several leaders, not least of which the king of France and a mistress that he is quite devoted to, but I cannot claim to understand the minds of men."

Margaret peered at Catherine more closely, wondering at what she did not say. She considered asking but knew that speaking negatively about the king was a line that Catherine would never cross, even with her oldest friend.

Seeing her friend's examination of her features, Catherine closed that path of conversation. "I cannot be sure, but I believe that Henry will have Montague and Bergavenny released."

"Soon?"

"I hope so." It was the best encouragement Catherine could offer.

The sun's warmth streamed into the room, despite the inhabitants having little interest in the golden beauty. Margaret swirled the wine in her goblet as her mind went back to Catherine's comments inferring degradation of her relationship with the king.

"You know that the Buckingham title has been revoked," Catherine spoke again, breaking Margaret from her thoughts. "I am so sorry if you had not heard, but Ursula will not be the duchess of Buckingham. At least not for now."

Margaret laughed, earning a bemused look from her friend. "It is all dust, as God tells us," she said, still laughing. "I have planned and negotiated, put everything I had into creating the best future for my children that I could. I married Ursula into the best family in the land, and now her husband is without title. Henry sits in the Tower with his father-in-law, from whom he was meant to inherit riches that will now go to the progeny of his new wife. Arthur and his wife can barely tolerate one another, and Reginald will likely never marry. I should leave poor Geoffrey to his own devices."

Catherine frowned as Margaret attempted to rein in her maniacal laughter at fortune's wheel taking its turns regardless of her efforts.

"The Princess Mary will require a spouse of fine family, good reputation, and prudent mind," Catherine mumbled as if thinking aloud.

"What?" Margaret was shocked from her fit. "What are you

suggesting?"

"That one of your sons should be the one to marry her."

Margaret shook her head enthusiastically. "Do not take offense, my dear friend," she said, taking Catherine's hands. "But the king would never agree to the match. Even suggesting it puts Geoffrey at risk of his wrath."

"Reginald then," Catherine said, unperturbed.

Margaret could only look at her friend in wonderment. The king had been considering matches for his daughter since the moment of her birth. None of those plans included the Pole family.

"I have brought this up at the wrong time," Catherine apologized. "Think on it and rest assured that I will speak no word of it to another soul."

Nodding in response, Margaret seemed unable to speak. She dared not consider one of her sons married to England's next queen. When she attempted to envision it, she only saw Tower Green.

May 1522

Catherine had been correct on all counts. The king was terrified of Richard de la Pole's potential and had called up troops to take the battle to King Francis once again. Montague had been released and was in attendance upon the king in France, either believed innocent of the treachery that had doomed Buckingham or deemed sufficiently warned.

Margaret was on progress to evaluate the status of her various renovation projects. The king's mercy had not extended quite completely to the entire Pole family, and Margaret had lost her position as Princess Mary's governess. Although she was disappointed, Margaret considered it a small price to pay for her son's return to favor. She also did not regret the time she could now spend seeing to her own affairs, though she missed the bright and sometimes surprising observations of the precocious young girl.

As Margaret's caravan made its slow way through the countryside, she was thankful. Ursula would never enjoy the title of the premier duchess of the land, and Henry could no longer count on Jane's inheritance. But they were alive. If her almost half a century on this Earth had taught her anything, it was that you could take nothing, not even life itself, for granted.

August 1525

The decorative chimneys of Thornbury peeked over the trees at the approaching sea of green and blue liveried people and horses. The estate, which Edward Stafford had not quite seen completed, was now to become the outpost for the princess of Wales, with the countess of Salisbury reestablished as her governess.

Margaret had never thought to return to this castle after the arrest and execution of the duke of Buckingham and was surprised when Catherine informed her that she was to be the head of Princess Mary's household once again. She was not sure if she should be grateful or displeased that her family had found its way back into close connection with the royal family. Since Arthur and Henry continued to serve the king, she supposed it made little difference if she again waited upon his heir.

Princess Mary was riding securely in a litter at her parents' insistence. It was too dangerous for her to make the trip on horseback, regardless of how much she pleaded to be allowed to for just a while. The girl longed to enjoy the sweet August sun with just enough breeze to keep it from being stifling, but the king and queen were unmoved. Margaret wondered if she would make the same decision with the kingdom's future dependent upon this one fragile life. Yes, she thought, she would.

Others claimed that Princess Mary would not feature in England's future. The king had not only recognized Elizabeth Blount's son, he had made him earl of Richmond. Certain that a girl was incapable of ruling, they looked to see Henry's bastard son take the throne. Margaret did not believe this would happen. A bastard? If that was all it took, Stephen and Matilda would not have had to plunge England into anarchy in their fight for the crown. Henry I's son Robert could simply have taken charge. Mary would just need the right husband to increase men's faith in her, just as her grandsire had needed Elizabeth of York.

She had even heard that some people believed Henry would betroth FitzRoy to his half-sister in order to give them each a greater claim. No one old enough to remember the outcry when people believed that Richard III would marry his niece were likely to give that rumor any credence. Margaret did not.

More of Thornbury was coming into view and Margaret had great appreciation for the care that had gone into its planning and construction. She had discovered a passion for her own building projects and noticed details that Edward Stafford had designed that others probably overlooked. The carved stone, mullioned windows, and elaborate towers took her breath away. Tears threatened to spill when Edward Stafford's carefully carved coat of arms came into view.

Margaret tilted her face into the wind to dry her watery eyes as she entered through the stone archway that welcomed Princess Mary's retinue to Thornbury, which was to become her seat of power as the governess of Wales.

At nine years of age, Mary was expected to do very little on her own, but councilors and agents made up a great portion of the retinue that quickly filled Thornbury's expansive courtyard. Built with housing of troops but not defense against an enemy in mind, Thornbury's construction was unique and ideal for setting up Mary's first household away from London.

Few questioned the decision to send Mary to the Marches. It was what had been standard practice for heirs to the throne for decades, but Margaret knew that there was more to it than that. Her last conversation with Catherine reverberated through her mind as she sought quiet rooms and left the unpacking and organization to Mary's capable steward.

Margaret had assumed that the king must be relieved when

Richard de la Pole was killed in battle at Pavia. Catherine had agreed that he was, but she had greater concerns.

"He has stopped sharing my bed," Catherine had confessed, blushing as she had when she was Arthur's young bride at Ludlow.

Margaret had been uncertain what to say. Catherine was unlikely to bear Henry another child, but this move seemed to indicate more than a lack of fertility. Had he no affection for his wife?

"I believe he loves another."

Catherine's tone revealed more than her words. It told Margaret that Catherine was concerned about more than a convenient tumble. She had endured Henry's affairs and would not have bothered to mention a casual romp.

"He is sending Mary away in order to punish me," she had concluded.

Attempting to reason with her had done no good. When Margaret pointed out that most princes spent their formative years practicing their ruling skills on the people of Wales, Catherine had simply stated that this was different.

She had stopped short of confiding to Margaret the name of the woman that she believed had stolen her husband's heart so completely that he wished his daughter to be far from his own presence as well as her mother's. Now that she had spent much of the trip considering Catherine's words, Margaret had decided that she would not dismiss them. Her friend was intelligent and discerning. She would not have shared these fears if there was no substance to them.

Constance, Geoffrey's wife, had joined the household as Margaret's primary attendant. Though she did not break Catherine's trust by sharing her concerns, Margaret did instruct the young woman to inform her of any rumor that floated through the castle, regardless of its implausibility or unimportance. Margaret would be in complete control of what reached Princess Mary's ears.

Dropping to her bed as soon as her ladies had prepared it, Margaret fell into a deep sleep where she could escape the conflicting thoughts and emotions that plagued her waking hours.

September 1526

"My mother seemed sad, Lady Salisbury. Why would that be?"

Princess Mary's question tore Margaret from her private thoughts. She had tended to her own estates while Mary had spent the summer on progress with her parents, who had apparently underestimated her powers of observation.

"Did you ask her, your grace?"

Mary slowly shook her head. "No. It did not seem right, somehow, though I know we should always be prepared to show God's comforting love to others. I sensed that she would be less happy if I indicated that I could see through her..." she paused. "What is the word?"

"Façade," Margaret supplied. "She was trying to look happier than she really felt."

"Yes, that's it," Mary smiled as she stored away the new word, but frowned again as she returned to the topic at hand. "Do you know what cause she has to be discontent?"

Margaret had enjoyed only a brief conversation with the queen upon Mary's return, but none of its content could be shared with her charge. She decided that was the only way to address the question. "If your mother did not wish you to know, then it is probably best that you do not concern yourself with the cause. I do know that she was extraordinarily pleased by the time she shared with you and seeing your impressive progress in your studies."

Mary politely smiled again, though Margaret could see that she recognized the distraction for what it was.

"She seemed particularly pleased with my accomplishments in Latin and French. My mother proclaimed that my skills have already eclipsed her own and that these languages will be useful diplomatic tools for my future." Mary bowed her head as she related this praise that was just as much Margaret's as it was her own.

"That is wonderful, your grace. I am blessed to work with such a willing student and supple mind. I believe you share your love of learning with your cousin, Reginald. He alone among my children has your passion for improving the mind. It shall serve you well. I am also pleased that you enjoyed your time with the king and queen."

Margaret had been nervous sending the small girl away for the summer. She knew that Catherine would shower her with affection, but was worried that Henry would be more challenging. Was he looking for evidence that his legitimate daughter was a better choice of heir than his strapping, but illegitimate, son? There seemed to have been no evidence of it or anything else to justify the reluctance that Margaret had harbored regarding placing Mary in her father's care for a few months.

Henry was pleased with his daughter, but less so his wife. Catherine had revealed to Margaret that Henry stayed away from her bed and their relationship seemed to continue to deteriorate. Some couples could enter this new stage of life, free of intimacy and childbearing, by building friendly comradery, but neither Catherine nor Henry seemed interested in this type of relationship. Catherine wanted a full marriage, while Henry pushed his wife further away. Where would it all end? And what would it mean for Mary?

Kathryn Craddock quietly entered the room and indicated that Mary's tutors were ready for her. Margaret sent Mary to continue her studies and then waited for Kathryn to speak what was clearly upon her heart.

She and Kathryn were of a similar age and each had been burdened with more than their share of heartbreak within their lifetimes. While Margaret had watched her father and brother be executed for treason and lost her mother and husband to deaths that had come far too soon, Kathryn had been bartered for and betrayed as the wife of a pretender. She had truly loved Perkin Warbeck, back when she had been Kathryn Gordon and he Richard Plantagenet.

Both women were now comfortably into their old age and did not often speak of the turbulent past, but they did not need to. It gave them common ground upon which their strong relationship was built. Their joint highest hope was that they could create a brighter future for their ward. With Kathryn as her chief lady-in-waiting and Margaret as her governess, Mary had no idea just how much effort went into ensuring her future happiness.

Unlike Margaret, Kathryn continued to search for her own happily ever after. Now on her third husband, she seemed content enough with Matthew Craddock, whose Welsh estates kept him relatively close to his wife as she waited upon the princess. Kathryn never spoke of Perkin Warbeck.

"Did Mary enjoy her time at Warblington?" Kathryn asked. Her voice remained a souvenir of her former beauty. Though years had greyed her hair and slightly thickened her figure, her voice was musical to hear.

"She did," Margaret said with a nod. "But you should tell me what is bothering you for neither of us appreciates beating around the bush."

Kathryn laughed, softening the lines around her eyes and filling the room with the pleasant sound.

"Very well, my bold and demanding Lady Salisbury." Her wink took the edge from her words, but her face turned serious once more. "She did not mention a lady that her father has been spending time with?"

Fear caused pain to grow deep in the pit of Margaret's

stomach. Fear for Catherine if Henry was not content with his wife. Fear for Mary if Henry had another child.

"Tell me."

Kathryn nodded and indicated two comfortable seats. Once they were settled, she asked, "Do you know Anne Boleyn?"

With brow wrinkled in thought, Margaret searched her memory for the name that was, in fact, familiar.

"She is one of Queen Catherine's ladies," Kathryn prompted.

This shed light on the girl, and a picture of a young, sophisticated woman sprung into Margaret's thoughts. "She has dark hair and a pointed chin, unfashionable of face but makes up for it with her clothes."

"Ah, you do pay attention, Lady Salisbury."

"She is Perseverance to her sister's Kindness."

"Yes!" Kathryn exclaimed, almost clapping her hands together before becoming solemn once again. "That is her."

Margaret considered the girl. She was no girl, was the first mental correction she made for herself. Though she had served the queen of France and now Catherine, she had never been married. Mary Boleyn, her sister, was a buxom woman, a little too friendly and free with her favors as one who is constantly searching for love and affection. Anne gave the impression that she could go a lifetime without love and affection, which of course made men desperate to give her theirs.

"This is the woman that has caught the king's eye?" Margaret asked, wondering if Kathryn knew that Henry had once tumbled Mary Boleyn during Catherine's pregnancy.

"She has," Kathryn had a knowing look on her face that told Margaret there was more to this than she was seeing.

"He has had mistresses before, though not usually when he

could be sharing his wife's bed."

"Which he refuses to do."

"Refuses. Is that the word used at court?" Margaret's hopes sank further. If openly discussed at all, she had hoped that people would say Henry worried for his wife's health and kept from her bed to avoid what could be fatal childbearing.

Kathryn nodded, her eyes soft with understanding. Even on the wrong side of fifty, Margaret could see what men loved about Kathryn.

"There is no way to soften the blow," Kathryn said, shaking her head. "He is seeking an annulment."

"No! He wishes to marry the Boleyn girl?"

Shrugging, Kathryn said, "If not her, then surely someone else. It is our Mary he wishes to replace as much as your dear Catherine. He wishes for a new queen for his bed and a prince for his throne."

Margaret's hands rubbed her temples as she sank into her seat, deflated that her best efforts had not been enough. Nothing Margaret could do would make Princess Mary a boy. She wanted to cry for Catherine who had been a devoted wife first to one Tudor prince and then his brother, only to be discarded after bearing half a dozen dead children.

"He is only whispering it now, but soon it will be public knowledge. The king will use Leviticus as his justification," Kathryn explained, almost as if she had read Margaret's thoughts.

"Leviticus?" Margaret repeated with a sneer. "It took him almost twenty years to determine that he should not have taken Arthur's wife? He has Papal dispensation!"

Kathryn shrugged again. "Kings have a way of getting what they want, regardless of facts." She leaned closer, the dismissiveness gone from her face. "The question is, what can we do for our Mary?"

They locked eyes, and unspoken agreement growing between them that their own unhappy fates would not be visited upon the princess they both loved.

Margaret decided to participate in something she had vowed to never do: get involved in politics. She had her own connections, not least of these her son, Reginald, who was studying in Italy closer to the Pope than most of them could ever hope to be. For Mary, only for Mary, would she rally against the king.

November 1527

Margaret looked out of her study window at the Bisham grounds. Clear finally of construction debris and wandering craftsmen, her gardens had been given new life throughout the summer months. As winter overtook autumn, those efforts seemed in vain. She tried to remind herself that the life there would reemerge in a few months' time, but she could not shake the feeling of foreboding, the certainty that death had a hold upon the roots.

The year had served an unkind turning of fortune's wheel, and Margaret had found herself coping with setbacks that kept her from dedicating herself to the battle against King Henry's annulment. Kathryn had been correct, Henry was no longer keeping any secrets about his feelings for Anne Boleyn or his lack of them for Queen Catherine. However, Margaret had done no more than write two letters, one to Mary's godfather, Cardinal Wolsey, and the other to her son Reginald.

A great many of the passing months since that seemingly innocuous conversation at Thornbury had been spent here at her own estate while others saw to her governess duties. Margaret had come home to care for another of her sons. She had been forced to watch Arthur die.

At first, she had been certain that he had simply worn himself out and brought on a minor illness. When he had written that he needed her, she was shocked but also assumed that he was being dramatic. Arthur loved to be the center of attention and this was his way of ensuring that he received hers. So, she had left Thornbury for Bisham, leaving instructions for the upcoming month.

She had, therefore, been completely unprepared for Arthur's appearance when he arrived at the peak of summer, dressed warmly as though warding off chill, thin and pale with an appearance that

Margaret recognized too well. It was the visible manifestation of death creeping up on one who has not quite noticed yet.

Arthur was in the prime of his life. In his early thirties with a young wife, he was a tournament champion and boon companion to England's noble sons. But he was dying, a truth that was painfully obvious to his mother.

This knowledge had not colored her greeting, which was joyous and gave nothing away. She would not be the one to inform him that he had a dark, merciless rider with him on his courser. Arthur would be forced to acknowledge him soon enough.

"I have comfortable rooms prepared for you," Margaret said as she embraced her son. Quickly, she was able to assess his temperature: too high, and weight: too low. His hands felt softer than normal, indicating that he had not been riding, hunting, and jousting regularly for quite some time. A reprimand died upon her lips. He should have come to her sooner. She could have cared for him. But, no. She would simply be thankful for the time that God did grant to him.

"Thank you, mother," he said in a raspy voice, throat dry with sickness and road dust. He seemed to be thanking her just as much for what she was not saying. His dark hair hung limply about his face as he allowed her to guide him into the house.

He had told her about his little Henry, Mary, and Margaret, and she had shared news about Princess Mary. If he had any greater insight into the king's plans for Mary, Arthur did not share it. Margaret doubted that her son had spent much time discussing the girl with her father. Arthur was a tool for keeping Henry young through physical challenges and light conversation. Discussions of his heir would be held with Cardinal Wolsey and other older, wiser counselors.

With her son tucked snugly into bed as if he were still her

little boy, Margaret made her way to Bisham's chapel. Should she pray for miraculous healing or the strength to watch her child waste away? Which prayer would be most likely to touch the heart of God and convince him to not put her through this?

On her knees in front of the altar, Margaret was stunned to find that her eyes remained dry. She wished it was because she felt God's comfort as she submitted herself to him, but she felt as alone as before. It seemed that her creator had formed her for sorrow and loss, relieved only by fleeting joy.

It would be strength he would give her rather than a miracle. She knew as certainly as if it had been whispered in her ear by the voice of his angels. And he said his burden was light.

She sighed and her knees made popping sounds as she rose. It was still within her power to provide Arthur with love and comfort while he remained hers, so she called for her steward to ensure that his favorite foods would be served to tempt him.

Arthur was propped up with pillows when Margaret had a tray brought to him. She impatiently waved away other helpful hands and pulled a chair up to his bedside. This was a duty she would not delegate. It would be her hand that fed him his last as she had fed him his first.

"It is too much," Arthur protested, looking at the overflowing tray.

"Then you will choose what you would like to sample, and I will send the rest back," Margaret argued with a shrug.

Arthur smiled. She had done the same thing for each of her children when they had been young, thinking nothing of creating a hard day of work for the cooks in providing the delicacies they preferred in order to tempt them into a few bites. He wondered if that made her a thoughtful mother or a demanding housekeeper.

"The marzipan," he said, lifting his chin to better survey his buffet.

Margaret gave him a look that said he should start with something not made entirely from sugar but fed him a piece, nonetheless. He closed his eyes in contentment as the sweetness melted on his tongue.

After tasting a few other morsels, Arthur was surprised to feel some measure of strength return.

"I am sorry, mother," he said.

"That's ridiculous," Margaret replied. "What have you to apologize for?"

He took a long breath and adjusted his position on the pillows. "For failing you. For not making success out of the plans you made for me." He saw her shaking her head and preparing to protest, so he held up a hand to stop her. "I know that I'm not as serious as Reginald and have not made my wife happy as Henry has, but neither am I wallowing in self-pity." He sighed again. "I just thought I would have more time."

Her lips pressed together into a thin line, Margaret took her son's hand. If she could have, she would have given him years of her own life. She had experienced enough of what the Earth had to offer. Before she could form a response, there was a knock at the door of Arthur's rooms.

"It is a messenger," whispered Margaret's chief lady-in-waiting who knew that she wished not to be disturbed.

"Very well," Margaret sighed, rising stiffly from the chair that had not left the side of Arthur's bed since his arrival.

She was absent only moments, but Arthur could see that she had taken another blow in the paleness of her countenance and ghostlike movements.

"What is it, mother?" he asked, pulled from the sleep that beckoned by the worry he discerned in lines of her face.

"It is Cat."

He blearily screwed up his face in thought. "Your cousin? Henry Courtenay's mother?"

"The same," Margaret whispered, falling gratefully into her seat. "She always seemed the very embodiment of life." Her voice had a dreamlike quality until Arthur spoke.

"She has died?" he asked, confusion stamped into his features by his mother's odd behavior.

Margaret's eyes snapped back into focus, and she realized that she was not taking proper care with her words. "Accept my apology, Arthur. It is just that I cannot believe. . . Yes, Cat has died at Devon."

"Once again, I must offer you condolences. I am sorry, mother."

"She was the last," Margaret started to say before realizing that she was wrong. She, herself, was the last of the children born to those Plantagenet princes, proud York boys who were so certain that they would rule forever. She had never felt so alone.

Her eyes met those of her son. His were searching hers though filled with fever and announcing the approach of death, and hers filled with the tears that had not come on schedule when she was alone in the chapel. Suddenly, she was sobbing, feeling nothing beyond the warmth of her dying son's arms wrapped around her. She had been ready to curse God for his heartlessness until that moment. Arthur's embrace broke her heart but saved her faith.

~ ~ ~ ~

"You must be prepared to forgive Jan."

Arthur's words pierced Margaret's heart. It felt like a pincushion since the day he had arrived at her door, so this was just one more wound that would harden into a scar once he was gone.

"That is not something you need concern yourself with," Margaret snapped. It still rankled that her children's marriages had not reflected their auspicious beginnings. While most of them were content or even happy, the Buckingham and Bergavenny inheritances had been lost. The fact that Arthur was cared for by his mother rather than his wife at this time spoke volumes on their relationship.

"I cannot remain silent on it," Arthur insisted. "Jan and I have made the best of things, and you have four grandchildren to show for it. Do not ask her for more than that."

"You mean do not ask her to mourn her husband or demonstrate love for you toward your children?" She was sorry as soon as the words had left her lips. How could she speak so coldly toward him as he lay wasting away? "Arthur, I wish I could take back my words," she said, rubbing his hands too enthusiastically but he lacked the strength to pull them away. "I will be gentle with Jan and do my very best to see your children well situated."

"Thank you, mother," he said wearily. "I know you will."

His eyes closed, and Margaret realized how much this small request had cost him. Arthur had not needed his mother to remind him that his wife did not love him. Of course, any husband would know. Poor Arthur, chivalrous knight and companion to the king, had been married to one of the few women in England who did not adore him. Margaret hated herself for making the match, even more so now that Arthur's time for earthly joys was cut short.

His breathing had the slow rhythm that informed her he slept. For a moment, she could convince herself that his health would be restored. He appeared so young and free of pain in the depths of his dreams. Lines of fatigue and pain relaxed as he took refuge in unconsciousness. However, it was an empty promise and a fool's dream. Margaret knew she was spending his final days with him.

The next day, Arthur was too exhausted for conversation, so he asked his mother to regale him with stories of court from the past summer.

"Princess Mary was in a whirlwind over the invitation to court. Spending the previous summer with her parents had given her such joy, despite the coolness between them, and this time there was her betrothal to celebrate. "

A faint smile crossed Arthur's face as he closed his eyes and imagined the beautiful little girl twirling around in her new dresses as she dreamed of her prince. He wondered if Jan had ever thought her marriage would be that way.

"Your brother, Reginald, was there. He interested me much more than the French ambassadors, of course," Margaret admitted with a girlish grin. "The king has made a great investment in him and his serious demeanor and intellect are a great reward for it. Henry has provided him with the deanery of Exeter now that he is returned from Italy."

"Do you think he will stay?" Arthur asked without opening his eyes.

"In England?" Margaret was surprised. She thought that she was the only person able to perceive the tension between Reginald and the king. Her son was a model of decorum and respect, but somehow she could sense that he wished to return to the continent.

Arthur peeked at her through slitted lids. "I have not spent as much time with my younger brother as our illustrious king, but I can tell you that they are oil and water. England may not be big enough for the both of them." This short speech had tired him, and he closed his eyes and rolled over before Margaret could question him further.

Light snoring soon escaped Arthur's bedcovers, and Margaret wondered if she would get the opportunity to learn more about his unexpectedly insightful observations. Why would Reginald not have a flourishing relationship with the man who had sponsored his education since childhood?

Wearily shaking her head, Margaret stood and hailed a girl to clear away the remnants of Arthur's last barely touched tray from the kitchens. Henry had favored Reginald and each of her children more than she could have ever hoped for. She dismissed Arthur's fears as the result of fever.

~ ~ ~ ~

Before Arthur had arrived, Margaret had concentrated upon bringing new life to the Bisham estate. She had purposely avoided thinking of or visiting the graves of her ancestors who were spending their eternal rest within the priory. Her brother and Neville grandfather were just two of many who had given their lives for causes of the kings of England. Arthur would join them, a novel addition to a collection of men who had died in battle or been executed, since Arthur was a Plantagenet son who had managed to die of natural causes.

The funeral arrangements had been made, but she did not remember doing so. The fortnight since his passing was a blur of prayer and tears. As she thanked her savior for welcoming her son into his arms, Margaret sobbed for the vibrant little boy who should have outlived her.

It was poor comfort that he would lie here among distinguished Neville and Montague relations, going back to the first earl of Salisbury. So many of their deaths seemed pointless now, Edward's execution chief among them for his youth and innocence. She had never even met her grandfather, who died after deciding he would like to replace the York king he had helped elevate. His bronze effigy revealed no clues to her of why he had decided it was worth his life to switch sides. Her father had soon followed him, executed for treason by his own brother.

Margaret dropped her hand, which she had subconsciously lifted to reach out to the kingmaker. She released a sigh and shivered at the thought of how cold and lifeless the golden face would feel. No different than the body that lie below it or the body of her son that would soon lie at its side.

She waited, but new tears did not fill her eyes. With a nod, she accepted that now was the time to carry out her last duties to her second son. Surely, more tears would come, but later, after her work was complete. Walking away from the tombs, she formed a picture in her mind of the monument that she would have crafted to memorialize Sir Arthur Pole.

~ ~ ~ ~

As if burying her child was not difficult enough, Margaret then had to deal with her daughter-in-law. She had strictly ordered her household not to spread word of Arthur's death. Jan may not care enough for her husband to sit at his deathbed, but no one deserved to hear about their spouse's death by chance gossip.

Margaret had sent messages to Jan, requesting that she come to Bisham. She had finally agreed and was making her way, unknowingly too late. Their marriage must have held some passion if not love, for the union had produced four children. It was these four whom Margaret's concern shifted to now. More important than consoling her son's wife, she must ensure that care was taken for his children's future. She only hoped that Jan shared her feelings.

No one would deny that Jan was a lovely woman. Her

parents had taken advantage of the fact and arranged a marriage for her early. She had been wed and widowed twice already, though her first marriage had not produced children due to her still being a child herself at the time. When Margaret looked upon her, she wished that her personality was as beautiful as her countenance.

That was not entirely fair. Many, men and women alike, were drawn to Jan. The young woman's failure to create a happy home for Margaret's beloved son colored her feelings for her. In her eyes, none of the fault lay on Arthur.

After breaking the news to Jan, Margaret presented her request.

"I would like for you and I to take a small pilgrimage to Syon Abbey."

Jan wrinkled her normally smooth forehead at the unexpected demand. Though she had not despised her husband, she felt no great love for his family or need to continue relations with them now that Arthur was gone.

In a deceptively sweet voice, she asked, "Why Syon when you have such a lovely chapel here?"

"Thank you, daughter," Margaret said, accepting the praise with a tilt of her head. "I believe it will provide us both with great healing. Have you seen the newest building completed?"

Jan's shoulders relaxed. She knew of her mother-in-law's obsession with building projects. Still unsure why she was included in the trip, she acquiesced, assuming that it would be the last time she spent extended time with her.

When they approached the impressive complex of Syon Abbey a few days later, Margaret's broad grin was caused by more than the great evidence of men's dedication to God.

"Jan, is it not a sight like none other?"

The stone structures sprawling along the bank of the Thames

were breathtaking, to most. Jan remained uninterested and slightly suspicious.

"Yes, mother," she responded dutifully.

The river sent up a great stink that invaded the nostrils and stuck fast to the clothing of anyone downwind, as they were. Jan, quite indiscreetly, covered her nose with a bit of perfumed cloth, but Margaret kept her nose high as though she did not notice.

As they entered the gates of Syon, Henry stepped forward to assist his mother from her coach. She greeted Henry casually, sharing a victorious look with him that Jan would have had to have been blind to not notice.

"Lord Montague," Jan said as she curtseyed. Her words and movements were as politeness required but no more. She could not be faulted for coldness nor praised for warmth. "What a surprise to find you here."

With a quick glance at his mother that seemed to ask how much Jan had been told, Henry bowed to his sister-in-law to gain time for forming his response.

"You have my condolences on the loss of your husband," he said gravely. "It is trying enough that I have lost a brother, but your loss is the greater one. May God have mercy on his soul and also give you peace."

Like her words, they could not be faulted though they did not answer her question.

"I thank you for your concern and your prayers," Jan said with her head appropriately bowed in a posture of grief.

"The abbess is busy?" Margaret interrupted their act with more practical matters.

Henry looked as though he was holding back a rather inappropriate grin. "She welcomes us to join her after midday prayers when she has reserved her time for us until vespers."

"Well done, Henry. Let us take this time to refresh ourselves from the dust and discomfort of the road." She turned to Jan. "Come, daughter. A room has been prepared."

Margaret ignored her daughter-in-law's small hands balled into fists so tight that her knuckles shone white. Jan would see that this was what was best for the children.

The delicate stonework and elaborate riches of the abbey could not distract Margaret from her purpose today. At any other time she would have been entranced by the carvings and stained glass windows. Today, they melted into the background of what she must do.

Jan seemed to have selected silence as the best defense, though she clearly believed her in-laws were up to something. Margaret could see it in her narrowed eyes and pursed lips, as well as the tiny line that was forming between her eyes. It was left to the older woman to make small talk as their dresses were brushed and a small meal was brought. She babbled about the history of the Abbey, as if anyone was still under the impression that pilgrimage was their true purpose.

Jan's eyes glazed over as Margaret talked of each king that had improved upon Syon and Richmond Palace which faced it across the river.

"Did you know that my cousin, Elizabeth, was in residence when the old manor of Sheen burnt to the ground?" Margaret asked.

"Yes, mother," Jan responded blandly. All England knew about the Christmas fire, some blaming it on Perkin Warbeck. However it had started, the first Tudor king had used the opportunity to build a new palace that demonstrated his magnificence.

"This is a beautiful place," Margaret continued, ignoring

Jan's disinterest. "It is no wonder so many serve God here at Syon."

"Yes, it is," Jan muttered with no hint that she was following Margaret's train of thought. She was concentrating on perfecting the arrangement of her light golden hair and inspecting her dress for specks that her ladies may have missed. Satisfied, she looked to see if Margaret was also prepared to do what they must before they could leave.

Margaret smiled and did not realize how it gave the younger woman chills. "Let us visit the chapel to pray before we meet with the abbess."

Jan followed obediently. As Margaret admired tapestries and fine stonework, Jan noticed the cold of the hard floor seeping through her velvet slippers. She hugged herself for warmth and support.

When they arose from their prayers, Margaret brushed a nonexistent bit of debris from Jan's sleeve. "It is a balm to the soul to be here. Wouldn't you agree?" She tried, unsuccessfully, to keep the question from sounding loaded.

"Prayer is always a tonic to me," Jan gave her hesitant agreement.

"That is good, daughter," Margaret said, gripping her arm and directing her away from the altar with some excitement. "That is very good."

Margaret ignored Jan's quizzical gaze. She would have her answers soon enough. Henry was rejoining them as they reached the vast entrance to the narthex. Margaret allowed herself to momentarily forget her mission to take in the view of the high ceiling, intricately carved by men who had already gone on to receive their reward in heaven. She hoped that God saw some part of her life as a worthy sacrifice to him as well.

"Mother, are you ready?" Henry asked.

His arm was offered and taken firmly by his mother as Jan followed behind. Her head was already bowed in defeat, though she knew not yet what she had lost.

The abbess enjoyed opulent luxuries that the nuns in residence were told kept them from depending fully upon God. Clearly, their leader had learned how to resist the temptations of warm fires, fine food, and glittering jewels, for she was often surrounded by them. As the trio entered her chamber, they felt as much at home as they would visiting a fellow member of the nobility.

Greetings exchanged, Margaret was quick to get down to business.

"I would like to speak to you, mother abbess, regarding my beloved daughter-in-law."

She felt slightly guilty about the misleading statement, especially when she saw Jan's eyes widen in realization of what was happening.

"Of course, Lady Salisbury," the abbess responded in a smooth voice. Turning to Jan, she offered condolences that seemed barely heard.

"It is the loss of my dear son, Arthur, that brings us here," Margaret continued, grasping Henry's arm for support though she sat on a firm chair.

Henry took up the conversation to spare her. "I believe that it would be beneficial to the entire family, and especially my dear sister-in-law, if she were to serve God here at Syon. Were you to take her as a novice, Jan could gain great comfort that comes only from our God who knows her grief."

"I have seen many widows find overwhelming comfort from prayer and the sisterhood," the abbess agreed without looking at Jan.

However, Margaret did look at her and saw surprise, but more than that, hurt. Margaret knew that she would be rending the woman from her children when she only just lost her husband, but this was the best way to protect their inheritance. If Jan were to remarry, which her position and beauty made rather likely, Arthur's children would be forced to split all that he had left to them with half siblings who had never known him. It simply would not do. Jan must see the sense of it.

"Jan has spoken to me about the joy that prayer brings her, and I am confident that this is the course that God has prepared for her," Margaret stated more confidently than she felt.

The abbess nodded and opened her mouth to speak when Jan's voice filled the room.

"Will no one ask me what I think? Does anyone wonder how I feel about spending the rest of my life cloistered with chaste women?"

Tears sprung to her eyes, and she swatted angrily at them for giving evidence of her weakness of character.

"I have not been a part of these discussions, though it is clear I have been the topic of them," Jan finished with a sneer that marred her perfect features.

Henry frowned at her before addressing the abbess as if she had not spoken.

"You can see that my sister-in-law is quite upset by her loss and the decisions that are required of her at this time. With her children taken into my household and that of Lady Salisbury, we wish to free her of these demands and enable her to find peace at Syon."

The abbess shifted her eyes slowly between them. Margaret lowered her own when the abbess looked her way, not realizing that this was far from the first time the nun had sat in discussions just like this one. She knew the secrets of many aristocratic families and kept them well.

Finally settling her gaze upon Jan, she spoke, "You understand that a vow of chastity would be required?"

Jan opened her mouth to speak, but not a sound escaped. Red blotches began at her eyes and spread slowly across her face as she attempted to control her feelings or at least stop crying. She closed her mouth and stared at a tapestry featuring Hannah giving Samuel over to the priest Eli rather than respond to the question posed to her. It seemed that in reverse of Hannah's decision to devote her long awaited child to God, she would be expected to give up her own life while her children went on to have theirs.

Margaret watched as Jan studied the tapestry and did not rush her. She silently prayed for God to guide them, though she hoped that he would guide them along the path she had already determined. He seemed to be listening, for as she finished the thought Jan turned back to them.

"I will do as my wise mother and brother prescribe, for I know that my eternal salvation and spiritual peace is the motivation for their actions," she said, leaving no doubt within the mind of any in the room that she did not believe this for a moment.

"We welcome you with open arms," the abbess said without moving to embrace her at all. "May God bless you through your service here."

Margaret winced at the coldness of the blessing. Should not service to God be heartfelt and sincere? And willingly entered? She looked again to Jan, afraid that she would see an accusing glare. However, the girl was staring at the table as though memorizing the swirls in the wood grain.

Good. Margaret could live with that.

October 1529

In the two years since Arthur's death, Margaret had found comfort in her responsibilities to Princess Mary. A bright thirteen-year-old, Mary provided Margaret with a welcome distraction from her grief. Margaret was also blessed to have her granddaughter, Katherine, as part of Mary's household, along with Geoffrey's wife, Constance. With Kathryn still Mary's chief lady-in-waiting who had tirelessly filled in for Margaret while she cared for Arthur, Margaret had a cozy household at Thornbury.

Katherine was Margaret's oldest grandchild, and she was close in age to the princess. When the two tipped their auburn heads together in some girlish conspiracy, Margaret could not help but smile and pray for God's blessings upon them as they grew up together as leading ladies in the country. Henry may not have the Bergavenny inheritance she had hoped to secure for him, but his large family gave him great joy and his favor with the king did not leave him wanting.

Margaret looked on as Kathryn oversaw the girls at their embroidery. Both had the talent to create beautiful work, but neither seemed willing to apply herself at the moment. Kathryn was attempting to be harsh, however her students knew her too well. In moments, the older woman was giggling alongside the girls, work forgotten.

Leaving her private alcove to approach the party, Margaret noticed the girls quickly take up their fabric and aspire to appear busy. Kathryn felt no need to join in this attempt. She brushed loose hairs from her face and smiled up at Margaret as if to say these are the moments that make it all worth it.

Margaret agreed, but felt that she was the one who must always remain stern, keeping the entire household on task at the sacrifice of her own joy at times.

"Let's see how you are progressing," Margaret said, holding her hand out to Katherine.

"Oh, do look at mine first, Lady Salisbury," Mary exclaimed. She jumped up and stood between Katherine and Margaret's outstretched hand, but bowed her head to keep from becoming entirely disrespectful.

Margaret took the elaborately stitched fabric from Mary's hand, while raising her eyebrow at Kathryn. Should she praise the girl's work and appreciate her willingness to shield her friend or remonstrate the insubordination? The question was forgotten as she peered at Mary's fine, tiny stitches.

"It is beautiful, Mary. Your mother will be quite pleased to see this."

"Thank you," Mary said submissively with her chin almost touching her chest. "I wish to make it a cover for the prayer book I am writing for her grace."

Now Margaret did smile. She could not be angry with the daughter who brought one of her closest friends such joy with her love and thoughtfulness. As she reached out to touch Mary's face and force her to look up, Margaret noted the difference between her lined and wrinkled hand when set next to the smooth skin of the princess. Her smile faded slightly, and she wondered at the passing of time. She brightened once again as Mary's inquisitive grey eyes sought hers.

"It will be one of your mother's most prized possessions," Margaret assured her, forcing her thoughts to remain in the present.

"Will you assist me when it comes to the binding?" Mary asked, turning her body slightly to block Margaret's view of Katherine as she attempted to salvage her poorly stitched project.

The lopsided smile on Kathryn's face as she immediately saw

the ruse finally broke through Margaret's impressive self-control. Mary went wide-eyed as her elderly governess threw her head back and laughed. She had thought she was being quite clever, but the knowing look on Lady Craddock's face indicated that she had not been as discreet as she hoped.

A flush crept up Mary's neck, and she breathed slowly and deeply to fight it. She hated to appear embarrassed or for her emotions to be too clearly written upon her face. Poor Katherine was practically in tears as she tore at sloppy stitches and became confused by the behavior of her grandmother.

"Dear girl," Margaret said in a breathless voice. She stepped around Mary with an appreciative grin and covered Katherine's hands with her own to stop their destructive work. "You must be patient. Not every woman naturally excels at needlework."

Katherine's eyes were bright blue with unshed tears when she raised her face to her grandmother. "I cannot do it! My stitches look nothing like Mary's."

"Princess Mary," Margaret corrected, as she did every time any member of the household did not address her properly.

Katherine closed her eyes, and Margaret had the feeling that she was rolling them behind her closed lids.

"It will serve you well to remember that, while Princess Mary is a dear friend, she will also be your queen," Margaret instructed the teary eyed girl.

"Yes, grandmother," Katherine whispered. She looked utterly defeated, a failure at needlework and too low to address her best friend by her Christian name.

Kathryn injected herself into the scene at that moment, nodding at Margaret to say that she would handle it from here. Margaret stepped back, allowing Kathryn to comfort where she had been forced to discipline. A pain grew in her chest as she walked away, and her arms ached to hold her own crying granddaughter.

~ ~ ~ ~

Later on, Kathryn bustled into Margaret's room. An excited flush made her face look radiant and much younger than Margaret knew her to be. She could not stop her mouth from turning up at the corners, catching Kathryn's contagious happiness.

"What is it?" Margaret asked, her brow lined in bemusement.

"You have a visitor," Kathryn announced in a sing-song voice. She took Margaret's hands and pulled her from her seat as though she would lead her in a dance.

Margaret pulled her hands back and searched her memory for news that a guest was expected. She did not like forgetting things or the fact that Kathryn seemed to carry their shared age so much more lightly. Kathryn just giggled and grabbed Margaret by her upper arms instead.

"It is a surprise," she explained, answering Margaret's unasked question. "One that will bring you great joy." The smile broadened on her face causing a sunburst of lines to stretch out from the corners of her eyes.

"Well, who is it?" Margaret demanded, not enjoying this nearly as much as her friend.

"Very well," Kathryn gave in, shrugging off Margaret's poor spirits. They would be lifted soon enough. "It is Reginald!"

Finally, Margaret's countenance lit up, and Kathryn's smile somehow broadened.

"Reginald? Now what is he doing here?" Margaret asked, patting her hair and skirts into place as though meeting a suitor. Suddenly her hands stopped. "You do not think something has happened."

"No," Kathryn insisted quickly, cutting Margaret off before she could put her imaginings into words. "I have no reason to believe that he is a bearer of bad news. He is simply here to see his beautiful mother."

Margaret scoffed and looked up to the ceiling as she shook her head at Kathryn's theatrics, but a smile also crossed her face again.

"I will have him sent up," Kathryn practically sang as she pranced from the room.

Only moments had passed when Margaret heard Kathryn gaily conversing with a deep voice which held tones of sophistication and intellect. It was a voice that spoke with authority and a pace that indicated each word was carefully considered before it was released. Her son's voice. Her arms tightened around herself and her lips pressed tightly together, as she realized the learned man about to enter the room was her boy.

Her nervousness was eliminated in one swift motion when Reginald knelt before her in greeting. "May you bless me, dearest mother?"

She felt a weight lifted from her shoulders as she sketched the sign of the cross upon his forehead as she had done since he was a newborn babe. He stood and embraced her, tucking her head comfortably beneath his beard.

"It is you who should be giving me God's blessing," Margaret said when he had released her. She saw that Kathryn had already left the room, enabling them to share a few private moments.

Reginald grinned and did so. Margaret closed her eyes to focus on the feel of his soft hands, scholar's hands, tracing Christ's cross on her head. "Amen," she whispered.

Pleasantries exchanged, they sat and selected morsels from the plate of sweetmeats that Kathryn had sent up.

"This unexpected visit gives me great joy, my son, but I must ask if there is a higher purpose than a mother's happiness."

Reginald took a sip of wine as he considered his words. She was proud of the way he was unafraid to pause and think before he spoke. He was not one to misspeak in anger or a desire to be heard before others.

"I will be leaving soon for Paris," he said, placing his cup on the table and averting his eyes from hers.

Margaret cocked her head to the side. "Is this your plan or the king's? Are you not content with Exeter?"

Reginald nodded, slowly answering once again. "I feel that you are the only person with whom I can be completely candid. Is that a fair assessment?"

"I am your mother." What more could she say?

He nodded again, indicating it was enough.

"The king wishes his marriage annulled."

A deep breath was captured and released by Margaret before her son continued.

"He also wishes for me to write a defense of his annulment, utilizing the education he has provided to establish a solid case for him to set the queen aside and marry Anne Boleyn."

Now Margaret gasped. "Marry her?" When Reginald simply nodded again, she shook her head in disbelief. "God preserve us. He wishes to set Catherine aside?"

"Just so," Reginald agreed. "He likely will, but I cannot in good conscience support him or give him the ammunition he needs to kill his marriage."

"Leviticus," Margaret whispered.

Reginald was not expecting this. He raised his eyebrows and almost smiled. "You are better informed than I gave you credit for, mother. I will not do as the king requires, and so I am leaving

England until this situation is resolved without my participation."

Margaret lay her head in her hands. Conflicting arguments swirled in her mind. Should she tell Reginald to stay and follow the king's orders? The tombs of those she had so recently buried Arthur near called out to her and insisted that nothing was worth defying the king over. Then she felt the outline of the cross where her son had just blessed her, and she understood that he had a higher calling than following King Henry.

"I understand you are concerned for me," Reginald said, taking her shaking hand. "Do not be. Henry's temper always cools with time, and I have duties to attend to. It will not be widely known that I leave in order to avoid his wishes."

"Are you sure?" Margaret asked in a whisper. She thought of her father, her brother. Executed for treason. "Maybe you should write..." The look on his face halted her words.

"If faced with the choice between serving my king and serving the king of kings, I do not feel that there is need for time to consider my options."

Margaret screwed her eyes shut and nodded once. He was correct, but she had to press her lips together and bite her tongue until a metallic taste filled her mouth to keep herself from contradicting him. She should be proud of her son, but instead she was terrified for him.

~ ~ ~ ~

Some of Reginald's news had been more optimistic. Henry and Geoffrey both had places in Parliament. The king's sister, Mary, was unashamedly standing up to him, insisting that he put away any thoughts he had about marrying Boleyn. That eased Margaret's fears somewhat. Mary had been queen of France and was currently married to Charles Brandon, the king's best friend.

She was a solid asset in any debate and would provide some protection for Reginald if necessary.

"Just remember that to most people I am returning to Paris on the king's orders to further my studies," Reginald had tried to reassure her.

What most people believed did not concern her. What the king thought of him did.

Margaret was seated in the gardens at Thornbury, allowing the fresh autumn scents and vibrant colors to sooth her when Princess Mary appeared at her side.

The princess curtseyed and asked if she could join her.

"I welcome your company," Margaret said, indicating the spot next to her.

"I hope that you will not think me impertinent," Mary began with downcast eyes. "But I must ask you about my mother and my father's intentions toward her."

A blush flamed across Mary's cheeks, and Margaret averted her eyes knowing that it would upset the girl further to know that Margaret had noticed.

Margaret breathed deeply, deciding where to begin. "This is a conversation that is overdue between us," she began. "You are no longer a girl and have a right to understand the situation, as it has the power to affect your future."

"I am not worried about my future," Mary snapped. "I am worried about my mother."

"Of course, you are," Margaret soothed, laying a hand on Mary's tense shoulder. "You are a dutiful daughter, and the queen could not ask for anything more."

Mary simply looked at her, urging Margaret to fill the silence with the answers to her questions.

Sighing, Margaret continued. "You may have heard that your

father seeks an annulment."

Mary's face was not readable. Margaret was not sure if she should be proud or uncomfortable to see the control the girl had gained over her emotions.

"He will argue that his marriage to your mother was never a true marriage because she had been his brother's wife."

"According to Leviticus, I know," Mary interrupted impatiently. "But will the Pope grant him his annulment?"

Margaret wished that Mary could go back to asking what made the sky blue and the grass green. Those had seemed like difficult questions once upon a time.

"I do not know," she admitted.

Mary looked startled. Her governess always knew everything, and it shook her world's foundation to realize that this most important question was an unknown to her.

"But what about me? Will he make me a bastard?" she cried in opposition to her earlier insistence that she was not concerned for her own situation.

Margaret wished that she could console the child, but she was no longer a child. She was a young woman and a princess who needed to know the truth.

"I do not know," Margaret repeated.

October 1530

"Henry!"

Margaret's excitement got the best of her and she practically flung herself into the arms of her firstborn son. He easily caught her up, grinning at her exuberance. She was surprised to notice fine lines stretch out from the corners of his eyes. Had she grown so old that even her children were getting old? No one thinks of these things when they are young.

"It restores my soul to see you. You must share stories of the other children. It is a joy to have your Katherine here with me, though I sometimes see too much of myself in her."

"Has she grown stubborn and demanding since leaving home?" Henry asked in false concern.

Margaret swatted at him. "She is emotional and expects too much of herself. She reminds me of my younger self, but she will benefit from a better upbringing. She and Princess Mary are good for each other."

"Good," Henry said, his head bobbing in approval. "I am eager to see her as well."

His eyes were surveying the courtyard, and Margaret felt momentarily disappointed that she was not the one he most desired to see. She was nobody's most desired companion, always a second choice.

"She is completing the day's lessons, and will greet you promptly," she assured him, and his focus fell back to her.

"That will give us time for a little talk and some refreshment."

His smile and strong arm held out to her buoyed her mood, and she gladly led him inside.

"I will not mince words," he started as soon as they were settled. "There are some things that you should know, for Princess

Mary's sake and that of our family."

Cold fear settled like a stone in her stomach, but she only said, "Carry on."

"The king plans to offer the Archbishopric of York to Reginald," he said and then paused to examine her for a reaction.

"Well, that is good news, is it not?" she asked.

"That depends," Henry continued, slowly moving his head from side to side as though considering two sides of a coin. His dark hair flopped from side to side with his movements, and Margaret wished she could push it away from his face for him.

"Henry will expect Reginald's support in return for the position."

Margaret had spoken to no one, not even her oldest son, about her conversation with Reginald before he departed England a year earlier. Henry seemed to be fully informed, nonetheless.

"Reginald will not deny his God for his king," Margaret stated flatly.

"But would he be?" Henry asked. He moved to the edge of his seat, and Margaret could see that this was the question he had been waiting to ask. "The king is a godly man rewarded with the title Defender of the Faith for his pamphlet opposing the heretic Luther. He sincerely believes that he was in error when he married Catherine. Why does Reginald think he is wrong?" Henry sat back, having concluded his argument.

Margaret composed her thoughts before responding. She had not expected to mediate between her sons on this topic. She examined Henry's face and realized that he did not believe it either. He was afraid.

"Henry," she began in the voice she had used to explain harsh truths to him since he was old enough to hear them. "The king had approval from the Pope to marry Catherine. Her marriage to Arthur was never consummated." She forced herself to maintain eye contact as she said this. It was not something she enjoyed discussing with her children, but she had been in the best position to know if Catherine and Arthur had shared a bed. "The king may have convinced himself of the truth of his argument because it is what he wants, but I do not believe that he has truly persuaded you or that he will ever convince Reginald."

As she said it, she knew that it was true. If the king insisted on pressing his case for an annulment, her family may once again be on the wrong side of a king. She seemed destined for sorrow.

When the young ladies arrived, Henry set aside his conversation with his mother in order to give his daughter his full attention. Margaret wondered if he realized how very much like his father he was, especially when interacting with his children. What would he do to protect them? Would he lie for his king the way he was asking Reginald to? Yes, Margaret decided as she watched Henry offer his arms to the girls for a stroll through the gardens. He would, but Reginald, unburdened by the divided loyalties of family versus church, would not.

April 1533

"He has done it."

Margaret allowed the missive to fall from her hand, careless of who may see it because the news would travel like wildfire regardless of her efforts or wishes.

"Done what, love?" Kathryn asked.

Margaret had almost forgotten that she was in the room when she had whispered to herself in horror. "See for yourself," she said with a shrug toward the parchment but no other movement to retrieve it.

Kathryn's normally friendly features shriveled into doubt and concern as she bent to pick up the note that Montague had sent to let his mother know to prepare Princess Mary for heartbreak.

A gasp informed Margaret that Kathryn's eyes had discerned the key portion of the message.

"He did not!" she said with uncharacteristic anger.

Margaret could only move to the window and face the outside in order to hide the tears forming and threatening to spill. Richmond's gardens were in vibrant bloom, promising a colorful summer filled with pleasant scents and beautiful bouquets. Unreasonably frustrated that the scenery was not grey to match her mood, Margaret spun away and swiped at her eyes.

What could she say?

After the devotion that Catherine had given the king, he had still chosen to shove her aside. Arthur had died before making her a wife in the true sense of the word, and his brother insisted that she was not his either. Nearing her old age, Catherine was without a place in this world. What would she do? What could she do?

Nothing.

She would have to go where Henry sent her and accept his

new wife. Not only because she had no power to do anything else, but because her concern now must be for her daughter. What if Anne Boleyn bore Henry a son? What would happen to Princess Mary?

Margaret was frustrated that only questions coursed through her mind. No answers ran to chase them.

"She will not accept this," Kathryn stated, reminding Margaret of her presence once again.

Scoffing, Margaret held out her hands toward her. "What else can she do? The king has already married that woman, and my Henry says that he believes she is already with child," she added, indicating the note still in Kathryn's hand.

Kathryn's fine, light hair escaped its pins as she furiously shook her head. "He does not know her as well as he thinks she does. These Tudor kings think that marriage means whatever they wish it to mean!"

Margaret sucked in a breath, finally understanding Kathryn's underlying feelings. The current king's father had felt certain that Kathryn would not love her first husband once she was convinced that he was not Richard of York, and now this Henry Tudor set aside his royal wife with a false argument. She had not considered the similarities since Henry VII had been utterly devoted to his wife, Margaret's cousin. However, she saw things differently from Kathryn's point of view.

"Oh, Kathryn," she whispered, taking her into her arms. "I did not think."

"It is not your fault," Kathryn insisted, pushing Margaret's arms and affection away. "I do not wish to think of my husband or my son."

Now Margaret's heart truly broke for her friend. Kathryn had never had another child after the king had taken away the son that Kathryn had conceived with Perkin Warbeck. Born to be a prince, his father's failure sent his future veering off course. Kathryn had never been able to discover what had been done with him, and could only take comfort in envisioning him living happily with a loving family. She could not believe that the king had killed him as he had executed the boy's father. Surely not, he was just a little boy.

Kathryn had turned away sobbing as Margaret replayed scenes from the past in her imagination. She had been young, married to Richard, and raising a family of her own when Kathryn was going through her personal hell. At the time, Margaret had not given Kathryn a second thought, but now they were bound together by many common threads.

When Margaret saw that Kathryn's shoulders were no longer shaking and heard sniffling dry up, she approached again, gingerly placing her hand on Kathryn's elbow.

"Forgive me for my thoughtlessness," she whispered.

With tears still clinging to her wet lashes, Kathryn turned and nodded. A new firmness was evident in her tense jawline and line forming between her eyebrows. "We will do what we must for Princess Mary. She will not be the next woman whose future is carelessly ruined by a Tudor king."

Gazing deeply into Kathryn's steely blue eyes, Margaret nodded. She was still not sure what they would do, but they would do it together.

The first task they must bear was notifying Mary that she had a new stepmother.

Of course, it had been foolish of them to assume that the girl was so poorly informed. As they quietly approached Mary, where she sat in close conversation with her cousin, Margaret Douglas, they realized that the young women were already discussing the possibilities that were now Mary's future hopes.

Kathryn motioned to Margaret to be silent, and Margaret obeyed though she felt guilty about eavesdropping on the girl she was supposed to be helping.

"Mary, you will simply find yourself a husband on the continent and leave your heretic father to his own devices," the younger Margaret was insisting.

The older woman's eyes grew round, and she was just about to remonstrate the girl when she noticed Kathryn urging her to remain silent. She pressed her lips together and waited to hear Mary provide her own correction. But she did not. In fact, she laughed out loud.

"Yes, the princes of Europe will be lining up at my door now that my father is an adulterer who hopes to make me the bastard sister to a sinfully conceived son." Mary raised an auburn eyebrow at her cousin, but their moods remained light.

"Very well, you can go to Scotland then," Margaret stated, unperturbed.

"And marry who?" exclaimed Mary in growing concern for her friend's sanity. "A minor nobleman reigning over a frozen sheep pasture?"

The Douglas girl simply shrugged, her bright red curls bouncing on her shoulders. She and Mary were good for one another, one so serious and the other too frivolous. But on this topic they seemed to agree. Mary must find a way to escape her tyrant of a father. They knew how to go about this no more than Mary's governess, however.

"He will grow weary of her," Mary said, sounding not at all certain of her words.

It was Margaret's turn to giggle at her friend's suggestion. "Weary of the woman he has chased into his bed for years?"

Mary's eyes warned her cousin to take care, and the girl held up her hands in surrender. "Very well. What do you suggest?"

Margaret was eager to hear the answer to this herself, and she felt herself creeping closer until Kathryn thrust out an arm to bar her way.

"I will wait."

"That is all? You will wait?" Margaret Douglas' face was a study in disdain.

"Yes," Mary insisted, rising from the bench and twirling to look down upon her cousin. Her governess was afraid that they would be spotted, but Mary was too focused on the conversation at hand. "I will wait. The concubine may die giving birth, my father may see the error of his ways, or he may choose to affirm my status as his heir. Impetuous action at this time will not serve me or my country well."

Her argument made, Mary lifted her chin and regally stormed off, never noticing her governess hiding in the bushes looking most undignified.

~ ~ ~ ~

Margaret did not wait long to approach Mary within her rooms. Sending away listening ears, she indicated that the girl should take a seat while handing her a goblet of watered wine.

"You know why I am here, and I know that you know why, so we can start from there," Margaret announced, heavily dropping into the seat nearest Mary's.

Mary smirked. "You have become like a mother to me," she began. "Except that my mother would never start a conversation like this so informally."

"Your mother has her lighter side as well."

"Not with me and surely not now," Mary locked her gaze on

Margaret and demonstrated that she was no longer a little girl with the knowledge that was swimming in the pools of her eyes.

"No," Margaret admitted after a sip of wine. "Not now. We must decide together what course will best serve you and the queen."

Finally, Mary smiled. She would never refer to her father's concubine as the queen and it felt like a small victory to find an ally in that.

"My cousin says that I should find a way to leave the country. That is what some will choose to do, but I do not know if it is what God intends for me."

"You refer to Reginald," Margaret said, her shoulders drooping slightly. Her son had written a letter harshly criticizing the king and his annulment. She wondered if she would ever see him again before their heavenly reunion.

"I do, but I do not fault him for it," Mary quickly reassured her. "How could I when he is my mother's greatest supporter and you are mine?"

Warmth flooded Margaret's heart as Mary took her hand and pressed it near her heart.

"Thank you, my dear girl," Margaret said, her voice heavy with emotion as she placed her other hand on Mary's soft cheek. "You have become a beautiful young woman, but even more importantly, you have a wisdom that belies your years and great understanding."

Mary did not blush, as many young women would in the face of such praise. A small, pleased smile crossed her lips before being replaced with a look of determination.

"I also believe that you are correct," Margaret continued, allowing her hands to fall back into her lap. "You must forgive me, but I overheard you in the garden."

Mary had grown accustomed to controlling her features, but Margaret noticed some fear of reprimand flash past.

"Waiting for your moment is what you should do. Watch for the path that God will open to you. Please your father, but not at the risk of your conscience or good name. He has already lost his."

"And what about my mother?" Mary wondered. "My father will not let me see her, and I am concerned for her health and well being."

Margaret held up her empty hands. "Pray for her."

June 1533

Margaret sat in the chapel at Richmond with her prayer book open in her lap. She so desperately longed to feel God's presence, but she felt completely alone, surrounded by cold, lifeless stone. Her prayers were rote, though she wished to beg God to set things right. The requests she meant to form were lost as she remembered the king as a child.

He had been precocious and engaging. When he danced at Catherine's first wedding to his older brother, he had stolen the limelight from the boy who was meant to be king. Not because he was cruel or selfish, at least not then. It had simply been the way he was. People had flocked to him and loved him.

How had that vivacious little boy become the man who would set aside the wife he had called beloved and put his own desires above the word of the Holy Father? Margaret hoped that it was true that there were no tears in heaven, because that would mean that the king's mother could not see the havoc her son was wreaking upon those he claimed to love.

Giving up, she slammed the prayer book closed and was leaving the chapel when a page almost collided with her.

"My apologies, your grace. A messenger awaits you in the hall."

Margaret closed her eyes and gathered breath to sustain her through what was almost certainly bad tidings. Weren't they always?

"Have Princess Mary join me," she ordered before moving on. They had quickly become partners, their relationship evolving from one of student and teacher to equal conspirators and allies. Whatever the news, Mary would hear it as well, and they would decide what to do together. The king may have been able to cleave mother from daughter, but he had not given a thought to the countess of Salisbury.

With long, confident strides, Margaret made her way to the hall. She was just fine with the king not realizing her worth. She knew what it was and would use it to ensure that Mary received justice.

The messenger was one she did not recognize, so she sent him to refresh himself before Princess Mary arrived. As she waited, she came to the realization that she no longer even knew what news to expect. Anything could happen in an England under Henry VIII.

Once Mary was properly enthroned for a regal image that would be whispered of when the messenger returned to court, he was recalled to impart his message.

"It falls upon me to bring news that I would rather not," he began, and Margaret wondered if he wrote poetry in his spare time. Mary simply nodded that he should continue. "Your grace, with great sorrow I must inform you of the death of your good kinswoman, her grace of Suffolk, the king's sister."

Even braced for disappointment, Margaret had not been expecting this. Henry's sister, Mary, had been Catherine's greatest supporter, and an outspoken one as one of the few people who could speak their mind without retribution in the presence of the king. She knew that concern must be written on her face, but when she looked at Mary she seemed carved from stone.

"Thank you for traveling to bring me news of my dear aunt's passage to heaven," Mary said with a tip of her head that made onlookers feel that a crown should be resting upon the red-gold hair. She rose and continued, "I must spend time in prayer for her soul."

Without another word, Mary turned and left her household staring after her. Margaret knew it then. She was looking at a future queen.

~ ~ ~ ~

"I would like to write to Frances and invite her to stay with us if it would offer her some comfort."

Mary made this announcement in a distracted manner, clearly establishing that she no longer felt she needed to ask her governess for permission, but rather simply inform her of her wishes. Margaret did not mind. Instead, she was proud of the woman that Mary was becoming. She knew that advice or correction would be respectfully received if Margaret had any to offer.

"That is very thoughtful of you," Margaret agreed, thinking of the girl who had lost her mother but would not see her father mourn her. Charles Brandon, Mary Tudor's widowed husband, was almost certainly comforting himself in another woman's bed. Margaret had long since stopped feeling sorry for the duchess, who had known who she was defying her brother to marry, but she did pity their children. "Frances enjoyed her time with you this spring and may enjoy being around other young woman of an age with herself."

Mary nodded once, that topic settled. She would see that a messenger was sent to her cousin before the day ended.

"Have you heard from my mother?" Mary asked in a tone that she attempted to force into casualness, but Margaret knew that she was anxious about the forced separation.

"Unfortunately, I have not," Margaret said, keeping her eyes on her needlework to avoid looking Mary in the face. She knew that they could both better control their emotions that way. "I do not believe that your father is allowing her much correspondence."

Mary tossed her own work into the basket at her side. As she stormed from the room, she growled angrily, "He has already taken away her crown. Will he not be content until he has taken her very life?"

July 1533

The summer sun was welcomed for its cheery warmth, and Margaret chose a cozy arbor for reviewing Mary's latest writing. Red and white roses that had been commissioned by Mary's grandfather covered the wooden slats, providing shade that was speckled with light where the brightness made its way through. The air was made sweet by those same roses, and Margaret was content that the unity they indicated would be personified in Mary when she became queen.

"Your Latin is without error," Margaret praised without looking up from the parchment. "Such a brilliant young woman you have become." She would not say aloud that her charge had surpassed her in every subject, but she was sure that Mary knew.

"I thank you for your kind words and guidance," Mary demurely replied.

Margaret finally looked up to see the rogue dashes of sunlight glimmering in Mary's coppery hair. With her head bowed and face partially in shadows, Mary was the image of her grandmother and Margaret's cousin, Elizabeth of York. Enough time had passed that the memory brought a smile to Margaret's face rather than pain or grief. Had it truly been three decades since the first Tudor queen escaped this world for her heavenly home?

Reaching out and tucking a stray lock of hair, Margaret said, "You remind me of your grandmother."

Mary lifted her face to look for indications of where this was leading but remained silent.

"She was devout, as you are, and beautiful."

A hand to Mary's cheek told her that she shared this trait with her York grandmother as well.

Margaret shifted to face Mary more directly and straightened her aching spine. "But you will rule, while she was submissive. She united England, but you will hold it together. This is the path that God has lain before you."

Not quite sure what had made Margaret say it, she nonetheless knew it to be true. She was no more certain now than she had ever been what would happen as a result of Mary's father taking a new wife and bearing another child, but she knew that Mary would be queen of England and it was her duty to prepare her for that day.

"Lady Salisbury," the voice of a page interrupted Margaret's revelation.

"Yes?" she said, removing her hand from Mary's face and emotion from her own.

"It is Lord Hussey, your grace," he wishes to speak with you. Something in the page's tone made Margaret think that this was a conversation that would not be enjoyed by any of the participants.

"Very well," Margaret said, gesturing that the page was dismissed she turned to Mary. "You will join me. This is your household, and you should be the ruler of it. I will be at your side."

A girlish grin appeared and was quickly squashed by the princess. "Let us go see what Lord Hussey has to say then, shall we?"

The women stood and left their comfortable hideaway together to confront the chamberlain the king had appointed to his daughter's household. When they arrived in the hall, Mary confidently stepped up to the large chair that Margaret had appointed for her without glancing at her governess for direction or approval. Pride for her swelled in Margaret's heart as she took a less ornate seat at Mary's right hand.

Lord Hussey approached, his discomfort palpable and sweat dripping into his eyes. "Lady Mary," he said, bowing low before his mistress but using the title that the king had determined was more appropriate for his daughter than princess. Margaret frowned and steeled herself for a fight, lines appeared in her forehead like a freshly plowed field.

As Lord Hussey straightened, his face was apologetic. Margaret felt an inkling of pity for him somewhere deep within her. He was stuck in a difficult position between Mary and King Henry. So was she, but she had no problem making the right choice. The compassion that she naturally felt was snuffed out by righteous indignation.

Thin, grey hair formed a ring around Hussey's head, and he moved his hands to flatten it in a motion that must have been necessary in the days when he had been younger. He bit his upper lip once before charging on to say what he must.

"His majesty the king has requested that I deliver the crown jewels currently in the Lady Mary's possession to his beloved wife, Queen Anne."

Margaret watched Mary's face, emotions bubbling just beneath the surface. She buried them well enough that only an observer who knew her as well as Margaret did would see the shock quickly replaced by hurt and then overwhelmed by anger.

"The queen is my mother and she would never make such a request," Mary stated firmly.

Shifting her eyes back to Hussey, Margaret felt as though she was surveying a field where armies prepared for battle.

"My lady," Hussey began, his eyes begging her to understand his unenviable position. "I am but a humble servant, doing my best to fulfill a royal demand." He twisted the edge of his doublet in his hands, making a wretched mess of the fabric.

Margaret saw the same sympathy that had threatened her own heart blossoming in Mary. Before the younger woman could speak again, Margaret stood.

"I regret to inform you, Lord Hussey, that I am uncertain

which items the king could be referring to and sorry to say that any search for them would be most inconvenient at this time. I am sure you can appreciate how difficult it would be for Princess Mary to be forced to part with beloved items that she received from the hand of her mother, the queen."

Margaret had forged her spine into steel as she looked down her Plantagenet nose at the squirming Lord Hussey. She did not need to be so cruel, she knew. Hussey loved Mary, but he was weak, giving in to Henry's will. Maybe he would take strength from Margaret, who had just placed herself in a position she had sworn she would never allow her family to take again, that opposed to the king.

Hussey frowned, but Margaret was uncertain if it were due to her opposition or the fact that he had been unwilling to stand up to the king himself. He looked to Margaret and back to Mary as if waiting to see if either would change their mind. They remained firm, like statues except for the fiery eyes that bore into him.

"Very well," he acquiesced with a nod. "I will, of course, have to notify his majesty of the difficulty in granting his request."

"We all will do what we must," Mary replied, her confidence restored by the support of her governess.

Hussey bowed again and left the hall in silence.

A moment passed as each woman replayed the scene in her head and wondered what she could have done differently. As if at an appointed time, each turned to the other. Exchanging grim smiles, they agreed without speaking aloud that battle lines had been drawn.

"Would you like to retire to Bisham?" Mary asked.

A scoffing laugh escaped Margaret's throat. "You wish to offer me escape from my decisions?" she asked, raising a single greying eyebrow. "That is unnecessary. My son, Reginald, took his stance and in doing so gave me my example. I have vowed to keep my family safe while also seeing that they receive the positions they are due. You are my family, too."

Mary would not try to convince her that she should leave, that the safety and security of Henry, Ursula, and Geoffrey depended upon it. She would not insult Margaret's intelligence by suggesting that she did not understand the significance or potential consequences of her decision. Instead, she stood to face her. The family resemblance was clear as they grasped each other's hands with determination and silently agreed that they would see this through together.

September 1533

Autumn splendor once again surrounded Margaret as she travelled by coach with Mary to Beaulieu in Essex. She was thankful to be putting distance between the princess and London. It would provide Mary with the opportunity to hold an informal court of her own but not seem to be in direct opposition to her father. As he was the one who must name her his heir, she could push him only so far. It was a fine line to submit to him yet not relinquish her position.

Beaulieu, with its red brick and octagonal towers, reminded Margaret of Thornbury. She and Mary had spent happy years there before Henry had decided that his daughter was a bastard. Perhaps they were doomed to repeat the cycles of betrayal and destruction. Edward Stafford had also enjoyed his brief time at Thornbury before King Henry had his head struck from his body.

That would not happen to Mary. Surely, not his own daughter. Margaret discreetly searched the young woman's face and posture for signals of her emotions, but she had grown expert at revealing nothing. If she feared her father, she did not show it. Longed for his approval and love, yes, but she was not truly afraid of him, regardless of their not insignificant differences of opinion.

Margaret despised riding in the coach but had been forced to admit she could no longer ride long distances the way she had once enjoyed. Mary was more content with it and had comfortably settled into the soft cushions provided for her, but Margaret kept leaning out to view the countryside and gaze longingly at the sleek horses in their retinue.

When she settled back into her seat, she was reminded why she was not on horseback. Her knees crunched unpleasantly as her weight shifted and a dull ache never seemed to leave her lower back. She looked down at the hands that had lovingly caressed Richard

Pole and saw the arthritic claws of an old woman. In Mary, she saw her younger self, though she had never seen herself as lovely as she could recognize Mary to be. It was unfortunate that she had not appreciated her beauty when she had it.

She let out a sigh, which attracted Mary's attention. "Are you comfortable?" Mary asked dotingly, but Margaret brushed her question aside.

"Do not treat me like an old woman."

Mary smiled at the brisk tone, knowing it was not truly aimed at her. "I've had a letter from my mother," she said to pull her governess from her dreary mood. It worked, and Margaret's face was transformed by the smile that lit it. They had both grown accustomed to the king not allowing their visits and took joy in what communication they did have.

"She claims to be well and is pleased that Chapuys, at least, is given entry. It is good for her to have some company and friendship."

Mary's face was turned toward Margaret, but her vision was of the kindly Spanish ambassador as he sat before her mother. They would both be smiling as they chatted. Mary's imagination would not include Catherine's anger at her imprisonment or grief over their separation. She wished to paint an optimistic picture of the mother she was in no position to help. In the moments when she could not ignore reality, her anger toward her father and his concubine threatened to bubble over into words and actions that she would likely regret and never be able to call back.

Margaret did not feel the same comradery for Eustace Chapuys that Mary and her mother did. Maybe it was because she did not speak Spanish and therefore felt that he was betraying her in some way when he did. Perhaps she simply wished to be Mary's only pillar of support and Chapuys offered the possible strength of an Emperor. How her mind wandered in her old age!

Mary continued to share the inane details of her mother's letter. Catherine had nothing more consequential to share after two years in exile, and Mary was satisfied to simply see her sprawling script and read her words of love and affection.

The towers of Beaulieu were by this time so close that they seemed to lean over them, so Margaret began to mentally prepare the list of orders she must delegate once she was released from this infernal coach. Most of Mary's household would already know exactly what they needed to do, but hearing it from Margaret reminded them of her position and authority. She had trained Mary to similarly order her ladies-in-waiting, ensuring that they would never forget that they served a future queen.

She was surprised to find a messenger awaiting their arrival. He had made the trip from London more quickly as a lone rider than they had as a caravan. He had made his face inscrutable, giving Margaret no clue to the news he had carried with him. When he approached Mary and bowed respectfully but not servilely, she knew.

"Lady Mary," he began without waiting for her to bid him speak. "I am pleased to announce the birth of your father's daughter, the Princess Elizabeth."

The smile faded from Mary's face, and she quickly composed her countenance to look like an effigy of herself. Those around her had suddenly gone silent, all eyes and eager ears waiting for her response. None had missed that the newborn babe was called princess, while they had been instructed to address Mary as lady. Margaret was preparing to step forward and release the man herself, when Mary spoke.

"I thank you for traveling such a distance to impart your news," she said dully, as though the man had informed her of market prices. Her back was turned to him so swiftly that her skirts almost flew up to touch him. Yet she strode away with dignity, not running or slouching but marching away with her head held high.

Margaret cleared her throat, and the swarm of eyes that had been following Mary focused on her. "Princess Mary will send a response to her father as she sees fit. You are free to go."

She was moving to step around him, when his voice broke the stunned silence. It seemed to be tinged with amusement, causing her to narrow her eyes at him.

"You misunderstand me, Lady Salisbury. There is more to the king's message." He stood, speaking to her as though he were equal to the countess. "Lady Mary is instructed to cease use of the badges and livery that decorates this display." He spread his arms to include the ornamented coach and horses. "Further instructions will be sent on the king's expectations on how the Lady Mary may serve Princess Elizabeth."

After a shallow bow, he leapt onto a waiting horse and trotted out of the courtyard. It seemed that he had been expecting to be immediately dismissed all along.

Margaret felt her jaw drop at the man's audacity, so she clamped it tightly shut.

"As you were," she almost shouted at the members of the household surrounding her. "You will continue to serve Princess Mary as you have until you are informed otherwise."

Bowing, curtseying, and mumbled assent slowly dissipated as each attended to their own duties. Margaret had thought she would feel relief if Anne gave birth to a girl, but it was terror that tore through her body like a sharpened sword.

Margaret thought to find Mary in her rooms, but she could not locate her until she entered the chapel. Mary was on her knees, but it was easy to see that she was sobbing rather than praying.

While Margaret internally debated whether to go to her or leave her in privacy, her heart was torn apart by the heartbreak evident in the quaking of Mary's shoulders and whimpers that reminded Margaret of a beaten dog.

Tilting her head heavenward and closing her eyes, Margaret pleaded with God. She would not call it a prayer, for her prayers so rarely included this form of raw begging for blessing. Mary was pious while her father tore the church apart to force it to do his will. Her father in heaven must see that and raise her up.

Had they made a mistake treating the king's messenger as they had and refusing his requests for jewels and plate to be returned? Margaret had thought that they should not accept Mary's reduced position, but what could they do to deny Henry's will if he chose to tear Mary's badge from her household livery? Margaret took a deep breath and heard Mary's sobbing abruptly stop. Opening her eyes, she saw Mary's turned upon her, red and swollen with tears like she had not seen her in years.

"Oh, sweet Mary," she groaned, hurrying to her side. "My poor, lovely girl." Her hands smoothed the red gold hair that identified Mary as her father's child in an effort to soothe her bruised heart, but nothing could repair her shattered dreams.

"He will send me into exile, as he did my mother," she whispered, her voice thick with emotion. "She was stubborn, but it did her no good," Mary argued, shaking her head back and forth against Margaret's skirts. "He will disown me for his bastard child! How could he?"

Margaret had never seen her so out of control and did not know what to say, so she said nothing but continued the consoling patting and rubbing of Mary's head and back.

"Will you stay with me?" Mary tilted her head back to peer up at her governess. Her heart was bare and her face was splotched from crying. Torn from her mother and abandoned by her father, she clung to the one constant in her life, and suddenly Margaret knew why men fought battles for causes that they knew to be lost.

"I will never leave you," she vowed passionately. "Never."

~ ~ ~ ~

Mary wrote a letter to her mother, offering the consolation that few others would give her. If she hoped that the action would inspire pity or a change of heart in the king, she misjudged him. Lord Hussey, who continued to serve as Mary's chamberlain, was ordered to reduce the household of "the king's daughter, Mary," in a missive sent by the man in charge of seeing her father's will fulfilled in all things, Thomas Cromwell.

"She is to keep her ladies-in-waiting as they are?" Margaret asked Hussey as they met to discuss the ordered reduction of the household.

"Yes, your grace," he said, lowering his head respectfully.

Despite their clash over following the king's orders regarding Princess Mary's jewels, Margaret recognized that Hussey had a great love for the king's daughter. Not everyone had the courage to stand up to King Henry. Sometimes Margaret wondered if she were being brave or foolish. What did she hope to achieve? Then she would see Mary or receive a letter from Catherine, who Chapuys whispered was dying, and her zeal would be renewed.

"Very well, we can manage," she announced, closing her household account book. "Give the servants leave to address the princess as the king requires of them. I will not be responsible for anyone's treason but my own."

Hussey regarded her with shock evident on his face. "Lady Salisbury, what do you intend?"

Margaret picked up her things and turned to leave him.

"That will depend upon the king."

Hussey watched her shuffle from the room, her arms loaded with books and parchment and grey overtaking the auburn of her hair but her head held high and her back straight as an expertly honed sword.

November 1533

"Did you read Princess Mary's letter to her father?" Hussey demanded of Margaret with uncharacteristic boldness.

Margaret set aside the needlework she had been attempting to concentrate on and rubbed her eyes. It became more difficult to see the tiny stitches and she felt weary of pretending it was not. She blinked to clear her vision and squinted at the chamberlain.

"I did not. The princess does not require my approval for her communications."

"Maybe she should," Hussey replied, stepping close enough to hold a parchment out to her.

She closed her eyes and sighed, preparing herself for the struggle of making out the elaborate script that was sure to accompany the wax seal that was cracked and broken from Hussey's prior examination. The bottom of the letter bore the king's signature, and Margaret's breath caught in her throat. This was more serious than another order from Cromwell or other sycophant of the king.

"She has said too much!" Hussey was almost shouting. "Patience must be practiced to bear this trial, but Princess Mary refuses to recognize her father's wife and goads him by referring to her mother as queen." He threw his hands up in the air as one who has given up on a lost cause. "She tells her father that she will obey him in all things before going on to list the areas in which she cannot obey him. He is the king for heaven's sake!" Now he was shouting, and all tiredness flew from Margaret's mind as she realized the seriousness of the situation.

"Just tell me what it says," she insisted in frustration at her failing vision and Hussey's reprimand. The royal letter was thrust back toward him in distaste.

Hussey took it with a wild look in his eyes. "He has dismissed you, Lady Salisbury." His voice was quieted and tinged with compassion as his face relaxed from anger to sympathy.

For a moment, Margaret's expression did not change. She remembered Henry greeting her as cousin when he first became king. He had made her countess of Salisbury and ensured that each of her children had a position worthy of her family's name. She had been made governess of his heir, but now she was released. Mary was no longer his princess and she was not needed to care for her.

Fortune's wheel turned so cruelly and interminably.

"I will write to him myself," she said confidently, not willing to accept the hand she had been dealt. Placing her needlework in the waiting basket, she stood as though to attend to the task immediately.

"Is that wise?" Hussey questioned, failing to remove his bulk from the doorway she was attempting to pass through.

"Of course it is," she insisted as she stepped closer, threatening to push her way by. "The king is my cousin, and Princess Mary is just a girl. His temper was roused by her disobedience, and it is my duty as her governess to offer apology and correction."

~ ~ ~ ~

After her first letter was met by cold rebuff, Margaret frantically wrote again. Through tears that made it almost impossible for her to compose the words, she offered to cover the expenses of Mary's household herself if she would just be allowed to stay at her side.

Henry was quite insistent. Lady Mary's household was to be dismantled. She would serve her sister, Princess Elizabeth, as a member of her household.

Margaret's sons, Henry and Geoffrey, came to assist her in

relocating to the Bisham estate. Both offered their sympathy and promises of future support to Mary, but no one offered any alternative to accepting the king's plan for the time being.

"You will see in time," Montague encouraged Mary. "The king will see that an intelligent young woman makes a far superior heir than a squalling infant."

"If the brat even survives," Geoffrey added from behind his mug of ale.

"Mind your tongue," Margaret snapped. "It is the king's daughter that you speak of. Loose speech is not worth the consequences."

He tilted his head to his mother in unspoken apology. Henry glared at his brother before turning his attention back to Mary, who listened in rapt attention. Montague was exactly what she needed, a man mature and intelligent who was on good terms with the king yet supportive of her. She hung on his every word.

"Patience will see you achieve your destiny, but God may ask that you humble yourself for a time," Henry continued.

Mary examined her hands in her lap and whispered, "Nothing could be more humbling than serving in my bastard sister's household."

"You think not?" Henry asked. He held up a hand to silence his mother's objection and carried on. "Your father is the king and few stand up to him. No one besides your mother understands why better than you." He leaned closer to her as his words gained intensity. "He could make you a chambermaid or marry you to a merchant. Do not give him a reason to."

Mary's grey eyes had widened as Montague spoke to her as nobody else in her life had dared to. He held her gaze until she broke it then nodded in satisfaction. Margaret swallowed her objection, seeing that her son was right. The time for fine words had passed. Mary was being put in her place and the best thing to do for the moment was to accept it.

"Do not lose heart," Henry followed his instructions with encouragement. "There are many who are prepared to support you when the right time arrives. Bide your time until then."

Until the king dies, he meant. Margaret considered whether the inference alone was treason. She was no longer certain. Edward Stafford had died for similar words.

Mary's eyes filled with tears but she nodded her acceptance. "I will follow your wise counsel, Lord Montague," she said. "God give me strength because it will take more than my own to humble myself before the concubine's daughter."

"Your father will not allow me to be there for you in person, but rest assured that I will be in constant prayer for you before our heavenly father," Margaret said, her words filled with fervency as she held Mary's hands in a tight grip. It was nothing like the vise gripping her heart as she realized that she must soon leave Mary's side. Would she ever see her again, or would they be kept apart as the girl and her mother were? She gulped, not daring to consider the answer.

"I thank you," Mary said, her eyes moving between them as if memorizing faces she would never see again.

Geoffrey stood and bowed casually, as if he had already altered Mary's status in his mind. Henry, however, knelt before her in a fashion that somehow made him seem more dignified though he prostrated himself before a young woman.

"I would have your blessing, Princess Mary, before we go on our ways that shall be separate, but only for a while," he requested quietly in a voice that deeply resonated through the dimly lit room.

Mary's training served her well, and she crossed Montague as though noblemen requested her blessing on a daily basis.

"Go in peace and serve the Lord with all your heart," she said in a barely audible whisper.

Margaret embraced Mary for what she prayed was not the last time before allowing her sons to bundle her off to Bisham.

December 1533

Having arrived at Bisham in time for Christmas revelries but completely unprepared for them, Margaret spent a quiet season, praying for Mary and Catherine. And England.

Henry and Geoffrey had stayed with her for a time before returning to their own families. One of the last conversations she had shared with Henry had taken her back into parts of her past that she kept deeply buried.

"Is this what it was like when your cousins were bastardized?" he had asked as they sipped his favorite wine before a welcoming hearth.

Margaret's breath had caught in her throat. She had not considered the similarities between King Richard disinheriting Edward's children and Henry delegitimizing his own. Was this the way of kings, to simply write off children whose existence had become inconvenient?

"I was so young," she had tried to evade him.

"Not so young," he countered.

A wry smile lifted one side of her mouth. "I had been in the household of my cousins since the execution of my father," she admitted quietly, as if afraid to disturb the rest of the ghosts she spoke about.

Henry leaned forward, appearing young and boyish in the firelight. He had never heard his mother speak of her father's execution.

"I was devastated, though my memories of my father were vague. He was a knight in shining armor who lit up a room when he entered. That was my impression of him as a little girl, anyhow." Her eyes took on a dreamlike quality as she attempted to travel through the years to a time when she was considered a princess rather than a difficult noblewoman with an excess of royal blood.

"He was handsome and charismatic, but impetuous and discontent. I did not know all that at the time of course, but have come to understand it. Geoffrey reminds me of him." Returning to the present and focusing her yes on her oldest son, she demanded, "You must be your brother's keeper. He will be in need of your wise counsel and prudence."

Caught off guard, Henry frowned and cocked his head questioningly to the side. "Do not speak as if you will not be here to knock sense into him yourself, mother."

They laughed gratefully, the tension of the moment broken. But as the laughter died, Margaret was sure that she felt the presence of her old ghosts crowding in around them.

~ ~ ~ ~

With her sons gone, Bisham felt cavernous and lonely. Margaret had never before had the opportunity to realize how little she enjoyed being alone. Though the duties of governess to the princess had seemed arduous for one her age, she missed the bustle of activity and presence of friends now that the household was broken up.

She had been so proud of her position as countess of Salisbury and eager to complete the construction work at Bisham and her other estates to demonstrate to onlookers that her star was once again ascending. Her family was not plagued by the name of traitor, and the king had favored her. Yet, somehow, as she walked down the beautiful but empty corridors, that did not seem to matter.

The sound of footsteps reached her long before the servant was visible. The hurried pace informed Margaret that they were on an important mission, and she prayed that they would be looking for her.

"Lady Salisbury," a wheezing voice reached her, and Margaret sent up a silent prayer of thanks that someone required her attention. She needed to be needed.

Margaret turned and recognized her granddaughter, Katherine, whose voice had been disguised by her breathlessness. The lessons of Princess Mary's household had been ingrained into her, and she rarely referred to her grandmother by anything less formal than her title. Margaret embraced the girl, encouraging familial closeness now that they were at her own estate, but Katherine remained stiff and Margaret wondered if she had disciplined her too well.

"What is it, Katherine?" she asked, infusing as much kindness into her voice as she could.

"Baron Hussey awaits you in the hall," she said, still gulping breath. "He indicated that he wished urgently to see you."

"Then I will not keep him waiting."

Margaret strode with renewed purpose to discover what Mary's chamberlain might need to discuss with her. The passageway already seemed full of life now that Margaret was called to action. Instead of being vacant, she noticed scurrying chambermaids and dogs sniffing for dropped crumbs. Had they been there before, she wondered. Curious.

Entering the hall that was freshly decorated to her specifications, Margaret did not even notice the tapestries and stonework that she had spent lavishly upon. Her eyes found only Hussey, standing still but seeming to vibrate with energy. He, too, had a look that exuded a desire to be at his work. His face was lively and appeared younger than the last time they had seen each other, parting company along with the rest of Mary's household.

When he caught sight of her, he rushed forward and reached out in eagerness, rather than bowing as he typically would. She no longer minded. There were greater concerns than precise manners now that she was not ordering the household of a princess.

"It delights me to see you," she said when they almost collided in their mutual enthusiasm. The smile he treated her with was one that she felt certain was seen by few people besides his beloved wife, Anne.

"And I, you," he replied, the words coming in a rush. "I would speak to you about a shared interest in a private place."

He spoke far less discreetly than he believed, but Margaret did not mind. The few members of her household who were near were those she trusted implicitly. Without another word, she gestured for him to follow her. Soon, they enjoyed the privacy of her sitting room, where Katherine had laid out refreshments, foreseeing that they would retire to that spot. Clever girl, Margaret thought, mentally noting that she must thank her granddaughter and find a way to bring her under her wing more intimately.

They each took a small plate of bread and cheese as well as a welcome cup of wine before settling in conspiratorially.

"Tell me about Princess Mary," Margaret demanded. "Is she treated well in her sister's household?"

Hussey sighed. He had hoped to delay Margaret's temper by discussing Catherine first. "The new queen's aunt serves as governess to Princess Elizabeth, so you can be sure that she offers Princess Mary no more respect than she feels necessary. Probably does so upon the queen's orders, possibly the king's."

"Surely not!" Margaret tilted her chin up defiantly at the idea that Henry would order his daughter taken down a notch by his concubine's family.

With a shake of his head, Hussey insisted, "I'm afraid it is true, Lady Salisbury. Mary is treated as a bastard sister serving a legitimate one. The position would not be untenable if it were the one she had been raised for, but..." he let his voice trail off. They both understood that Mary had been raised for a very different position indeed. "She does give as well as she gets though," he added with a wry smile. "She is as stubborn as her former governess and fights Lady Shelton at every turn."

A sharp bark of laughter escaped Margaret, but she immediately sobered. "Will the king punish her further if she does not submit?"

Shrugging, Hussey exhaled a heavy breath, "That, I cannot know any better than the next man. Henry has become unpredictable and his temper increases with his age." He lifted his shoulders in a hopeless gesture once more before filling his mouth with soft Leicester cheese.

Wheels of thought were turning in Margaret's brain, but she could conceive no path for Mary to follow for the time being besides following her father's orders.

"I have also spoken to Catherine," Hussey said through the bread that had followed the cheese.

The wheels grinded to a halt, and Margaret eyed him curiously. Very few people managed to gain access to Catherine these days. Henry seemed to be hoping she would die of loneliness.

"She would like for you to visit her."

Margaret's mouth fell open as her eyes wandered the room for a response. "There is no chance of the king approving such a plan," she settled on lamely.

"True," Hussey agreed with a movement of his head that seemed to indicate he was agreeing with her and saying no at the same time. His grey head bobbed on a diagonal line in result. "My advice is to not ask him."

Was that a wink?

"How did you manage to see her?" Margaret asked. She felt

excitement bubbling inside her at the thought of seeing her friend after such a long absence, but she shoved it down like placing a heavy lid on a pot's boiling contents.

Hussey lowered his voice though there was nobody near and jutted his face forward as a cat would if it were stalking a bird. "Her household is small and she is gaining their loyalty despite the king's best efforts to keep it staffed by those loyal to him. He has more important appointments for sycophants than guarding his former wife, so he has become lax. If we are careful, it can be arranged."

He leaned back into his chair, taking comfort in the cushions and his position as one sharing unexpected good news. His face fell slightly, and he added, "You will have to make your way to her bed chamber."

The turbulent contents of Margaret's stomach were joined by fear. "She is bedridden?"

Hussey responded with a reluctant nod, admitting that Catherine was not kept as a queen should be, but neither was she neglected. An evil seemed to be eating at her from the inside out. Chapuys agreed that she was likely more ill than she admitted, and even Catherine had relented to being treated as an invalid.

Margaret had experienced too much loss for her to become overwhelmed by this news. "Then it is all the more vital that I reach her as soon as we can secretly make the trip. I would know what Catherine's wishes are for her daughter if she is truly approaching her ascendance to her heavenly home."

Hussey raised his eyebrows but nodded in agreement. His wife had cried with much sniffling and grief when he had shared the same news with her, and she was not the lifelong friend of Catherine that Margaret was. The countess was made of sterner stuff.

"My Anne serves within the princess' household. She is

therefore able to communicate with Princess Mary without the need for written letters or messages."

Margaret looked at the man before her in a new light. He had served the king, and still did if truth be told, but he had also just put himself and his wife at risk in order to help those opposed to him.

Opposed to the king. Yes, it was time she accepted that she was. When it came down to choosing Henry or Mary, she did not need the urging of the Holy Spirit to tell her which was the future of England.

"I thank you for your loyal service. You do understand the risk you are taking, even in having this conversation, but also in what we plan to do next?" she asked gently.

"Of course I do," Hussey exclaimed looking somewhat miffed. "I know you stood up to the king when I did not where plate and jewels were involved, but this is somewhat more important than that."

A snort of laughter escaped Margaret again, and she nodded with a slight frown. He was right. She had no idea at the time how serious the situation would become. Had she and Mary submitted from the beginning, they may be quietly continuing their lives together now. Or Henry may have come up with another reason to reduce Mary's circumstances. It mattered not now.

"Then I will consider you a valued advisor and ally," she said and was rewarded by a ruddy blush across old Hussey's face.

June 1534

Margaret felt that she, rather than the palfrey beneath her, was chomping at the bit to be on their way. Six months had passed since she and Hussey had decided that a clandestine visit to Catherine was a worthy mission, but it had been more difficult to bring it to fruition.

She had begun riding again, telling her ladies and granddaughter that she felt the need for more exercise to fend off the effects of old age creeping up on her. As a cover story it was a good one, and she did feel years younger after spending much of her time preparing her body for the rigors of travel without coaches or attendants. Her hands smoothed her stomacher and felt leaner muscle beneath than had been present there in years.

That was not on her mind, though. Each item in her saddlebags was mentally checked off as she prepared for a journey like none she had ever taken in her life. Alone, with a man not her husband, she would sneak in like a spy to visit the queen of England. How had her life come to this?

Yet, she was excited. If this was what God required of her, she would see it done and trust the results to him.

Leaving Bisham was simple enough. She had built up the expectation that she would take short trips in her eccentric quest for exercise, so her household thought nothing of her trotting away with the well-known and trusted Hussey.

He had mapped out a path that would keep them from meeting those who might recognize the countess of Salisbury. Stopping to water the horses and pulling biscuits from a sack, Margaret smiled at Hussey and joked, "It is good that your wife trusts you."

"It is good that she trusts you," he countered. Formality had disappeared between them in the last year. It had no power to aid in their success and was therefore discarded.

As she laughed freely, Margaret drank in her surroundings. The ugliness that Henry had poisoned the kingdom with could not make the summer sky less warm and comforting or the scent of honeysuckle less sweet. It was as if she were on a pleasant afternoon ride rather than a treasonous adventure. Why had she not appreciated the smell of crushed grass or vibrant shades of blue that filled the sky when she was younger? She supposed all old women asked themselves that question.

Would Catherine be asking herself why she had not appreciated her freedom? Margaret loved her friend and understood that she did what she knew to be right in the eyes of God, but had it been worth it? Soon, she would be able to ask her.

"Let us be off," she insisted, standing near her horse and waiting for Hussey to lift her up.

He did so with a groan, and Margaret was reminded that if she was old, he was ancient. Their eyes met in silent understanding that it would be worth it.

Margaret felt guilt at her thankfulness that Catherine had been moved to Kimbolton. It made this trip possible, being a quite reasonable distance from Bisham, but she knew the castle to be aged and not well-kept. If Catherine was as ill as her few visitors indicated, it was a poor situation for Henry's neglected queen.

Kicking her horse quite unnecessarily, Margaret hardened her features in determination. This was no longer about Catherine. Her future had been forfeit, but her daughter's had not. Not yet.

Following obscure paths that Margaret wondered how Hussey had known of, they made their secret way through trees and across quiet meadows. Much time had been spent in prayer that God would veil their progress, and he must have heard. The roof of Kimbolton came into view like teeth biting into the sky before they spotted a single soul.

Tension that she had not realized was there left Margaret's shoulders as the honey colored stone filled her vision. She scanned the dirty windows, wondering which one Catherine lay behind.

Hussey had precise directions regarding the approach of the castle and where to enter unnoticed. Gesturing to Margaret, he led the way. She crouched low and followed through the brush. Rather than fearing capture, she was exhilarated.

The ground was soft and damp under her feet, and she was thankful for the boots that she had thought were ridiculous but Hussey had insisted upon. Margaret felt mud ooze over the toes without the moisture leaking through as she swatted at an insect that was intent upon landing upon her face. The air was thick in the summer heat and humidity, and Margaret wondered if she would be able to wring liquid from her clothes at the end of the journey.

How would the heavy air feel to one who was unwell as Catherine was reported to be? The thought restored Margaret's determination to reach her old friend and find a way to help her.

She hoped that she would continue to be in a position to help Princess Mary as her father's demands grew increasingly tyrannical. In his most recent fit of frustration, he had outlawed appeals to Rome. Only King Henry VIII ruled over Englishmen, not the Bishop of Rome. These concerns were shoved aside as Margaret peered through the dusk at Hussey's back. Catherine and Mary inspired devotion and courage, while Henry ruled through fear. For how long?

The expanse of lawn would be the riskiest portion of their journey. After crossing eighty miles and having Catherine almost within reach, they could fail here, spotted within the cleared area surrounding the castle.

God was watching over them again. Catherine's reduced household had higher priorities than keeping the grounds manicured, especially with their mistress unable to step outside. Grass was overgrown and bushes in need of trimming. Margaret felt like the snake in the Garden of Eden as she slithered through the growing darkness to sidle up to a wooden door.

The rough planks of the small entryway marked it as a service door used solely by servants. When it opened with only slight creaking upon Hussey's knock, Margaret saw that it led to a storage area that would be more often visited through a larger opening on the opposite wall. The girl who had received them appeared to be younger than Katherine, making Margaret wonder if her granddaughter supported secret causes. Surely, her children were fighting for their princess and their God in their own quiet way.

Brushing aside dark blond hair, the girl pointed to a narrow stairwell without speaking a word. Hussey nodded to her and squeezed past, so Margaret followed suit. She caught the girl's eye and was shocked to see no fear there. Strength shone from the deep brown pools, created by experiences that young Katherine would always be shielded from.

"My thanks," Margaret offered in a whisper as she reached the bottom step.

Dust motes floated in the dim shafts of light that weakly streaked into the stairwell. As they rose higher, Margaret grew in her appreciation for Hussey. How had he made these contacts and received such precise directions without discovery? His wife, Anne, had shown her value as well, refusing to call the king's daughter anything besides Princess Mary until the king had given up and removed the elderly woman from the household.

Margaret sensed that they were nearing their final destination as Hussey's weary posture straightened and a happy glow lit his face. Maneuvering within the castle had been easier than anticipated, and they had encountered little evidence of anyone living there as they snuck down corridors and up a wider set of steps to pause before a broad, heavy door.

"This is it," Hussey whispered excitedly. "At this time of night, she will be unattended for several hours as she sleeps."

The dying queen would get little sleep this night. Her clandestine visitors shoved the door open just enough to slip through before silently latching it closed.

Moonlight streamed into the room, and the cloying fragrance of scattered pomanders greeted them. The exotic petals and spices failed to cover the unmistakable scent of withering life. Margaret's final hopes fell. She had prayed to find Catherine healing and preparing to continue her righteous battle with the king, but a single step into Catherine's chamber convinced her that God's path veered in another direction.

As her eyes adjusted to the soft light blended with deep shadows, Margaret saw Catherine. She saw only her face, her body was too thin to make a perceptible shape under the heavy bedcovers that the ill woman required even in the summer heat. The bed curtains had been left open, either because the attendants were lax in their duties or Catherine had requested the light be allowed in. Catherine's cheeks were sunken except where bones that had previously been pleasantly padded now thrust sharply forth. Was she breathing? Had they arrived too late?

Seeming to sense their presence or somehow hear Margaret's unspoken questions, Catherine opened her eyes. Without searching the room, she looked directly at Hussey and Margaret with eerie precognition. A single blink indicated that she recognized them, as though a smile or word would have taken more strength than she had in supply.

Forgetting the need for quiet and the requirements of their mission, Margaret rushed forward and fell to her knees at the bedside of her friend.

"Dear, Catherine," she cried. "Why did you not call for me sooner?"

She knew the question was ridiculous. Catherine had neither power to issue orders nor permission to request visitors, but Margaret's heart was shattered by the sight of Catherine so depleted. The rosy cheeked girl who had rode into London at Prince Arthur's side, so full of hope and joy and sure to reign with the reincarnation of the glorious king of old, now lie in a damp bed, alone and unwanted.

Dank smells of the swamp mingled with the sweet scent of oncoming death as Margaret buried her face in Catherine's bedcovers. The pomanders, one of the few items in the castle fit for a queen, could not fight this battle. They were losing, as all do when they attempt to instill their own will over God's.

Margaret wriggled a hand through the layers to find Catherine's, clammy and fragile beneath the blankets. "Oh, Catherine," she moaned. She had intended to be optimistic, dignified, and full of reassurances. Instead, Margaret was on her knees sobbing for the impending death of her friend, their faith, and England's future.

"Meg," Catherine whispered, using a name Margaret had not heard in years. Richard used to call her Meg. Catherine would see him soon.

Forcing herself to raise watery eyes to meet Catherine's, Margaret saw that an inner strength remained there that could not be squashed even as her earthly body wasted away. If Catherine could offer what little strength she had, Margaret could carry on.

"I'm here," she said, emphasizing the truth of her words by

squeezing Catherine's hand. "I would know what my queen wishes of me."

Catherine's lips twitched. Few called her queen anymore, not if they valued their position and freedom.

"Mary?" The single word asked an exhaustive list of questions. Was she well? Had she given in to her father and signed the Act of Succession? Did her father find new methods to creatively punish her?

A flash of fear told Margaret that she would never learn what she must from Catherine if the poor woman was able to communicate solely in single whispered words, but she told Catherine what she knew.

"Your daughter is strong as a future queen must be," Margaret whispered, forcing herself to smile encouragingly. "She has taken her wise mother's advice and informed the king that she wishes nothing more than to obey him and will do so in every way that is in accordance with God's wishes as well."

The twitch again, and Margaret knew Catherine was pleased. She kept to herself that she wondered if it was wise for Mary to take up her mother's failed argument and logic, but Mary was a woman now and no longer under the direction of her governess.

"Mary," Catherine whispered again, making Margaret wonder if she had heard her or if her mind was failing. Her face must have scrunched in confusion because Catherine gave a miniscule shake of her head and added, "Reginald."

First squeezing together in growing frustration then widening as understanding struck, Margaret's eyes locked on Catherine's in astonishment.

"You wish for Mary to marry Reginald?"

Blink.

Struck speechless, Margaret stared mouth agape at her

queen. Of all the tasks she had thought Catherine might assign her, this was not one she would have ever considered.

"Let me help you, your grace," Hussey interjected, swiftly swooping in to rescue her. She had forgotten he was there.

But he was not addressing Margaret. He moved to the opposite side of the bed, taking a cup of water in one hand and lifting Catherine to a seated position with the other. Margaret almost cried out that he must leave her, that he would hurt her, but she was silenced by his practiced movements and gentleness. Catherine's look of gratefulness spoke louder thanks than any word could have.

After a few moments, Catherine was settled with pillows behind her back and a worn notebook in her hand.

"It takes her a bit to rouse from her sleep, but she will be fine," Hussey commented under his breath to Margaret. Fine in this case meant that Catherine would be well enough to express her last wishes to her dearest friend. Fine did not mean that she would recover her health, her daughter, or her crown.

Margaret nodded. It was no less than she had gone into this scheme expecting.

Hussey lit a candle, and its soft light gave Catherine's skin the illusion of a healthy glow. Everyone looked beautiful in candlelight, Margaret mused. It was the harsh sun that revealed every flaw and line while adding its own burning redness to cheeks and noses.

"Reginald, will he have her?"

The question startled Margaret, and she gave a small gasp as she realized that the low scratchy voice had been emitted by her vibrant friend. She took a deep breath, slowly moving her head from side to side.

"I do not know." Honesty seemed the best policy. "He has

not set foot upon English soil – cannot now that he has so vociferously rejected the king's annulment and remarriage."

Hussey spoke up. "Henry has sent assassins to target Reginald without success. There is no hope of reconciliation in that quarter. He is the most hated man since Richard de la Pole."

He did not look to Margaret as he made this revelation, though he doubted she had understood the extent of the situation between the king and her son who had formerly enjoyed his favor and support in education.

"He was going to make him Archbishop of York," Margaret whispered, but Hussey knew that she required no response.

He continued addressing Catherine. "Princess Mary, of course, is prepared to marry him if it becomes possible and is your will."

Margaret turned toward Hussey, once again astonished at the depth of his loyalty. She had been underestimating him still. She would have the return journey to ask him how he moved between Mary and Catherine without anyone, friend or enemy, knowing it. He ignored her for the task at hand.

"She remains strong, but the animosity between she and the king increases," Hussey continued. "He cannot stand defiance, but feelings against him grow in all quarters. I respect your continued loyalty to your husband," he said, dipping his chin to her, "but I believe he is more hated at this moment than the late King Richard ever was."

"The people at Anne's coronation seemed more curious than enthralled," Margaret said as though thinking aloud. "Did you see some of the men?" she asked Hussey. "They did not even remove their hats."

He nodded and turned back to Catherine. "It is true, your grace. Princess Mary is beloved, and even more, trusted, while her father is increasingly seen as a tyrant who dictates the lives of men to suit his own purposes."

His face reddened as he realized that nobody would understand that phenomenon more than Catherine, but it was thankfully unnoticeable in the forgiving candlelight.

"Princess Mary refuses to recognize Anne as queen or Elizabeth as princess," Margaret added. "Are these gestures worth the wrath of her father? How can she expect to be named his heir if she puts such distance between them?"

It was the wrong thing to say.

Catherine seemed to grow taller, even as she sat in bed. "Mary is the only Princess of Wales," she said in a voice reminiscent of the Catherine Margaret remembered. "When she is wed to Reginald, the York families will support her."

What was left of them, Margaret thought. However, that was not exactly true. While the Plantagenets of her own generation were gone, another generation was rising up. The Courtenays, Poles, and Howards - could they wrest power from the Supreme Head of the Church of England and give it to his daughter? Would Reginald be king?

Margaret had never believed that one of her children would reign, even when Edward Stafford had spent many years attempting to convince her that Henry and Ursula would be next in line. She had no trouble supporting Princess Mary because she did not feel that her children had been displaced. But Mary wed to a Pole son, this was an idea she had never proposed to herself with all but Reginald married and he devoted to the church.

"If it is your wish and Princess Mary's," Margaret stated with fresh certainty. "I believe he would be honored to pledge himself as her husband."

Hussey looked bemused. He had assumed this to be the case

and had not required the internal process that Margaret had needed to come to the conclusion. Catherine, however, understood and pressed her friend's hand in weak yet meaningful appreciation.

"But Reginald cannot enter England," Margaret pointed out. "What if the king marries her to someone else?"

"You must take Mary to him."

"Escape?" Hussey whispered. Rather than pointing out that this was impossible - insane even - he appeared thrilled by the challenge.

"How on earth could we possibly smuggle the princess to the continent?" Margaret exclaimed. They should be advising patience and reconciliation, not encouraging dangerous schemes. "Princess Mary is of delicate health. How would she even manage the journey if we were able to extract her from Hatfield? We are not even allowed visits."

Disappointment was evident on Hussey's face, and Margaret was ashamed of her outburst. Yet, they must be reasonable. Surely, an escape plan was not realistic.

"She cannot take the oath," Catherine insisted, ignoring Margaret's objection. "That would be handing her crown to that Boleyn bastard." A fit of coughing followed her emotional outburst, and Hussey was immediately at hand with her water.

Margaret watched the pewter edge touch Catherine's puckered lips and followed the fine lines away from her mouth. The network of lines helped calm her though she had no more answers than before. How could Mary be obedient but not sign her inheritance away? How could any of them remain faithful to their God and their king? Her gaze had shifted over the cup to the man holding it. She smirked, wondering at the unexpected ally God had given her. Maybe he had other miracles in mind.

One thing was becoming painfully clear to Margaret. The

safe place that she had created for herself, for her children, the place she had hoped to keep Mary – it did not exist. Not in King Henry's England. She was being forced to take a stand. They all were. You were either for Henry or against him. The grey area she had attempted to reside in since the execution of her father was no longer an option.

She steeled her spine. Margaret was over sixty years of age and did not fear what the king could do to her. Riches would not benefit her much longer and her soul had always been eager to meet God. It was thoughts of her children that closed her throat and made pain emanate from her heart. When Henry had been arrested with Edward, she thought he was going to go the way of many young Plantagenet men. However, he had been spared. He had taken the oath as a member of Parliament just a few months earlier, and she had been relieved. He was safe again. She had thought that was all that mattered. It was all that had mattered to her at the time, but God had given her greater purpose now. Each of them must stand up for his truth or nothing else mattered.

"What can I do?" she asked.

It seemed like only moments later when Hussey turned to the window and announced that they must be departing soon. Surprised, Margaret followed his gaze and realized that the room was beginning to fill with early morning sun rather than candlelight. The candles had burned down to stubs and attendants would soon be arriving to bring food to break Catherine's fast and send news through discreet channels that she still lived.

Margaret had gained confidence from the discussion and planning that had carried on through the night, but now it evaporated as she was forced to face what would almost certainly be the final farewell between her and her oldest friend. Her eyes found Catherine's and saw her feelings mirrored there.

She swallowed her emotions that had formed a giant lump in her throat.

"I will serve your daughter until my dying day," Margaret vowed.

"I know," Catherine whispered, her strength waning after a tiring night. "Give her my love."

Margaret pursed her lips, causing lines to etch her face. It was unjust that Henry kept Mary from her dying mother when mercy would cost him so little. "I will, and know that you have mine."

A small smile was Catherine's only response. She seemed to be slipping back into the weak state that they had found her in. Margaret thanked God that she had been given strength enough for their meeting and prayed for success in turning Catherine's last wishes into reality.

Hussey's large hands were on her shoulders, beckoning her to action. He would never have touched her that way before this trial they had faced together, and it was not over. They must still leave Kimbolton undetected and make their way back to Bisham. Margaret took a deep breath and realized that all she smelled now was the pleasantly spiced pomanders. Curious how things we find unacceptable slowly go beyond notice with enough exposure.

Catherine had closed her eyes, but they slowly opened as Margaret made the sign of the cross upon her forehead. "God bless you, Queen Catherine," Margaret whispered before kissing her for the last time. She crossed the floor, leaning on Hussey's arm. He seemed strengthened by the challenge and her need for him. Margaret looked to Catherine once more and then shut the door with a quiet sound of closure.

After becoming comfortable in the castle during the hours of their visit, Margaret almost laughed at how nonthreatening the dim passageways were. They were quickly down in the storage room, preparing to make a dash across the lawn.

Margaret did not feel like dashing. She was feeling her sixty-one years, the ride of the day before, and the fact that she had not slept in more than twenty-four hours. Hussey handed her a sack of provisions and assured her that they would find a hidden spot to rest once they were well away from Kimbolton.

Nodding in acceptance of his plan, Margaret edged the door open just enough to peer outside. The sunrise was breathtaking and the air still held the coolness of night. Somewhat revived, she shoved it far enough to allow their escape and sprinted across the long grass in a way she would not have thought she was capable of six months ago. The dew clung to her skirt, weighing it down and chilling her ankles. She was thankful again for the clunky boots.

A dog barked in the distance, sending a shiver down Margaret's spine. Had they been spotted? Without turning to look for pursuers, she increased her pace as she made a beeline for the grove where they had left their horses.

Hussey overtook her. Because he was afraid she would not know the way or because he was frightened of pursuit? She was not sure. The bravery she had felt in the dim chamber as she made her vow to the queen was quickly evaporating into the dawn.

They reached the horses and fell against them, straining for breath and scanning their path for those they hoped were not there. A dog bark. The call of a bird. The sounds could be innocuous or they could indicate the end. Did she hear the approach of a horse or was that the furious beating of her heart?

Her haggard, windblown face turned toward Hussey.

He took one look at the countess in a damp dress covered in road dust, her hair in disarray, and her face ruddy with sweat and started laughing. Margaret looked around and behind her before realizing that she was the source of his mirth. Secure in herself enough to see the jest, she joined him in laughter that freed them from the fear and ghosts that had been the only things chasing them.

By unspoken signal, they both became serious at the same moment. Hussey quickly made the horses ready and handed Margaret onto her grey palfrey. It being much better rested than she was, her horse pranced in readiness. She prayed that she would not fall asleep and fall from her mount. It would be a rather undignified way to go.

Once they had placed some distance between themselves and Kimbolton, Margaret felt emboldened to speak to Hussey about the future of their cause.

"What will you and Anne do now?"

Hussey cleared his throat and frowned, weighing what he might say. "At my earliest opportunity," he said. "I will encourage the Holy Roman Emperor to invade England."

He gave his horse a firm kick, pulling out in front of Margaret before she had time to respond. It was not a decision that he wished to give her the opportunity to talk him out of.

August 1534

As weeks crept by following Margaret and Hussey's clandestine visit to Catherine, Margaret began to wonder if it had all really happened. Overseeing the day to day operation of her estates and receiving letters from her children seemed so ordinary compared to the wild ride across the countryside to make treacherous plans with the displaced queen.

A visit with Ursula would take her mind off things that she could not control and wished she knew more about. Hussey had been serious when he said that he would ask Charles to invade, and he did not think he would be alone. Henry had been making some dangerous enemies and might live to see his daughter handed his crown.

After ensuring that each of Ursula's favorite foods were being created in the kitchen, Margaret settled into a chair with her most recent parcel of messages to await the arrival of her daughter. It had been too long since she had spent time with Ursula. She and Harry tended to keep to themselves, especially since the death of his father. Margaret could not blame them, her life with Richard had been much the same. Even when they ordered the household of the Prince of Wales, they felt away from the center of politics out on the Marches.

A basket of wooden swords and scrap fabric dolls sat in the corner to serve as small gifts for the passel of grandchildren that would accompany Ursula. The thought of the cheery faces, one babe coming quickly after the other, brought a content smile to Margaret's face.

Harry and Ursula had been crushed by the loss of their first child, but it had not created distance between them. In fact, the shared grief had seemed to bring them even closer together, finding comfort in one another they were soon expecting another child.

And then another.

In the fourteen years of their marriage, they had produced six more children and lost one more, a beautiful little girl who would forever be the image of a golden curled toddler. The second loss had been easier to bear with the distraction of other children. Ursula had also been with child at the time. It was not lack of love that made Ursula mourn little Anne less, but the outpouring of love that she received from her growing family.

Margaret had reached an age where she took comfort from the thoughts of those who would greet her in heaven on a day that grew ever closer. It had plagued her as a younger woman to think of all she had lost, but as she aged her anticipation of reunion swelled. Her little grandchildren would be there holding the hands of her own lost babes. And Arthur. How she missed her joyful son. No reverie on those she missed was complete without Richard's face, now eternally younger than hers, coming to the forefront. "How I still love you," she whispered, hoping that God would relay the message.

The sounds of shuffling feet and more hurrying than typically took place at Bisham told Margaret that her daughter had arrived. Soon the laughter of children and an older scolding voice confirmed it. She set aside her letters and stood, subconsciously smoothing her skirt and hair. At a quick, yet dignified, pace, Margaret strode toward the hall to greet her family.

Margaret's heart swelled and tears sprung to her eyes at the sight of Ursula and the children. They must be the picture of what I looked like when Ursula clung to my skirts, she thought. Ursula was the image of her mother's younger self, auburn hair shining in the sun and heart shaped lips pursed at the children's antics. At the sight of their grandmother, they fell into order.

They were surprised to watch their proper mother publicly

embrace and kiss the countess they had been trained to be perfectly behaved in the presence of. The boys cocked their heads in curiosity, while the girls smiled with grins that spoke of knowledge that mama could let down her guard every now and then. Margaret and Ursula were oblivious to them as they reveled in the warmth of each other's arms.

The scent of her daughter's rose water filled Margaret's nostrils, and she closed her eyes to memorize the sensation of the moment. How many embraces like this would she share with her daughter? It had become her habit to consider all items and events finite.

"I must have a look at you," she said, only releasing her grip when Ursula had loosened hers. Taking the smallest of steps back, Margaret's face crinkled in happiness and her eyes roved over her daughter from head to toe.

Ursula's hair was bright red-gold, where Margaret's had long gone grey. Her figure was pleasantly rounded with frequent childbirth, while her mother's had gone thin with age. Yet there was a similarity that could not be mistaken, despite the lines and sagged skin that affected only the elder of them.

"My little white rose," Margaret said in a voice choked with emotion.

"Mama," Ursula exclaimed. "You have not called me that in years."

It was the recent talks with Hussey and the visit to Catherine, Margaret knew, that had brought the old pet name to mind, but she could not share her reasons with Ursula. She wanted her daughter to be free of any bonds that the king might trap her in.

"It is seeing your girls, looking so much as you did when you were my lovely shadow," Margaret settled upon, and it was true. The little girls, who stood near each other for support without actually clinging to each other, had the Plantagenet appearance that was almost guaranteed for a child of a Pole and a Stafford. Thank God that Harry and Ursula kept them from court.

Ursula called them to her side and urged them to greet their grandmother. Perfect little curtseys and formally prepared words were her reward.

"That was very well done, girls," Margaret praised them as she struggled to lower herself to their level. "Now let me hold you a moment and remember what it was like when your mama was as small as you are now."

Dorothy looked up at her mother for guidance, but Susan happily flung herself into Margaret's arms, almost knocking her to the ground.

"Susan!" Ursula immediately had one hand on the enthusiastic child and another on Margaret's back to steady her.

Margaret chuckled and said, "Do not punish the dear child. She simply did as I asked." She tussled the hair of Dorothy, who had remained at her mother's side, as she rose with Ursula's support. "Only I was more capable of absorbing the impact when you attempted to knock me over," Margaret added with an affectionate look at her daughter.

Ursula laughed despite herself, and her daughters shared another knowing glance. It was interesting to learn new facets of their parents, and the information was stored away in their clever minds.

Margaret welcomed the boys and presented them with the wooden swords that were waiting for their first nicks and scrapes. The two older boys struck at each other immediately, while a younger one toddled after them. It was not long before they were receiving a lesson on chivalry from their governess as they rubbed purpling bruises. Only the baby was quiet with his nurse.

Arm in arm, Margaret and Ursula strolled to a cozy spot that had been prepared for them in an alcove. The girls moved to follow until they were halted by their own nurse. Instead of eavesdropping on their mother and grandmother, they would have to be content with the dolls that Margaret had stitched for them.

"It does my heart well to see you and the children, and looking so fine," Margaret said, attempting not to groan as she lowered into her chair.

"I only wish that I could bring them more often," Ursula agreed.

Though they both had much to say, they enjoyed comfortable silence for a few moments as they selected morsels from the tray that had been silently set before them. Each savored the fact that the closeness between them remained even as circumstances of life changed. Ursula was the first to break the calm quiet.

"Harry asked me to tell you that Anne Hussey has been taken to the Tower." She said it nonchalantly, knowing that the children were quick to pick up anxiety in her tone, but she had not wanted to bring the news. Best to get it out of the way from the start.

Margaret was no longer as accustomed to controlling her emotions, living on her own at Bisham so little required the skill. Her face tightened in anger, but she was pleased to realize that she felt no fear.

"Her husband understood that was a possibility," Margaret acknowledged.

"Why could she not simply call her Lady Mary?" Ursula asked. She was almost begging her mother to tell her that she would not take a stand on this. Stay quiet. Stay safe. Her eyes pleaded.

"Were I your age, surrounded by my husband and young children," Margaret agreed. "I would feel the same way." Ursula leaned forward and opened her mouth to protest, but Margaret continued without allowing her objection. "When you are my age, you will understand that those who still need you may require a different sort of sacrifice. Instead of my teaching or affection, you need me to be able to take this stand for you. Your children need you, and God would have you remain with them. He has different requirements for me."

"No, mama."

"Yes, Ursula. I do not know if I will be forced to directly oppose the king, but if it becomes necessary to defend our faith and our future queen I will not back down from him."

Ursula blinked away tears that were causing her eyes to appear a brighter blue than normal. She looked toward the wall so that her children would not see. After a deep breath, she faced her mother once again.

"Faith in our Lord is the most important thing you taught me, but I never thought to see it questioned. Who would have guessed that our king would set himself up as our god?"

Her slender fingers pinched the bridge of her nose to squeeze away a forming headache, but she quickly pulled them away. Her children would notice her distress. Margaret took the fidgeting hands into her own.

"Pray for our king, even as you pray for the daughter he oppresses. Ask God to reform his heart that he will repent of his sins. There can be reconciliation yet," Margaret insisted. "Nothing is impossible with God," she added, seeing Ursula's doubt. "I have witnessed treachery and bloodshed in my life," Margaret said with a sigh. "But I have also experienced love and have hope for my grandchildren's future."

They both turned to watch the children at play. Margaret had accepted that it was time for her to do whatever was best for them and for her God. Ursula felt the same, but her role in the events that must unfold was her own.

"We must speak of happier things," Ursula said, desperation clung to the words.

"The queen desires to make marriage arrangements," Margaret said quietly enough to be sure that the words reached only Ursula's ears.

It took Ursula a moment to realize that her mother referred to Catherine. Despite her feelings and preferences, Ursula now thought of Anne as queen, as the king ordered her to do.

"But she insists that she is the true wife of King Henry," Ursula said, her confusion imprinted on her brow.

Margaret's laughter was sharp. "Not her own," she said with a shake of her head. "She wishes for Princess Mary to be joined with your brother, Reginald."

If Ursula's eyes widened any further, Margaret worried that her eyeballs might actually pop out and roll to the floor. The expression was squashed in an instant, but it was clear that the younger woman still had not grasped the seriousness of the issue and the extent that her family was involved. Stay quiet. Stay safe. Her eyes again begged.

"But Reginald is pledged to the church," she pointed out quite unnecessarily.

Still shaking her head, Margaret corrected, "He has never taken orders. He would have done so had Henry made him Archbishop of York, of course."

She did not need to continue. Both women knew well that Reginald had chosen exile over the prominent position in King Henry's new church.

"But marriage to Lady – to the Princess Mary," she revised her words in the presence of her mother. "Is he considering it?"

"I am sure that Reginald considers everything with deep thought," Margaret assured her with a hint of humor. "If he has responded to the proposal, I have not yet heard of it. Both he and Hussey were to urge Emperor Charles toward invasion in the hopes of rescuing Princess Mary from her gilded prison. It is my hope that any success in that arena includes Queen Catherine." She purposely used her friend's title in order to emphasize it to her daughter.

Thankfully, the earlier shock had prepared Ursula to exercise extreme self-control. She wished that she had saved what she had thought was scandalous news for after the children had been taken to the nursery for the night. This conversation that had followed was much more than she had bargained for.

"Mother, I..." she trailed off, unsure what she could offer.

"There is nothing you can or should be doing," Margaret reassured her with a pat on her hand for good measure. "I simply wish you to hear things from me, rather than second or third hand through court rumors. If anything happens, I wish for you to know the truth." She placed a wrinkled hand on her daughter's chin as she spoke her next words, "I do not expect or desire for you to be involved in any way."

"Yes, mama," Ursula whispered. "Please be careful, though. My Harry says that Cromwell has spies everywhere, even in households that you would not imagine containing one who is not loyal." She spread her hands to indicate the sprawling building that surrounded their tiny corner.

"I will," Margaret ceded. "But I will do what I must."

They shared a look that silently closed the subject and agreed to tend to more trivial and joyful matters. Conversation flowed freely about the education and particular talents of each child, Harry's work in Parliament, and the skill required to smoothly run their respective estates.

From that point on, the visit took on the light hearted atmosphere of a typical daughter spending time with her aging mother. No further mentions of treason were spoken, and they could almost forget that danger crouched nearby, waiting to pounce.

January 1536

After a Christmas season that had been quietly spent, Margaret was preparing to welcome her oldest son to Bisham. Word had arrived only days before his expected arrival, so she anticipated that he had news for her that could only be spoken in person, not recorded in print. Knowing that the king had sent a request to Reginald in Italy for support with the new pope, she hoped that was not the cause of Henry's visit.

God had a new representative on Earth in Cardinal Farnese who had recently been named Pope Paul III. If Englishmen had hoped that their king would be reconciled to the new leader of the Catholic Church and life could go back to what it had been before the advent of Anne Boleyn, they were sorely disappointed. Margaret had heard that mention of this theory to Henry had been met with anger and firm rejection, as were any ideas that were not the king's own.

King Henry had become increasingly unpredictable and difficult to please, to the extent that Margaret almost felt sympathy for the upstart who had displaced her friend. Anne Boleyn was also said to be nervous and demanding of those who served her. They deserved each other, it seemed.

Even knowing that the royal couple was plagued by a toxic relationship that had failed to produce the children that Henry so desperately wanted had not prepared Margaret for the news of the past summer. Sir Thomas More, a lifelong friend and mentor of the king, had been executed for treason. The pious More had refused to sign the Oath of Succession, the very same stance that Princess Mary had taken. Allowing his Lord Chancellor far less mercy than his daughter, the king ordered More tried for treason. He had been executed under a pleasant July sun that belied the stew of discontent that was brewing below it.

The memory of receiving this news caused Margaret to go cold all over again. Fear had once again made her wonder if she was doing the right thing, not only failing to support the Boleyn faction herself, but encouraging the princess to insist upon her own rights. Maybe it would be easier to enforce Princess Mary's right to succeed after her father was dead. With only a baby girl and bastard brother to challenge her, victory was almost certain.

It was the almost that kept Margaret in the fight. That and her desire to present herself as righteous before God. How would she explain herself to her heavenly master if she were called to him before Henry was, as seemed likely given their respective ages? She would not be able to justify a life filled with sins of omission, of sitting back and doing what was easy rather than what was right.

When her mind became overwhelmed with these thoughts, she made her way to her private chapel to gain the comfort that only God could provide. Her deep green skirts swirled around her feet as she took swift steps in that direction. The areas without roaring fires were too cool for her aching joints, so she kept a cloak woven of warm, pure white wool wrapped tightly about her shoulders. She was glad of it as the icy cold of the chapel's stone floor seemed to reach up gnarled claws to snag at her ankles and knees.

A pillow rested before the altar. She had received permission from her chaplain to kneel upon it when the hard ground had become an undeniable distraction when she was at prayer. Better this indulgence than a heart not completely focused on her conversation with God. She gripped the pillow in her hands, still not relishing the idea of kneeling and then having to pull herself back up. She felt growing respect for the decrepit monks and priests who continued to prostrate themselves for long hours without outward concern for their physical pain and discomfort. Margaret was simply not that strong.

The cushion was just enough to keep agony from shooting through her hips and knees as she knelt. Her prayers did not include requests for physical blessings. Those she loved most had enough of those, but she pleaded for their safety. She prayed for renewed faith and forgiveness in the king, but felt that her heart was not in that hope. Nothing is impossible with God, she reminded herself as she had Ursula. But just how well did God know King Henry? Was he beyond the influence of his heavenly father though he proclaimed himself his representative to Englishmen?

Pushing aside her questions and doubts, Margaret prayed for her own children and for Mary, who she considered always in the same breath as the children of her own womb. Mary's mother was the next person in need of God's ministrations, and Margaret asked God for news of Catherine even as she dared not go so far as to ask to see her again.

Margaret was uncertain how much time had passed when she finally unbent stiff knees and massaged her sore lower back. A cleared throat from the back of the chapel alerted her that she was no longer alone.

Turning toward the sound, she recognized a relatively new page. He had joined her household recently enough that she was embarrassed to realize that she did not remember the young man's name.

"Yes, you have need of me?" she asked as he bowed before her.

"It is Lord Montague, Lady Salisbury," he said, never lifting his face to look into hers, though he stood at exactly her height. "His cavalcade has been spotted entering the village."

"I thank you for bearing wonderful news," Margaret

enthusiastically replied. She hoped to encourage the sheepish young man, but her excitement was also authentic. Always too much time passed between visits from her children. She hurried from the chapel to welcome Henry to Bisham.

A table had been prepared in her chamber. She had learned to assume that discretion would be necessary after Ursula's visit. Regularly managing visits this way with Hussey and her sons also took away any sense of secrecy that might have otherwise been created by not hosting a larger gathering of the household in the hall. Those who served the countess knew that she preferred intimate arrangements. It was simply the eccentrics of an old woman rather than the need to avoid listening ears and spying eyes.

Upon opening the finely engraved wood door, the scent of roasted foul filled air and made her body remember that it was hungry. She fasted often in her focus on prayer, but this day would be filled with feasting. One never knew how many opportunities remained.

Only moments passed before Henry was ushered into the room, exclaiming his joy at seeing her and declaring that he was ravenous. Losing no time, Margaret waved away all but those who would serve the food and directed her son to the table.

The meat steamed as it was carved and placed upon their plates. Thick sauce accompanied it because Margaret knew that Henry favored it. She ate sparingly, preferring to observe him enjoying the meal. She had happened upon one of the cook's boys grinding almonds into fine paste for the marzipan, and it made her wonder how many other dishes took hours to create only to be gobbled up in a moment. Henry put a sugared bite into his mouth, closed his eyes, and let it melt with pleasure written upon his face.

"All this with such a short time to prepare," Henry said when he eventually pushed back from the table. He remained seated but seemed to need the extra space after the courses of meats, cheeses, and wine. "You could manage the fine affairs at court."

Margaret was shaking her head. There were few things that would make her wish to return to court, none that she could think of. "I am eager for the news that you bring," she said in hopes of changing the subject.

Henry frowned and wiped his mouth, though Margaret could see nothing to make the action necessary.

"I wish that it did not fall to me to cause you pain, mother," he said, taking her hand.

She felt familiar feelings churning within her. Was it Reginald or Geoffrey? Not Ursula. Please God, not Ursula.

"You know that Queen Catherine has not been in good health for quite some time."

Margaret frowned. This was not what she had been expecting.

Henry cleared his throat to delay his message. "I'm afraid that she has died. I sent my message to you as soon as I heard, but would not have you receive the news in writing."

Her face clearing, Margaret was struck by the fact that she was not upset. Poor Catherine had been suffering emotionally for years and physically for only slightly less time. "She is finally at peace," she whispered. "I pray that God welcomes her as the faithful servant that she was."

"Amen," Henry agreed.

The memory of the former queen of England flew through the years to settle in the room. "I thank you for traveling through the cold and snow to tell me," Margaret added, remembering that stark parchment that gave no hint of the tragic news it contained.

"Of course," he said, moving to stand behind her and place his hands protectively on her arms. Their evolution was now complete. She no longer served and cared for him. It was his turn to protect his mother.

"You will hear rumors of poison," he did not continue, seeing his mother shake her head and hold up a hand.

"I know the truth of her terminal condition," Margaret reassured him. She almost told him of her wild ride and secret visit. What could be the harm now? But she did not. The less Henry knew, the less could be held against him if the king were to narrow his eyes at him.

"You have my deepest sympathy," he said. "Would you like me to escort you to the chapel? I would join you to say prayers for our dear queen's soul."

"Later," Margaret said, much to her son's surprise. "I have just come from there, and God knew the truth already as I prayed for Catherine's peace. She had already received it."

Henry nodded and moved back to his chair, finding another minute space for a bite of marzipan. He had waited for them to be alone before breaking the news to his mother. The entire country would hear of the beloved queen's death, though he hoped that not all heard that the husband she had been devoted to rejoiced at the news. Henry frowned at the thought.

"What is it?" his mother asked. He could hide nothing from her.

"I do not think that peace will come for the rest of us," he said, rubbing his chin and frowning at the stubble he felt beneath his fingers. "The king is disillusioned with Anne, but he awaits the result of her current pregnancy."

"She is with child again?" There were some disadvantages to being so far from court.

"Yes," Henry acceded with reservation evident in his voice. "The entire court seems to hold its breath until she gives birth.

After two babes lost with his new wife, there are whispers that it is the king who is at fault for his lack of sons rather than his queens."

Margaret remained silent, considering the import of this news. What would it mean for Mary if Anne produced a boy? If the king died while the boy was young, Mary may still be the clear choice of successor. Margaret knew well the lack of faith Englishmen placed in a child king, and for good reason.

"Anne is not only frantic about her condition," Henry continued. "She raves at whomever is near regarding her husband's wandering eye."

"It is more than his eye that wanders if he is anything like I remember," Margaret pointed out, causing a blush to rise on her son's face. "Really, Henry. You have your own children almost grown, but cannot hear your mother speak of the temptations of man?"

Henry just shook his head but could not contain his smile.

"He has no additional illegitimate children that I have not heard of?" she asked.

"Not that I am aware of, and he proudly presents Richmond so there's no reason to think that he would not do the same if there were others."

Margaret weighed this. "Unless he did not wish to add to Anne's anxiety."

"Maybe," Henry acquiesced doubtfully.

"No others then," Margaret agreed. "I am simply thinking of Princess Mary. Has anyone told her?"

"Chapuys. He was with her near her mother's end and will be the best person to comfort her, I think," his tone questioned, so Margaret nodded in agreement.

Chapuys would provide support and encouragement to stay strong where another might attempt to convince Mary that her cause was lost without her mother.

"I need to see her," Margaret stated. "What if I were to come to court. Maybe I could convince the king that I mean only to care for her as a mother does a child. I can be no threat to him."

Henry leaned back in his chair exhaling a heavy breath. His hand lifted to his chin again and his eyes narrowed in thought.

"It is not a bad idea," he agreed. "It cannot be long before the king receives a return message from my brother regarding his request for support of his new marriage. He may have it written and sent before hearing of Catherine's death. If I know Reginald, he will be bold. You could smooth the king's ruffled feathers."

This was not precisely what Margaret had in mind, but she saw the sense of it if such actions became necessary.

"I will write to Reginald myself and encourage prudence," she said, pouring more wine for each of them. "His righteousness is admirable, but we must also weigh what should be said and when. He must remember that this is a king who will punish those at hand if he cannot have the guilty party he desires."

Henry sat up alert at that. "Surely, Reginald would not write anything to put his family in danger. Remember Edmund de la Pole."

"I shall see that he does not."

~ ~ ~ ~

Henry was still at Bisham with his mother when he received a message from Geoffrey.

"Anne Boleyn has suffered another miscarriage," he told his mother, reading from the scribbled note. "Geoffrey does not believe she will be given the opportunity to have another."

"What does that mean?" Margaret snapped. She may harbor no love for the Boleyn girl, but she could feel a mother's sympathy

292

for a lost child.

Henry locked his gaze on her. "He believes that Henry means to get rid of her."

Margaret laughed and her son looked as though he was concerned for her mental health.

"All the pain he has caused. The people he has exiled or killed. The church he has sundered," she said in gasps, fighting to catch her breath. "All for this woman whom he would now replace."

Henry did not know if he was supposed to say anything, so he did not.

"At least it did not take him two decades to decide this time. Anne will have Catherine's example to thank as she quietly retires to a nunnery rather than fighting a drawn out battle that she cannot win. May God have mercy on their souls."

June 1536

Margaret's transition back to the foreign world of King Henry's court went more smoothly than she could have imagined. Few seemed concerned with the movements of a woman old enough to be considered irrelevant.

For Queen Anne, fortune's wheel made a vicious downturn. Even Margaret was surprised when the king's second wife was brought up on charges of treason rather than given the opportunity to remove herself to a nunnery. Henry used the situation to rid himself of a few others who had been overly fond of the Boleyn girl, accusing them of adultery with her and chopping off their heads. Margaret was scandalized that one of the men was Anne's own brother.

In the wake of Anne Boleyn's execution, few spared a thought for the aged remnant of the York family quietly inserting herself into court mechanizations.

Though none were allowed to let it show, the brutal trial and death of Anne had shaken even the king's most staunch supporters. An invisible fissure had opened up, with England's aristocracy on one side and Henry and Cromwell on the other.

Make that Henry, Cromwell, and Jane Seymour. The girl was either incredibly brave or astoundingly stupid, for she had become the third wife of King Henry just days after the head of his second was skillfully sliced off by a French swordsman. Margaret had to pinch herself to ensure that she was not dreaming or going insane. She supposed feeling the pinch did not mean that she was sane but knew of no other test.

Margaret was sitting within Westminster's great hall, observing the conspiracies and manipulations taking place when she looked up to find Kathryn Craddock examining her. No, she was no longer Craddock, Margaret reminded herself as Kathryn crossed the hall toward her. Deep blue silk enveloped the still beautiful woman. Her beauty was now that of a dignified older woman on her fourth marriage, but the beauty of her youth still twinkled in her ocean colored eyes and mischievous dimple. The woman who had thought to be consort to Richard IV was now the wife of gentleman usher of the chamber, Christopher Aston.

The old friends greeted each other warmly and agreed to stroll through the gardens while they caught up with one another. Margaret shared what she could, wishing that she could say more. It was not that she did not trust Kathryn, but she and Hussey had agreed to keep tight the circle of people who were endangered by knowledge of their activities. She already regretted telling Ursula. It would have been better to let the girl live her simple life with her children away from court manipulations.

"You are keeping something from me," Kathryn observed as they slowly made their way through the fragrant paths surrounded by the blooms of summer.

One side of Margaret's mouth crept upward, remembering that it was difficult to keep anything hidden from Kathryn. She was one who knew how to slip into the hearts and minds of her friends and cared about what she found there.

"Nothing of import," Margaret reassured her rather unconvincingly, but Kathryn let it pass. "I was surprised to find you here," Margaret added, changing the subject.

Kathryn's laughter was an echo of the past, and Margaret almost expected to glance over and see the woman who had turned all heads in 1497 standing there.

"I do spend the majority of my time on the lands left to me by my beloved Matthew," she agreed with a sad smile as she thought of her third and most loved husband. "The vast hills and sweet gurgling brooks are a balm for a weary soul. I love to ride out and pretend that I am the only person left in the world."

"At times, I do feel like the only person left. The only one from a certain time, I should say," Margaret said with wistfulness evident in her tone and watery eyes.

"But you are not," Kathryn denied. "You have me."

"And I am thankful for that," Margaret said with a smile that did not reach her eyes. Kathryn was a good person and a thoughtful friend, but she was not close enough to confide in. Nor had she grown up in the violence of the battles between Edward III's descendants, as Margaret had, even if her husband had been one of the last victims of it.

Instead of lifting her spirits as Margaret had been sure spending time with Kathryn would do, she felt morose. She would never learn to deny the ghosts of her past, so instead she welcomed them and let their presence wash over her like the tide coming in. She did not realize that she had halted her steps and closed her eyes.

"Margaret, are you well?" the concern all people kept on hand to use with the aged clung to Kathryn's words.

Margaret took one more moment to appreciate the feel of the sun on her face before bidding her spirits farewell, then took a deep breath.

"I am, and I apologize for worrying you," Margaret resumed her steps as she spoke.

Kathryn pinned her down with a quizzical look but did not prod. Margaret purposefully turned away from her to inspect a sprig of planta genista that was warring for dominance in a flowerbed. The grey-green leaves shielded tiny thorns from view. Bright yellow flowers gave the plant a cheery appearance that must have appealed to Geoffrey of Anjou when he wore the flower so often that it had given his son's dynasty its name, but the hidden barbs protected the invasive shrub from pests, animal and human. She was the last Plantagenet. Would its thorns protect her?

"Lady Salisbury," a deep voice announced itself. Without turning, Margaret knew it would be attached to a large man further puffed up with self-importance. Clothing chosen for the statement it made rather than its practicality would accompany a voice such as that one. It was the sound of a man who was accustomed to answering to no one besides his king.

Margaret grasped a branch of the Plantagenet shrub, mindless of the blood drawn as spikes drove into her soft palm. She silently prayed for strength before slowly shifting to face him as if he was the one at her command.

"Sir?" The tilt of her chin and raising of her eyebrow left no doubt that she expected his obeisance.

She would not receive it. His stern features faltered almost imperceptibly under the gaze of this York matriarch before he remembered that her position was not that exalted under the Tudor regime. He stretched to stand even taller, towering over the old women. "You have been ordered into the presence of his majesty."

Margaret swallowed and nodded, unable to speak. Only Kathryn noticed the drop of blood fall from Margaret's hand to the ground as she followed her escort to the king.

Prayers to God and all his saints raced through Margaret's head as she followed her silent guide. He did not turn to glimpse at her, unconcerned if his pace was too quick and certain she would follow. She did.

Despite her anxiety, she noticed the tapestries that seemed to cover every surface of the castle walls. Henry may have become notorious for his temper, dissolving beloved religious houses, and collecting wives, but he clearly also had an interest in the arts.

Margaret hoped that she would have the opportunity to inspect them more closely, that she would have the opportunity to do anything after this meeting.

A calmness came over her, and she was sure that it was her friendly ghosts accompanying her to her audience with the king. They reassured her that Montague was capable of leading the family. Reginald would stay firm in the faith and marry Princess Mary if it was deemed the right thing to do. And Geoffrey? He would have his older brothers to guide him.

They had come to a door so elaborately carved and painted that it could only lead to the king's chambers. As she was announced, Margaret prayed a last time for strength to remain faithful. She was led into the room with her head held high.

"Cousin."

The word hit her before her eyes had found the man who had once been little Harry Tudor. Margaret blinked to be sure she was seeing clearly. How long had it been since she had been in the presence of the king?

The vivacious little boy and athletic young man seemed to have been swallowed up by a thick puddle of a man reclining in a cushioned chair with one leg propped up on a short stool. He must have noticed Margaret's eyes widen, because he released a belly laugh that set his rolls of flab jiggling in a nauseating dance. Once he gained control of his mirth and his body settled into its preferred stagnancy, Margaret had renewed her dignity as well.

"Your grace," she said as she curtseyed as low as she was able.

"Do you know why I have had you brought here?" he asked in a low rumble that drew deeply from his gigantic girth.

To ensure that she knew her place, beneath him? To threaten her? To have her thrown into the Tower?

"I do not, but it pleases me to be at your mercy, and hope

that I may serve you in whatever task you have for me," she gave the expected response.

He chortled again, loud and long. "Your skills are wasted at Bisham," he stated coolly as if the echoes of his dying laughter were not still bouncing around the chamber.

The sudden change made Margaret's blood run cold, and her thumb rubbed the wounds on her palm like a sort of talisman. She did not speak, as he had not asked a question. The less said the better.

"I would like to share with you a letter that I have lately received," Henry announced, his words still tinged with a threat, though Margaret could not imagine what he meant. "Do you know who it is from?"

His beady eyes that had once been bright with intelligence and joy were now made smaller by the massive jowls attempting to bury them. His stare stabbed her like a sword, and suddenly she knew. But she would not confess that to him. He gestured to an attendant, who handed him a single piece of vellum.

"I cannot imagine what missive your majesty would deign to share with one such as myself," she said demurely, her head bowed low in submission. When had her chin reached her chest, she wondered? Had she not meant to keep it upright? Her strength was insufficient to raise it.

A grin that reminded Margaret of that painted in murals of demons trapping humans in sin filled Henry's face, rearranging the folds of skin. She repressed a shiver, or at least she hoped she had.

"This," he continued slowly, holding up the letter as if it were damning evidence in a trial, "is from a dear cousin of mine. I have supported him financially and taken much interest in his education and prospects from the time I took my throne. Above most others, he has reason to serve me well and gratefully."

Margaret tried not to swallow or blink or breathe.

"Do you still not know who wrote this?" He gave it a shake between his pudgy fingers as his eyes narrowed until Margaret was surprised he could see through them. "I think you do."

She remained silent, not because she thought it was prudent at this point but because she was unable to speak.

"It is from your son, Reginald."

And the world crashed down around her.

Still, she could not speak, and she knew she must. Those icy blue eyes were fixed upon her, waiting.

"You will know, of course," he continued as if they were discussing trivial matters, "that I have asked your son represent me before the Bishop of Rome. I have requested that he support me in marital matters the way I have supported him in all things."

Margaret could only nod in affirmation. Henry did not seem to mind.

"In response to these requests from his king, your son," he said the last two words as if they were daggers that he could throw, "has written this." Another shake of the mysterious vellum.

"When was the last time you communicated with Reginald?"

The question took Margaret by surprise. She had been hypnotized by the quivering of the sheet in the king's fingers as he crinkled the edges with anger that he wished he could take out on the author.

"Your grace?" she mumbled.

"When," he carefully enunciated each word, "was the last time you received word from your son?"

Her tongue searched her mouth for words, and she was appalled at the indecisive mutterings escaping from her. "I am not sure," she finished.

"You are not sure," Henry repeated so that she could hear

the lameness of her response.

"I apologize, your highness," Margaret attempted to recover. "This is all rather unexpected." She realized that the king had not actually revealed the contents of Reginald's letter. "What does he say?"

"Ah," Henry said, that grin filling his countenance once again. "That is an important question. You are a smart woman, Lady Pole, aren't you? Of course, you are," he answered his own question, and Margaret just watched the letter, willing it to flutter away. "You have managed to thrive when so many others have not. Warwick, de la Pole, Courtenay," he enumerated, not because she would have forgotten the fate of her house, but to taunt her with it.

"Your grace has been unfailingly generous," she forced herself to say.

"Yes, I have."

Tension sparked as they locked gazes, but Margaret was the first to look away. What else could she do?

"When your aged mind recalls the last time you spoke to your son, Reginald," he continued, "perhaps you can tell me if you encouraged him to support my unfortunate need to rectify my sinful position as husband to my brother's wife. I have no doubt that you informed him that I, your king, am supreme ruler of this kingdom of all earthly and heavenly concerns. You, as my loyal subject and dear cousin, surely guided your son - and all your children - in understanding that you owe me everything."

All her children. Why had he said that? Reginald was safely out of Henry's reach, and she had no fear for herself, but what of the others?

"I have," she boldly lied. "I will repeat my advice to him again, if you have a scribe available," she offered. "Reginald is my child but is not under my control, surely you can understand."

She hated herself for speaking against him. Why had he not warned her of what she would face? Margaret had no choice but to look to those she must protect and let Reginald take care of himself.

Henry seemed pleasantly surprised. "Is that so?" He gestured again, certain that his attendants could read his mind. "We shall do so now."

Margaret's fingers fidgeted at the dried blood on her palm. Could she do this? What would Reginald think? She watched a scribe brought in, settled with ink, parchment, and wax to warm for her seal. Instead of nervousness and doubt building in her, the peace that was stronger than she was came over her again. Reginald understood her position. He knew that preparing her would have convicted her of his crime, and he would also expect this result. Clever boy.

"Would you like to know what your son has written?" the king asked, and Margaret realized how much she had given him by not asking more questions. He knew that she expected Reginald to speak out against him. She closed her eyes and admonished herself for her stupidity.

"I can see that it is something that displeases your grace," she attempted to recover. "If it involves the points that you have stated, I am at your pleasure to remonstrate him as my child."

Henry nodded slowly, as if even this movement were retarded by his excess flesh. "Very well," he conceded, and Margaret felt she had averted the devil. "In your instructions to him, you may like to inform him that it is best not to refer to his king as 'a robber, a murderer, and a greater enemy to Christianity than the Turk.'"

Margaret gulped.

"You may also wish to remind him that I am the head of the Church in England. So much time away from his homeland seems

303

to have confused Reginald's allegiances. Please request that he return to our shores and submit to me as is his duty."

Never. "Yes, your highness."

Henry shifted his attention to the scribe, who seemed to have everything in its place after much shuffling and rearranging. Margaret felt her shoulders droop as if the king's gaze had been propping them up.

"Please take down the countess' wise words to our servant Reginald Pole," he instructed with a bit of amusement in his tone. He was like a cat playing with a mouse.

She found herself speaking the words that she knew the king expected to hear while praying that Reginald would comprehend them as a warning but not the one that was written.

"You have been a traitor and no son of mine."

"Serve our king as is your duty."

"You owe much to the benevolence of his majesty."

"Word of your folly has reached me from the king himself, and I ask you to consider the guidance of your mother though you are a man full grown."

As she scanned the scribe's final product, she was astounded by the words she had instructed him to pen. The king appeared pleased, and she could only pray that Reginald would read his mother's code. Her seal was brought to her that she might prepare the letter for sending in King Henry's presence. He had generously offered to see it delivered with haste.

"A mother bears many pains for her children long after the physical pain of bringing them into this world is a memory," Henry said once the deed was complete.

Margaret cocked her head and searched for the deep thinking young man that must still exist somewhere in this angry tyrant. Not finding him, she simply agreed, "She does."

Left weary by the interaction, Margaret hurried to her own rooms once the king had released her. She could think no more on whether or not she had done the right thing or if there was a way she could have turned things further in her family's favor. Ordering her attendants to leave her as soon as she was dressed for bed, she fell into a deep, restorative sleep.

Upon rising, she had word sent to her son, Henry, that she wished to see him. Knowing that the king would be likely to have her watched, she made no attempts to be secretive. Better to admit to the actions that could not incriminate her in order to make it appear that there were none that could.

She was certain that Henry would promptly reply, and, in the meantime, she returned to the garden. The planta genista was easily located. This time she had her clippers with her. Others may find it an odd arrangement, but Margaret's room would be decorated with the hardy yellow blooms.

Henry arrived as Margaret was fine tuning the arrangement of the flowers in a delicate vase. He glanced at them, but seemed not to recognize their importance. After Margaret had relayed her story to him, she was surprised by the intensity of his wrath.

He was unable to stay seated and paced the room angrily. "How could Reginald be so thoughtless to put us – you – in this position?" His words were emphasized by quick hand movements that made Margaret wonder how long until he knocked something over.

"I do not believe he thought to put us in danger," she replied calmly. "First, we must remember that Reginald has not had extensive contact with the king of late. He may have believed that Henry could still be convinced of his need for repentance and reconciliation. If he did fear the king's wrath, he likely expected it to be aimed solely at himself, from a distance to be impotent."

Henry shook his head, wishing to remain angry though his mother's words made a kind of sense. "I shall write him as well, admonishing him as an older brother. The king must see us as faithful servants rather than categorize us with Reginald as a traitor."

"If you feel it is wise," Margaret agreed hesitantly. One admonishing letter Reginald would see the need for. Two might convince him that he alone of his family continued to oppose the break with Rome.

Her son seemed to deflate as he let go of his resentment toward his brother. How he wished he could be so bold with the king!

"He has disinherited the Boleyn brat as well, you know."

"It is as we expected," Margaret agreed. "He hopes for a son with Seymour."

"I have no doubt that Jane's brothers, Edward and Thomas, wish it as well. They are no less hungry for power and position than the Boleyns were," Henry declared.

Margaret nodded as she quietly reflected upon the reign of this king that she had placed all her hopes in.

"She is not . . ."

"No," Henry said, finishing her thought. "But I'm sure Jane will be with child soon enough."

"What will you say to Reginald?" she asked.

"Nothing for now," he relented. "As you have said, the king is pleased and I shall leave the situation as it lies."

"I am grateful," Margaret said, approaching her son and lifting her arms before realizing how long it had been since she had held him in them. Men had little need for the embraces of mothers.

Yet he fell into her waiting arms now like a tired little boy searching for respite.

September 1536

Margaret's time at court had been brief. Returning to Bisham had seemed a wise alternative to remaining beneath King Henry's thumb. She would leave it to her sons to inform her if events occurred that she should be aware of.

Before leaving she had visited with Kathryn for what she was certain would be the last time. They were neither of them young nor desirous of a return to London, so their parting was bittersweet. Margaret had considered again sharing her burden with this woman who had endured her own harsh journey through life, but decided it would be selfish. She would be increasing Kathryn's load in order to lighten her own. Let her return to Berkshire in peace for the remainder of her days.

When Margaret had watched Kathryn and her small retinue prepare to leave, she was sure she had seen an image of the young woman who had thought to be queen superimposed upon her elderly friend. Rapid blinking cleared her vision, but Kathryn dimpled at that moment as though she knew exactly what Margaret had seen.

The memory of Kathryn's leaving brought simultaneous smile and tears to Margaret as she admired the planta genista that she had ordered planted near her rooms at Bisham. The gardener had argued that the shrub grew like a weed and was difficult to control. Margaret had attempted to hide a small smile when she responded, "Exactly."

He had strode away, shaking his head at the senseless demands of noblewomen.

Margaret's skin no longer healed the way it had when she was younger, and her palm bore scars from the sprig that had given her strength to bear the scrutiny of the king. She caressed the marks and prayed that they be a constant reminder of the greater wounds that her savior bore for her as he gave her strength in this life until he welcomed her to the next.

Montague was scheduled to arrive, he also requiring a refuge away from the Seymour faction that was now taking up the space that the Boleyns had been forcefully vacated from. Margaret clipped a sprig of yellow flowers to place upon his hat.

When he arrived, Henry clearly brought news that made him eager to burst. They had just sat down to bowls of honeyed fruit when he announced that the duke of Richmond had died.

"May God have mercy on his soul," Margaret whispered.

This was unexpected. Though illegitimate, Henry Fitzroy had been the hope of many who were opposed to either Mary or Elizabeth taking their father's crown.

"He was just a child," she mourned. It was impossible to find joy in the death of a possible enemy when he was a sweet child on the verge of adulthood. The king had married him to Mary Howard but refused to allow them to live as husband and wife, despite the boy's insistence that he was a man. Somehow the very insistence was what made him seem incurably young.

"Yes," Henry agreed, attempting to be sensitive. "But now the king is left to choose between two daughters that he has bastardized. Which will he choose?"

Margaret frowned in thought. "Jane?"

"Not yet."

They each selected bits of the sweet, sugared fruit as they considered what this meant for the future of the kingdom, if anything.

"Will Reginald marry Princess Mary?" Henry asked, sounding like a child asking his mother why a chicken laid eggs.

Margaret breathed deeply. "I do not know. Somehow, I cannot imagine Reginald occupying the space that Henry does today."

Henry barked with laughter. "That is an interesting picture. Our Reginald decked out in jewels and sitting where the current king dandles girls on his knee."

She glared at her oldest son. There was no need for frivolous remarks that could have grave consequences. He raised his hands in apology.

"Still, I think I will write to him while I am here. It is so peaceful," Henry sighed, popping a strawberry into his mouth.

"Take care what you put to parchment," Margaret advised. "Lady Hussey has just recently been released for a lesser crime than you purport to commit, and now only because of her ill health."

She need not remind Henry of the risks inherent in saying anything that varied from the king's views, but she was still his mother.

"I had heard," he said. "It was a pathetic move to attempt to make an example out of an old lady who simply wished to show the princess respect."

"You must take care what you say aloud as well," Margaret admonished, surveying their surroundings for how far his words might carry and what ears might be within range.

Henry bowed to her. "Then I will retire and hope that I have reined in my tongue before the morrow."

Margaret could not help but smile as she watched him walk away, the yellow petals upon his hat gleaming in the dying sunlight.

February 1537

Sitting before a crackling fire, Margaret and her granddaughter, Katherine, relaxed in companionable silence. Katherine had a book open on her lap, and the older woman envied her ability to see the small characters in the dim light. Since her brief and disastrous return to court, Margaret had been happy to spend quiet days at Bisham with Henry and Jane's daughter. She was getting too old for politics and was pleased to see that her efforts to become closer to the girl who had served her for so long had been positively received.

A letter from Reginald had been delivered earlier, but Margaret had saved it for this cozy time of the evening when it could be savored. Retrieving it, she held it where it would capture Katherine's attention and indicated that she would like her to read it aloud.

"What is this?" Katherine asked rhetorically, unfolding the note. "Ah, it is from Reginald." She smiled, but it faded almost immediately, her face paling and eyes bulging at the message.

Margaret had been expecting innocuous Christmas tidings. Clearly, Reginald was surprising her again. "What is it?" she demanded. She moved to tear the paper from Katherine's hand before remembering that she would not be capable of making out the print if she did.

Katherine tore her eyes from the words long enough to glance at her grandmother. "My apologies," she muttered, quickly refocusing on Reginald's news. "You will be very proud of your son," she added in false cheer. "He has been made a cardinal."

If Margaret thought the battle lines had been drawn before, there was no doubt now. She wondered if the king had already heard. Undoubtedly.

She realized that her mouth was hanging open, though she

had no words. She clinched it shut. An image of Reginald in his red hat brought her joy, despite the anger it would rouse in King Henry. "My son," she whispered. "A cardinal."

"Yes, grandmother," Katherine agreed, even less certain that this was a good thing. "He could be a rallying point for the pilgrims."

The Pilgrimage of Grace it was being called. Faithful Catholics had gathered together in the North of England and marched south. They were without armor and weapons of war but hoped that their number would encourage the king to consider their desire to return to the mother Church. Margaret pictured Reginald marching out in front of them, his robes scarlet against the dull colors of peasant clothes behind him, a scepter held high.

"But Princess Mary has just returned to court," Katherine pointed out, her confusion clear.

"That she has," Margaret agreed. "And I do not blame her. Reconciliation with her father may be her best course if she wishes to be chosen as his heir now that Richmond is gone and Elizabeth is bastardized."

"Will she deny the faith?" Katherine asked.

"I think not," Margaret said slowly. "She is a strong girl. Smart as well. I believe she will accommodate her father's wishes as far as her conscience allows, but nothing could shake the faith passed down to her from her beloved mother."

Katherine looked doubtful, and Margaret wished to console her.

"You do not know Princess Mary the way I do, sweet Katherine. She has reason to understand the mechanizations of the court far better than most. The experience of her mother's exile was not one to be thankful for but has prepared her for anything else she must face. Most importantly, we can trust her. Regardless of what her father does, when Mary is queen, she will restore the church and rule us well."

The cloud of doubt over Katherine's features dispelled somewhat if it did not clear completely. "I thank you for your wise counsel, grandmother. What about Reginald? Cardinal Pole," she corrected herself.

Cardinal Pole. Pride stirred in Margaret's heart as she replayed the words in her mind. "He will do as God leads him," she said. "And what better guide could he have?"

Katherine attempted a smile before fixing her gaze upon the roaring flames. Was she imagining them reaching out and searing her skin the way so many good men, women, and even children had lately experienced? Margaret wished that she could provide her with greater reassurance, but there was nothing left to do but trust their future to God.

October 1537

How many more times would she see the splendor of autumn, Margaret wondered as she moved slowly through her gardens. Though the colors were splendid, they were evidence of death. Dying leaves gave one last glorious show before falling to the ground to be trampled into the dirt that would sprout with new life in the spring.

The aged countess smiled to herself. When she went to God, there would be no fine last moment such as these leaves had. She was likely to simply find needed rest one night and wake from it in her new heavenly home. Or she might slowly deteriorate as Catherine did. She frowned at the thought.

Her Plantagenet shrub continued to thrust forth tiny yellow flowers late into the year, long after the more delicate roses had gone into hibernation. That was her, outlasting the beauties that should have enjoyed life longer.

It was the word that Kathryn had died that left her in a fatalistic mood. An illness that struck with the speed and violence of a sword had put an end to her rejuvenating daily rides. Her husband had not even had time to reach Berkshire from London before she had left him to return to her previous husbands.

What a stir Kathryn had made when she first arrived in England, Margaret remembered. Even without considering the drama of her husband's claim to be Richard, duke of York, Kathryn had turned heads. She had been the most beautiful woman anyone had seen since Elizabeth of York.

Four decades had passed since then, and so few people who had witnessed it remained.

One who had not yet been born when Perkin Warbeck attempted his invasion of England was striding toward Margaret along the well-worn garden path. She shook her head and blinked quickly, certain that she must be mistaken, but the image remained and grew clearer as he approached.

"Mama!" Geoffrey greeted her jovially as he swept her into his arms. He was the very image of her father as she remembered him, which was just one more reminder of how aged she had become.

Her hands slapped at him to release her. "What are you doing here?" she snapped, sure that his absence from court could be nothing but a bad omen.

"I wanted to see you," he said, managing to appear hurt by her cold welcome.

She examined his face. "What have you done?"

He sighed and relented the information that he had hoped to reveal only once buttering her up somewhat. "I have some debts."

She raised an eyebrow.

"Alright," he admitted. "More debt than I should. It is rather expensive to serve our benevolent king."

Margaret bit her lower lip. All courtiers had debt. Geoffrey's must be substantial to force him to come to her.

"But, mama," he exclaimed, trying to salvage the moment. "I did wish to see you and bring you news."

"I have no wish for news," she muttered. "It is always bad."

Geoffrey roared with laughter as if he had never heard bad news in his life.

"Come now, mama," he said, offering his arm. He took her hand and placed it there when she failed to move. "Let us spend some time together, just you and me."

She knew that he had come to take advantage of her and convince her to bail him out of his problems once again. Choosing to be happy to see her son rather than angry about his reasons, she gripped his arm and said, "That sounds fine."

After all, a woman only received so many opportunities to be the center of her adult son's attention. Money was a small price to pay for that.

Geoffrey seemed to have arrived with a minimal retinue, which either evinced his desire for a hasty departure from London or his characteristic lack of planning. Either way, his presence at Bisham did not create too much of a stir, besides among the female servants who fluttered as he passed.

Margaret found that she did enjoy his company and that his debt, though high by any standards, would not be a problem for her to cover. She would sell Wyke in Middlesex and have no cause to miss it. What had she to spend her fortune on at this point, if not her children?

Her beloved building projects seemed less attractive of a prospect as she reached an age that made her doubt she would see their outcome. How she wished she shared the optimism of masons who worked tirelessly on the soaring cathedrals, knowing they would never see their work complete. An elaborate chantry at Christchurch Priory was the work of her craftsmen now until the day she required it.

"Mother, let us ride out," Geoffrey exclaimed as he burst into the room.

Margaret could not remember him ever entering one quietly. As she recalled, he had come into the world announcing his presence – right before she had learned that her Richard had been taken from her.

"I will be sore for a week if I attempt such a foolish pastime," she argued, wishing she had kept up the habit after her trip to Kimbolton.

"Nonsense." Geoffrey was not one to be declined. "A calm

palfrey taking you on a slow walk about the grounds will be good for you."

"And you would limit yourself to a walk in order to keep pace with your old mother?" she asked, unconvinced.

He gave her a lopsided smile that reminded her of his father. "Probably not," he admitted. "But I shall always come back to you."

Too true, she thought. She considered continuing to deny him, but knew it would be futile. He was spoiled, she supposed, but it was too late to rectify that. Just enjoy the moment. That was what life with Geoffrey taught her.

She would never admit to him how often he was correct. Though she would never have even thought of riding out that day, with him at her side she was quickly invigorated by the crisp air that fought to overcome the heat of the sun. The combination was pleasant, leaving her cold in the shade of trees then embraced by warmth as they entered sunny patches.

"I have had word from my brother," he said when they were well away from the manor.

"From court?" she asked, knowing that communication with Reginald was no longer permitted except through the king's council.

"Yes. Henry sends word that Jane Seymour has managed to provide the king with his much sought after son and heir." He did not look at her as he said it, knowing his mother did not like to be caught unaware.

"A boy," she whispered. After years of preparing Princess Mary for queenship, making promises to her dying mother, and risking all to oppose the king. It came down to his newborn child. What did God mean by this?

She absently rubbed her hand along the silky coat of her mare in a soothing motion, and Geoffrey remained silent. He was more sensitive and perceptive than he was often given credit for, she realized, ashamed that she was often one to underestimate him.

"What else did he say?" she asked. But what else could there be to compete with the news that King Henry finally had a son?

"He writes that Jane is not expected to live."

Margaret gasped. Little as she admired the girl for her grasp at power, the Seymours were at least preferred to the Boleyns. Would Henry be content as a widower now that he had a boy or would he continue his quest for an heir and a spare? What poor woman might be next?

"But the child?" she asked.

"Said to be robust," Geoffrey answered the question she meant to ask. The mother would give her life for that of her son as so many before her had.

Margaret nodded, peering up at the array of colors that surrounded them, russet, gold, and chestnut. It was too beautiful for most artists to recreate, and she was blessed to be here in the center of it while a much younger woman, a queen at that, lay dying. God's ways are not our ways. Was there any truer statement than this?

"Does Henry advise anything at this time?" She could accept that they had begun the swapping of positions in life. Henry was the head of the family as much as she was, and he had the benefit of maintaining his quiet place at court. He excelled at being present yet inoffensive, despite the king's issues with his mother and brother.

Geoffrey's head bobbed in affirmation. His older brother seemed to perfectly anticipate his mother's inquiries.

"He suggests that we simply wait. The king does not seem to have a fourth queen in waiting, so the past whirlwind courtships are not expected to be repeated. Let the king make the next move, especially as Cromwell watches carefully for ours."

Margaret could see the sense of it though every part of her cried out that something must be done. But what? Should they put forth a potential wife acceptable to their cause and take the chance that Henry would continue producing boys or wait to see what unpredictable action he takes next? No clear alternative presented itself, so she agreed to await further instructions from Montague.

"I thank you," she said, the words out of her mouth before she knew she wanted to say them. In response to Geoffrey's raised eyebrows, she continued, "Oh, I know that you initially came here for your own purposes, but it has done my soul well to have you here. It is good for Katherine, as well, to have her uncle here when she misses her father."

Geoffrey inclined his head to her, almost embarrassed. He was used to praise but that of the more superficial sort. He was not equipped to properly respond and could only hope his mother understood how much it meant to him.

"He does share somewhat unrelated news as well," he turned the conversation back to his brother's missive.

Margaret appeared interested but not concerned. She had received what she thought was the most severe blow.

"Throckmorton has been arrested."

A chill shivered through Margaret's body though she was clear of shadows. Throckmorton had been an agent of the king's - and one of Reginald's - a fact that must have been discovered for the Tower to be his fate.

"What does this mean for Reginald?" she asked, praying that God did not damn her for her lack of concern for the poor man if her son remained safe from the king's clutches.

Geoffrey offered an unconcerned shrug. "He is as safe as he can be, though he is now without such a valuable spy."

Margaret sighed in relief and could spare some thought for the double agent. "And Throckmorton?"

"Will most likely be executed," Geoffrey admitted lightly.

"God have mercy on his soul," Margaret whispered.

May 1538

Receiving a summons to join Henry's court was as unexpected as it was unwelcome. Margaret's hands were shaking by the time she finished reading the note from the king's secretary. Placing the vellum on a table already covered with correspondence, she squeezed her hands together, willing them to stop. She closed her eyes and tried to imagine why he would want her there now.

There could be no favorable reason, of that much she was quite certain.

Her lips pressed tightly together and she forced herself to pray for strength. If she was being called to account for her loyalty to the princess, she would stand up to Henry for the sake of his daughter. Were he to question her on her reverence of relics and saints, she had her son, a cardinal no less, to point to as an authority higher than a man who had forced his people to revere him as a god. Little else could be the subject of the hearing. Which loyalty had made her a traitor to the crown?

For the first time in years, she wished that she was at Bockmer. It had long become much more Jane's than hers, but this moment when her death seemed so close she wished that she were there where she and Richard had lived.

A harsh laugh filled the still air and it startled Margaret. It took her a moment to realize that the discomforting sound was of her own making. Bitter laughter in the face of the demise that she had claimed she was prepared to staunchly face.

Sun beamed through the window and lent its warmth to her frigid outlook. Perhaps she should not so hastily assume the worst. After all, Montague was still at court, serving the king satisfactorily so far as she knew. Even Geoffrey had been welcomed back once Margaret had covered his latest debts and Henry had grown bored with less jovial companions.

Taking a deep breath and stiffening her spine, Margaret called for her ladies to begin packing. They would leave as soon as proper arrangements could be made. It was not wise to keep the king - or fate - waiting.

Watching her ladies stuff dresses, linens, and other necessities into large trunks, Margaret wished that she had a closer companion to travel with her. With Katherine settled in her own household with Francis Hastings and their three children, Margaret had many occasions to feel her absence. This was one of the more piercing moments since the girl, or rather young woman, had left to see to her own family. Margaret felt like a relic in a world that no longer needed her.

King Henry had not brought his court to Bisham in recent months as he had done in the past. Rather than being upset by this, Margaret had been content to retire into obscurity. Apparently, he was not going to give her that option.

She hoped to have the opportunity to speak to Montague before being presented to the king to ask if he had heard from Reginald. Could it be a letter from Cardinal Pole that had sent Henry into a fury? Again. If that were the case, would Margaret be equipped to protect her family from the consequences that Reginald need not fear? She could only pray that God would see her through whatever King Henry had planned for the Pole family.

She had trained her household to be efficient and was soon upon the London road. Spring blooms greeted them cheerily in their ignorance of the cavalcade's reason for travel. Pink apple blossoms kissed the sky and received warm yellow sun in return. The sight of Tudor roses made Margaret's stomach churn. York roses were not prominent in the area surrounding Henry's seat of power.

As country cottages were replaced by busy storefronts and

taverns in structures that leaned out over the road as if attempting to embrace each other, Margaret steeled herself for the confrontation to come. She had decided to stay with her son instead of renting a house because she hoped to leave as soon as business could be completed. Keeping arrangements simple would help make that possible.

Margaret was surprised to see her Henry waiting to welcome her when they arrived. His hair was disheveled if not as thick as it had once been. The athletic frame that he had once proudly displayed was shrouded in a layer of padding as a result of fine food and wine frequently enjoyed with close friends. He was still handsome, at least Margaret and Jane both thought so, but there was no denying that he was no longer young.

As soon as her coach crunched to a stop on the finely raked gravel, he was there to help her out. Margaret was touched that he was so eager to see her, until she glimpsed his face up close. She knew that fine lines had become Henry's lot as well as any who reach his age, but the haggard visage that greeted her was hatch-marked with buried anxiety. To all others present, he appeared carefree as he made inane conversation and was friendly with the servants, but Margaret could see that there was much hidden behind his façade.

She could hardly wait until they were safely out of earshot to plague him with questions. Holding up his hands, he promised to tell her everything he knew, including the likely reason that Henry wished to see her. If only she had an inkling of what she missed while snugly spending quiet days at Bisham.

Margaret knew, of course, that the king's right hand, Thomas Cromwell, was pressing for his fourth marriage. She assumed with only one surviving infant son, that Henry would not be difficult to convince. The problem seemed to be with the choice.

His last two wives had been conveniently prepared for him as ladies-in-waiting to their predecessor. For once, none of the ladies at court was waiting in the queue, so a foreign match had been suggested.

"A Lutheran?" Margaret exclaimed. She could not have been more shocked if Christ had chosen that moment to return to Earth. "How has Cromwell convinced him of that? He must be more persuasive than we have given him credit for."

Henry allowed his head to sag. Clearly he had more to reveal.

"Geoffrey's man, Hugh, has been arrested," he said in the voice of one who knows they must be resilient but lacks the strength. "He warned me that my brother and I would be quick to follow."

The heat rushed from Margaret's body and she was certain that she must have died, her body left lying cold in poor Henry's sitting room. How could her heart continue to beat if it were her sons, and not just her, who were targeted by the king? Her mouth had dropped open, so she shut behind tiny pursed lips.

"He would not. What charge would he bring?" she said, hoping she sounded more hopeful to his ears than she did to her own.

Henry burst out in laughter, making her wonder what she had missed. She prayed she was not one of those unfortunate souls who lost their senses at a certain age. He seemed incapable of controlling his mirth, and she felt anger returning the heat to her limbs.

"Perhaps you can explain what in God's green earth is humorous regarding our predicament?" she demanded.

"I'm sorry, mother," Henry apologized breathlessly as he struggled to regain control of himself. "I forget that you are not here to see that our king makes up his own rules as he goes along." Shaking his head and taking deep gulps of breath, Henry went on.

"He receives a dispensation to marry his first wife, then leaves the church to divorce her. He burns Catholics for denying that he is the head of the church and reformers for denying Catholic truths. Do you not see?"

"It does not matter what truth is when it comes to my cousin the king," Margaret whispered. She could have God, the Pope, and Martin Luther united at her back, but it would not be sufficient to bear the wrath of King Henry if she had displeased him. "Is he so separated from reality? From God?"

Henry shrugged. "He has always claimed to be a true son of the church, but the very woman he may marry confesses a faith that he has burned lesser men for. Then again, he may change his mind with the setting of the sun. He has become completely unpredictable. Only Cromwell enters his presence with an unconcerned air and dry brow."

But was that bravery or ignorance?

"Alright," Margaret brushed away the information to the back of her mind. "But why do you think he has called me here? Is it regarding Reginald? Have you heard from him?"

Henry held up his hand once again, slowing his mother's stream of questions.

"I cannot be certain of course. I believe it is regarding Reginald but not the way you think." He paused to sip his wine and Margaret resisted the urge to hurry him on. "I believe he may have heard whispers of the hope that many have for Reginald as king consort."

Margaret's eyes were wide and dry as air around an open flame. When heretics were burnt at the stake, did they notice how dry their eyes were before the flames made other pain unendurable?

"And because he now has a son, any plans for Princess Mary are a hope to usurp his own," she completed Henry's thought. She would not ask how the king would have heard. It was inevitable that a prayer so many years held would become less private than it should be. Margaret had no doubt that each one who was privy to Catherine's last wish would be discreet with it, but somewhere it had leaked. It only took a drop of conspiracy and treason to enrage a king, especially this king.

"Is there a way that you and Geoffrey could join Reginald?"

His face had darkened as she asked the question, and she was crestfallen to see that he would never consider it.

"And leave my children and dear Jane to his inconsistent mercies? You remember the fate of Maude de Braose, do you not?"

"That's ridiculous," Margaret snapped, shaking her head in insistent disagreement. "My cousin is a tyrant, but he is not King John."

Henry simply raised a single eyebrow in reproach but would not argue with his mother. "I will not leave them."

"Very well," she acquiesced. Part of her respected him and had a mother's pride for his refusal to leave his family as her grandfather, Richard of York, had when he left her father and uncle with their mother to fend for themselves at Ludlow while he retreated to safety in Ireland during the late wars. Grandmother Cecily, with young George and Richard, had been put under household arrest but not harmed. However, Henry was her son, no matter his age, and a small part of her wished to force him to flee. Surely, she could protect his family. No, she knew that she could not guarantee it.

"What shall be our strategy then?" Margaret asked him.

As he breathed deeply, Henry's eyes scanned the room as if taking an inventory of the rich tapestries and displayed plate. Their riches meant nothing, she could read the thought upon his face.

"Let us talk after your conversation with the king," Henry

advised. "He could be complaining about Geoffrey's gambling or raging regarding correspondence from Reginald. We cannot determine our next move without knowing his."

Disappointed that he had not been able to provide greater insight, Margaret agreed. Not one to waste time, even if what needed to be done was distasteful, she left to present herself to King Henry's secretaries.

As she had expected, Margaret was asked to wait in a hall that was filled with hopeful courtiers. Regardless of the king's increasingly despotic behavior, there were those anxious and willing to do his bidding if they saw advantages to their house in doing so. Margaret's lips disappeared into a thin line as she observed them in what was undoubtedly their finest doublets and hose. How she wished she could advise them to leave and be content in their life that did not include their king to an unnecessary extent. Go home and love your wives and children in peace, she longed to encourage them.

Some truths one had to learn for themselves and were only fully understood when it was far too late.

Before long, Margaret was called upon to present herself. The glares of those who had been waiting far longer prepared her for the reddened visage she expected to find behind the door.

King Henry appeared older than his years thanks to a recent illness that had left him closer to death than many knew. It was this topic that he promptly broached with Margaret after the required pleasantries were exchanged.

"I will include your majesty in my prayers to an even greater extent than I already do," Margaret assured him with her head bowed as if she would intercede for him at that very moment.

Henry was waving her comment off before she had finished uttering it. "You know quite well that I am not interested in that."

"Not interested in prayer, your grace?" she asked archly.

His smile indicated that he would not be trapped by his words. Not by her.

"It is schemes that blossom at the news that a king may be dying that concern me, not your bedtime prayers," he spat.

Moving her head from side to side, Margaret insisted, "I am sure that no such scheme would be necessary, given that your dear late wife blessed you with a strong son and heir."

He narrowed his eyes at her. "You have never been a good liar, cousin."

The statement hung in the air as he reclined into the cushions piled into his chair and continued to examine her. Margaret stood unwavering, knowing that the slightest expression of doubt would be jumped upon. She would not reduce her dignity by denying a vague accusation of a crime she had not committed.

"Your son is close to Exeter, if I am not mistaken," he finally said, then grinned to see that he had taken her by surprise.

"They are cousins," Margaret agreed, unsure what else to say or where this was going.

"Of course, they are," Henry rubbed his hands together as one preparing to grasp their prize. "My dear Yorkist cousins."

"Your mother and I were quite close before my marriage took me from court," Margaret said. She was not sure what had rekindled Henry's fear of his white rose relatives, but a mention of his level-headed mother seemed appropriate.

"Such a very long time ago," he countered, pointedly fixing his eyes on her grey hair and lined face until she lowered her gaze. "Could it be that you do not serve your current king as loyally as you did my mother? Even I know that you had no great love for my father."

Keeping her chin down, Margaret closed her eyes and

worked to control the anger that still simmered when she thought of Henry Tudor sending her brother to the block. That had been four decades ago and had not involved this king.

"My devotion to you has been complete, your grace," she insisted without raising her head.

He shifted uncomfortably in his chair. It was clear that his leg pained him, and he was absentmindedly rubbing his temples as though his head throbbed as well. However, his eyes never left her.

"The completely devoted countess of Salisbury," he mocked with a groan that brought an attendant to his side to help him settle more comfortably.

"Yes, my lord," she muttered.

"And are your sons completely devoted to me as well?"

"Lord Montague has served you in many capacities since he was old enough to do so, your majesty. As does my Geoffrey, though I know he is more impetuous and not as suited to prominent roles. You have judged them well in where you have placed them each in your service," she said, hoping the praise would balance the fact that she knew no mention of Reginald could positively affect his mood.

"I am so glad to have your approval," he replied with rich sarcasm. "You do not feel that they are at all influenced by their brother, the revered Cardinal Pole?"

Margaret could not resist glancing up at the mention of her exiled son. Henry's face was red with anger and pain. Why must she speak to him when all was stacked against her?

"They have not seen their brother in years, your grace. I believe that it pains them as much as myself that Reginald has not been reconciled to his prince."

"To be sure," he mumbled, unconvinced. "What if I told you that I know that your sons have, in fact, been corresponding with each other and that the topics of said letters were of great import?"

"I do not believe that is true," Margaret said in a rush. Too quickly. She could see by the smug grin that spread his tiny mouth and forced hanging jowls aside that he read her denial for what it was.

"Ah," he almost purred. The cat was happy with its toy. "Does Reginald write to his dear mother as well?"

"All of my correspondence with Reginald goes through your council since you requested that be so," Margaret said with greater confidence for this portion of her statement was true. Only Henry wrote clandestine messages and smuggled them to Italy. It had seemed safe. His position so secure. Why had she not done it herself, she with nothing to lose?

"I believe you," he said, but somehow it did not make Margaret feel any better. "Please escort Lady Salisbury from my presence," he ordered no one in particular. "I am in need of rest and her presence unbalances my humors."

She was quickly ushered away feeling as though she knew no more now than she had when leaving Bisham.

August 1538

Margaret had decided to remain in London. She dreaded the idea but could not leave with such an unfinished feeling and tension in the air. The one bright spot was the time she was able to spend with her oldest son. The years separating them seemed insignificant, and she spoke to Henry now as an equal rather than a child.

They had discussed the vague remarks made by the king but could determine no new path based upon it. If he had learned of the whispered scheme to bring Mary from England in order to wed her to Reginald, little could save them. Plan was too strong a word for the dreams of men who hoped to see Mary as a staunch Catholic queen in place of her inconsistent father or infant brother. That did not mean that men could not die for considering it.

Since her arrival, Margaret had heard of other ideas, such as Henry Courtenay's hope to marry his son, Edward, to Princess Mary. Margaret had thought that the idea had substance. As the grandson of Margaret's cousin, Catherine of York, young Edward possessed an equal portion of royal blood as Reginald. She could not determine whether she longed for the position for her son or thought it would be the final plague on her house. Thankfully, few thought to look for her opinion or support. Henry was considered the head of the family now, and he seemed to be carefully weighing the options so she left him to it.

If Princess Mary were to be married to Courtenay, the need to secret her from the country was removed. Finding a priest willing to wed the two would be no difficulty, since the couple would stand to restore the Church. But would Montague throw his support behind his cousin or his brother?

These were the questions and ideas that swirled through Margaret's mind throughout the summer of 1538, before she understood the true extent of Henry VIII's vengeance and power.

~ ~ ~ ~

"Mother, join me in my study, please."

Henry had rushed in at midday, his presence unexpected at that hour due to his duties at court. He had not waited for his mother to respond but continued on hurriedly toward his study. Margaret's brow creased in curiosity as she set aside the needlework she had been attempting. Her vision made it impossible to complete the fine work in anything other than full sun and even that was becoming a great challenge. She promptly followed her son's footsteps into the study that could be a mirror image of Richard's old room at Bockmer. Margaret would have smiled at her son's mimicry of his father if it had not been for the utterly crushed expression upon his face.

She dashed to his side. "What is it?"

To her surprise, tears filled his eyes. She could not recall the last time she had witnessed her eldest child in such pain. "Henry?"

"They have taken Geoffrey," he exclaimed as if each word wounded him.

"Geoffrey?" she parroted dumbly.

"To the Tower."

~ ~ ~ ~

Everything up to this point felt like a child's game now that Margaret was faced with the reality of her youngest child held in the fortress whose very name struck fear into noblemen's hearts. The idea that they had been scheming to arrange marriage for Princess Mary while her father lived and ruled with an iron fist seemed ridiculously dangerous and a wholly not worthwhile risk now that it was already taken.

Margaret pleaded with the king through every channel available to her. He would not see her, so she sent letters and advocates with a greater opportunity to have his ear. She did not request Geoffrey's release. That would not be well received. Her requests were sent with the simple request of a mother begging to visit her child.

She received no word in return.

It was as if Geoffrey had simply vanished. Montague heard nothing of his brother being questioned or charged with any crime. He was not seen walking within the Tower complex or upon its walls. No one seemed to even be sure exactly where he was being held.

Margaret had to settle for sending clothing and food in the hope that a compassionate party would see that at least a portion of it reached him.

As summer became autumn, the chill in the air was met by icy fear that surrounded Margaret's heart.

October 1538

Margaret sat at the table without seeing her family surrounding her or smelling the roasted apples that had been prepared to tempt her. Her mind was trapped in a cell with her youngest child, envisioning the worst because she still had no word on what was happening to him or even if he yet lived.

That was what plagued her most as she went through the motions of each day, losing hope a bit more with each sunset. She told herself that she would know somehow if Geoffrey had been tortured or fallen ill, but she could not convince herself. As her prayers were sent half-heartedly that he might be released, Margaret sank deeper into despair.

The image of Geoffrey as an infant, the only one she had nursed after she learned of the death of her husband, was followed in quick succession by his first steps, playing with a wooden sword, and her finding him sneaking a kiss from a kitchen girl. The pictures flitted through her mind in the way that her own life was supposed to flash before her eyes in those last moments. Was it the same thing he was seeing?

"Grandmother, will you not try a bit of apple? They are lovely," her youngest granddaughter urged her.

Margaret attempted to smile at the sweet girl and took a reluctant bite. She saw the bones protruding through her skin and knew that she was giving up. Let the darkness cover me, she thought. Her desire for scheming had dissipated like the fog chased away by the sun. The ideas that had brought them to this place seemed so irrelevant when faced with their consequences.

"I think I will spend some time in the chapel," she whispered, pushing back from her trencher and leaving without hearing the arguments that rose for her to stay.

As she knelt before the altar, she wondered how long the

king would allow it to remain with its crucifix and relics. Reform continued though little was changed within the Pole households to recognize it. They would be forced eventually to give up their precious items that had been deemed idols, but Margaret would not betray her faith willingly. Would that God rewarded her for her faith with the restoration of her son.

Did the heavenly father look down upon Geoffrey as Margaret prayed? Did he hear her at all? At times, she wished to leave the chapel and never return. She had seen too much bloodshed to believe in a peace loving God. Then she would return, needful of the comfort that only fell upon her when she was in prayer. Who was she to understand the ways of the eternal king?

When she finally rose, slowly with aches permeating her body, she saw that Jane was sitting on one of the elaborately carved benches. Stranger still, she was smiling.

"What is it daughter?" Margaret asked, surprised that fate continued to provide reasons for cheer.

"A message from Constance," gushed Jane. "She has received permission to visit her husband."

"Geoffrey is alive," Margaret whispered. "Thank God and all his saints."

"Amen," Jane dutifully replied.

November 1538

The joy that arrived with Constance's permission to visit Geoffrey was promptly extinguished. She reported that his condition was poor. Since his arrest, he had been held within a dungeon that normally housed only the worst criminals. This pampered son who was accustomed to luxuries had spent two full moons scraping out his living among fleas and rats.

Constance had hardly recognized him and only been allowed to see him for a moment when he was taken for his examination. Fully demoralized and reminded of the woman he had to live for, Geoffrey was dragged from the room as his wife screamed his name.

When Constance tearfully shared her experience with Margaret and Henry, they all agreed that nothing good could come of it. The king had known exactly who to target. They each loved Geoffrey but were fearful of what he would reveal under torture.

"They can prove nothing," Henry insisted. "I burn all of my correspondence. Certainly, Geoffrey has as well."

"Proof," Margaret scoffed. "Like the proof his father had against my brother or that my uncle had against my father? Kings do not need proof."

Knowing that their discussion could lead to no answers, Margaret stormed from the room.

"Mother," Henry pleaded her to return.

"I believe that my time would be better spent in the chapel," she snapped, angrier with the tears that began to run down her face than her son for wishing to discuss matters without resolution.

Was it fate that brought them to this place? Had she and her brother simply been born into a cursed branch of the family, and had she unwittingly passed damnation on to her children? She had not believed it to be true, but hearing of Geoffrey beaten into submission weakened her resolve and increased her fear for the future. For all their futures.

As Margaret was attempting to work out these eternal mysteries on her knees, Jane burst into the chapel.

"You must come!" she cried.

Margaret dropped deeper into the pit that was threatening to swallow her. The news she had been dreading must have arrived.

"Please, mother," Jane begged while Margaret moved slowly as if her presence could delay what had already occurred.

Tears ran in rivers down Jane's face, and confusion pierced the hazy veil over Margaret's thoughts. "Jane?"

It took her daughter-in-law a moment to be able to form the words, and then Margaret wished that she never had.

"They have taken Henry, too."

Just when Margaret thought she could fall no further, fortune's wheel turned again. She and Jane tumbled into each other's arms and wept bitterly. Margaret knew that she should be in prayer for their safety but never before had her prayers seemed so pointless. As she prayed for one child, God had allowed another to be taken.

The women had not had time to consider their next step before footfalls were heard outside the chapel. They held each other and turned in fear, watery eyes ringed with glistening eyelashes stared at the door as if they could hold it shut.

The pair of guards that entered did not offer an explanation, but the taller of the two spoke, "Lady Salisbury. Lady Montague. You are to come with us."

~ ~ ~ ~

The walls of Warblington Castle were as secure as any jail cell, and Margaret could only assume that she was held here while most members of her family were taken to the Tower as another subtle form of torture.

In all, Jane and Constance had joined their husbands within the Tower, as had Henry and Edward Courtenay. A shiver of foreboding shuddered through Margaret's body when she heard that their children had also followed. She knew better than anyone alive that no one was safe within the Tower, not even children. The fortress that had been built as a place of safety had become synonymous with death.

She could sense the king's hand in the decision to leave her to rot at Warblington, just as he had done to Catherine at Kimbolton. Originally a portion of her brother's Warwick estates, the castle had become the property of Henry VII when he rid himself of the York heir. Henry VIII had restored it to Margaret and then made it her prison. How poetic.

The castle and surrounding grounds were beautiful, which only served to increase Margaret's overwhelming sense of grief. As she gazed from the upper turrets at the crashing sea and golden hued forest, she could only think of her sons and grandchildren held in Tower cells. How many of them would escape?

Margaret struggled to find her comfort where she always had, in prayer. She asked God if the situation might be resolved by the ascent of a new English monarch in an attempt to veil her wish for the death of the king that surely did not fool her heavenly father. At this point, she cared not one iota whether that next monarch might be Princess Mary or the infant Edward. She would serve any king or queen who released those most precious to her.

Her mood was almost brightened by the arrival of her inquisitor. A man announced as Sir William Fitzwilliam had Margaret brought before him. It was surreal for her to be treated as a supplicant before this commoner and in her own manor, but she kept her head low and her back curved in submission.

Fitzwilliam likely thought that he had been assigned easy prey until he began his round of questions. This seemingly docile old woman had enough strength remaining to deny any wrongdoing and to protect her grown sons as if they were babes in the cradle.

He started with a jab at her youngest. "I have been told that you have been disappointed in your son, Geoffrey."

"Geoffrey has brought me joy since the day of his birth," she countered.

"But more recently," Fitzwilliam pressed.

"He has only ever strived to serve his king to the best of his abilities," Margaret replied. Her head remained inclined but her words would not be used against any of her household.

Fitzwilliam shifted in his seat and tried another tactic. "You know that he is guilty of the damning sin of suicide."

He smiled when Margaret's head shot up in surprise. Margaret's mouth went dry. It could not be. She would have heard. Surely, she would have sensed it if her child's soul had been plunged into the depths of hell for a sin that could not be repented of. Her mouth worked on words that would not come and she felt like a fish that has been tossed into the bottom of a boat, gulping for water in the poisonous air.

"Well, attempted suicide, anyway," Fitzwilliam amended, his point scored. He adjusted the belt around his substantial waist, his face never lifting its ever present scowl.

Margaret felt as if her heart had stopped. Geoffrey was not dead? How could he play this game with her? Dear lord, give me strength, she prayed.

Fitzwilliam continued as casually as if he had mentioned the weather. "Now, why do you think he would do that – stab himself in the chest? And not even well, since the poor sot survives."

What answer could she give? "Perhaps he felt that he was without hope, knowing how few innocents leave the Tower alive."

Fitzwilliam's lips formed a flat line, and Margaret realized that was his form of a grin. "Innocent of what?" he asked.

"I am quite sure that I do not know," Margaret snapped, her anger increasing her courage. "I attempted to gain information regarding my son's incarceration for several fortnights before being removed from London. Never did I receive an answer."

Her interrogator's face did not move. "Your oldest son, Lord Montague," he continued after examining her until she could not help shifting in discomfort. "He is in contact with his brother."

He looked down at the scroll before him, as if looking for an answer, "Cardinal Pole."

"Cardinal Pole is my son," she agreed.

"And when did you last hear from him?" Fitzwilliam asked in a voice that insinuated that the answer was not all that important to him.

Margaret knew that it was vital. "You would do better to refer that question to the king. His council oversees all correspondence with the cardinal. I am certain that their records are more accurate than an old woman's memory."

His eye twitched. "Was your son betrothed to the Lady Mary?"

"Which son?" she asked innocently. "I do not have one available for marriage."

That flat grimace of a smile appeared again. "The cardinal is not yet a priest if I am not mistaken," he corrected her.

"It is but a foregone conclusion," she lied, her eyes on her lap. When she looked up again, victory was in Fitzwilliam's eyes. Margaret pressed her lips together. He would not goad her into saying too much. She looked out a nearby window as if she were unconcerned and bored with the conversation.

"Montague, too, has been questioned," Fitzwilliam stated and then waited for her to take the bait. She did not. "Was he in the habit of having secret meetings with the earl of Exeter?"

"You mean his cousin, Henry?" Margaret asked in a tone that expressed doubt in his intelligence. "Of course he had conversations with him, though they were not any more secret than any other gathering of family."

"That is not entirely true is it?"

"Which part?" Margaret asked in a pleasant voice. "They are cousins. My cousin, Catherine of York...."

"That is enough," Fitzwilliam cut her off. His voice remained flat and the lack of consternation only made him more frightening.

The questions continued as the sun disappeared and Margaret's stomach grumbled audibly. Fitzwilliam seemed to neither tire nor require refreshment. The room cooled, but he did not order a fire. The cold sent pain shooting into Margaret's joints, but she refused to admit her discomfort to this scarily emotionless gaoler.

When he finally began gathering his things to leave, she became desperate for information that she knew he would not give her. What could she ask of this man who had so nonchalantly informed her of Geoffrey's suicide attempt? "Was that true?" she asked before realizing that she had spoken out loud.

His muddy brown eyes slowly shifted to her. He made no other sign that he had heard her or understood the question until he responded, "That was after his first interrogation." He stood and made his way to the door. Turning a last time, he added, "To my knowledge, he has been questioned several times since then. No need to even use the rack on that one. The threat of it is enough."

Margaret watched the door shut behind him, no longer

feeling any pride in her ability to evade his questions. Her entire family, everyone she loved, was at the mercy of King Henry and vulnerable to whatever testimony Geoffrey could be convinced to give. She had complete confidence that Montague could manage his inquisitors at least as capably as she had . . . but Geoffrey? Had he seen death as the only escape that could keep him from causing the downfall of his family?

Frustration built in her and she stood to pace with nervous energy. Spinning the rings on her fingers and scanning the room for anything that may provide help, she prayed for a way to stop the worst from happening. The view through the window continued to mock her with tranquil skies and the beautiful autumn setting.

Her movement stopped as she stared out at the beauty of God's creation. She stood and willed herself to pray and for God to listen. Nothing changed. It was too much. She collapsed to the cold stone floor and wept.

December 1538

A fortnight under house arrest was sufficient time for Margaret to realize how much she had taken for granted before that fateful day when her world had fallen apart. She missed her granddaughters who had served as her ladies-in-waiting. Her worry for them and all of her extended family ate at her continuously and as effectively as a cancerous growth. Margaret had grown thin and looked every one of her sixty-five years as she took up her post at a window that looked out upon the road approaching the castle and watched the seasons change.

Without a doting family to encourage her well-being, she took little care for her meals. Though her dress remained immaculate, each piece hung loose. She continued to pray to the God who had thus far abandoned them to the devil's demon and hoped that he might use her family to bring him glory. Margaret wondered how her family endured within the Tower. Were they fed and kept in rooms according to their rank and position or had they been tossed into a dank cell as Geoffrey had been?

Had they been tortured?

It had been unbearable to be ignorant of Geoffrey's fate. She had no idea how to cope with hearing nothing of her entire family.

The trees outside had lost their colorful foliage, leaving dormant branches stretching brown claws toward the sky. The sea was bleak with icy foam topping the waves. Margaret wished they could wash over her and end her suffering. Was she really any better than Geoffrey who had attempted to end his own? Her poor child. He was simply not equipped with the strength for the situation he had been placed in. Of course, that is why the king had placed him there.

Margaret sighed heavily wishing there was some useful way for her to pass these interminable days. Then a movement in the trees caught her eye. She squinted and cursed her failing sight. After a moment, she shook her head and mumbled about her hopeful imagination when it happened again. She could not pinpoint the movement or identify its source, but her prayers became more fervent that something, anything was going to happen.

Her prayers seemed to go unanswered for the remainder of the day, and she had almost forgotten about the mysterious sight when a sound at her door startled her out of her doze. She had been secured in her room for the night, and the quiet sound reminded her of the nighttime adventure to visit Queen Catherine. Her heart was ready to burst with hope when John Hussey slipped into the room.

The smile that lit her face was filled with wonder. "How did you come to be here?" she exclaimed.

"You know me better than that," Hussey said casually as though he secretly entered noblewomen's bedchambers on a regular basis. He bowed low to her in reverence and gave her the opportunity to cover herself with a nearby cloak.

"Your presence is an unexpected blessing," she said, still praying that she was not dreaming.

Hussey's voice clouded as he spoke, "I pray that you will welcome me as warmly after you have heard the message I bear."

Margaret swallowed hard and lifted her chin. "Anything is better than not knowing. Tell me."

She had risen from her bed with the cloak wrapped tightly around her for warmth and propriety. They stood facing each other, and Hussey inclined his head once to indicate that he would do her will though his frown expressed that he did not relish the role he was in.

"A trial has been held," he said, then stopped to clear his throat and gather his strength.

"Who was on trial?" Margaret prompted impatiently.

"Several men have been tried in rapid succession, most notably among them Montague, Exeter, and Edward Neville."

Margaret blinked to dry her eyes. Did Hussey believe by saying Montague rather than Henry that Margaret would fail to render up an image of him as a sun-kissed little boy? And Exeter, dear Henry Courtenay. A trial was for show only. The king's will would be done.

"The charges?"

Hussey seemed surprised by the question. "My dear Margaret," he said, addressing her more intimately than he had in their long years of friendship. "High treason."

Her hands tightened into fists and she closed her eyes. Let it all be a dream, she prayed. Hoping that Hussey would not be there, she opened them to see his face stamped in grief. She released the breath that she had been holding.

"Geoffrey?"

"Will not be tried," Hussey said crisply.

Rather than being thankful, Margaret was confused. Hussey seemed unwilling to say more without being prompted. "Why?" she demanded.

Hussey coughed and patted his doublet as though he searched for an answer more pleasing than the one he had on hand. Giving up the quest under Margaret's anxious glare, he wilted and admitted, "Because he has given evidence against the others."

The confusion cleared from Margaret's face as storm clouds are chased away by sun, but it revealed something she did not want to see. "Against his brother," she whispered.

"I am so sorry, my lady," Hussey's voice was a low grumble, heavy with sorrow for this lady he had grown to admire.

He reached a hand out to comfort her but pulled it back,

remembering that she was in her bedclothes. She did not see his effort because her face was buried in her hands. Every time she thought she could bear no more, trials were heaped upon her. Without uncovering her face, she blindly made her way to the bed and sat down heavily, sobs wracking her body.

"How could it have come to this?" she cried. "Brother giving testimony against brother, and I am here." She removed her hands from her tear-streaked face to indicate the stark room so far from her sons and so empty of hope.

Hussey allowed her a few moments to weep. He turned away and fixed his gaze upon the hearth that should have held a warm fire on this chilly night, but Margaret's gaolers had left it dark. When the sounds of sniffling quieted behind him, he turned back toward her.

"Forgive me, my dear lady," he began quietly. "But I have more that I must share with you."

Margaret shook her head vehemently. "No, please. I cannot."

He looked as if he were considering it. Just leave it at that. It was enough.

"I am sorry, Margaret," he said as one who knows he is about to break another's heart. "The sentence has been carried out."

Hussey was able to pinpoint the precise instant when the truth of his statement had been processed by Margaret's sharp mind. Her reddened eyes widened, the brows raising as if they would cry out of their own accord, and her jaw dropped in a most unladylike fashion. Then her face collapsed into uncontrollable pain as she realized that her firstborn son had been executed by his own cousin.

"His ways are not our ways . . . He leads us to green pastures . . . He prepares a place for us . . ." Margaret was muttering in an effort to soothe her own excruciating pain.

It took several utterings and fierce concentration for Hussey to discern that she was praying or attempting to recall God's promises to his children as if needing to convince herself of their truth.

"Let us pray together for the soul of your son," he said, holding out a hand to her.

As Margaret raised her own, it shook with tremors that she could not control. It felt as cold within Hussey's warm grasp as her son's hand must now feel in death, but he did not cringe or give away his thought. He smiled encouragingly at her and pulled her from the edge of the bed toward her small altar. Giving her the time she needed to collect herself and her thoughts, he then helped her to her knees before joining her in appealing to the almighty for comfort and mercy.

~ ~ ~ ~

The next morning dawned cold as the weight that sat firmly upon Margaret's heart. She and Hussey had exchanged few words after their time in prayer. Were it not for the heartache reminding her of the night's events, she would tell herself that it was not true.

A hand to her puffy eyes and cracked lips found further evidence that her nightmare was indeed reality. She pulled the bedcovers over her head and determined never to rise again. Within the warm dark, Margaret recollected the remainder of harsh news that Hussey had imparted before he was forced to leave with the rising of the sun.

Sir Edward Neville, Hugh Holland, and others less known to her had also met their fate while she had sat senseless at Warblington. Not for the first time, she was struck by the fact that so much life had been brought to an end without any portent brought to her notice. How had her firstborn died without so much as an omen or skipped heartbeat on her part?

The darkness provided her with no answers.

Margaret wondered what the scene had looked like as Henry and his Courtenay cousin went to their deaths together. Hussey had admitted only to the expected story of good death, well said prayers, and quick slicing off of their heads. She pondered whether that was truly the case.

Had her son cried as he was forced to leave this world as he had when he fell and scraped his knee when he was small? Did the two of them bear each other up and encourage manliness in one another? She prayed that the executioner had been skilled if he must be employed at all.

Did the crowd cheer as her child's head was sundered from the body that had been created within her womb?

The air had grown stale and her thoughts morbid, so she thrust the coverings back while making no move to rise from bed. She gulped in cool, fresh air, then felt guilty for doing so when her child could not. Could she ever take joy from this life again?

She had no company or distraction to make the grief bearable as she could do nothing but wait for more bad tidings to arrive. Hussey had happily assured Margaret that no testimony had been given which incriminated her. She almost wished that it had. Better to know that her own end was approaching than to wait helplessly while her family was butchered.

March 1539

The move from Warblington to Cowdray made little difference to Margaret. She knew that it would make another visit from Hussey impossible if she were held at the residence of Sir Fitzwilliam, but her only concern during this sentence of life surrounded by death was prayer. She had so many dead to pray for.

King Henry was apparently not content with the degree of his extinction of the York families. With Margaret close at hand, Fitzwilliam took it upon himself to interrogate her regularly, taunting her with incomplete tidbits of news regarding her remaining children.

Margaret had obtained expertise in hiding her feelings from him since she rarely experienced them anymore. When he entered her room unannounced, she did not even glance in his direction.

"I thought you would want to know," he said without greetings. Just enough of a pause let her think that she probably did not want to know. "Your son, Geoffrey, has been released and pardoned."

At that unexpected announcement, she did look to the dour man. His face held no more expression than it had when he had tauntingly informed her, he thought for the first time, of Henry's death. A spark of hope dared to brighten within her before he continued.

"He almost immediately attempted suicide once again," he continued with scorn. "But perhaps Constance will inspire him to be more of a man than he has been thus far."

Margaret dropped her eyes and allowed her shoulders to sag. She had let him trick her, the greater fool she was thinking that he might take pity on her. He pulled up a chair next to her, not bothered by her clear wish that he would not.

"I would like to speak to you about your other traitorous

son," he said conversationally. When she did not respond, he added, "The whoreson posing as a cardinal has been striving to cause trouble for the prince who so generously raised him up."

She fumed silently, biting back the retort she would like to make, as he had as yet posed no question.

"Does he yet have your support?"

Margaret almost laughed. After the seasons changing, soon for a third time, since her incarceration, Fitzwilliam must believe her to be a greater schemer than she was. Yet it was a question, so she answered, "It is unfortunate that my son behaves so toward one who has been so good to him."

She almost had to choke the words out, but any others were not worth the pain they would cause. The king had been sending assassins to target Reginald for years, so there was no point in her offering an empty defense of him that would convict others, including herself.

"Who is helping him?" Fitzwilliam pressed, leaning forward as though he smelled weakness.

Margaret did her best to appear helpless, no more than that. Clueless. "Besides the Holy Father and Mother Church, I know of none who give my child comfort."

A slight reddening of his cheeks was the only sign of anger that Fitzwilliam unwillingly demonstrated.

"What about you?" he asked vaguely.

"I am a good woman," she stated firmly. "And have given no offense to my cousin the king."

The slight twitch of his lips was the closest thing to a smile that Margaret had seen on Fitzwilliam's face. He stood, wishing to waste no more of his time on this aged woman's clever answers.

"If you could," Margaret surprised him by saying. "This room is rather cold. Could you see a fire made? Also, my dinner was quite unsatisfactory. I would like some roasted partridge to help balance my humors, and surely you have a higher quality wine on hand than that which I have been served."

Fitzwilliam's eyebrows raised just a fraction of an inch before he bowed and left without responding to her requests.

He would not be an easy target, Margaret knew, but with steady pressure she would see herself removed from this house. She had begun making her requests to the servants and then to Fitzwilliam's wife when she had come to see what the fuss was about. In Margaret's unique position as a countess and cousin of the king but also a prisoner, her keepers were obligated to do what they could to see her wishes fulfilled, so she made them plentiful.

It took more time and patience than she had anticipated, but the longed for move finally occurred. That is when Margaret discovered that God can have a rather dark sense of humor.

November 1539

"I have informed his majesty that my wife will no longer accommodate your noble desires, nor will I trouble myself with questioning you further. Quite frankly, my lady," Fitzwilliam informed Margaret. "You are not worth my time."

Without waiting for her to ask any question or respond to his brusque announcement, he parted with saying, "Prepare to leave and not return."

A sliver of joy shone itself, but Margaret was reluctant to allow it growth. Fitzwilliam had not said where she was going, and that seemed an evil omen. He was not one to put hope or trust in, as she had learned well in the past year. He had informed her of Geoffrey's miserable condition and her grandson's continued imprisonment as if they were jolly stories he had picked up at the tavern. He had not mentioned where she was going on purpose. Because it was a victory for her that he did not want to admit?

The caravan that was prepared for Margaret's travel was present to prevent her escape more than for her protection, but it would serve as both if need be. Despite her efforts to smother any remaining hope, she found she was glad to be leaving. She was no longer able to ride and would use a litter, but that no longer bothered her. She had taken so many things for granted and was content simply to be leaving, even if her destination remained a mystery.

As they rode out, she recognized their course was set toward London but would learn no more from any of those traveling with her. Fitzwilliam must have instructed them that she was to know nothing, and he clearly paid well. Margaret's questions were met with blank stares and one or two sympathetic apologies but no answers.

She had her answers soon enough as the whitewashed stone

of the Tower of London came into view.

December 1539

Margaret was enclosed within a small room, relatively clean but not at all comfortable, with nothing to entertain her besides the enumeration of the ancestors she joined within these blood soaked grounds.

Her father was a vague memory. She had been so young when he died and so many years had passed since. Her brother. If her end was near, she must find a way to forgive those who had conspired to end his days so that she could, in turn, be forgiven by God for her own sins. He had been a sweet child, taking happiness in the small joys in life, even after he was committed to this bleak prison.

Elizabeth had not been a prisoner of the Tower, but it had taken her life and that of her newborn daughter just the same. Had the secret of her brothers been revealed before she drew her final breath?

Margaret could at least take comfort in the fact that she had so many to welcome her to heaven when the inevitable day came.

It should have no longer shocked her to receive an unexpected visit from John Hussey. When he was escorted into her cell, she knew not whether to jump for joy or close her ears.

"You should not be here," she admonished him. "Any favor toward me will be interpreted as disloyalty to the king."

He nodded, seeming to consider her advice. "You are probably correct. It is a good thing that the guards currently on duty are in the pay of a common friend."

Realization dawned on Margaret. "All this time?" she asked.

Hussey only smiled. Of course, Margaret thought. How else would he have managed all that he had without the support of Princess Mary?

"Still, I will not have much time," he continued as he

emptied sacks of practical items like dried meat and a woolen blanket.

"Thank you," Margaret murmured, humbled by the items that she could no longer provide for herself. She waited for Hussey to speak, but he seemed content to gift her these necessities. "Tidings?" she prompted.

He shrugged. "Much is as it was and you know of. Your grandsons remain here, though I doubt you will be able to see them. Gertrude Courtenay has been released."

"But she is guiltier than anyone!" Margaret snapped. "Her ambition to wed Edward to Mary was the scheme that sent her husband to his death."

Another shrug. "I know it as well as you do, as does the king. It must serve some purpose of his to forgive her." He paused to check the bottoms of his bags and found them emptied. "You may be interested to know that he will be taking his fourth wife."

Margaret's eyebrows shot upward. She did not need to ask what woman could possibly think that all the riches of England were worth marrying a temperamental tyrant.

"She does not know him," Hussey answered her unspoken inquiry. "Anne of Cleves was the option put forward by the king's secretary, Thomas Cromwell."

"He takes a Lutheran bride?" Margaret was stunned. It seemed Henry still had the power to surprise.

"It would seem so," Hussey agreed. He seemed convinced that anything could happen and none of it would shock him given what he had seen.

"How are my sons?" Margaret asked, not wishing to spend any more time thinking of the king.

"Reginald does well, as he always does. It is good that he left when he did." They shared a look that spoke volumes of what they may have done differently had they only known. "He has loudly proclaimed his brother and cousin as martyrs of the Holy Church," Hussey added with a smile that reflected a father-like pride. "Geoffrey," he paused to cough, and Margaret knew it to be a signal of choking on words that he would rather not say. "He struggles with guilt. I pray that you will not be offended if I say that I believe he wishes that he had died with his brother."

Margaret nodded in understanding. Geoffrey's sentence was to live with what he had done.

"I do not know how vital this will be to you at this point," Hussey went on. "But Jan has revoked her vow of celibacy and married Sir William Barentyne."

Anger flared, and Margaret slammed her hand down on the table with more force than Hussey would have thought possible. "She cannot," Margaret insisted sternly.

Hussey seemed taken aback by her vehemence. "She has."

"I have done little to protect my children's lives but will see that their inheritance goes to their children," Margaret stated with her old fire. "See that the marriage is challenged," she ordered before adding more demurely, "If you would."

"Why not?" Hussey said with a sigh. He had believed the news to be inconsequential and now he had another tedious task to accomplish. Yet, he would accomplish is for Margaret. She deserved that much.

A light tap on the door alerted them that their time must end, and Margaret suddenly felt as though she had misspent it.

"Hussey," she pleaded not knowing what she would ask of him. She simply did not want him to go. "Will I see you again?" she asked.

"That is known by God alone," he said as he returned the soft knocking. "I pray that he will bless and comfort you, Margaret."

Then he was gone, and Margaret was left feeling more alone than ever before.

December 1540

Margaret passed more than a year in the confines of the small room with little besides the comforts that Hussey had provided or those that she complained loud and long enough to receive from the king's hand. Henry never had her brought before him or had her questioned. She was held just as her brother had been, with no hope of release or resolution. How many more years would pass before God himself affected her release?

Most of her time was spent in silent meditation and prayer. Initially, she had tortured herself. No need for Henry's men to do the dirty work. Replaying each moment of her life, every decision and each word, had been worse than the rack. In so many instances, she found ways that she could have saved her son. She should have been content to submit to the king in all things. Princess Mary could fight for herself when the time came, and God would be content with her worship regardless of the liturgy. Margaret had sunk into a deep depression with no one around her to pull her out.

It had been the comfort of the Holy Spirit that had finally drawn her out. At her deepest depth and all alone in prison, God was her rock. Though she continued to struggle with forgiving herself for the choices she had made, she knew that God had already done so and that her Henry was rejoicing in heaven. He was there with his father and Arthur. Margaret longed to join them, so her prayer time was the closest route she had.

During her year in the Tower, the world went on around her, but she only caught snippets of it. The king married and divorced Anne of Cleves. Lucky girl, Margaret thought. His new wife, for he had not waited long before choosing another, was young Catherine Howard. Margaret knew little of her, for she was of an age with her grandchildren. More than that, she no longer cared.

Hussey had managed to press the suit that had Jan's new marriage annulled, and Margaret was content with that. Arthur's children would have their inheritance. It was the last of her scheming. God's will, rather than hers, would decide the future.

It had not even brought her any satisfaction when Thomas Cromwell had been executed. The man who had sent so many good men, women, and even children to their deaths for not taking up the reformed faith finally had pushed his king too far. Margaret had, however, reached the point where she was more curious as to whether she would see the man in heaven than gratified by his downfall.

Would Reginald someday be king consort to Mary? Margaret doubted that she would find out, and God had given her peace in that uncertainty. She had done all she could, and Reginald had proven time and again that he was capable of looking out for himself. Margaret still hoped, of course, to see it but was no longer consumed by it.

She had made her peace and could only wait.

March 1541

Geoffrey was in too low of a place himself to attempt to visit his mother. Reginald continued in happy exile, and Hussey had little reason to take the risk. At least that was what Margaret believed. She had no way of knowing that John Hussey had also made his walk to the scaffold for treason. Therefore, Margaret was pleasantly surprised to see her door opening after many moons without a visitor.

The first thing that caught her eye was the bright auburn hair, so like hers had once been. She almost fell to reminiscing before reminding herself that this was a person who had come to see her, not a ghost of her past. The rich dress also appeared like something out of another lifetime. Margaret had worn such silks before the damp and cold of the Tower forced her to choose warm wools.

Bright blue eyes and a sweet smile were found on the face of the woman that Margaret barely knew and certainly had not expected to see.

"Catherine Howard!" she exclaimed in a rusty voice. "Queen Catherine," she corrected after clearing her throat. How odd it felt to use her old friend's name for this youthful beauty.

The young woman dimpled, appearing honored that the old countess had recognized her. "I have brought you some warm clothes," she said in a high, sweet voice. "I also asked the tailor to make them fashionable, as your rank demands."

Margaret watched as the girl, for she was hardly more than a child, draw out lovely clothing from the trunk that had been dropped just outside the door for her. Each item was held up and admired, and Catherine did not seem to mind that Margaret was unable to form words of thanks. Once each rich piece had been paraded by, Margaret finally found her voice.

"Catherine, you should not have taken this risk," Margaret whispered. She felt wholly ungrateful in admonishing the girl for her generosity, but Margaret understood how dangerous it was to demonstrate favor to the wrong people.

"Nonsense," Catherine brushed her objection aside. "My husband is aware that I placed this order with you in mind. I am not solely a plaything for his majesty."

"No," Margaret agreed, though she had the distinct feeling that the comment was directed at someone other than herself. "It was remarkably kind of you to think of me," Margaret said more confidently, daring to touch the soft, thick fabrics that were ideal for the cool, moist interior of the Tower. "May God bless you," Margaret said. She began moving to her knees to ask for the queen's blessing, but Catherine stopped her with a hand upon her shoulder.

"Do not, Lady Salisbury. It is not needful and would cause you pain." She made the sign of the cross upon Margaret's forehead, and Margaret closed her eyes to memorize the sensation. It had been so long since anyone had touched her. "May the Lord bless you and keep you," Catherine said in a simple blessing.

"And you," Margaret replied, inclining her head. "I thank you, Catherine. Please take care."

"I am always careful," Catherine said with a playful wink.

Margaret watched Catherine stride away and prayed that the girl had what it took to survive King Henry.

May 27, 1541

As the weather warmed, Margaret found she could wear fewer layers of the fine clothing that Queen Catherine had brought her. The visit still gave Margaret reason to smile when she remembered the young queen who had cared enough to ensure the comfort of an aged traitor. She had not heard of any rumors regarding the girl and wished her well in what was certain to be a trying marriage.

Not that Margaret heard much in her little room. It was as if she were separated from the entire world. As this new day dawned bright but cold, Margaret wondered how much longer she would be here. Would they simply forget that she was there as she outlived everyone who had once cared for her?

The creaking of her door was unanticipated that early. The meager ration brought to break her fast normally came at erratic times but much later than the sunrise. Margaret turned without much curiosity, but the dark face of the guard caused her to flinch.

"Lady Salisbury," he grumbled with the slight incline of his head. "It is my duty to inform you that your sentence will be carried out this morn."

"My sentence?" she asked in confusion. "I have never stood trial. What is my crime to justify this mysterious punishment?"

Margaret stood firm as she asked these questions which she already knew the answer to. King Henry, so accustomed to committing legalized murder, was not bothering to go through the legal niceties anymore. And why not? Guilt was a foregone conclusion in Tudor England's treason trials. It was unfair to make this lackey squirm, but she would not get a chance to do so to the man who deserved it.

After a moment spent in search for the proper words, the guard stumbled over those he had chosen. "You are to be executed by the axe two hours hence."

Now it was Margaret's turn to be lost for words, but the guard did not mind. He left quickly, glad that his task was complete. As the door shut on Margaret for the last time and she heard the locks secured, she was suddenly afraid.

Two hours. She had felt ready since Henry's death, but now every fiber of her being screamed out that the timing was not right. Yes, she was aged, even unneeded, but did that sentence one to death?

Why now?

Margaret had been sitting in this room and at Cowdray and Warblington before it for more than two years. What drove the king to make his move at this point when she had not made one to spur it on?

She could only guess that anger against Reginald pushed the king to vengeance. Since his assassins failed in their attempts to bring down the cardinal, they would hurt him through his mother.

Very well. She gladly stood proxy that one of her children would live.

Looking around the room that had seemed so bare only moments before, Margaret noticed details that had slowly turned it into something of a home during her lengthy stay. A letter from Jane. Her rosary beads. A small bunch of wildflowers handed to her by a shy kitchen maid when she delivered Margaret's dinner a few days previously. Had the girl a notion of what was to come when she made that kind gesture?

It did not matter. None of it mattered.

She fell to her knees to pray for the last time.

~ ~ ~ ~

An unfamiliar guard arrived after what seemed to be only

moments, but Margaret was prepared. One does not spend a life surrounded by death and not know how to greet it. She followed him with another guard close behind as if they were afraid that a sixty-seven year old traitor may attempt escape.

Should she make a run for it, just for fun? A small smile enhanced the wrinkles around her mouth.

Arriving on the Tower Green, her nerve failed her and her bowels turned watery. There was no scaffold in sight, but she noticed that her guard was looking to a small block that had been placed unceremoniously upon the ground.

She furrowed her brow. The secrecy and suddenness felt wrong. What was behind this?

"Lady Salisbury," a deep voice beckoned. "Have you any sins to confess?"

The priest that accosted her would surely take any confession back to the king, but Margaret did not mind. He would be disappointed. "Bless me, for I have sinned, Father," she began and saw the gleam in her confessor's eye. "I am a sinful woman, sinful from birth. I have failed to do all the work my lord set before me and ask him to welcome me now into my heavenly home."

She was offered a half-hearted absolution before the priest stalked off disappointed. Her guards shoved her closer to the block.

"What is the meaning of this?" she demanded. "I have had no trial of my peers, and know of no crime brought against me." She fixed her gaze on the guard who appeared weakest. "This is a mistake."

He made to grasp her arm and she moved a step away. "Do you know that I am one of the highest peeresses in the land? That the king is my cousin? You should be aware of what you do before you do this."

She moved another step as he grabbed for her.

"Our orders come from the king himself. Now prepare yourself," this came from the other guard, who held her in a firm grip until she was standing before the pathetic block.

This must be how Lord Hastings felt all those years ago, she thought and then wondered why a crime of almost sixty years ago would spring to mind at this moment. Then she remembered something far more important.

She scanned the small crowd. So few. Her sentence must not have been announced. She would never know why events had unfolded this way. She needed just one friendly face.

And there it was.

Katherine, Henry's daughter but not dressed as a noblewoman, was standing dangerously close. Her peasant's garment caused most to look past her, but not Margaret. She would take one final risk.

"Please, girl. See this sent to my family," she begged. She could not let on that she recognized her granddaughter, but she did press a note into her hand before being forced back to the block. Margaret did not dare look at her again. The risk she was too great.

Margaret shook off the grasping hands of the guards. "I am well aware of how this is done."

The executioner knelt before her and asked for forgiveness for what he was about to do. "May the Lord forgive you as I do," Margaret said automatically with the fleeting thought that it must leave wounds on the soul to have his occupation.

She took one last deep breath of clean spring air and smiled, because she knew the air would be much sweeter in heaven.

Epilogue – May 1541

King Henry VIII wished to clear the Tower of traitors before his planned progress to treat with James V of Scotland. It seemed easier and safer to leave London without the passel of schemers gathered together. That one of these prisoners was his aged cousin bothered him little, if at all.

The maid sent to clear the room that had been Margaret's home for longer than a year found a poem etched into the cold stone wall.

> *For traitors on the block should die;*
> *I am no traitor, no, not I!*
> *My faithfulness stands fast and so,*
> *Towards the block I shall not go!*
> *Nor make one step, as you shall see;*
> *Christ in Thy Mercy, save Thou me!*

Afterword

Margaret Pole is often referred to as the last Plantagenet, and she was indeed the last of her generation. Her remaining children did manage to continue the spread of the family tree.

Geoffrey Pole did not inherit his mother's strength of character. After Margaret's execution, he joined his remaining brother in Europe where he seems to have aimlessly wandered until Queen Mary's reign. He died shortly before his queen, leaving several daughters and four sons, two of which would die in the Tower and one who would be exiled.

Ursula bore over a dozen children for Henry Stafford and lived well into old age, an unusual feat for a Plantagenet. She did, however, suffer the execution of one of her sons. Thomas Stafford was ironically executed for rebelling against Queen Mary in an effort to stop her plans to marry Philip of Spain. Ursula's daughter, Dorothy, became a prominent member of Elizabeth I's household.

Reginald Pole returned to England in order to serve Queen Mary, but not as her husband. He was made Archbishop of Canterbury within the Church of England and served in that role until he and his queen died on the very same day, November 17, 1558.

Henry Pole, the son of Lord Montague, was never released from the Tower and is believed to be one of many York sons to meet his death too early under mysterious circumstances within those cold stone walls.

Additional Reading

For those interested in reading more about the historical figures featured in this novel, I recommend the following sources:

Margaret Pole: Countess of Salisbury 1473-1541 by Hazel Pierce

The First Queen of England by Linda Porter

Last White Rose: The Secret Wars of the Tudors by Desmond Seward

Reginald Pole: Prince and Prophet by Thomas Mayer

Tudor: The Family Story by Leanda de Lisle

Author's Note

The story of Margaret Pole demonstrates the epitome of what medieval people would have referred to as fortune's wheel. Her highs were astronomical: the daughter of the heir apparent, later Countess of Salisbury. However, her lows were worse than most people experience: the execution of her father, brother, son, and eventually herself.

Tudor England was a dangerous place to live.

As this is a work of fiction, I would like to take the opportunity to explain where I have taken artistic license. Some of these are minor, such as the changing of names to avoid having dozens of Henrys and Catherines. I have used different spellings and titles as much as possible to clarify who I am referring to. For example, Arthur's wife, Jan, was truly another Jane, and Ursula's Harry was another Henry. As spellings in the sixteenth century were not used consistently, I felt little license was required in this strategy.

More serious decisions were made regarding Margaret's thoughts and relationships. I used historical facts as an outline, and created the 'mother bear' attitude in Margaret to justify them. The personalities of her sons are established to some extent in their statements after arrest. Geoffrey truly did give testimony against anyone he could and then attempt suicide more than once in guilt. Henry, on the other hand, remained firm and unafraid, just like his mother.

Regarding dates, I had a few more decisions to make. Precise dates are not always provided for the birth of children and other events that we record thoroughly today. Some examples in Margaret's life include the dates of her children's births and Arthur's death. I have chosen to follow the research of biographer

Hazel Pierce in dating these events though they are not always the most often repeated dates proclaimed in online sources. For example, Pierce states that Margaret's children, besides Geoffrey, were born by 1500, while Wikipedia gives 1504 as Ursula's birth year. In most cases, it is the people themselves that are more important than the exact dates that cannot be known.

The relationship with John Hussey, including the wild ride to visit Queen Catherine at Kimbolton, is completely my creation. It is true that his wife was imprisoned for refusing to refer to the princess as Lady Mary, so I chose to make him an active member of the White Rose faction. I also gave dear Hussey an extra lease on life with his final secret visit to Margaret in the Tower. In truth, he had been executed the year before.

It remains unclear why Henry VIII decided to have Margaret executed when he did, other than as part of a heartless cleaning of house. The commonly repeated story that Margaret attempted to run from her executioner was not written by a witness and does not seem to fit what the remainder of historical evidence tells us about her character. I chose to write this final scene the way I did to indicate her protest, but not in such an undignified manner.

Writing about Margaret Pole was a unique experience after spending so much time with Elizabeth of York. The two York women chose vastly different ways of coping with the trials that life threw at them, but they shared the strength that must have been infused in their royal blood.

Connect with Samantha
at SamanthaWilcoxson.blogspot.com
or on Twitter @Carpe_Librum.